THE
Regency
COLLECTION

VOLUME
—6—

THE Regency COLLECTION

VOLUME —6—

Ravensdene's Bride

by

Julia Byrne

Hidden Flame

by

Elizabeth Bailey

*MILLS & BOON and MILLS & BOON with the Rose Device
are registered trademarks of the publisher.*

*First published in Great Britain 1999 by
Harlequin Mills & Boon Limited,
Eton House, 18–24 Paradise Road,
Richmond, Surrey, TW9 1SR.*

The Regency Collection © by Harlequin Enterprises II B.V. 1999

The publisher acknowledges the copyright holders of the
individual work as follows:

Ravensdene's Bride © Julia Byrne 1996
Hidden Flame © Elizabeth Bailey 1993

ISBN 0 263 81712 1
106-9910

*Printed and bound in Spain
by Litografía Rosés S.A., Barcelona*

RAVENSDENE'S BRIDE

by

Julia Byrne

Dear Reader

Regencies are my very favourite romances. Like most fans I started with Georgette Heyer and have been hooked ever since. Funnily enough, my first three books were medieval romances – the thought of following in such august footsteps was daunting – but once I discovered how much fun Regencies were to write I took a giant leap from the Plantaganets to the Hanoverians.

I don't have a degree in history, but worked in the History Department of a Melbourne university for many years, which certainly helped with research. My husband and I now own a Tobacconist/Confectionary shop in a seaside suburb. I don't smoke, but the chocolate is a temptation! We have one daughter, and have recently been adopted by a lost kitten. He likes taking a shower with anyone foolish enough to leave the door open and thinks he ought to eat at the dining-table, but we're used to cats who think they're people.

Spare time is rare – my latest cross-stitch project has been sitting in a corner for years – but I enjoy genealogy because I like solving puzzles. And, of course, I love books. I hope you enjoy this story as much as I enjoyed writing it.

Julia Byrne

Julia Byrne lives in Australia with her husband, daughter, and two overgrown cats. She started her working career as a secretary, taught ballroom dancing after several successful years as a competitor, and presently works part-time in the History Department of a Melbourne university. She enjoys reading, tapestry, and playing Mah Jong.

Other titles by the same author:

Gentle Conqueror
My Enemy, My Love
Mistress of Her Fate
Scandal and Miss Smith

CHAPTER ONE

HE WAS living in a state of siege. There was no other word for it. And no one at Comberford Place seemed to have the least idea of how to deal with such a sorry situation.

Nicholas Everard Dalton, 5th Earl of Ravensdene, glared at the door of the breakfast parlour as it closed behind his late grandfather's butler. This was the third time in as many days that he had been obliged to inform Winwick that unknown females were not to be ushered into his presence, regardless of such heart-rending tales of woe as their favourite puppy escaping onto the grounds through the open gates, the feeling that they were being followed by villainous—but invisible—persons that had come upon them just outside the gates, and, not five minutes ago, a painfully turned ankle, also just outside his gates.

Soon he wouldn't be able to get *through* the gates for the females staging accidents there.

'It's no use sitting there scowling at the door, Nick, old boy.'

The only other occupant of the breakfast parlour, a fair-haired gentleman who was steadily eating his way through a breakfast of gargantuan proportions, looked up to wave an admonitory fork at him. 'It's not poor old Winwick's fault he's a soft touch. Probably never had occasion to deal with predatory women before. Don't suppose your grandfather was hunted right and left when he was alive.'

Nick shifted his lowering gaze to the other end of the table. 'Stow it, Dev.'

A friend of long-standing, Viscount Devenham had no trouble in ignoring this terse piece of advice. He grinned. 'Do you think Miss Smisby, or whatever her name was, will consent to being conveyed home in ignominious defeat?'

'If she declines my offer of a carriage, she can limp home for all I care.'

Devenham winced. 'Amazing what a man can get away with when he's suddenly become so dashed eligible,' he observed with patently false gloom.

'I would have done the same thing before I came into the title,' Nick retorted dryly. But a wry smile tugged at his lips. 'Besides, I'm no more eligible than you are.'

The Viscount shook his head. 'Not the same. According to m'sisters, I have superior address, but you have an air of danger about you.' The fork was brandished again for emphasis. 'Fatal to females.'

Fatal to my investigation if I don't put a stop to it, Nick thought grimly. But Dev's remarks had touched another nerve. He looked down the table at his friend's pleasant, open countenance and smiling blue eyes, and his own smile faded.

They had both experienced the destruction of war, but Dev had come through it almost unchanged, he realised. His friend's war had been fought across the impersonal distance of battlefields, whereas his own had taken place in the secret, twilight world of the spy. A world where you watched your opponent's eyes as his life snuffed out. A world where you had to be harder and faster than anyone else if you wanted to survive. A world where the line between right and wrong was sometimes very indistinct.

With a swift stab of memory he recalled the proud, young lieutenant who had left England over a decade ago with his new bride and his high minded notions of honour and glory, and found himself comparing the image with the lean face that had stared back at him from his shaving mirror that morning. There had been no trace then of youth or idealism in the cold, green eyes set beneath frowning black brows, nothing soft in the grim, unsmiling line of his mouth, and, not for the first time in recent months, he wondered precisely what it was he had become—and if he could live with the answer.

'Of course the real problem is your mother,' Devenham went on, apparently sensing nothing amiss. He picked up the coffee pot and poured himself another cup with the air of a man needing sustenance. 'I know you were bored with sorting out the mess your brother made of Ravensdene Hall, but inviting her ladyship to accompany us to Comberford was the action of a desperate man. Now that she's put off her black gloves she's had us out to some party or another just about every night, and look at the result— husband-hunting harpies calling on us before we've even swallowed our breakfasts.'

Despite his own annoyance at the situation, Nick had to laugh. 'A hideous prospect, to be sure. But in fact I didn't invite my dear mama, Dev. She invited herself. Perhaps I should have refused her.'

The Viscount looked shocked. 'Good God, no! You couldn't do that. Girlhood home. Hasn't seen the place for years, I daresay.' He paused for a moment, then added rather too casually, 'Didn't know your mother had asked to accompany you. Thought all this gadding about you've been encouraging her to do might mean you're contemplating marrying again.'

A slight narrowing of his friend's eyes was the only intimation Devenham had that this remark wasn't entirely welcome. 'Perfectly reasonable assumption,' he murmured apologetically. 'Know Marianne's death knocked you for six, old fellow, but now you've come into the title... Well, duty and all that. And since you've been perfectly willing to escort her ladyship to every social event in Sussex, she probably thinks you're hunting for a wife.'

A rather tense silence seemed to hang in the air, then Nick stretched his long legs out, crossed one ankle over the other and contemplated the toe of one highly-polished Hessian. 'Not quite,' he said at last. 'Actually I thought my mother's presence might give more credence to my cover. You see, Dev, I am hunting.' He looked up, his gaze steady on his friend's face. 'For a pair of traitors.'

The Viscount promptly choked on a mouthful of coffee. 'Damn it, Nick,' he wheezed when he could speak. 'You ought to be more careful what you throw at a man. Hunting for a pair of traitors? *Here*?'

'One here; the other in town.'

'Good God!' Forgetting such mundane matters as breakfast, Devenham stared back at him. 'You're *not* funning. Who...? What ...?'

'"What?" is the easy part. For several years, it seems, information has been passed from the Foreign Office to the continent by someone in this part of Sussex. One of their agents was put onto it two years ago when the leak was discovered and he eventually found where and how the information entered France and back-tracked from there. He ended up on the beach a couple of miles away and hit a dead end.'

'And then?'

'And then nothing. The idiots pulled their man off

the case when Napoleon abdicated and was sent to Elba last year.'

Devenham groaned. 'Don't tell me. Now they're panicking because Boney's running amok again. What a damnable situation, Nick. There's nothing to say the fellow at this end is still working from here, but you can't ignore the possibility. The Frogs would give anything to know Wellington's movements.'

'A situation I may be able to turn to our advantage, although one would think a man who has evaded detection for years would see through any amount of traps set for him.'

'You're here to spring a trap? For whom? Do you suspect anyone in particular?'

Nick shrugged. 'Sir Jasper Lynley interests me, but he isn't the only gentleman retired from active service who still has contacts in London.'

'Something a touch smokey about the Lynleys,' agreed the Viscount, nodding sagely. 'Don't know about Sir Jasper, but whenever Miss Lynley's name is mentioned everyone clams up. And yet all she seems to do is spread good works or some such spinsterish thing. Sounds pretty harmless.'

'I daresay, but I would like to know more. Unfortunately, Sir Jasper apparently discovered a pressing need to remove himself from the area just prior to our arrival.'

'Would he suspect anything?' Devenham asked doubtfully. 'I mean, you inherited Comberford Place from your grandfather a couple of years ago. Perfectly good reason to be here now you've had to sell out, and—'

He broke off suddenly as Nick held up a hand in warning. Two seconds later the door of the breakfast

parlour was opened by a footman and the Dowager
Lady Ravensdene floated into the room.

'Remind me to ask you how your hearing got to be
so dashed acute,' Devenham murmured in a frustrated
undertone as both men rose to their feet. 'Your mother
never makes a sound.'

The comment was perfectly justified. Hermione,
Countess of Ravensdene, was an ethereal creature
whose slender, blonde beauty had made her an accred-
ited Toast in the days of her youth. The tresses, at
present covered by a cap of Brussels lace, were now
more silver than gold, but her deep blue eyes still held
a soulful expression that, together with her fragile
appearance and soft voice, never failed to assure her of
the most assiduous attention.

The fact that she had managed to present her lord
with four strapping sons, all of whom had inherited the
tall, athletic physique, black hair and green eyes that
characterised the male members of the Dalton family,
was, according to the *ton*, nothing short of a miracle.
Only the most discerning sensed that, beneath the
delicate, pastel-shaded silks and gauzes with which her
ladyship draped her willowy form, there was a back-
bone of pure steel.

Her son was definitely one of the discerning. Fixing
his parent with a considering eye, Nick drew a chair
out for her. 'Good morning, ma'am. You're astir
unusually early. Have you come to take breakfast with
us?'

Her ladyship shuddered delicately. 'How can you,
Nicholas? You know I take only a cup of weak tea
before noon. Good morning, Barney.' The Dowager's
gaze fell to the slices of ham still reposing on his
lordship's plate. She closed her eyes momentarily and

sank into the chair her son was holding for her as though in dire need of its support.

'Shall I ring for Winwick to bring you some tea, then, ma'am?' enquired Devenham, casting a rueful look at Ravensdene.

'Thank you, Barney, but my maid always brings my tea to my room. Besides, Winwick appears to be involved in a most extraordinary argument with someone on the front doorstep. I cannot imagine what it is about.'

'Miss Smisby,' supplied the Viscount helpfully, resuming his seat. 'Haven't met her. Thought she could throw herself in Nick's way, but Winwick is heading her off at the crossroads.'

The Dowager appeared slightly confused. 'Heading her off at the crossroads?'

'Never mind,' Nick interposed sternly. 'Mama, I'm afraid you will have to endure the sight of the breakfast table until Winwick has rid us of our morning caller.'

'If she lays eyes on you, we'll be in the suds,' Devenham explained, apparently feeling that this terse remark needed some clarification. 'Use you to scrape an acquaintance with Nick.'

'Oh, no,' she murmured vaguely. 'A scarlet-and-puce striped walking dress. Not suitable at all.'

'Not suitable for what, may one ask, Mama?'

'Why, for paying morning calls, dearest. What did you think? And speaking of calls, I came to ask if you would be so kind as to escort me to the Wribbonhalls'. Augusta and I are going into Eastbourne to shop, and it seemed foolish for her to fetch me when it means going out of her way. After we depart, you could take Miss Wribbonhall for a drive about the countryside. I am sure she would be happy to point out all the changes that have occurred since you were last in Sussex. She has the most obliging nature.'

Nick exchanged one brief glance with Devenham. 'Unfortunately, mine is not so obliging,' he stated in the bluntest of tones. 'In case you have forgotten, ma'am, I am here to bring some sort of order to the Place—which necessitates my being upon the premises occasionally. That does not mean, however, that your own pleasures have to be curtailed. The carriages are all at your disposal, and you may take as many footmen with you as you like if you feel the need for an escort, but—'

Recognising the ominous signs of danger as the Dowager leaned back in her chair and withdrew a bottle of smelling-salts from her reticule, he forcibly bit back the rest of his lecture.

'Really, Nicholas, there is no need to speak so roughly to your poor mother. Or to loom over me in that odiously threatening manner. Naturally I don't expect you to accompany me everywhere. Although, I must say that, until now, you seem to have been perfectly happy to do so.'

'Getting a bit much,' confided Devenham, observing the way his friend's lips compressed and hastening into the breach. 'Nick's been out of society a long time. Not used to falling over females every time he sets foot out of doors. Why, only yesterday we were waylaid by a bunch of giggling girls on horseback, challenging us to a race. And take the chit who decided to faint in his arms at the Langdons' soirée last night. All a put up job. Can't blame him for feeling a trifle hunted and going to earth.'

Her ladyship revived with unexpected vigour. 'Never have I been so mortified in my entire life as I was upon that occasion,' she declared, gazing reproachfully up at her son. 'I do not hesitate to inform you, Ravensdene, that your behaviour was atrocious. How could you step back in that callous way and let Miss Sherington crash to the floor?'

'Because the little fool was shamming it,' growled Nick.

Devenham started to laugh. 'I should say so. Never seen a female recover her senses so fast in my life.'

In the face of this conspiracy of male heartlessness, the Dowager abandoned scolding for her usual dulcet tones. 'Well, the provocation to teach Miss Sherington a lesson was certainly great,' she conceded. 'However, most young ladies, I am happy to say, are more modestly behaved. I am sure Miss Wribbonhall, for one, would never—'

'Now, look, Mama, before you go any further, let me make it quite clear that—'

Once again Devenham hurried to avert a threatened relapse. 'Be happy to escort your ladyship to the Wribbonhalls' this morning,' he intervened, smiling winningly. 'That is, if you don't object to cutting a dash in a sporting vehicle for a few miles, ma'am. Been teaching Miss Wribbonhall to drive a high-perch phaeton, you know.'

Lady Ravensdene bestowed a seraphic smile upon him and gave him to understand that she was still quite capable of cutting dashes. 'Dear Barney,' she murmured. 'Always so obliging.' She rose from her chair and, after patting Ravensdene's arm in an absent-minded way which nevertheless managed to convey noble forgiveness, drifted towards the door.

Nick stepped past her to open it. 'Dev will be with you in a moment, Mama,' he said, shutting it firmly behind her. He turned to the Viscount. 'If ever a female has matchmaking on her mind,' he stated grimly, 'it's my mother. Bloody hell!'

'Yes, well, I hate to break this to you, Nick, but she isn't the only one. Look at the past week, not to mention the female who dropped her basket at your feet in the middle of the village the other day. If it continues like this, the next thing you know they'll be armed and dangerous. What the devil are you going to do?'

Nick leaned back against the door and folded his arms across his chest. 'Recruit you to distract my mother,' he returned, smiling evilly.

The Viscount put his head in his hands. 'I knew you invited me down here for more than the occasional game of chess,' he groaned. 'I'm to be fobbed off with your mother. You, I suppose, are about to have the pleasure of interrogating some dark, suspicious character.'

'I don't think the vicar quite falls into that category, but, yes, I do intend to speak to him today. He may be the one person in the county who can tell me about the Lynleys.'

'Not if you roll him up the way you just did me,' said Devenham dolefully. He stuck his fork in a slice of ham and shook his head. 'Not subtle, Nick. Definitely not subtle. You'll have to use more delicacy with the vicar if you're going to interrogate him about the neighbours.'

But later that day, when Nick caught up with the Reverend Butterlow in the small garden surrounding Comberford vicarage, he was forced to admit that delicate interrogation was not his strong suit. The trouble was, he reflected wryly, he was more used to holding a knife at his quarry's throat while he asked his questions. It might not be delicate, but at least it got results.

Reminding himself that he was now a civilian, and was obliged to act in a correspondingly civil manner, he tried again to extract some information about his nearest neighbour.

'So the owner of the Grange moved here nine years ago. You are well acquainted with him, no doubt.'

'Sir Jasper Lynley, my lord? Yes, I know him well. And his niece, Miss Sarah.' The vicar interrupted a close examination of his precious roses to beam up at his visitor. 'A most capable girl. Most capable. Feels just as she ought on subjects of a more serious nature. Not one given over to the constant pursuit of frivolity, if you take my meaning, dear sir.'

Nick inclined his head as though in agreement, while he wondered why it was that the Reverend Butterlow's mind, like that of everyone else with whom he had conversed on the subject, seemed incapable of running along more than one track—that of Sir Jasper Lynley's niece. Since it was highly unlikely that such a paragon of virtue was employed as a spy for Napoleon in her spare time, he didn't need to hear anymore about the good works of Miss Sarah Lynley.

Her uncle was another matter.

'I haven't made Sir Jasper's acquaintance as yet, although his land marches with mine. He's staying, at present, in Tunbridge Wells, I believe.'

'Left the day before your lordship's arrival three weeks ago,' confirmed the vicar, bending to tug at a weed that had had the temerity to show itself in the middle of a garden bed. 'But I saw Sir Jasper's carriage pass through the village yesterday evening, my lord. I daresay, if the journey has not proved too much for his constitution, he will invite you to call on him. Seldom

goes out himself, but likes to be upon amiable terms
with his neighbours. How many times have I heard him
say—?'

'They live retired?' Nick cut the vicar off with ruthless despatch. 'That must be somewhat restricting for a
young lady.' *And very helpful to a man selling secrets to
the French.*

'Oh, Miss Lynley is not in the first blush of youth,'
Butterlow informed him. Then added rather hastily,
'But not an antidote, as the saying goes. No, no. She
was always a pretty child, and the sweetest, happiest
nature—'

But at that point the chatty little vicar broke off of
his own accord, his smile vanishing as he shook his
head, quite as though Miss Lynley's sweet, happy
nature was a matter for the deepest sorrow.

Nick ground his teeth together to prevent the emis-
sion of a curse totally unsuited to the hallowed ears of
his auditor. He had had enough. This was the last
straw.

It was bad enough that no one could stick to the
subject of Sir Jasper without digressing to that gentleman's niece, but if one more person began a panegyric
on Miss Lynley's sterling qualities, only to break it off
with a shake of the head, a melancholy sigh or any
other equally lachrymose expression, he wouldn't be
answer-fjable for the consequences.

Fortunately for the cordial relations that had
always existed between the vicarage and the occupants of Comberford Place, the Reverend Butterlow's
housekeeper appeared at that moment with the
announcement that another caller was waiting in the
parlour. Nick managed to wind up his conversation
with the vicar and depart with mutual expressions of
goodwill. But by the time he had indulged himself with

a gallop across the Downs that took him to within sight of the Sussex coast, and was on his way back to the Place, questions about the Lynleys were again nagging at his brain.

Was Sir Jasper the harmless old invalid he was depicted to be, or was he the traitor Nick had been sent here to apprehend? And if Sir Jasper was exactly what he seemed, what was it about his niece that had everyone commiserating with her situation? There must be something. Butterlow was not the only person whose remarks had been irritatingly mysterious. His grandfather's ancient groom, now living in a snug cottage on the estate, had started it on the very day Nick had arrived.

'Neighbours, my lord?' Peake had said in answer to his query. 'Well, there's the Fishbournes. You'll remember them from the days you spent here as a boy. Good, solid country folk. And to the south there's Sir Jasper Lynley and his niece, Miss Sarah. A godsend she is, my lord, a proper godsend. What I would've done without her this past winter when the rheumatism got so bad, I can't tell you. And the number of times she pops in to the cottage to see how the wife goes on—'

Then he'd stopped and heaved a sigh that had seemed to come from his very boots.

His elderly housekeeper had been next. 'The dearest, sweetest girl that ever walked the earth, my lord. Why, when my Becky's youngest got herself into wrong company, if you take my meaning, M'lord, Miss Lynley took the girl in and found her respectable work, and never a word of blame. But 'twas only to be expected, I suppose, when you consider—'

And on that tantalising note, Mrs Winwick had shut her lips tight and become alarmingly formal.

The same thing had happened, with sundry variations, whenever Miss Lynley's name had cropped up. And as he and Dev had been towed about the neighbourhood in his mother's wake, it had cropped up with annoying regularity. He had thought he might finally have an answer when he'd returned the Fishbournes' formal visit earlier this afternoon. Waving away his spouse's offer of tea, Lord Fishbourne had become quite locquacious over a glass of wine.

'I hear Jasper Lynley is back, my lord. His land lies between your southern boundary and the coast, as you probably know by now. Sound chap. Ex-military like yourself. Lives with his niece. Sensible gal. Make some man a damn fine wife, if it wasn't for—' And he'd stopped dead.

At that point Nick had felt his patience disintegrate rather drastically. 'What?' he'd demanded baldly.

But Lord Fishbourne had encountered a gimlet-eyed look from his wife.

'Oh...um...nothing, really, my lord. Females, you know. No making head nor tail of 'em. Girl's taken a notion to remain single. But a very nice little rider. And speaking of riding, do you want to hear what that stupid young cub of Marsham's has done now?'

And the conversation had taken an abrupt turn to the iniquities of the local youngsters.

Nick stared frowningly ahead between his horse's ears and wondered if he was making too much of the fact that, while everyone appeared perfectly happy to gossip at length about their neighbours, whenever the Lynleys were mentioned he met a stone wall within seconds.

It was his misfortune, he decided irritably, that just when he had his hands full with the burden of Ravensdene Hall and the title that went with it, follow-

ing the unexpected death of his childless elder brother
a year ago, his erstwhile superiors had decided that a
visit of inspection to his Sussex estate was the perfect
cover and had persuaded him to pick up where their
last agent—since then mysteriously deceased—had left
off.

Not that he'd needed much persuasion. Though busy
with the responsibilities of a position he'd never
expected to inherit, he'd been conscious of an increasing restlessness within himself, a sense of something
missing in his life. He didn't want to think that the
missing element was the feeling of living constantly on
the edge of danger. Because if it was. . .

He frowned, considering. If it was, then he had left
it too late to sell out. And far too late to question what
it was he had become.

A gust of wind whipped through the woods, carrying
the scent of rain and causing the branches overhead to
rustle and sway violently. Nick glanced up, distracted
from his suddenly grim thoughts. He could barely see
the sky through the dense foliage, but the rapidly
fading light was all the warning he needed. There was
a storm coming. One of the easterlies that periodically
lashed this part of the coast.

Pushing his questions aside for the moment, he loosened the reins a fraction and nudged the powerful
black horse he was riding to a faster pace.

The wind swooped down from the east just as Sarah
reached the top of the steps leading up from the beach.
It snatched at the skirts of her old cherry-red pelisse,
tangling them about her legs, and fought for possession
of her plain chip hat. Below her, the sea began to whip
itself into a white-crested fury.

'Stupid,' she muttered, as a brief splatter of rain

brushed her face. Why hadn't she kept an eye on the weather?

Clutching her heavy reticule with one hand and clamping the other over her bonnet, she scurried across the exposed cliff top towards the shelter of the woods. Once beneath the trees there was some respite from the wind, but the light was dim. It wasn't an improvement in her circumstances.

Sarah hesitated, eyeing the narrow, inhospitable-looking path in front of her, and wondered what perverse fate had decreed that there should be a storm on the very day she had mustered the courage to walk alone through the woods after eight years of avoiding the exercise. If wind and rain were to be her reward for trying to be more courageous then she would rather have saved herself the trouble.

In the next breath she told herself not to be so foolish. So what if the stunted bushes on either side of the path looked like crouching, misshapen creatures lying in wait for her? She knew they were only bushes. And the eerie moans above her head were merely caused by branches rubbing together. She was perfectly safe. What was more, she could find her way through these woods if there was no daylight at all. And if she walked very fast she might even beat the rain.

She would *not* run.

A low branch smacked her smartly on the arm as she plunged forward, nearly causing her to drop her reticule Sarah clutched it with both hands, cursing both the branch and her pounding heart. Perhaps she shouldn't have tried to be courageous all the way to the beach. A turn around the rose garden would have been sufficient.

On the other hand, she hadn't had the annoyance of a groom dogging her footsteps and telling her to

'Watch out for that tree, Miss Sarah', or 'Go slow on them steps now, Miss Sarah, they weren't meant for the use of ladies.'

A giggle bubbled up as she remembered the stunned looks on the faces of her well-wishers at the Grange when she had declared her intention of walking unaccompanied to the beach that afternoon. She had caused as much consternation as if she had announced that she was going to catch the stage-coach to London to join the Circus at Astley's Amphitheatre.

Then as another violent gust of wind buffeted her, the tiny sound of amusement faded. Other memories began crowding into her mind. Memories that never quite went away. Memories of the day Amy had died.

Scarcely noticing that she had done so, Sarah quickened her pace until she was almost running, as though trying to outpace the invisible ghost at her heels. She didn't want to remember Amy in these woods. She only thought of her sister when she was safely at home, surrounded by warmth and lights and people.

But warmth and lights and people were at least ten minutes away. And the memories kept coming, taking shape in her mind even as she fought against remembering; for it had been a day like this...almost exactly like this. The fading light that kept her gaze fixed on the ground immediately in front of her...the swaying trees, branches creaking in the wind...the scent of rain...the distant, sullen mutter of thunder...

She could almost feel Amy beside her. Amy the Beauty. Amy the wilful, the flirtatious, the reckless one, telling her to stop dawdling or they'd be caught in the storm. It had been here on this very path. She had laughed and told her sister that a few drops of rain wouldn't hurt them, that Amy was only concerned about ruining her new muslin dress.

And then just ahead, just where the path crossed a narrow ride, she had glimpsed movement and—

Sarah looked up and screamed.

Out of the wind-torn shadows before her, rising from the very ground at her feet came a creature of horror, a towering black demon, its gaping mouth emitting a shriek that was a hideous echo of her own. She tried to recoil, to slow her headlong pace, but it was too late. The apparition was upon her. She couldn't stop. Couldn't even draw breath to scream again.

Then the black monster was wrenched violently away to the side. Hooves thudded to the ground bare inches away and a blistering curse scorched her ears.

'Oh, dear God!' Sarah stumbled to the side of the path, almost sobbing with relief. She put a shaking hand to the nearest tree and almost collapsed against it. 'It's only a horse.'

A second later she saw the rider.

He seemed to loom even larger and more menacing than the horse, a giant black shadow against the lighter shadows cast by the surrounding trees, his face an indistinct blur in the gloom. He reined the horse around, bringing the frightened animal under control by sheer muscular force, then began to dismount.

No!

He hadn't heard her. The cold fingers of fear clutching at her throat stopped her voice. Sarah backed away, cannoning into another tree as she pulled frantically at the strings of her reticule.

It was a stupid place to keep a pistol, she thought crazily, as her fingers closed around the weapon. The wretched thing weighed a ton, but she managed to level it, hoping the horseman couldn't see how wildly her hand was shaking. 'Don't move!' she cried, the words emerging thin and high. 'Don't move or I'll shoot!'

The rider went utterly still. So, incredibly, did the horse, the two figures seeming to blend with one another as if she was looking at a vision of an ancient centaur. Then—

'This,' he ground out in a furious voice, 'has gone far enough.'

CHAPTER TWO

IT WASN'T the voice of her nightmares.

Sarah sagged limply against the tree trunk at her back, overwhelming relief flooding through her. The voice was deep, rough-edged, and savage with anger, but she had never heard it before.

It was also, unmistakeably, the voice of a gentleman.

'Oh, dear,' she murmured. She blinked several times, trying to think. Now what? Here she was backed up against a tree, holding an unknown man at gunpoint, and she didn't know what to do next. She would gladly have sunk into the ground, but that didn't seem to be an option.

'What's the matter?' the stranger demanded. 'Not quite sure how to go about it?'

Sarah had been thinking of lowering the pistol. Now it seemed like a good idea to keep it where it was. 'Go about what?' she asked cautiously.

'Blackmail, I imagine, Madam Footpad.'

'*Footpad*!' He thought she was a footpad? *Were* there lady footpads?

Sarah shook her head. It didn't matter. She had to extricate herself from what promised to be an extremely awkward, not to say disastrous, situation. 'I think there's been a small mistake,' she began.

He didn't let her get any further. 'Oh, I can assure you there's no mistake,' the dark voice purred. 'You do have the right victim. I *am* Ravensdene.'

'Ravensdene?'

Good heavens! She knew Ravensdene. At least she

28

knew *of* him. He was old Lord Comberford's heir and their nearest neighbour and—

'Oh, dear,' Sarah said again. The hand holding the pistol wavered and fell to her side.

An instant later she was slammed back against the tree with a force and speed that didn't even give her time to gasp. Her legs were immobilised between two hard thighs, long, powerful fingers wrapped around her throat, forcing her chin up, and the hand holding her pistol went completely numb under the bone-crushing grip on her wrist. His voice spoke in her ear, the tone so cold and merciless that every muscle in her body turned liquid with fear.

'Never lower a pistol,' he advised softly, 'until you're quite sure you won't lose the advantage.'

She couldn't answer. She simply couldn't speak. Terror paralysed her voice as surely as the hand about her throat. He was huge; his weight brutal, crushing, as he held her pinned to the tree. Sarah squeezed her eyes shut, struggling against the sickening, helpless panic sweeping over her. Had it been like this for Amy? Oh, dear God, *Amy. . .*

Her fear hit him first. He had, in fact, intended to give the little hussy the fright of her life. What he hadn't expected was that the soft flesh beneath his hand would go ice-cold with shock, or that she would turn so white he could see the blood wash out of her face even in the dim light, could see the damp sheen of fear on her brow where her bonnet had been pushed aside.

Nick knew all about fear. He'd seen it in men before a battle; he'd even used it, made a weapon of it. But he'd never seen such stark, mindless terror in a woman. This was more than alarm at suddenly losing the upper hand. She was in the grip of real panic, almost senseless with it.

The thought shook him—badly. And, shaken, he felt the softness. And the trembling. Sensations shot through him that were violently at odds with the anger still simmering in his veins. Desire, sharp and swift and hot, but more than that; a need to gentle, to reassure, to cradle.

God! What was wrong with him? Six months out of the field and he was in danger of forgetting one of the basic rules for survival.

Releasing the unknown's wrist, he pried the pistol from her clenched fingers and examined it briefly. It was loaded.

'Damned little fool.' Muttering beneath his breath, Nick pocketed the weapon before shifting his hands to her arms to hold her upright while he eased his weight from her. She stayed where she was, scarcely seeming to breathe, her lashes dark crescents against the pallor of her cheeks.

'Damned little fool,' he snarled, suddenly furious that she had made him use such force against her. 'What the bloody hell did you think you were doing?'

The rough question jolted Sarah back into the present, burying the hideous clamour of screams and harsh curses echoing inside her head beneath the sounds of here and now. Gradually the sounds became distinct, separate; the wild drumming of her heartbeat, the sibilant rustle of leaves above her, a deep male voice she didn't recognise.

'All right.' The voice was softer now, more controlled. The hands wrapped around her arms flexed, but not in any cruel way. 'It's all right. I'm not going to hurt you. Do you hear me? You're safe.'

She knew that. Somewhere in the confusion of her mind was the knowledge that she wasn't hurt. But. . .

She was angry, Sarah realised with a jarring sense of shock. Furious! Rage was welling up inside her with a force that made her want to scream aloud with the pressure of it. Why should this happen to her? *Why?* What had she done? For years—*years!*—she had been afraid of her own shadow, haunted by the memory of violence, hovered over, protected, stifled. And just when she had tried to be brave, just when she had steeled herself to take the first shaky steps towards facing her fear, *this* had to happen. It wasn't fair. It simply wasn't fair!

Her eyes snapped open to glare straight up at the face of her captor.

'Better now?' he asked quietly.

'If I am, it's no thanks to you,' Sarah flung at him, then promptly fell silent as an instant impression of darkness and power hit her like a blow. Darkness that had nothing to do with the midnight shade of his hair and his shadowed eyes. Power that was more than physical strength, more than a strong masculine jaw and a hard, sharply etched mouth that looked utterly, indomitably, ruthless.

Sarah shivered, suddenly grateful that she couldn't see him clearly, that the daylight seeping through the trees behind him left his upper face in shadow. Had she been foolish enough to lash out at him because he was the Earl of Ravensdene and a member of polite society and thus safe? She peered at the hard face above her and knew that Ravensdene was capable of exactly the kind of brutality she had armed herself against. Tough-looking rather than handsome, he made her think of a predator, fierce, savage and dangerous. He belonged in a jungle, in a dark, deadly jungle.

'You won't get away with this,' she warned, her voice husky and trembling with the strange mixture of fear and rage still roiling inside her.

'I should be saying that,' he retorted. 'But we'll sort out that little detail later. Who are you?'

'Sarah Lynley. Not that it's any of your—'

'*What*?' She was freed so abruptly she would have stumbled if not for the tree at her back. Ravensdene stared at her as if she had just produced another pistol.

'*You're* Miss Lynley?'

'Yes,' she stormed. 'And if you've quite finished assaulting me, my lord, you may remove yourself from my uncle's land. Immediately!'

Nick didn't even listen to the order. He was too busy trying to reconcile the tiny spitfire confronting him with his mental image of Sir Jasper Lynley's spinster niece.

This was the mature woman who shunned frivolity and spread good works all over the neighbourhood? He rapidly reviewed all the conversations he had had about Miss Sarah Lynley and decided that none of them had prepared him for the reality of dark, wildly tousled ringlets and huge long-lashed eyes set in an exquisite face that, at present, combined feminine delicacy and fierce determination in equal measure.

She reminded him irresistibly of a small kitten confronted by a large predator. Panicked, outweighed and cornered, but fighting nonetheless. The impression was heightened by the faint tilt at the outer corners of her eyes. Eyes, he decided, that, heated with fury, were the warmest shade of amber he had ever seen.

His gaze slid swiftly over the rest of her, noting that the prevailing fashion for high-waisted garments suited her slender figure to perfection. Her pelisse was rucked up at the side, exposing one neatly-turned ankle and a small foot encased in a suede half-boot. Beneath her bonnet, which had been pushed to a haphazard angle, her sable-brown tresses were liberally adorned with leaves and twigs. He had an insane urge to brush them away, to thrust his fingers into those thick curls, turn her face up to his and kiss away the anger that had her deliciously curved mouth set in a firm line.

Until he remembered that her uncle was possibly the most promising candidate for the role of traitor.

And she'd been armed.

His eyes narrowed abruptly on her face. 'Do you always make a point of confronting strangers with a pistol, Miss Lynley?'

'Of course not,' Sarah muttered. She had just discovered that long tense silences were not conducive to maintaining outrage. That intent stare was horribly intimidating. So was his question. Especially when she thought about the various and disastrous consequences of aiming loaded pistols at strangers who turned out to be neighbours. 'You gave me a fright because it was getting dark and I wasn't expecting to meet anyone.'

'I gave you a fright so you whip out a pistol? Good God!'

'I was only being cautious.' She shifted uncomfortably.

'Cautious! You think it cautious to wave a loaded pistol at anyone you happen to meet?'

'I didn't just *happen* to meet you. You nearly ran me down! You had no business to be riding so fast through these woods, and in fact,' she added, grasping at the first frail straw to occur to her, 'if you hadn't been trespassing in the first place, my lord, none of this would have happened.'

'I understand Sir Jasper Lynley allows this bridle-path to be used as a right-of-way to the village,' he retorted instantly. 'However, you may correct me if I'm wrong.'

'Well, no, but. . .'

'In that case, Miss Lynley, I am at a loss to understand why your uncle allows you to walk about unattended when you appear to be of an extremely nervous disposition.'

She flinched. 'I am not—'

'Or is he unaware of the situation? Such freedom would not be permitted in London.'

'This isn't London,' Sarah muttered. She lifted her chin. 'And my uncle is perfectly well aware that I walk about unaccompanied on our own land. There is nothing improper in that.'

When he raised one black brow, she bit her lip. The accusation hovering in the air of the impropriety of brandishing loaded pistols at all and sundry was almost visible. Words of apology began floating about in her mind. Perhaps that would placate him.

'In that respect, Miss Lynley, if in no other, I am obliged to admit you are right,' he owned tersely. 'In which case I suppose I should count myself fortunate that my head is still attached to my shoulders.'

The words of apology vanished. In her opinion, sarcasm did not deserve an apology. Besides, a rather horrible reaction was setting in. If she stayed here much longer she was going to collapse.

'Yes, well. . .' She took an experimental step to the side, hoping her trembling legs would support her long enough for her to escape before she made a bigger fool of herself. Her reticule knocked against her knee with the movement. There was a faint clunk.

Ravensdene's gaze narrowed even more menacingly than before. 'Not so fast,' he ordered. He reached out and plucked the bag from her nerveless fingers. 'Let's see what else you have in this handy little receptacle.'

Before she could utter one word of protest, he upended the reticule and shook it. The contents fell to the ground and shattered.

'What the—?'

'Shells,' Sarah informed him righteously.

'Shells?' He stared at her as if she'd lost her wits.

'Yes. You know—' she waved a hand furiously towards the beach '—*shells*. I happen to collect them. And now look what you've done! A particularly fine specimen of—'

'You drew a pistol on me for a handful of shells?' he demanded incredulously. 'What the devil did you think I was going to do? Steal them?'

Sarah glared up at him. She had forgotten all about escape. The perverse sense of satisfaction filling her that it was now Ravensdene who was in the wrong was too revivifying to abandon.

'Why would you want to do that?' she demanded. 'They're in a thousand pieces. And I can assure you, my lord, that it will take a more delicate touch than you possess to piece them back together again.'

That sardonic eyebrow shot up again. His voice went very soft. Very soft and very interested. 'Would it?' he murmured.

Sarah had a sudden desire to take several steps back. Unfortunately, the tree behind her showed no inclination to move out of her way.

'Anyone who smashes people into trees after frightening them out of their wits does not have a delicate touch,' she informed him, trying to rally her wits. 'And as if that is not enough, you've killed all my shells.'

She looked pointedly at the shattered wreckage at her feet, wondering if the words sounded as idiotic to

Ravensdene as they did to her. So much for rallied wits. Then she heard an odd sound. Her head came up. Surely that hadn't been—a laugh?

There *was* a faint difference in the set of his mouth, she thought bemusedly. Somehow his lower lip looked . . .fuller. Softer. The sight sent the most peculiar tingles through her.

'Once again, Miss Lynley, I am forced to agree with you,' he acknowledged, the merest hint of a tremor in his voice. 'If it is any consolation, however, the sight of you with that pistol aimed at my head had a rather unnerving effect on my wits, as well.'

Sarah's gaze flew upward. For the first time she wished she could see the expression in his eyes. Would it match the faint gentling of his mouth? The subtle change in his voice? More tingles shivered through her. Very strange tingles. It was definitely time to put an end to this whole ghastly encounter.

Before she could decide on the best method of removing herself, preferably instantly, from Ravensdene's vicinity, however, he stepped forward a pace, reached for her hand and slipped the strings of her reticule over her wrist. He seemed to take a great deal of care over the exact placement of the ribbons, then his fingers closed around hers.

'I hope that under those circumstances you will accept my apologies for frightening you out of your wits, smashing you into a tree and slaying all your shells,' he murmured.

'I. . .um. . .' She was completely unable to think of anything more intelligent to say. All her awareness was focused on the size and strength of the large hand that was enveloping hers and the utterly astonishing gentleness of his hold. How could his grip edge towards brutal one moment, and then...and then...become almost *protective*?

'I accept your apology,' she managed at last, dragging her hand from Ravensdene's warm clasp and clutching her reticule to her breast as if she feared he might try to snatch it back at any moment. 'Good day, my lord.'

There was a bend in the path only a few steps away. Sarah forced herself to start walking. Head high, she managed to maintain a dignified pace until she was out of sight. Then she gave in to her instincts. Picking up her skirts, she clamped a hand over her bonnet, broke into a run and fled home as if every dark spectre she had ever imagined was at her heels.

Nick was left staring at the empty path in front of him and wondering if he'd suddenly gone soft in the head. He couldn't believe he'd let her get away with it. One minute his would-be assassin had been almost senseless with fear, the next she had treated him to the cutting edge of her tongue, and finally she'd left him with...

What? No apology. No explanation. Just threaten to shoot him over a bag of seashells and then saunter off with a 'Good day, my lord.'

No wonder everyone was so damned mysterious about the woman! Now he knew what was wrong with her. She was mad. Insane! A prime candidate for Bedlam!

And the most intriguing little creature he had ever met.

A searing wave of heat hit him as he recalled in sudden, excruciating detail how Miss Sarah Lynley had felt crushed against him from shoulder to thigh. Soft. Incredibly soft. And fragile. He'd almost torn his hand from her wrist in case the delicate bones had snapped beneath his fingers.

Which would really have left him without a head on his shoulders, Nick concluded disgustedly. She would probably have shot him then and there.

But even that grim thought couldn't prevent his fingers curling into his palm as though he still held that delicate feminine softness within his grasp. Nor had desire been the only emotion that she'd aroused in him. She had fought back fear and defied him with the kind of gallant courage he'd seen in men about to charge a battery of cannon.

And once, just for one infinitesimal second when he'd accused her of possessing an overly nervous disposition, there had been such a look of pain in her eyes that he'd felt something stir deep inside himself. Something he hadn't felt for a long, long time.

Beside him, his horse snorted, nudging his arm as if reminding him of the rapidly worsening weather. The movement shifted the gun in his pocket and Nick reached for the weapon, testing the aim and balance before laying it across his palm. For some reason, the sight of the weapon made him recall something else about Miss Sarah Lynley.

She had made him laugh.

He regarded the slim, deadly looking pistol for a moment, then lifted his gaze to the point where Sarah had vanished. A faint smile edged his mouth. A smile that would have caused the battle-hardened guerillas he had once commanded to tread very cautiously around him indeed.

'I'll let you go this time, Miss Lynley,' he murmured. 'But you are going to tell me why you held me up. Very, very soon.'

*   *   *

'*You held him up*?'

The stunned question reverberated around the elegant drawing room at Wribbonhall Lacy as though the walls themselves had spoken. Even the blue and gold brocade curtains seemed to quiver with shock.

Sarah turned from her contemplation of the sheltered courtyard garden beyond the long windows and nodded confirmation. Horrified comprehension was dawning in Miss Julia Wribbonhall's soft grey eyes, but clearly she was still struggling to absorb the tale she had just heard.

'You held up Lord Ravensdene?'

Sarah nodded again.

'You held up the *Earl of Ravensdene*? With a *pistol*? Sarah. . .?'

'I know. He had trouble with the idea, too.'

Julia sank onto a convenient sofa, distractedly brushing away a blonde curl that had strayed over her shoulder. 'I can understand why,' she said faintly. 'He must have thought you were out of your senses. And you say he still has Sir Jasper's pistol? Oh, Sarah! What are you going to do?'

'Get it back before Ravensdene goes to Uncle Jasper. But don't ask me how. I haven't thought of a plan yet.'

'Before Ravensdene goes to Sir Jasper? Good heavens!'

'I wish you would not repeat everything I say, Julia,' Sarah commanded sternly, beginning to pace up and down in front of the windows. 'It is not at all helpful.'

'How can I think of anything helpful with you whizzing about like that?' Julia retorted with spirit. 'Come here and sit down. I swear my head is spinning.'

Sarah obliged, seating herself on a matching gold brocade sofa on the other side of the fireplace. She kicked a fold of her green velvet riding habit out from under one small foot and gazed hopefully at her friend.

'Do you suppose. . .?' Julia leaned forward, frowning intently. 'Do you suppose, if you were to explain about Amy—?'

She was cut off by a laugh that wobbled desperately in the middle. 'What do you suggest I tell him, Julia? My lord, the reason I held you up was because my sister and I were set upon at that very spot and she was assaulted and murdered while I did nothing to help her, so I've avoided the woods ever since unless I'm with someone, and since I was unaccompanied for the first time in eight years yesterday, you happened to be unfortunate enough—'

The rapid spate of words at last dried up. Sarah swallowed hard, fighting back tears. 'Can you imagine what he'd think? That I am positively unbalanced.'

'You know it wasn't like that,' Julia reproached gently. 'You couldn't have helped Amy, so there would be no need to say anything about that part of it. For goodness' sake, Sarah, you were knocked unconscious.'

Sarah stared unseeingly at her hands. 'Not quite,' she whispered. 'I knew. . . I could hear. . .'

'Oh, Sarah, I'm sorry.' Springing up from her seat in a flurry of white muslin skirts, Julia rushed across the small space between them to fling her arms around her friend. 'I'm so sorry. This is all my fault. I should never have reminded you.'

'Hush, it's all right.' Sarah returned the embrace, blinking rapidly until her control was restored. 'I can always go to Comberford Place and demand that Ravensdene give my pistol back,' she said bracingly. 'I can hardly make a worse impression than I already have. Not that I care what he thinks of me,' she added hastily. 'But poor Uncle Jasper would collapse from mortification if he ever found out.'

Julia's eyes grew round at this display of courage but before she could comment, the door opened.

'Sarah, dear child, welcome.' Lady Wribbonhall, a plump, still pretty matron as fair-complexioned as her daughter, crossed the room to enfold Sarah in a scented, blue-silken embrace. 'How is Sir Jasper after your sojourn in Tunbridge Wells? I know Dr Salcott considered that taking the waters would prove beneficial enough to offset the disadvantages of the journey. I trust it was so?'

'I'm afraid Uncle Jasper drank very little of the waters, ma'am,' Sarah responded with a rueful smile. She resumed her seat, exchanging a speaking glance with Julia as Lady Wribbonhall disposed herself comfortably on the opposite sofa. 'In fact, after the first swallow he refused to take another drop.'

Julia giggled. 'And you were stuck there for three weeks with all those elderly invalids! Why didn't you return earlier?'

'In this instance Uncle Jasper had another reason for going in the first place,' Sarah muttered somewhat grimly. 'He thought some poor, lonely old gentleman would be misguided enough to offer for me.'

'No doubt with your welfare in mind, Sarah,' Lady Wribbonhall reproved, frowning as her daughter went off into peals of laughter. 'Perhaps he thought an older man might suit you.'

Sarah sighed. She did not feel in the least inclined to share her friend's mirth. 'I know, ma'am. In fact, it is because of Uncle Jasper that I came to see you today. I have a favour to ask of you, if it should not prove to be too much trouble.'

Lady Wribbonhall leaned over and patted her hand.

'You know you have only to ask, dear child. It is to do with Sir Jasper's health, I collect.'

'Not quite, ma'am.' Sarah took a deep breath. 'But you are right about Uncle Jasper being concerned about me...about my future to be precise. I had no idea...that is, I thought he had accepted...'

'That you don't wish to be married?' Lady Wribbonhall concluded for her. 'You were only fourteen when you made that decision, Sarah, and still very...hurt.'

Sarah knew 'hurt' was not the word Lady Wribbonhall had been about to utter. 'Hurt' didn't begin to describe what everyone had thought of her eight years ago.

Extremely disturbed. A severe shock to the brain. Must be kept very quiet. The doctor's verdict had been whispered from manor to hall. From village to farm.

'Yes, well, when I twitted Uncle Jasper about his plans for me—only joking him, you understand—he confessed how worried he's been since that bad spell he suffered at Christmas. And I know he was thinking of what will happen after he...after he dies.'

Lady Wribbonhall nodded. 'Very sensible,' she approved. 'I don't mean to sound harsh, Sarah, but Sir Jasper would be most remiss not to be thinking of your future, especially as his health is now so frail.'

'Yes, I can understand that, Mama,' put in Julia, frowning thoughtfully. 'But surely he will provide for Sarah.'

Sarah shook her head. 'I won't be destitute, of course, but everything is entailed on my cousin, Alfred. Uncle Jasper explained it to me. What is left over would not be sufficient to set up my own establishment, which means I'd have to engage in some respectable employment, or make my home with Alfred and his wife.'

'Alfred and Charlotte? You'd be turned into a drudge,' stated Julia, not mincing matters. 'And an unpaid one at that.'

Sarah spoke before Lady Wribbonhall could reprove her daughter for this brutally honest appraisal of the situation.

'What I've come to ask, dear ma'am, is if you would be so good as to chaperon me whenever we're invited to the same social events. Only until you go to London for the Season, of course. I—'

'My dear child, as if you need to ask. I will be delighted to see you go about in society a little more.' A warm smile spread over Lady Wribbonhall's face. 'You know I have always said you may call upon me at any time. As for the Season—with half the *ton* in Brussels at present, we have decided to remain in Sussex for several more weeks. One or two little country gatherings will be just the thing to accustom you to society.'

'Strictly speaking, Mama, our little country gatherings are not so little these days.' Julia gave Sarah's hand a surreptitious squeeze. 'In fact, I was about to tell Sarah about the exciting new arrivals in our midst when you came in.'

'I expect you have already heard about Lord Ravensdene, if you've been home for a day, my dear,' Lady Wribbonhall said with a wry smile. 'The neighbourhood is in such an uproar that you never did see. One would think the Regent had come amongst us.'

'Mama, how can you speak so?' demanded Julia. 'When you and Lady Ravensdene have become as thick as thieves. I didn't know you were even acquainted with her until recently.'

'Lady Ravensdene?' Sarah's eyes widened.

'Hermione Ravensdene and I have been acquainted for years,' responded Lady Wribbonhall placidly. 'She was presented a few seasons ahead of me, but was kind enough to come to my assistance one night at Almack's when her partner put his foot on the hem of my gown. When I married and came to live in Sussex our friendship was kept up mainly through the occasional letter, your papa having no taste for town life. And when *you* made your come-out, my love, she was in black gloves for her husband, and then for George, her eldest son, so you have never met her until now.'

'Then you also know the present Lord Ravensdene,' murmured Sarah. She wondered why she had felt so strange when Julia had mentioned the existence of a Lady Ravensdene. And why she felt even more peculiar now that she realised the lady in question was the Earl's mother and not his wife.

'We've met, of course,' Lady Wribbonhall agreed. 'But I doubt if anyone, with the possible exception of Lord Devenham, can claim to *know* Ravensdene. There is a certain reserve, a coldness one might say, that is extremely daunting, and quite unlike the rest of his family.'

'I daresay it may be caused by his years in the army,' offered Julia, clearly hoping to allay any alarm Sarah might feel at having to confront a cold, daunting Ravensdene and demand the return of her pistol.

'It is far more likely to be caused by all the caps that are being set at him, my love,' responded Lady Wribbonhall dryly. 'For all the good it will do them.'

'Why is that, ma'am? Does Ravensdene not wish to be married?'

'As to that, I cannot say.' Her ladyship reached out to tug at the bell-pull hanging beside the fireplace. 'He certainly had no objections to the married state twelve years ago, for he wed Marianne Moreton before she was scarce out of the schoolroom and carried her off to Sicily where he was posted. Quite in the teeth of her parents' misgivings, I might add, not to mention his own family's doubts. But he wouldn't settle for a betrothal. It was marriage or nothing and, as he was perfectly eligible, the Moretons eventually capitulated.'

'Well—' Julia looked doubtful '—it sounds very romantic, but I don't think I'd like Ravensdene to be pursuing me so relentlessly. Was she happy with him, Mama?'

'I should think Marianne was very happy,' Lady Wribbonhall replied. 'Remember, my love, that ten or twelve years makes a difference in a man. Ravensdene was still a boy himself at the time, had scarce attained his majority, and Marianne was exceptionally lovely, and quite angelic so I've been told. I imagine she saw a side to him that others might not.'

Sarah shivered inwardly as an image of darkness and power returned to her mind. 'What happened to her, ma'am?'

'There was an accident only a year after their marriage. It was very tragic. They were still living on the continent, but I remember how shocked everyone was to hear the news. Marianne was expecting a child and had some sort of fall. Both she and the baby died.'

'Oh, how terrible!' exclaimed Julia. 'No wonder Ravensdene is so cold and intimidating. It must have been dreadful for him to lose his wife and child like that.'

Sarah didn't comment. For some reason the knowledge that Ravensdene had known tragedy just as she had, that he had grieved for his wife to the extent of never remarrying, both fascinated and frightened her. She remembered the swiftness of his attack, the devastating strength with which he'd disarmed her and shivered again. She hadn't even seen him move. She couldn't believe she had stayed there in the woods and argued with him. The very thought of what might have happened made her blood run cold.

The sound of voices intruded and she glanced up to see that Lady Wribbonhall's butler had answered her summons.

'And see that a message is conveyed to Sir Jasper immediately, Humby, that Miss Lynley will be spending the day here and that she will be attending our party this evening. Naturally we will see her safely home. In fact, I had better write him a note if you would be so good as to sharpen a pen for me. One of the grooms can deliver it when he returns Miss Lynley's horse.'

'Returns my horse? But, ma'am...I don't think...' Feeling as if the ground had suddenly been cut from under her feet, Sarah glanced down at her riding habit. A party? She wasn't ready for a party! 'I haven't got anything to wear,' she finally wailed, falling back on the age-old feminine excuse. 'And I can't spend so much time away from Uncle Jasper—'

'Nonsense, my dear.' Clearly, since her new charge was already in her clutches, Lady Wribbonhall was not about to let her escape. 'If Sir Jasper is as concerned about your future as you say, you can best set his mind at rest by contracting a respectable alliance, which I gather is your purpose in entering society. And what better place to start than a small gathering of friends, most of whom you already know. As for a gown, I am sure we will find something in Julia's wardrobe that will suit you admirably. This isn't a ball, you know, although there will be music if enough young couples wish to dance.'

'*Dance*?'

Lady Wribbonhall swept over this alarmed interjection. 'Now, let me see. There is an Assembly at Eastbourne next week which we should attend, and the Sheringtons are giving a waltzing party— We will have to go shopping as soon as possible. And a visit to my dressmaker must be arranged. Julia, take Sarah upstairs so she may choose a gown for tonight, while I make some plans.'

Sarah found herself swept out of the room before she could voice another protest. They passed Humby bearing notepaper and a selection of quills on a salver. Obviously, a protest on the grounds of leaving her uncle to his own devices would be useless. Besides, she knew Uncle Jasper would be positively delirious with joy that she was going to a party.

'I have just the gown for you, Sarah,' Julia confided as she prodded her unwilling guest up the stairs. 'I've never worn it because Mama thought it should have an over-dress of white gauze or some such thing, but thank goodness you are two-and-twenty and need not feel obliged to wear white all the time. The jonquil silk will look charming with your colouring, and if we can prevail upon Mama to lend you her gold-spangled shawl you will outshine every lady present.'

'I don't want to outshine anyone,' Sarah muttered rebelliously, but without much expectation of being attended to. Julia was as carried away with plans as Lady Wribbonhall. Somehow she had to regain control of the situation. If she was constantly attending social functions under Lady Wribbonhall's aegis, people would naturally assume one thing—which fitted in with her plans up to a point. But beyond that point, how was she to let Uncle Jasper think she was on the lookout for a husband, while making sure every other male in society knew she wasn't?

Nor could she confide her true reason for going into society to Lady Wribbonhall. She was quite sure her ladyship would not be receptive to the idea of her making contacts for the express purpose of hiring herself out as a governess or housekeeper at some later date.

'This is going to be such fun.' Julia's voice bubbled over with excitement as she threw open the door to her bedchamber. 'Mama was right, you know, Sarah. There won't be many strangers here tonight. Why, you even know Lord Ravensdene.'

'Wonderful.' Sarah balked on the threshold and glared at her friend. 'I can ask him to return my pistol. That should enliven the evening considerably.'

'That pistol is not a matter for ill-timed jests,' Julia said severely, pushing Sarah through the doorway and heading straight for her wardrobe.

She then ruined the entire effect of this stern rebuke, however, when she emerged from the closet a moment later, yellow silk spilling over her arms and laughter in her eyes. 'But I have to confess, Sarah, I would have given anything to have seen Ravensdene's face when you aimed that pistol at him yesterday.'

Sarah plumped herself cross-legged on Julia's bed, propped her chin in her hands and resigned herself to the inevitable.

CHAPTER THREE

SEVERAL hours later Sarah was wishing she hadn't been quite so resigned. So far the only ray of light on her horizon was that Ravensdene had not yet put in an appearance. Aside from that, however, she had had to endure an endless line of people exclaiming at seeing her in tones that would have led the uninitiated to suppose she had been incarcerated in a dungeon for years, and at the same time had had to deflect a good deal of curiosity, albeit politely veiled.

And Julia had reverted to scolding.

'Sarah, will you stop pulling at that gown. You look delightful.' She glanced down at her own gown of white sarsenet, its scalloped hem caught up with knots of sapphire ribbon, and added with deeply feminine satisfaction, 'We both do.'

'I should have worn the shawl.' Sarah twitched the tiny puffed sleeves of jonquil silk higher on her shoulders. The adjustment merely caused the bodice to gape. Even the row of gold and white silk roses bordering the neckline didn't make her feel more comfortable. Sighing, she pushed the sleeves down again. 'Really, Julia, how did your mama come to countenance such a low-cut bodice? I feel positively naked.'

'If you were naked people would be staring. Do you see anyone staring?'

Sarah glanced cautiously around at the groups of chattering guests. The first thing she saw had her clutching her friend's arm. 'Oh, no! Julia, it's him!'

'Who?'

'*Who*?' Sarah's voice soared to a hastily stifled squeak. 'What do you mean "who"?' She turned incredulous eyes on her friend and saw her gaze fixed on the entrance to the drawing-room. 'You're looking straight at him.'

Julia's gaze shifted fractionally. 'Oh! You mean Ravensdene. He must have come with Lord Devenham.' And to Sarah's utter amazement, she blushed.

She had never seen Julia blush in her life. Stunned, she looked back at the doorway, momentarily diverted from the unnerving prospect of meeting Ravensdene again.

The gentleman standing next to the Earl and conversing easily with his hostess was possessed of a pleasant countenance and average build. His fair hair was cut short in the military fashion and he was dressed with quiet propriety in black evening clothes. Sarah could not see anything about him that would cause a female to blush. She was perfectly happy to go on studying him, however. Because it was preferable to looking at the tall, black-haired nemesis beside him.

'I take it that is the friend who knows Ravensdene better than anyone,' she murmured.

Julia nodded. 'Yes. Viscount Devenham. Actually, we've come to know him quite well. In fact—' she paused and faint colour tinted her cheeks again '—he's been teaching me to drive his phaeton.'

'Drive his *phaeton*? You hate driving! You can't even drive a gig!'

'Yes, well, that was when Papa was teaching me, and if you only knew how impatient he used to become merely because the stupid horse would go through a garden bed, or if I chipped the paint on the gates. But Lord Devenham is everything that is kind and patient.'

'Kind and patient,' repeated Sarah weakly. All of a sudden she felt very odd. As if the world had shifted in some indefinable way. As if Julia, though three years younger, had somehow stepped past her, to discover something that was beyond her comprehension. How could that happen in just three weeks?

She glanced back at the group by the doorway, telling herself it was her overwrought mind at work, only to have that and every other thought fly right out of her head as her gaze met Ravensdene's with an impact that shook her all the way to her toes. He was looking at her as if she was the only person in the room. As if he would look straight into her soul and discover all her secrets.

Then before she could recover from the shock of his intent gaze, he detached himself and Lord Devenham from the group around Lady Wribbonhall and came striding across the room towards her.

Sarah's mouth went dry. In the brightly lit drawing-room he looked even taller than she remembered. Bigger. Darker. But it was not the threat of his size that had her heart pounding as he approached. It was the way he moved. She had been right about the jungle, Sarah thought. He moved like a large hunting cat; lithe, powerful, intent on his prey. And this time there was nowhere to flee.

'Good evening, Miss Wribbonhall. I see you have quite recovered from our narrow escape yesterday.'

The cheerful voice wrenched Sarah back to an awareness of her public surroundings. She took a step closer to Julia and tried to control the urge to grab at her friend's hand.

'Oh, yes,' Julia was saying gaily. 'Though it is most ungallant of you, sir, to remind me that I nearly sent us into the ditch when I have been telling my friend, Miss

Lynley, how my driving has improved out of sight. Oh, Sarah, I don't believe you have met Lord Ravensdene and Viscount Devenham. Gentlemen, Miss Lynley.'

Both men bowed. Beneath an exchange of polite pleasantries, Sarah could only marvel at her friend's aplomb. While her own mind was still in a turmoil, Julia, with a neat turn of phrase and a blithe pose of ignorance, had left it to Sarah to acknowledge any prior encounter with Ravensdene.

Not that she was going to acknowledge any such thing. Indeed, she hadn't dared raise her eyes above the level of either gentleman's exquisitely tied cravat.

She was just hoping that Lord Devenham's apparent ignorance of the situation was as genuine as Julia's was false, when he offered his arm to her friend.

'I see they are forming a set in the next room, Miss Wribbonhall,' he said. 'Will you do me the honour?'

Julia's poise promptly deserted her. 'Well, I—' She sent Sarah a frantic, questioning glance.

'I advise you to accept, Miss Wribbonhall,' Ravensdene said gently. 'Dev was a member of Wellington's staff, you know, and considers himself, quite erroneously of course, to be the master of any number of intricate steps. You can't have him making a cake of himself in your parents' drawing-room.'

'Well, of all the dashed insults!' exclaimed the Viscount. 'See if we don't take the shine out of everyone.' And taking advantage of Julia's confusion, he whisked her into the upper half of the drawing-room where a string quartet was preparing to play.

Sarah was left marooned with Ravensdene on an island of silence amid the sea of conversation going on around them.

'Your little friend did that rather well for an amateur,' he murmured, far too softly for anyone near them to hear. 'But I should warn you, Miss Lynley, that Dev and I have had a great deal of experience in strategy.'

Sarah gasped and looked up. And promptly forgot what she was going to say.

Ravensdene was looking down at her, his face as hard as she remembered it. Hard and lean, with sharply-chiselled cheekbones, a straight aristocratic nose and twin lines bracketing the firm, cleanly etched mouth. All that, she recalled. It was his eyes that startled her into silence. Though framed by thick black lashes, they weren't dark as she had expected, but a clear, crystalline green, as cold and brilliant as winter sunlight on an emerald sea.

And like the sea, she thought with a small shiver of awareness, the glittering surface hid depths that could prove dangerous.

'You mean you planned—' she began faintly.

'I'm afraid so,' he answered. And then the cool intelligence gleaming in those ice-green eyes warmed with amusement. 'A risk, I know, but it seemed fairly safe to approach you. That piece of nonsense you have on your wrist isn't large enough to hold a pistol.'

Sarah's mouth opened. Nothing came out. Clamping her lips shut again, she glanced around at her very respectable neighbours and almost choked on a giggle. It was partly caused by nerves, she knew, but the picture conjured up of herself holding Ravensdene at pistol point in the middle of a party was suddenly too much. Laughter bubbled over and escaped in a delighted gurgle of sound that had his eyes narrowing briefly.

'Oh, it is a great deal too bad of you to remind me of such an embarrassing situation, my lord,' she reproached, laughter still dancing in her eyes as she gazed up at him more naturally. 'How was I to know you would turn out to be Uncle Jasper's neighbour?'

Nick's mouth quirked. The little devil had turned the tables on him very nicely, he thought wryly. Disarming him with her mirth. He wondered how amused she'd feel if he followed his baser instincts and put his mouth to the pulse he could see fluttering in her throat.

'Most disobliging of me,' he agreed instead. 'But as my mother will be only too happy to inform you, Miss Lynley, I am disobliging.'

'Oh, no. I don't think you are at all,' she said, surprising him again. 'I am sure most gentlemen would have gone straight to my uncle to complain of my hoydenish behaviour, or whatever word they might have put on it.' The animated little face upturned to his was suddenly very serious. 'I am glad you did not,' she confided. 'Uncle Jasper's health is rather fragile at present, and I don't wish to cause him any concern.'

'Very commendable,' Nick returned. He saw the almost imperceptible renewal of tension in her body at his dry tone and smiled down at her. 'We do, however, have unfinished business to attend to, Miss Lynley. Would you prefer to discuss it here, although I should warn you that we may attract unwanted attention, or shall we join Miss Wribbonhall and Lord Devenham?'

The tentative poise Sarah had been gathering about her shattered in an instant. 'What?' she stammered.

'Would you like to dance?'

Dance! With *him*? 'No!'

Oh, good heavens! Had she lost her manners along with her wits? What if someone had heard her? 'I. . . that is. . . I don't dance, my lord.'

He didn't even hesitate. 'In that case, let us take a turn in the courtyard, Miss Lynley. I see the windows are open and several people seem to be finding this room as oppressively warm as you are.'

'It. . .it is particularly close in here,' Sarah managed, and laid the barest tips of her gloved fingers on the arm he offered her.

One dark brow lifted fractionally, but, to her everlasting relief, Ravensdene had no opportunity to comment on her obvious discomfort at even that light contact. Their progress across the room was constantly hindered by those guests who had not had an opportunity earlier of remarking on how delightful she looked, and how happy they were to see her.

Sarah answered automatically, glad of the few minutes' respite in which to pull herself together. Her nervousness at being alone with Ravensdene was quite irrational. There were plenty of people admiring Lady Wribbonhall's courtyard garden. All she had to do was remain calm, and politely ask for the return of her pistol. There was no need to be thrown into a panic over that.

'Why do I have the impression that your appearance here tonight is something quite out of the ordinary?' Ravensdene demanded as he eventually drew her through the long windows opening onto the courtyard.

Since he chose that moment to take her hand and tuck it firmly beneath his arm, Sarah barely heard the question.

'I. . .don't go into society very much,' she finally stammered. How was she supposed to answer questions when all her senses were being overwhelmed by the male heat and power beneath her fingers, when she knew that beneath Ravensdene's formal clothes and cool, polite manner he was capable of exploding into violent action when he was pushed too far?

The memory had Sarah quaking inwardly. She had

escaped him once, but now she was in a trap of her own making; not even the presence of several other guests in the garden calmed her nerves. Ravensdene was taking her as far away from them as propriety allowed. By the time they reached a small marble bench set beneath a hedge of greenery, her heart was beating so hard she could scarce hear anything else.

'Dear me.' Ravensdene halted at the bench and looked up at the topiary in front of them. 'Is that supposed to be a mermaid, do you think?' Then he looked down at her and his voice changed. 'Stop it,' he ordered softly.

'I beg your pardon?' Her voice was no more than a whisper.

'I brought you out here to discuss the return of a certain object, Miss Lynley, not to exact whatever dramatic revenge your overly vivid imagination is conjuring up.

He pressed her gently down onto the bench as he spoke and seated himself beside her. Sarah edged further away at once, but Ravensdene's curt tone had stung her pride. Her imagination really had run amok. She took a deep breath and felt the cool air clear her head a little. The garden seemed to come into sharper focus, the lanterns in the trees casting a soft glow over the flower-bordered paths and strolling guests.

Now if only she could banish a lingering vision of a large black panther cutting his intended prey from a herd of brightly coloured, exotic creatures, she might recover her usual calm, sensible manner.

'You were right, my lord. It is much more pleasant out here. But we should conclude our business before anyone remarks on the length of time we spend conversing. After all, we have only just been introduced.'

His mouth curved slightly. 'I am glad you didn't claim

to have only just met me, Miss Lynley. You would seem
to have a fine appreciation for the exact truth.'

'Well. . .'

'That alone makes you a rarity,' he murmured
before she could enter a caveat in the interests of self-
preservation. 'But you appear to be a most unusual
female in other ways, too. You don't dance. You don't
go into society in the normal way of things. I am forced
to conclude, therefore, that you ventured forth tonight
for the sole purpose of regaining your. . .er, property.'

'Well, actually, the pistol is not precisely mine,' she
confided, relief at his ready understanding loosening
her tongue. 'My uncle has a collection of firearms, you
see, and I. . .*borrowed* one. Just in case. I mean, I was
on the beach. And one cannot be too careful, can one?
We used to have smugglers in this area, you know.'

He raised an eyebrow.

'Yes. Smugglers are very dangerous persons, my lord.
And I was by myself. Collecting shells,' she tacked on
in case he might be wondering why she had ventured
to the beach alone.

'Ah, yes. The slaughtered shells.' The faint smile
reached his eyes. 'A most perilous expedition. I can see
why you would feel the need to arm yourself, Miss
Lynley. I can also see the impending peril confronting
you should your uncle discover that one of his pistols
is missing.'

Sarah glared at him suspiciously, then decided to
ignore Ravensdene's descent into levity in favour of
forming a plan. She nodded. 'All too likely, I'm afraid.
Uncle Jasper's collection is quite extensive and he likes
to reminisce over it from time to time. In fact, quite
often,' she concluded gloomily.

'Obviously there is no time to lose. Be assured, Miss
Lynley, that I will call upon Sir Jasper tomorrow and

contrive to slip the pistol to you without anyone noticing. I hope.'

'You *hope*?' She glared at him again. 'Don't you
know?'

In the light from a nearby lantern, she could see the
gleam in his eyes. 'I see you have no comprehension of
the delicacy of such an operation, Miss Lynley. One
must consider every aspect of the situation. For
instance, would it be preferable to pass the pistol to
you as we shake hands? But what would you do with it
in full view of your uncle? Or perhaps I could stuff it
beneath a sofa cushion for you to retrieve later. However, if your uncle were to wave me to a chair without
a cushion we would be forced to think of something
else. And even if that small setback could be overcome,
there is always the possibility of some unsuspecting
person sitting upon the cushion and setting the pistol
off before you have a chance to—'

'Oh, stop!' Sarah almost bounced with the force of
her impatience. 'You are not taking this seriously, my
lord. You know perfectly well that it is Uncle Jasper's
place to call on you, or leave cards, since you are newly
come to Comberford and have never met him.'

Ravensdene merely smiled. 'But I have met you,
Miss Lynley.'

Sarah only just managed not to fall off the bench in
shock. Even the thought of her uncle's reaction—not
to mention the reaction of everyone else in the neighbourhood—to the Earl of Ravensdene calling on her
after one brief meeting at a party, and before he had
been properly introduced to her guardian, was enough
to overset every faculty.

The suspicion that Ravensdene knew precisely what
he was doing and why, prevented any such frivolous
feminine weakness.

'I am glad to be able to provide your lordship with an evening's entertainment,' she informed him tartly. 'No doubt you consider that I deserve it after giving you such a fright yesterday. However, I assure you that you were never in any danger. I am an excellent shot.'

He just looked at her. 'An excellent shot.'

'Yes.' She suddenly remembered Ravensdene's assessment of her truthfulness and hoped the muted light in the garden hid the blush creeping into her cheeks. She had never fired a gun in her life. But on the other hand, how difficult could it be? You just aimed the thing and pulled the trigger.

One look at the Earl's expression, however, convinced Sarah that he would not subscribe to this simple philosophy. In fact he continued to regard her as if he was examining some strange and hitherto undiscovered form of life.

'Do you know, Miss Lynley, I believe I did you an injustice before. You are not merely rare or unusual. You are unique.'

This time he succeeded in robbing her of breath. Her lungs constricted and her heart began beating in a light, rapid rhythm that reminded her of the fluttering of butterfly wings. The butterflies seemed to be migrating to her stomach. 'I do not know what you are talking about, my lord,' she said with distressingly less forcefulness than she'd intended.

'No, I can see you do not,' he murmured. 'That is part of your singularity, Miss Lynley. And—' he paused and a crooked, unexpectedly appealing smile curved his hard mouth '—if I explained it to you, I would sound like a veritable coxcomb. Suffice it to say that a lady of less character might not be so nice as to object to a man calling on her before he had obtained an introduction to her nearest male relative.'

'Character has nothing to do with it,' Sarah muttered, unnervingly aware that her eyes were fixed on the softened line of his mouth. She wrenched her gaze upward. 'I do not wish to be the subject of gossip. It may not make any difference to you, being a. . .a. . .'

'Gentleman?'

Her brows met in a severe frown. 'That was not the word I was searching for,' she enunciated with great precision. 'If you were a proper gentleman, sir, you would not sit there making idiotic suggestions when I may be faced with disaster at any moment. You claim to be the expert in strategy. Think of something!'

He could think of any number of things, Nick reflected ruefully. And none of them had anything to do with pistols, stolen information or traitors. Having succeeded in making Miss Sarah Lynley forget her nervousness, he was becoming fascinated by the imperious little creature who had taken her place.

And yet he sensed that her instinct to flee was never far from the surface. There was a soft, almost vulnerable curve to her mouth that contrasted intriguingly with the delicate feminine strength in her firm little chin. And though her amber eyes mirrored annoyance, he knew that if he touched her he would feel the tension quivering within her slender body.

The image had him setting his teeth against a sharp stab of desire. He forced it back, suppressing an urge to reach out and run his fingers down the fragile line of her throat to the gentle upper swell of her breasts nestling in a row of silken flowers; to find out if she was as soft as she had felt yesterday. He was here for a purpose, damn it. And that purpose was to gain an entrée into Sir Jasper Lynley's home. One social step at a time.

'I am trying to think of something, Miss Lynley,' he

told her, more brusquely than he intended. 'However, our options are severely limited. If I am not to call upon your uncle, and if the risk of discovery is probable before he calls upon me, then we shall have to meet somewhere else.'

'Do you mean. . .at another party?' Sarah quailed at the thought. This was not turning out to be as simple as she had supposed. And her own brain was very little help. It seemed to be far too occupied with trying to fathom Ravensdene's quick changes of mood than in thinking of ways out of her predicament.

'Where precisely is my pistol, sir?' she demanded, as if the answer might solve everything.

He stared down at her rather thoughtfully. 'Locked in the desk in my library, Miss Lynley. Were you going to suggest that we meet there?'

'Good heavens, no! Of course not!'

'We could, however, meet again in the woods.'

The suggestion was so smoothly delivered that for a moment Sarah simply stared at him. Then an unnerving memory of herself, Ravensdene and woods took hold of her mind. She swallowed and gripped the edge of the bench while her thoughts scurried to and fro in search of an alternative. There was none.

'When?' she managed to whisper.

'I will be inspecting a farm several miles away in the morning,' he answered, still watching her closely. 'Shall we say three o'clock, Miss Lynley? At the same place?'

She nodded, her senses slowly going numb. That was probably a good thing. If she couldn't feel anything. . .

'Miss Lynley.' He waited until she raised dazed eyes to his. 'The last thing I wish to do is cause you distress,' he said very softly. 'And it would be plain to the meanest intelligence that you are extremely reluctant to meet me in such a clandestine manner. Why not ask your friend, Miss Wribbonhall, to accompany you? She knows what happened.'

'She does?' Sarah struggled to collect her scattered wits. 'I. . . I mean. . .how do you know that?'

'She was watching me earlier as if I was about to sprout horns and a tail.' He didn't add that the expression had been shared by several other people who had encountered him in the past under less than salubrious circumstances. 'And,' he continued, 'I think she knows why it happened.'

Now Sarah couldn't speak at all. Ravensdene held her shocked gaze for a moment, then reached out and covered her hand with one of his. The warmth of his touch startled her, making her aware of how chilled she had become.

'Miss Lynley, you did not arm yourself yesterday against smugglers, real or imagined. Apart from anything else, smugglers seldom operate in broad daylight, a fact which I am sure you know well. If you are in any kind of trouble—'

'No!' She tried to pull her hand free. 'It's nothing. . . whatever you're thinking. . .it's not. . .'

'You're afraid of something,' he persisted, overcoming her attempt to escape with terrifying ease. 'And you were afraid yesterday. Panic-stricken, in fact. That's why you were hurrying. Was it something you saw? On the beach? In the wood?'

She shook her head frantically. Why was he asking these questions? Why wouldn't he let her go?

'There was something,' he said, and the absolute certainty in his voice sent a convulsive shudder through her. 'Tell me.'

'I'm sorry,' she said in a stifled voice. 'I'm afraid that is not possible.' She felt the colour seep out of her face and trembled, knowing her words had been an admission of sorts but helpless against his stronger will. She wished she could look away from the intense green of Ravensdene's eyes—heaven only knew what he could see in her own—but his gaze held hers captive.

'Are you sure?' he asked quite gently. 'I might imagine something far worse than the truth.'

'No,' she whispered. 'You couldn't. Nothing could be worse than the truth.'

She turned away at last, blindly, trying to rise, instinctively seeking the lights and warmth she needed to replace the dark chill of her memories, only to be stopped as Ravensdene's hand tightened around hers.

'Wait,' he said softly. 'You can't go back inside like this. You're as white as a ghost, and trembling as if you'd just seen—'

A sudden burst of talk and laughter interrupted him as several young couples came through the french doors into the courtyard, all seeming to be chattering at once. The rather voluptuous red-head leading the fray spotted them immediately and waved.

'Sophie Sherington,' Sarah whispered. 'Oh. . .'

'Yes, a feather-brained ninnyhammer. Leave her to me.' Still holding her hand, Ravensdene stood, drawing her up beside him but half-shielding her from the crowd while she struggled to retrieve what was left of her composure.

'Sarah, dear,' trilled Miss Sherington, reaching them at last and smiling sweetly. 'You sly creature. I had no idea you knew Lord Ravensdene so well. Here I thought you such a retiring miss, but you have been sitting outside chatting with him for the longest time. Oh, good evening, my lord.'

'Miss Sherington,' acknowledged Ravensdene.

Despite her still shattered senses, Sarah's eyes widened at the ice in his voice. Without any warning whatsoever, he was the chilling, ruthless stranger who had terrified her yesterday. Then his long fingers squeezed hers gently and he released her.

'No doubt you also are in need of some cooler air,' he continued with a smile that frosted over at the edges. 'As I recall, your senses are somewhat susceptible to overheated drawing-rooms.'

Miss Sherington's fair complexion took on a hue that clashed hideously with her red tresses and amber gown.

'Jupiter, yes.' Her escort, a callow young gentleman who was apparently oblivious to his partner's discomfort, nodded owlishly. 'Wouldn't want you swooning again, Sophie. Dashed uncomfortable situation. Not but what she's right, Sarah. You shouldn't be—'

He encountered Ravensdene's frigid stare and blanched visibly.

'Don't be such a goose, Harry.' Feeling as if *she* could swoon with very little assistance, Sarah stepped forward. Her legs were shaking and her voice sounded rather far away, but she could not stand by and let young Mr Marsham, whom she had known since he was in short-coats, be annihilated. And from the look on the Earl's face, Harry Marsham's annihilation was imminent.

'Surely you remember that when Lord Comberford became too ill to venture out, he and Uncle Jasper continued their chess matches using me as their proxy. I swear I wore a path between Comberford Place and the Grange. Lord Ravensdene wished to thank me, and naturally asked to hear more of his grandfather. They were very close when he was a boy. Isn't that so, my lord?' She looked up at Ravensdene in silent appeal.

The cold glitter of his eyes was hidden, shadowed by half-lowered lashes as he gazed down at her. For a moment Sarah thought he was going to ignore her plea, then he inclined his head slightly. 'Yes, Miss Lynley,' he murmured, his voice a deep, dark purr. 'As a matter of fact, we were.'

She smiled shakily.

He did not return her smile but glanced away at once, using his impressive height to look over the heads of their stunned audience as if the small crowd did not exist. 'Are you ready to return to the drawing-room, Miss Lynley? I see Lady Wribbonhall signalling to us. Shall I take you to her?'

'Oh, yes. Thank you.' Aiming a vague, meaningless smile in the general direction of her friends, Sarah took the arm he offered her as if it was a life-line. For once the strength in him was welcome. Not a threat but a haven; something to cling to while they approached the lights and chatter of the bright drawing-room.

How could that be? she wondered, confused. Ravensdene might have been compliant a moment ago, but he still frightened her. The daunting steel of the forearm beneath her fingers should have been enough to make her run as fast and as far from him as she could. And yet. . .when she pictured herself doing that, she saw herself halting, and looking back. Even, heaven help her, being drawn back.

She must have taken leave of her senses! He was male, therefore unpredictable. He was larger and more powerful than her, therefore dangerous. And if Julia could not accompany her tomorrow, she would have to face him again without any defences at all.

A second later that fact was brought home to her in no uncertain terms. As Lady Wribbonhall's kind face appeared in her line of vision, Ravensdene bowed and left her—but not before he had murmured for her ears alone, 'Until tomorrow, Miss Lynley.'

CHAPTER FOUR

SHE was doing the right thing, Sarah told herself for about the fiftieth time that morning as she turned her mount onto the narrow path that branched off the main road just before it reached the charming little village of Comberford.

Knowing her rider's destination, the chestnut mare responded eagerly, trotting briskly along the laneway that was bordered on one side by the high stone wall surrounding the gardens of Comberford Place, and on the other by a hedge dividing the lane from cultivated fields. Several hundred yards further on, the path veered westward at a pair of wooden gates to eventually disappear somewhere in the grassy folds of the Downs, but Sarah had no interest in the magnificent vistas to be seen in that direction.

She reined in her horse and dismounted to open the gates, then, being country-bred, carefully shut them behind her. The mare danced with impatience as Sarah climbed onto the second bar of the gate to mount again.

'You might as well calm down, Honey,' she warned, regaining her saddle with some difficulty. 'No one is expecting us, so there won't be any treats for you today.'

Honey merely snorted in disbelief and set off along the faint track that skirted the fields of the home farm before her mistress had given her the office to start.

Sarah sighed and let her horse have her head. Life was very uncomplicated for those of the equine persuasion, she mused. The track ended at the stableyard where such delicacies as apples never failed to materialise. Honey apparently saw no reason to believe that today was going to be any different.

Not that she herself wanted to dawdle. Sarah frowned as she ran through the plan she had devised after discovering that Julia was engaged elsewhere this afternoon, and again assured herself that she was doing the right thing. Retrieving her pistol from Ravensdene's library was a good deal safer than meeting the Earl in the woods. And probably a good deal easier as well.

In fact, the circumstances could hardly be better. As the guests had been leaving last night, she had overheard Lord Devenham arranging another driving lesson with Julia for this morning, while Ravensdene's delightfully vague mother had said she would visit Lady Wribbonhall at the same time to gossip about the party. As for Ravensdene himself, she knew he was out inspecting farms. The only people she expected to encounter, therefore, were the servants, and they were accustomed to her comings and goings.

Of course the senior members of Ravensdene's staff might think it a little odd that she would call at the servants' entrance with a fresh pot of salve for Mrs Winwick's bunions while the family was in residence, but they would very likely dismiss it as force of habit. After all, in the months prior to old Lord Comberford's death and during the two years since, she had been a regular visitor to Mrs Winwick's sitting-room.

She even had a ready excuse if anyone caught her sneaking into the library. And she would leave a note for Ravensdene. He would probably be very grateful to be saved from a third encounter with a female whose nerves and brain turned to mush whenever she was in his presence.

Sarah nodded. Yes, her plan covered every aspect of the situation. She was doing the right thing. Certain persons who would remain nameless might think her cowardly—and it was true that she had been dreading her next meeting with Ravensdene—but she didn't care what he thought. *She* knew the truth. It had not been dread alone that had kept her awake half the night, planning, but a faint, whispering sense of anticipation. It had scared her witless.

She was definitely doing the right thing.

'My God, it's true.' Devenham looked at the pistol held casually in his friend's hand then collapsed onto the nearest chair and started to laugh. Again.

Raising his eyes towards the library ceiling, Nick propped himself against his desk and waited for the paroxysms to subside. It was not the first time he had been obliged to do so. Since regaling Devenham with the story of his initial encounter with Miss Sarah Lynley, the Viscount, between bouts of disbelief, had been doubled over with laughter for a good ten minutes.

'If you've quite finished cackling like a maniac,' he said when Devenham finally sat up and mopped his streaming eyes, 'we can get on with discussing the situation.'

'Sorry, old boy.' Devenham grinned unrepentantly. 'Couldn't help it. I know I said the next female chasing after you would be armed and dangerous, but I didn't expect it to actually happen.'

Nick felt a reluctant smile tug at his own mouth. 'Believe me, Dev, if I thought it was that simple you could laugh yourself silly, with my compliments. But it's not.' He glanced down at the pistol and frowned thoughtfully. 'It most definitely is not that simple. Miss Lynley did not know who I was two days ago when she brandished this gun in my face, and last night I received the distinct impression that she would have preferred to remain in that ignorant state of mind.'

'So the lady isn't joining the ranks of females falling over you.' Devenham chuckled. 'You ought to be grateful. Pretty little thing,' he added judiciously. 'Shame she's so timid. Although if she pulled a pistol on you. . .'

'Precisely.'

'Good God!' The Viscount's jaw dropped. Suddenly he was completely sober. 'Surely you don't think. . . A *woman*?'

Nick shook his head. 'You're going too fast, Dev. I don't suspect Miss Lynley of being a spy, but I think she knows something. Perhaps she's known it for some time, or maybe she stumbled onto something the other day, which would explain why she was going full-tilt along that path from the beach.'

'There was a storm coming,' Devenham reminded him.

'She didn't arm herself with this against thunder and rain,' Nick said quietly. He tossed the pistol gently into the air before straightening and returning it to the half-open drawer in his desk.

Devenham watched him lock the drawer and pocket the key. 'Lynley is supposed to be a recluse, but you're going to contrive a meeting with him using his niece, aren't you?'

'Using her or anyone else who'll oblige me,' Nick returned. He glanced at his friend. 'Including the Wribbonhalls if I have to.'

'God, Nick, you don't have to say that as if you're

warning me. Whoever is selling information to the French has to be stopped.' He paused, frowning. 'If Lynley is your man, though, it'll cause the devil of a scandal.'

'And an innocent girl will be hurt. At the very least she'll feel used. Probably others will also. Is that what you're thinking, Dev?'

'Hard not to think it,' Devenham said shortly. 'It's the truth.'

Nick met the Viscount's frowning gaze for a moment, then turned and walked over to the window. He propped one broad shoulder against the wall, shoved his hands into the pockets of his riding coat and stared out at the view of the lake and the home-wood.

'Yes, it's the truth,' he admitted. 'But you see, Dev, I can be very. . .discreet.' His mouth twisted. 'It's a rather particular talent of mine .'

In the hazy reflection in the glass he saw Devenham rise swiftly to his feet and knew his friend had picked up the faint trace of bitterness in his tone. Before the Viscount could speak, however, the door opened to admit Winwick.

'Excuse me, my lord, but Lord Devenham's phaeton is at the door and Holcot has instructed me to inform his lordship that the greys are, er, damned nasty devils to hold, begging your lordship's pardon. He wishes to know if he should take them for a turn along the carriageway.'

'Good God!' The Viscount strode forward, seized the hat and gloves he had thrown carelessly onto the desk earlier, and headed towards the door. 'Not unless he wants a broken neck. Thanks, Winwick, I'd forgotten the time. Tell Holcot I'm coming, would you? Her ladyship, too. Can't keep your mother waiting, Nick. I'm taking her to the Wribbonhalls'. I'll convey your thanks for the party last night.' He reached the open doorway and stopped to look back. 'And don't think this conversation is finished because I have to dash off,' he warned.

'You're allowing Miss Wribbonhall to drive your greys?' Nick queried politely, ignoring the rest.

'Are you mad? Of course not. She only thinks she is.'

'Indeed? That must be an interesting method of teaching a lady to drive.'

Taking hold of the door handle, the Viscount prepared to depart. 'It is,' he said, and grinned. 'You ought to try it some day.'

Nick was still smiling as he turned back to the view beyond the window. For some reason Dev's suggestion held a definite appeal. He was just wondering whether Miss Lynley had ever driven a high-perch phaeton when, far to the left, he glimpsed movement. It was brief, nothing more than a flash of colour among the trees, but to senses honed by years of danger it was enough. His eyes narrowed on the spot where he thought the flash of chestnut would come again. When it did he smiled in satisfaction. It was always gratifying to have one's suspicions confirmed.

He stood there for a moment, thinking rapidly, then strode over to the fireplace and reached for the bell-pull to summon Winwick back into the room.

Sarah couldn't understand it. There was no one around. The Place appeared to be deserted.

True, there had been plenty of bustle in the stable-yard, with grooms and stableboys tending their high-strung charges, but since she had left Honey with a young undergroom and stepped into the small entryway serving the kitchen wing, she had not encountered a single soul. It was all very odd.

On the other hand, she mused, as she slipped into the vacant dining-room at the far end of the passage connecting the kitchens and the main wing of the house, perhaps she should be grateful. She could complete her errand in peace, and then look into the kitchen on her way out as if she'd just come in. Surely the chef and his minions would be present. She would leave a message and the pot of salve for Mrs Winwick and make good her escape. Simple.

Sarah closed the dining-room door behind her and spared a quick glance at the charming view of lawn, lake and woods to be had from the two bay windows in this corner of the Place. She was really very fortunate, she told herself again. Comberford Place being built in the shape of a U, all the rooms along the south wing opened into each other: dining-room, breakfast parlour, drawing-room, library. There was no need to go into the hall, even if everybody did seem to have vanished.

Less than a minute later she reached her goal. Sunlight streamed through the long windows at the far end of the library, illuminating the big mahogany desk that stood there. The rest of the room was furnished with comfort in mind, from the thick flower-patterned carpet to the commodious chairs and sofas grouped about the fireplace, above which hung a portrait of the late Lord Comberford.

The black and white marble chess table, its pieces set out as if the absent players were in the middle of a game, caught her eye as she sped down the long, book-lined room, but Sarah didn't pause until she reached the window alcove. Her story of a lost glove, possibly mislaid weeks ago when she had last visited Mrs

Winwick and had found the housekeeper in the library, would do to explain her presence. It would hardly be reason enough to be rifling through Ravensdene's desk. She would have to be quick.

A qualm shook her as she realised just what she was about to do. Then she thought of the alternative. Taking a resolute step forward, she bent to tug gently at the middle drawer of the desk.

It was locked, of course. Ravensdene had said as much last night. But that was not a problem. Fate was still on her side. She had not exaggerated last night when she had mentioned her many visits to Lord Comberford. The elderly baron had become quite fond of her. She had even penned the odd letter for him. She knew exactly where the keys to the drawers were kept.

Steadying herself with one hand, Sarah leaned forward and reached for the ornate silver quill-holder on the far side of the desk.

'I'm afraid I neglected to tell you, Miss Lynley, that my habits are rather different to my grandfathers. I keep my keys upon my person.'

A most unladylike shriek echoed through the library before the last words were out. Sarah jerked upright as if she'd been seized by the neck of her riding habit. She collided with the chair behind her, staggered forward again and ricocheted off the edge of the desk to land in a dishevelled heap, this time *in* the chair. Clutching both its arms she watched, frozen with shock, as Ravensdene rose slowly from a high-backed chair near the fireplace and paced down the room towards her.

He came to a halt on the other side of the desk, tilted his head slightly and raised an eyebrow in silent enquiry.

The barely suppressed amusement gleaming in his

eyes had Sarah wishing she had her hands around his
throat rather than the chair arms. Stunned by this
hitherto unsuspected propensity for violence in herself,
she uttered the first words that sprang to her lips.

'Are you out of your mind?' she yelped. 'How dare
you give me such a fright when you're not supposed to
be here!'

His lips twitched. 'My apologies, Miss Lynley. However, you may have noticed that I, er, live here.'

'That's no excuse!' she raged. Then, as he burst out
laughing, she moaned and sank back in the chair, one
hand over her closed eyes. What on earth had made
her say such a thing? What was the man doing to her?

The discreet creak of expensive leather had her eyes
flying open again. She peered out from under her hand
to find that Ravensdene had drawn another chair up to
the desk and was sitting down.

'Are you going to have a fit of the vapours?' he
enquired, regarding her with great interest.

Sarah lowered her hand immediately. 'No, I am not!
But if I was it would be all your fault.' She suddenly
realised how ridiculous she must look sitting there
behind the huge desk while Ravensdene occupied a
visitor's chair. Not that he seemed to be conscious of
the absurdity of the situation. In fact he looked as if he
was prepared to spend the entire day right where he
was.

She scowled at him suspiciously. 'Why are you sitting
down?'

He merely smiled in answer and stretched his legs
out. As one transfixed, Sarah watched him settle back
in a lazy masculine sprawl that made her heart start to
pound. She had a strong urge to spring to her feet,
except that such a move would make Ravensdene feel

obliged to stand also, and she wasn't sure she could cope with him looming over her.

Even sitting he looked far too big and dangerous. The panther at his ease, she thought, shuddering. Relaxed, but alert and powerful.

'I think you and I should have a little talk, Miss Lynley, don't you?'

'Talk?' Sarah tried to moisten suddenly dry lips. 'What about?'

Ravensdene's gaze lowered to watch the small, betraying movement of her tongue, then lifted again. All traces of humour had vanished from the gem-like green eyes gazing into hers, to be replaced by a rather disturbing gravity, and behind it, for a fleeting second, something more intense, and infinitely more disturbing.

'Would it have been so very terrible to have met me in the woods?' he asked quietly.

Sarah groped frantically for a response that wouldn't require any complicated explanations. 'It was. . .it would have been. . .quite improper for me to do so, my lord.'

He raised a brow. 'And stealing into a gentleman's house without so much as a maid to lend you countenance, is not?'

'I intended to meet Mrs Winwick,' she muttered, feeling extremely put upon. 'But I should have known it was too good to be true when I didn't see anyone at all.' Anxious to get off the subject of her improper behaviour, she scowled even more ferociously. 'Which reminds me, sir. What have you done with everybody?'

He eyed her for a moment, then gave a short, rueful laugh. 'You must indeed consider me to be a dangerous character, Miss Lynley, if you believe I can cause an entire houseful of servants to disappear. Would it set your mind at rest to know they are in the west wing, cleaning?'

'*All* of them?'

'I'm afraid so. My mother intends to entertain shortly, you see, and she seems to be set on a larger gathering than can be accommodated in the family wing. I put Winwick onto the task of preparing the state drawing-rooms this morning.'

'Oh.' She mulled that over for a few seconds before seizing on his other iniquity. 'You were supposed to be inspecting farms.'

'And so I did.' He smiled. 'Wasn't it fortunate that the property was in such excellent condition that I could return in plenty of time to meet you?'

'Fortunate for whom?' Sarah muttered, trying to ignore the odd little shivers coursing through her at the sight of his smile.

At her disgruntled tone the smile broadened into a grin of such blatant male wickedness that she blinked. For an instant she had a sudden unnerving vision of the boy Lady Wribbonhall had described yesterday; of how he must have looked before personal loss and war had carved the twin lines bracketing his mouth and hardened the devilish light in his eyes into glittering green ice.

And yet she had seen the ice melt last night, she remembered, feeling strangely shaken. More than once.

'There is no need to be so nervous, Miss Lynley,' he said, his voice lowering again. 'I am fully aware of the reason you came here this morning.'

Sarah wondered if he thought that dark, purring tone was soothing. She could have told him it wasn't. Shivers ran up and down her spine every time he used it. 'It's just that. . .and then there was. . .'

'Perfectly understandable.'

'Yes, well, it would have been most improper,' she mumbled, feeling like an idiot.

'Most. And since your reputation may be at stake the longer you remain here, Miss Lynley, the sooner we are on our way the better.' He fished a key out of his pocket and tossed it across the desk. 'Here. Catch.'

Her eyes widened in surprise a split second before she managed to loosen her grip on the chair and catch the key. Sending him a look of uncertainty, she fitted the key to the lock and opened the drawer. Ravensdene looked on in silence as she removed the pistol and, without so much as glancing at it, stuffed it into the reticule dangling from her wrist. Taking a deep breath, she rose to her feet.

'Thank you, my lord. I am very gr—' She stopped dead, her eyes going wide again with alarm as he rose also. 'What do you mean, *we* can be on our way?'

He indicated her reticule. 'Surely it is obvious, Miss Lynley. When a young lady feels the need to arm herself with a lethal weapon merely to ride about unescorted, it is the duty of any gentleman worthy of the name to offer his protection.'

'But—'

'Besides—' he walked around the desk and took her arm in a light clasp '—in the interests of public safety, I really must insist on accompanying you. . .'

'*Public safety*! Just what do you think I—?'

'Oh, don't worry about the proprieties,' he continued, ushering her through the adjoining rooms as if her spluttered protest had not been uttered. 'You can go out the way you came in and I'll meet you as though by chance in the laneway. No one need ever know you ventured further than Mrs Winwick's parlour.'

'But—'

'And so you feel quite safe during our ride, I'll have

my groom, Figgins, accompany us. At a discreet distance, of course.'

Before Sarah could open her mouth to suggest that Figgins' escort would be quite sufficient, Nick opened the dining-room door, pushed her gently into the room and shut the door again on her bewildered countenance.

He leaned back against the wooden panels, feeling as though he'd had a rather narrow escape. As if his quarry had almost got away from him. He frowned at the thought. He wasn't hunting Sarah, damn it. It was her uncle he had to investigate. Why did he keep forgetting that?

Pushing away from the door, he strode determinedly across the breakfast parlour and out into the hall, more than a little annoyed with himself. The only question remaining unanswered about Miss Sarah Lynley was why she had felt obliged to defend herself in such a drastic fashion on her own land. But did he have an answer? No, he did not. Because for some ridiculous reason he had found himself reluctant to push her just now, reluctant to say anything that might end their strange, almost private, relationship.

He slammed the front door behind him with rather more force than was strictly necessary. He was definitely losing his edge. This was not the time to be distracted by a woman, no matter how intriguing he found her. For one thing, Sarah was not a candidate for a brief seduction. And for another, whatever else she might be, he had no illusions that he would find her politely waiting for him in the lane. If he didn't get to the stables in the next two minutes, she would be more than halfway home before he caught up with her.

* * *

It was no use blinking at the facts, Sarah mused gloomily as the rugged Sussex coastline came into view. She had been outwitted and outmanoeuvred by an expert in strategy.

Of course, he had received some unexpected assistance from her horse, she remembered, bending a fulminating look upon the chestnut fiend she was riding. No sooner had they reached the laneway than Honey had objected strenuously to returning home after a mere two-mile ride. Several minutes later, Ravensdene had found her involved in a most undignified tussle with her suddenly recalcitrant mount, and when he had suggested they shake the fidgets out of their horses by taking a long roundabout route to the Grange which included the scenic path along the cliffs, her mare had taken off as if she'd understood every word, and before her mistress could think of an excuse to refuse.

If she hadn't been such an experienced rider, Sarah fumed silently, she would have found herself left in an ignominious heap in the middle of the road while Honey galloped off after Ravensdene's black stallion.

She stole a glance at her escort and had to admit that the huge horse suited him. Both males were big, dark and powerful. Both were capable of making any sensible female think twice about approaching them. She was forced to the conclusion, therefore, that her horse had no sense at all.

'Behave yourself, Honey,' she admonished in a muttered undertone as the mare frisked closer to Ravensdene's mount, flicking her heels out in what Sarah considered to be a decidedly flirtatious manner.

The Earl turned to smile at her as he slowed the black to a walk. 'Honey?'

A tide of hot colour flooded Sarah's cheeks. 'Short for Honeycomb,' she elaborated hastily. Really, when he'd said 'Honey' in that dark, purring tone, her insides had threatened to melt to a similar consistency.

'She is certainly the right colour,' Ravensdene observed, running an expert eye over the mare's points just as if he hadn't managed to addle her wits. 'And you appear to have excellent hands, Miss Lynley. I suspect you ride regularly.'

'Oh...yes.' Deciding after a moment to take this unobjectionable remark at face value, Sarah launched into a monologue on the advantages of riding this particular path. 'Especially along here. I love to watch the sea. It's so changeable. Serene one day and the next like a playful child with the sunshine dancing on the water as it is now. But I like it best when it's wild, and the waves are hurling themselves against the cliffs as though daring the land to break them.'

'Which the land does,' he murmured.

Carried away by her descriptions, she scarcely noticed the amused interest in his eyes as he watched her. 'Yes, but the sea wins in the end, doesn't it?'

He smiled at the triumph in her voice. 'A lesson in patience over resistance, Miss Lynley,' he acknowledged softly.

She was promptly struck dumb again.

'However, I doubt if the crews manning the ships out there share your love of wild seas,' he added smoothly.

'Er...no.' Carefully avoiding his gaze, she looked out across the sea roads named for the Sussex Downs. Scenery and the weather, she told herself grimly. Two very innocuous topics of conversation. There was no need to suspect some deep, hidden meaning in Ravensdene's every other remark. 'We do get some dreadful weather here,' she continued with rather determined chattiness. 'I remember when a troop ship was nearly driven onto the rocks not far from this spot.

But unless we grow wings and fly, ships are our only means of crossing the Channel.'

'Oh, I don't know. Were you aware that several years ago there were plans for a tunnel to be built beneath the sea?'

'A tunnel! Beneath the Channel?'

'Yes. It was all going to be very elaborate: underground staging posts for changes of horses, air shafts sunk from mid-Channel islands, and the whole lit by candles in the finest chandeliers.'

'Good heavens! Whose idea was that?'

'I'm not sure. Napoleon was very enamoured of the plan, however. Needless to say, the English government was not.'

Sarah looked across the sunlit expanse and shivered. 'One can hardly blame them,' she said. 'I, for one, would rather take my chances with the weather than go burrowing beneath the earth. Or the sea in this case.'

'I agree with you, but one day in the future it may not be such an impractical alternative for negotiating a very treacherous stretch of water. I remember my grandfather telling my brothers and I about a terrible gale that blew up in the year his father was born, when hundreds of ships were caught in the Downs and destroyed.'

'I was very fond of your grandfather,' Sarah mused. 'Lord Comberford was very kind to me.' She remembered the way Ravensdene had backed up her explanation for the amount of time they had spent together at the Wribbonhalls' party, and retreated hastily to safer waters, 'And I do believe he told me that same story.'

He laughed softly. 'I must confess it was one of our favourite tales. Especially the part about the local

fishermen launching their boats in the teeth of all
danger to rescue the sailors who were struggling
towards the shore.'

'They still do so, whenever the need arises.'

'Yes. I suspect that was the reason my grandfather
was rather lenient when some of those same fishermen
turned to the occasional spot of smuggling,' he said
dryly. 'Despite his being a Justice of the Peace.'

'You don't approve of such leniency?' she asked,
momentarily forgetting that she, herself, had suppos-
edly been armed against such dangerous persons as
free-traders.

Ravensdene shrugged. 'I can understand how a man
with a family to feed could be tempted to trade in
harmless commodities, Miss Lynley, but sometimes
more than brandy or lace is conveyed across the Channel.' As they turned their horses inland towards a wider
path than the one Sarah had taken two days ago, he
looked at her rather intently. 'Sometimes information
is traded.'

'Oh. You mean. . .about the war?'

'Yes.'

'It's hard to believe anyone would do that.' She
glanced away, suddenly uncomfortable with the conversation and aware of the narrow-eyed gaze with which
Ravensdene was studying her, of a strange tension in
him, as though he was waiting for her to say more.

In the distance the sun glinted off the rail at the top
of the steps she had mounted with such haste two days
ago, and, unbidden, her mind began retracing the path
through the woods to the spot where she had first
encountered Ravensdene. And perhaps it was the talk
of smugglers, or maybe the sudden, unaccountable
grimness about his mouth, but all at once she recalled
the initial words he had spoken that afternoon.

'Was that what you meant the other day?' she asked, turning back to him impulsively. 'Did you think I was a smuggler? Is that what had gone far enough?' It would be rather reassuring if he had meant that, she thought, without quite knowing why.

But to her amazement, he appeared momentarily disconcerted, as if he had not expected such a response. Then that wicked male grin flashed out again, and the impression was gone.

'Miss Lynley, I have a confession to make,' he began. 'I'm afraid I was guilty of judging you by the standards of some of the other ladies in this area. To tell you the truth—' his smile turned rueful '—and at the risk of sounding insufferably puffed-up with my own consequence, I have been living under siege. Miss Smisby was the last one—a sprained ankle. During the two days preceding that, we had lost puppies, invisible footpads—Well, I won't bore you with the rest, but, believe me, an armed and dangerous female was the next logical step. At least, according to Lord Devenham, who, by the by, thinks the whole situation is absolutely hilarious.'

Sarah couldn't contain herself any longer. The disgusted note in his voice as he finished the tale was too much. She leaned over Honey's withers and burst out laughing. And if there was more than a little relief in her amusement, she ignored the fact.

'My lord, I forgive you instantly,' she gasped when she recovered. 'It sounds to me as if the Miss Smisbys have been trying to scrape an acquaintance with you.' She looked up at him and nearly choked on another gurgle of laughter when she saw Ravensdene staring at her with a kind of horrified fascination.

'Good God! Do you mean there's more than one Miss Smisby?'

'Three,' she managed, trying to control herself. 'They're really very good-natured girls, you know. Very. . .enthusiastic.'

'Good God!' he said again.

'Yes. The sprained ankle sounds like Leopoldina, and the puppy—'

'*Leopoldina*?'

Sarah succumbed to another fit of the giggles. 'I'm afraid Mrs Smisby indulged herself in choosing unusual names for her daughters,' she explained kindly. 'Averilla probably imagined the footpads—she is rather prone to melodrama, you see—and the puppy must belong to Euphemia. She is extremely fond of animals, which is not very appropriate really, because she was named for a martyr who was consumed by wild beasts.'

'I suppose it is too much to hope that the dog will eventually grow large enough to—?'

'Oh, no! You must not say it, my lord.' Sarah clapped a hand over her mouth to stifle her laughter. 'Poor Mrs Smisby is forever trying to instil notions of propriety into her offspring, with little success, unfortunately. She herself is quite respectable, you know. She is the widow of a gentleman who owned a manufactory somewhere in the north, and after his death she sold the business and decided to move to a genteel neighbourhood in the country.'

'Aha! Trying to marry them into the squirearchy.'

'Not an unreasonable ambition given her wealth,' Sarah reproved him, trying to look properly severe. 'And one cannot blame her for wishing to establish her daughters creditably.'

'Believe me, Miss Lynley, I have no argument with that. Mrs Smisby may aim as high as Almack's if she likes, so long as she keeps those girls away from Comberford Place.'

'I'm sure it must have been very annoying for you,' she said soothingly. 'But now that you've been settled at Comberford for several weeks, I daresay all the excitement over your arrival will calm down.'

'You're an expert in these matters?'

'Of course not.' She levelled her brows at him. 'To be quite blunt, sir, I have no understanding at all as to why so many girls behave in such a peculiar fashion. Anyone would think marriage to some man, who in many cases is little more than a stranger, is the only way of life available to an intelligent female.'

'From that remark, I deduce that you have not gone hunting at Almack's, yourself, Miss Lynley.'

Sarah shuddered. 'Never!'

'You have no hankering for a London season?'

'I am perfectly happy in the country, my lord.'

'And the, er, joys of wedlock hold no appeal for you?'

'That very word is a masterly description of what a woman can expect of marriage,' she informed him tartly. 'Locked away, at the mercy of some man, for the term of her natural life.'

'Hmm. Don't you think that *you* are becoming rather melodramatic, Miss Lynley?' he queried gently.

Sarah blushed and looked away, suddenly aware of what she was saying. Heavens, what was the matter with her? She couldn't remember when she'd last lost control like that in front of a man. Probably not for eight years. She thought back over the last few minutes and frowned again.

'But I don't quite understand,' she said, prudently ignoring his last remark. 'How would holding you up with a pistol force you into marriage? If that was indeed what you assumed I was intending the other day.'

He smiled faintly. 'Miss Lynley, it is plain to see that you have no idea of the lengths to which some people will go to have their way. We were quite alone in the woods. Once the opportunity had presented itself, all you would have had to do was disarrange your clothing, accuse me of luring you to a clandestine meeting and trying to seduce you or worse, and then run screaming to your uncle that you'd been compromised. He would have stormed over to Comberford Place, probably armed with a shotgun, to demand that I marry you.'

Sarah had only heard one thing. 'Or worse?' she whispered.

He looked straight into her eyes. 'It would not be the first time, Miss Lynley, that a woman has acquired a husband, or otherwise extricated herself from trouble, by accusing a man of raping her.'

CHAPTER FIVE

SHE couldn't move. She couldn't even breathe. She sat rigid in the saddle, staring blindly at Ravensdene, while heat swept over her in a sickening, suffocating wave that blurred her vision and threatened her senses. Her lips parted, she tried to drag in some air, but every ragged gasp seemed to catch in her throat, choking her. An instant later she was shivering as violently as if she'd been plunged into a pool of ice-water. Then the heat returned. Terrified she was going to be sick, she clenched her teeth together.

'Miss Lynley! Sarah!' Ravensdene's hand shot out and closed over hers. He pulled both horses to a halt, dropped her reins and without any hesitation at all, passed his arm around her waist.

Just in time Sarah sensed his intention of lifting her out of the saddle and onto his own horse. She regained her powers of movement in a hurry. 'No! Let me go!'

'I will when you're better,' he said, with a calmness that contrasted sharply with her frantic efforts to escape his touch. 'Be still now. You know I'm not going to hurt you. We're not even alone. Figgins will be coming up with us at any moment.'

He was right. Sarah obeyed, ceasing her struggles as the knowledge that Ravensdene was merely supporting her seeped into her consciousness. But even as her body went limp in his hold, her mind seemed to lurch into action, setting words and images swirling about in her head in a dizzying, bewildering jumble. She could still hardly breathe, let alone speak, but somehow the words were spilling out.

'How *could* you? How could you say that? No woman would ever. . . It is men who. . . Do you think a man has never done *that*. . .in order to acquire a *wife*?'

'Hush,' he murmured. 'Don't try to talk.' He pressed her head gently against his shoulder with his free hand, removing her hat as he did so.

And she let him. How could she do that, Sarah wondered dazedly? He had said a terrible thing. Made an unforgivable accusation, and she could only rest limply against him and feel the warm strength of his body wrap her around, sheltering her.

'That's it.' The deep velvety purr washed over her shattered nerves like a caress. 'Take a deep breath. You're going to be all right. Ah, Figgins.' The tone of his voice changed and Sarah felt him look around. 'Miss Lynley has been overtaken by an unfortunate bout of dizziness. Ride on ahead and warn them, would you?'

'No.' Quite unaware that her hand was clutching Ravensdene's lapel for support, Sarah raised her head. 'I don't want to worry Uncle Jasper. I'm much better now. Quite well, and—'

'You're as white as a sheet,' Ravensdene muttered, glancing down at her. But he didn't insist on his order being carried out, merely gestured slightly to his groom.

The man nodded. 'There's a gate up ahead that opens into the field behind the Grange stables,' he said. 'I'll wait there, me lord.'

Sarah watched him go, eyes wide with surprise. 'How did he know that?' she asked.

'I don't know. Perhaps he takes this path occasionally when he exercises my horses.'

'But this is private prop—'

'It doesn't matter,' he cut in impatiently. 'Sarah—'

The sound of her name brought the world crashing back with a resounding thud. Sarah found herself staring in stunned astonishment first at Ravensdene, then at her hand clasped tightly around his lapel. At the same time she became intensely aware of the solid pressure of his arm around her, and the way she was all but nestled against him. The last time they had been this close she had felt the crushing imprint of his body against hers for hours afterwards.

The memory had her unlocking her fingers and wrenching out of his hold with a violence that almost sent her toppling from the saddle.

The horses, who had both been standing obediently motionless until that moment, flung up their heads in startled reaction to her sudden movement. Honey pranced sideways, wickering nervously, while Ravensdene's black reared up sharply and nearly went over on his hocks.

He was brought under control immediately. Ravensdene reined the stallion in close again and caught Honey's bridle, steadying the little mare. 'Are you all right?' he rapped out.

Feeling like an idiot, Sarah snapped back just as sharply. 'Of course I am.'

She wasn't anything of the sort. She felt horribly weak, her insides quaking madly and her hands barely able to grip the reins. She would have given anything to have been able to ride away, but the effort of keeping her seat had taken every ounce of strength she had left.

'I'm sorry I barked at you like that,' Ravensdene said in a milder tone. 'I was concerned about your ability to hold your horse in your present fragile state of health.' He released the bridle and handed her hat to her. Its bright green plume had been sadly squashed during his tussle with his horse, and Sarah realised he had managed to control the huge beast with only one hand and the power of his thighs. The knowledge stirred up another unnerving memory of his strength. She jammed the hat down on her ruffled curls and glared at him.

'My health is not the issue here,' she retorted. 'It is my. . .my sense of propriety that is outraged, my lord. How dare you make such a contemptible accusation?'

His brows snapped together. 'I wasn't accusing you, for God's sake!'

'I realise that, and am happy to know that you don't believe me to have any designs on your. . .your. . .'

'Yes, you don't have to search for a socially accept-able euphemism, Miss Lynley. After this encounter, I am quite sure my lack of delicacy has given you an ineradicable distaste of me. I can only apologise. Your understanding of my situation, and your questions, led me to believe you would prefer a candid answer.'

Sarah gasped. 'That was no candid answer, sir. You traduced the entire female sex!'

He reached out and captured her wildly gesturing hand. 'No,' he said. 'I didn't. And I agree with you that there are men who have used force to acquire a wife. But I was speaking of the type of manipulative female that you, fortunately, know nothing about.'

When she tried to tug her hand free, his fingers tightened and he looked directly into her eyes. All at once his voice was very low, very soft, and wholly serious. 'Miss Lynley, when you asked me for an expla-nation I had no thought of distressing you so cruelly. I see I was appallingly blunt. Please forgive me.'

'I. . .' She couldn't go on. She couldn't speak. The utter sincerity in his voice shook her unbearably. She had the most absurd desire to burst into tears, and at the same time wanted to go on railing at him for the dreadful things he had said. Both reactions were so horribly unlike her usual self that for several nerve-racking seconds she felt as if every faculty was suspended.

'I can't believe we're having this conversation,' she finally managed, bewilderment clear in her voice.

'I'm not surprised,' he muttered. 'Since our rather singular meeting, I seem to have spent a great deal of time upsetting you and then apologising.' He released her hand and indicated the path. 'Shall we ride on, Miss Lynley? I daresay you wish to gain the privacy of your home as soon as possible.'

Again she couldn't answer but merely allowed him to set a sedate pace towards the open fields of the Grange. Honey, as though sensing her mistress's distraction, kept to the steady walk without argument.

Sarah was feeling anything but steady. As well as all the other emotions roiling around inside her, she was now coping with a hefty dose of guilt. She risked a quick glance at Ravensdene, riding stern-faced alongside her, and was painfully conscious that she hadn't accepted his apology, nor barely even acknowledged it.

'I can see where you might have received a...a mistaken impression of me, my lord,' she got out, keeping her gaze fixed on a point between Honey's chestnut ears. Swallowing the lump in her throat, she added valiantly, 'You must think me quite unbalanced.'

'No,' he said curtly. 'I don't.' Gallant under fire, thrown into panic by close proximity to him, and utterly free of feminine wiles, Nick added silently, but not unbalanced.

Nor was the mystery surrounding Sarah going to be solved today. Already he felt as if he'd been pulling

wings off butterflies. Whatever terrible secret it was
that caused her to go from delightfully natural and
amusing one moment, to the verge of panic the next,
she had endured enough for one day. He couldn't
probe any further.

Besides, it was becoming perfectly obvious that her
fear arose from some incident that had nothing to do
with spying. Or smugglers. He didn't need to be a
genius to see the way she flinched from any close
physical contact. With any man, or just with him? he
wondered grimly, remembering their first stormy
encounter. And then he wondered why he should
suddenly feel so savage about the matter. It was none
of his business; he already had enough to worry about.

So why was he unable to leave well enough alone?
he asked himself wryly. Why was it so difficult to wait
until the warm, red-brick walls of Sarah's home came
into view and he could see Figgins waiting for them
before he felt he could turn to her and ask, 'Has it?'

As he hoped, the cryptic question at least aroused
her feminine curiosity.

'Has what?' she asked in a very subdued voice.

'Has my lack of finesse given you an ineradicable
distaste of me?'

She should say yes, Sarah thought. Say yes and be
done with it. Now that she had her pistol back, there
was no reason for her to speak to Ravensdene again,
apart from the usual polite acknowledgement when she
saw him in public.

But she couldn't bring herself to do it. She couldn't
bring herself to be so cruel when he had been so
understanding. He had been kind last night also. And
the other day, even when furiously angry, he hadn't
hurt her.

'You do not lack finesse, my lord,' she said before

she lost her courage. 'And—' she kept her gaze resolutely forward '—I do not have a distaste of you.'

'Thank you, Miss Lynley. May I presume, then, that you will still present me to your uncle? I should very much like to meet him.'

'It was my intention, my lord.'

'Again, thank you. I shall not stay long, I assure you.'

'I believe twenty minutes to be the correct length for a first visit, my lord.'

Nick set his teeth and persevered. 'Then I will endeavour to redeem myself by keeping your uncle occupied while you return his pistol to its proper place.'

She sent him a very swift, very shy glance from beneath her lashes that had him forcibly suppressing a violent urge to take her in his arms and shield her from whatever spectre was haunting her. Fortunately, before he could do anything so calculated to chase her away for good, she nudged her mare into a canter that quickly brought them up to Figgins and the gate leading to the stableyard.

Neither of them said another word until they had dismounted and Sarah had led him along a path bordered by garden beds to the main entrance of the neat, square Georgian house. They rounded the corner in time to see a tall, white-haired gentleman descending the portico steps with the aid of a cane. He glanced up and smiled.

'Sarah, my dear,' he said gently, holding out a thin, frail hand. 'I've been wondering where you were.'

'Oh, Uncle Jasper, I'm sorry. Am I very late?' Sarah hurried forward with an alacrity that had Nick clenching his fists in silent self-reproach at her eagerness to leave his side. She took her uncle's outstretched hand and stood on tip-toe to kiss his wrinkled cheek. Clearly, whatever nightmare she feared was not here, and it struck him again that although she was afraid—of men? Of *something*—he had never seen her completely give in to it. She had always managed to rally herself and recover.

'It was all Honey's fault,' she was saying now, with a droll look that Nick knew had to be forced. 'She simply would *not* return home before she'd had her gallop along the cliffs, and then what should happen but that Lord Ravensdene must come upon me losing the argument. However, he very kindly offered his assistance, and I knew you would wish to thank him, so. . .'

Before this breathless speech was over, Sir Jasper had released Sarah's hand and was turning to greet his visitor. Nick found himself meeting a kindly, blue-eyed gaze that for all Lynley's age was still surprisingly shrewd .

'So, you're old Comberford's grandson, my lord,' he said in his soft voice. 'I am very happy to meet you. I had formed the intention of calling on you in a day or two, you know, and am much obliged to you for saving me a trip in that rattletrap of a carriage Sarah insists that I use. But I hope in assisting her you did not have to go out of your way?'

'How do you do, sir?' Nick returned the handshake, instinctively softening both grip and voice. Most people, he reflected, would respond that way to the old man's gentle, curiously old-world air. 'No, I'm not out of my way at all. Miss Lynley exaggerates. I merely escorted her home.'

'Well, I am grateful to you, sir. To tell you the truth, I cannot like this notion she has taken into her head to start walking or riding alone. And now we see what has come of it.'

'Now, Uncle Jasper, I told you—'

'Yes, yes, my dear.' He patted her cheek. 'I daresay I am sadly behind the times, but there it is. You will have to indulge an old man who worries about you.'

She dimpled at him. 'Dearest Uncle Jasper, there is not the least need, I assure you. But I'm sorry to have made you fret. What is to be done? Shall I lose our next match?'

'Cheeky puss.' He chuckled. 'You see how it is, my lord. Little did I think it would come to this when I introduced Sarah to a chessboard. But what are we doing standing about in this wind? Come in, my lord, come in. Your grandfather told me you are no mean chess player yourself. Learned it from him, I expect. Perhaps you will give me the pleasure of a game one day?'

'I'm afraid you will find me sadly out of practise, sir, but I would be happy to oblige you.' Nick reached out to hand Sarah up the steps, frowning slightly at the almost imperceptible tremor that shook her the moment his fingers closed around her arm.

He saw her glance quickly at her uncle, but Sir Jasper was busy with the careful placement of his cane and hadn't noticed anything amiss. Still chatting away in happy ignorance of any undercurrents, he led the way into a small, well-lit hall. Doors led off it on either side and, opposite the front door, a narrow but elegant staircase rose to the upper floors.

As soon as they were inside, Sarah extracted herself from his hold and gathered up the skirts of her riding habit, obviously preparing to flee at the first opportunity.

'Yes, off you go, my dear,' Sir Jasper approved, waving a vague hand towards the upper reaches. 'No doubt you will be wishing to change your gown. This way, my lord. Let me show you the state of play your grandfather left me in. Never got to finish our last game, you know. Sarah offered to take Jonathan's place, but that wouldn't do. The little minx always wins. No respect for her elders at all.'

'Don't believe a word of it, my lord.' Sarah turned to him with a carefully polite smile. 'Uncle Jasper gives no quarter.'

Sir Jasper beamed modestly.

'Indeed?' Fully aware that she was trying to make an unobtrusive retreat towards the stairs without any further contact, Nick stepped into her path and held out his hand. 'In that case I shall count on your good advice, Miss Lynley, to avoid any pitfalls your uncle has in store for me.'

She hesitated a moment then placed her hand lightly in his, her colour rising as his fingers enveloped hers. 'Good day, my lord,' she managed to utter in a very formal, very small voice. 'Thank you for your assistance earlier.'

Nick released her, stunned to discover that for the first time in his life it was difficult to keep his mind on social conventions that should have been second nature. Quite simply, he did not want to let her go with this constraint between them. He watched her ascend the stairs and he knew, as surely as if she had admitted it aloud, that she was fiercely resisting the urge to run.

She would not run, Sarah told herself as she mounted the stairs. She would not run and she would not look back. She would keep her eyes straight ahead until she got to her room. She would not even peek. She would *not—*

He was standing where they had parted, one hand resting on the newel post, the other clenched at his side, looking up at her. Sarah felt her steps slow. Her gaze was caught, held captive. It was as if he had been waiting for her to turn, to glance back. She stopped, her hand gripping the bannister, waiting also. . .

And then he smiled. A crooked smile of such wry understanding that her heart stopped in mid-beat. Time stopped, stood still. And to her utter astonishment she felt her own lips part and curve in an answering smile. A shy, hesitant, fugitive smile, but still a smile, that perhaps held everything she wanted to say, and could not. Gratitude, tentative friendship, the beginnings of trust, reassurance.

Reassurance?

The smile was wiped off her face in a flash. Sarah whirled about and fled up the stairs and into her room with nary a thought for what her uncle might think of such peculiar behaviour. Far from stopping, her heart was now racing like a panicked deer. Reassurance! What on earth had put *that* idea into her head? She had never in her entire life seen anyone who looked less in need of reassurance than the Earl of Ravensdene.

If anyone needed comforting and reassurance, it was her. Because she was very much afraid that she was taking leave of her senses. Ravensdene scared her. Of course he did. That was absolutely indisputable. He was a man. She was frightened of him. Of his strength, his size, the compelling force he seemed able to command at will. And yet there was gentleness in him, in his voice, his touch, in that last long look they had exchanged. It disturbed her. Terribly.

And she didn't know why.

'Very easy on the eyes, the little lady, me lord.'

Nick shifted his frowning gaze from the road in front of him to his henchman's inquisitive face. They had left the Grange five minutes ago; he knew from long acquaintance that five minutes was about the limit of Figgins' silence when he had something to say.

'Very,' he agreed repressively. 'She also happens to be intelligent, Figgins, so mind what you say in her hearing.'

'Aye, sir.' The groom thought this over and added, 'Not that we'll need to slum the place from the outside anymore now that you've met the lady's uncle.'

'*Slum* the place? I won't ask where you picked up that thieves' cant.'

'No need, sir. Probably the same places you've been in your time, sir.'

A reluctant grin tugged at Nick's mouth. 'Very likely,' he said. 'You know, Figgins, this is getting damned complicated.'

'Never known a job o' yours that weren't,' Figgins remarked with laconic understatement. 'If you'll pardon the liberty, me lord, what did you think of the old gentleman?'

Nick narrowed his eyes thoughtfully. 'That's what's so damned complicated, Figgins. He *is* old. Older than I would have expected an uncle of Miss Lynley's to be. He must be close to eighty, more my grandfather's generation.'

'Well, he weren't much more than a likely prospect,' Figgins observed, apparently feeling the need to offer some consolation. 'Funny how everyone talks about the Grange folk, though. . . Well, they *don't* talk about 'em. That's what's strange.'

'No doubt. However, from this moment on, Figgins, you also will maintain a like silence on the subject of Miss Lynley and her uncle. At least while we search further afield.'

An expression of resigned suffering appeared on Figgin's rough-hewn countenance. 'I'm to stay friendly-like with every fisherman up and down this blasted coast,' he said, as if reciting a standing order. 'And here I was thinking after we left France that I'd never have to set foot in a boat again. Give me a horse every time.'

Nick grimaced faintly. 'Console yourself with the reflection that you'd feel even more out of place in a drawing-room. I'm the one who'll have to observe my neighbours a little more closely than I have been doing.'

'Ah, well, 'tis probably for the best.' Figgins cast a shrewd, sidelong glance at his master. 'If the little lady's gettin' her hooks into yer lordship, things could get a mite lively.'

There was a frozen silence.

'How long have you been with me, Figgins?' Nick asked at last in a very soft voice.

The groom pursed his lips and looked cautious. 'Er . . .about eight years, me lord.'

'Ah, yes. I remember the occasion of our meeting. You saved me from a rather nasty encounter with a knife.'

'Never did approve of coves stabbing people in the back,' muttered Figgins.

Nick's voice became even softer. 'A sentiment I applaud. However, if you wish to remain in your present post for as long as another eight seconds, you will not again refer to Miss Lynley as "the little lady" nor that she has her hooks into anyone.'

'Aye, me lord.'

'And while we're on the subject,' he added as Figgins looked uncharacteristically crestfallen, 'you ought to know me better. Women do not get their hooks into me.'

'No, sir.' Figgins revived somewhat. 'Well, not those

kind of hooks, anyroad. I ain't forgetting that hussy three years back who thought she had you caught good and proper. Tried to get information out of you and ended up flat on her back telling *you* what we wanted to know.' He chuckled. 'Sang like a bird, she did.'

'Thank you, Figgins. I hadn't forgotten. Perhaps you could contrive to do so, however.'

'If you say so, me lord. But you was always very cool with the ladies. Very cool. Talk of the troop, it were.'

Having had the last word to say on the subject, Figgins finally subsided and the ride back to Comberford Place was accomplished in silence, leaving Nick to the contemplation, not of the task he'd been set, but of a certain small female who seemed to have the knack of arousing some very primitive emotions in him.

Desire he could understand, even if he couldn't so easily dismiss it; not only was Sarah uncommonly pretty, there was both humour and an innocent, enquiring intelligence in those soft amber eyes that was appealing in its very rarity. But beautiful women had come and gone before in his life without disturbing his concentration. They had occupied their place, usually very briefly, and he had parted from them without regret.

Simple physical attraction, therefore, did not explain the quite disproportionate sense of relief he felt at the possibility that Sarah's courtly, frail uncle might be precisely what he seemed. It didn't explain the near-savage rage he felt every time she flinched from his touch.

And it didn't explain the sudden sharp need he had experienced to have her run to him, and not to her uncle, for protection, to fold her in his arms and keep her safe. Once again she had reached a part of him he thought had been closed off forever, and he was discovering, much to his surprise, that the steel walls he had constructed years ago were being shaken to their very foundations.

By an elusive slip of a girl so fragile he could have broken her two days ago without even meaning to.

'Oh, dear, why did we not bring a footman with us to carry some of these parcels? How on earth are we ever going to manage? We shall have to return to the inn and then set out again. Sarah, do you have that russet cambric walking dress wrapped up safely? And where is my new pelisse?'

Talking non-stop, Lady Wribbonhall emerged from her dressmaker's establishment onto the busy street and began counting packages, to the vast inconvenience of several passers-by.

'Oh, Mama, do stop worrying. Sarah and I can manage perfectly, and we have only the haberdashery to visit now.' With a good deal of dexterous juggling, Julia transferred the strings of several bandboxes to one hand and relieved her flustered parent of yet another.

'Yes, but there are so many things still to purchase. Silk stockings, gloves, dancing slippers, ribbons. I think some knots of cherry ribbon will be just the thing to set off the cambric, Sarah. And we positively must return to Celine's for that russet and ecru bonnet to wear with it. Oh, dear. Why cannot things be in the same shop? It would make everything so much easier.'

'Dearest ma'am, there is not the least need for you to be running all over Eastbourne for a particular bonnet,' Sarah ventured. 'I am sure I already have a score of hats and gowns for every possible occasion. You must be exhausted, and—'

'Exhausted?' Lady Wribbonhall looked at her charge in the liveliest astonishment. 'When there are clothes to be bought? Never, dear child. Come! The haberdashery!'

Lady Wribbonhall might as well have said 'Charge!' Plunging into the crowd, she set off down the street like a velvet-clad ship of the line, accompanied by two small frigates. Sarah could only marvel at her ladyship's stamina.

On the other hand, such constant activity was at least keeping her mind from the contemplation of a certain exchange of smiles that had been haunting her dreams for the past couple of days.

'Two pairs of dancing slippers, I think,' Lady Wribbonhall decreed, as if they had just been discussing the subject.

Sarah blinked away yet another mental image of glittering green eyes and a hard mouth that could curve without warning into a crooked, heart-shaking smile, and tried to drum up some interest in the current conversation.

'Two, ma'am? But—'

'At least two, my dear. There is the Assembly tomorrow night and ever since the invitations went out for the Sherington's waltzing party next month, everyone is determined to give a ball of their own. Which reminds me. I have been meaning to warn you, my love, on no account must you dance more than twice with the same gentleman, and should anyone solicit your hand for the waltz—'

'I have *no* intention of waltzing,' Sarah broke in with more haste than grace. She flushed and tried to soften the abrupt interjection. 'I remember when you warned Julia that she must not waltz before she had been approved by the Patronesses at Almack's, dear ma'am.

Besides, I truly don't wish to find myself in such an intimate situation with any strange gentlemen.'

'Well, I don't think you will meet anyone precisely *strange*,' mused Lady Wribbonhall, completely missing Sarah's meaning. 'The Assemblies are quite well-conducted, you know, and when performed correctly, the waltz is a most charming dance. However, there are several young officers quartered in the town who perhaps may not be counted upon to keep the line, and you may be sure those dreadful Smisby girls will turn the whole evening into a romp.'

'Mama, be assured that Sarah and I shall sit virtuously on the sidelines,' promised Julia with a mischievous smile.

'Nonsense, my love,' Lady Wribbonhall declared, responding to this sally with all the comfortable assurance of one who knows her charges will not suffer the fate of less attractive damsels. She turned the corner onto another street, causing a gentlemen in a buff-coloured coat to dodge hastily to one side to avoid a flying bandbox, and continued with her lecture. 'I was only advising Sarah to exercise discretion in the case of the waltz. But if there is any gentleman with whom you do not feel comfortable, Sarah dear, you need not feel obliged to dance with him. Which leads me to another point. It is an unfortunate fact that some men do not know how to accept a refusal gracefully. If that should happen, you have merely to say your card is full.'

'Thank you, ma'am,' returned Sarah with real gratitude.

'Well, I am not usually an advocate of falsehood, but sometimes it is a lady's only recourse. I recall a gentleman at a ball many years ago who kept insisting that I dance with him, although he did not know his left foot from his right. He simply would not take "no" for an answer.'

'I know precisely what you mean, ma'am,' Sarah agreed with a rueful smile. 'I met a very similar gentleman at Tunbridge Wells who had accompanied his invalid parent, but who spent more time trying to persuade me to go driving with him, or take a turn about the town, than he did with his mama. I am sure she considered me to be a most unscrupulous female, out to ensnare her precious child, but for my part I was heartily glad of her presence.'

'Oh, dear. You did not consider him to be at all eligible, my love?'

'Not at all,' responded Sarah, dashing Lady Wribbonhall's hopes for a possible suitor. 'And to top off his very unfortunate manner, he looked just like a frog. He even wore a green coat.'

'Well, rest assured that you are unlikely to be pestered by any frogs while you under *my*— But here we are. Gracious! What a press of people. Why must everyone choose to shop here at once? How will we ever. . .?' Lady Wribbonhall subsided once more into flustered incoherence as she forged a path through the doorway and into the crowded haberdashery.

'Now, Mama, there is no need to fuss. We will just have to separate.'

'But—'

Julia took command. 'Sarah, you will have to try on dancing slippers, so you had best wait for a chair to become available. Mama, you are in charge of purchasing ribbons, and I shall buy gloves and silk stockings. We shall meet back here by the door as soon as we are able.'

Lady Wribbonhall acquiescing to this sensible arrangement, they each went their separate ways. Not

without some difficulty, Sarah acknowledged as she
was beaten to the only vacant chair in the immediate
vicinity by a stout lady in purple grosgrain. The lady
settled herself triumphantly on her perch and straightened her turban which was dipping drunkenly over one
eye after her dash through the crowd.

Sarah retired from the lists to a tiny space near one
wall and considered the possibility of lacing up slippers
while balancing on one foot and while her hands were
full of parcels. That was if she managed to attract the
notice of one of the clerks who were scurrying back
and forth behind the counters like so many ants.

Around her all was bustle and confusion. Nearby,
two ladies were arguing loudly over the selection of a
cashmere shawl, while their respective offspring were
busily employed in emptying the contents of a large
glass buttonjar onto the floor. Several buttons had
already been crunched underfoot, much to the delight
of the small miscreants.

She was just beginning to wonder if her old evening
slippers would survive several parties and balls, when
she noticed another lady who looked as hot and tired
and uncomfortable as she did. Like the two patrons
who had by now all but buried their attendant clerk
beneath a pile of discarded cashmere shawls, her fellow
sufferer also had a little boy with her. Unlike his
contemporaries, however, the child had hold of his
mother's hand and was looking up at her with an
anxious expression on his round, cherubic face.

Sarah smiled in sympathy. The poor little fellow
probably thought he was going to end up like the
buttons. She glanced up to see if the mother had
noticed anything amiss with her offspring and suddenly
understood the reason for the boy's concern. The lady
was now as pale as she had been flushed a second ago,

and even as Sarah watched, she swayed and put out her free hand.

Sarah sprang forward, narrowly avoiding a collision with a passing clerk and grasped the lady's arm. 'Forgive me, ma'am,' she said quickly as the lady turned a pair of startled blue eyes on her. 'I couldn't help but notice that you are unwell. There is a chair over here. I am sure that lady in purple won't object to—'

'Oh, no. Please.' Shaking her head, the lady straightened and took a deep breath. 'Please don't disturb her. I am not ill. It is just so hot in here, and when one has been standing forever. . .'

'It is a wonder we are not all laid out upon the floor,' Sarah finished with a smile.

'Yes, indeed.' The lady smiled back at her and seemed to recover a little of her colour. 'What we females will put up with for a new shipment of India muslin.'

'Is that what has caused such a crowd? Good heavens! We shall be here all day. Are you alone, ma'am? Can I—?'

'Of course my mama is not alone,' piped up a small voice from the vicinity of her knees. 'She has me.'

'And I am sure she could not wish for a better escort,' Sarah responded instantly, smiling down at the indignant face upturned to her. 'Do you think, sir, that if I make a path for us, you will be able to guide your mama outside?'

The cherub nodded and puffed out his small nankeen-covered chest.

'Oh, please, dear ma'am. Giles and I can manage. There is not the least need—'

'Nonsense. I shall be glad to leave this place myself.' Sarah bent to retrieve the bandbox she had dropped when she had leapt to the rescue and indicated the door. 'Come, Master Giles, follow me.'

'My name is really Master Giles Beresford,' the cherub announced importantly once they found themselves safely out on the street again. 'And my mama is Mrs Major William Beresford.'

'How very clever of you to introduce us,' Sarah said, charmed by the little boy's quaint manners. 'My name is Miss Sarah Lynley. How do you do?'

'As you can see, Miss Lynley, Giles does very much better than his mama,' Mrs Beresford answered ruefully, as her son solemnly shook hands with his new acquaintance. 'Thank you. You are very kind. It was foolish of me to wait in such a horrid crush in my present situation, but the fresh air will soon put me to rights, I assure you.'

'Oh. Yes. Of course.' Feeling remarkably foolish herself for not noticing what should have been patently obvious from the start, even in the confines of the crowded shop, Sarah struggled to hide her shocked reaction. She didn't even know why she was shocked. Mrs Beresford was certainly not the first lady she had encountered who was expecting an interesting event.

As the lady concerned bent to straighten Master Beresford's small coat, Sarah studied her more closely, startled again to discover that Mrs Beresford appeared to be only a year or two older than herself. She was a pretty girl, with large blue eyes, a tiny rosebud of a mouth, and an exquisitely fair complexion that was set off by a wealth of red-gold hair. She also looked as if the interesting event was going to take place in a matter of weeks, not months.

'Er, should you not be sitting down, Mrs Beresford?' she asked diffidently. 'There is a bench over there near the gardens, or perhaps your carriage. . .'

'Oh, we walked.' Mrs Beresford straighted and smiled. 'And my name is Lydia. I know we have never met, but I am sure I have seen you in the town before. Forgive me, but you are so pretty, I couldn't help but remember you.'

Sarah blushed, hardly knowing how to reply to this forthright speech. 'You are staying in Eastbourne?' she asked.

'Yes, my husband has taken lodgings for us only a block or two away. He is on leave for a while, until his wounds heal—' A shadow crossed her face briefly and was banished. 'But we must not detain you further. The bench will be the perfect place to wait for him. He is to meet us at this corner, you know, after he has seen his doctor.'

'I see,' Sarah murmured somewhat awkwardly. 'Your. . .that is, Major Beresford's wound was serious?'

'Yes.' Lydia Beresford glanced quickly at Giles, but the little boy's attention had been drawn to a dashing phaeton and pair being tooled along the other side of the street, and he was no longer listening to the conversation. 'Poor William was in a French hospital in the most appalling conditions for months,' she explained in a low voice. 'He was eventually exchanged with other prisoners of war, but it was almost a year before he began to regain his health.'

'I'm sorry. You must have been very anxious.'

In the face of the grim memories still lingering in Mrs Beresford's fine eyes, Sarah felt her remark to be utterly meaningless. She could have bitten her tongue. But what else could she have said? Any dutiful wife would have been concerned for the health of a wounded husband. Why then did she sense that, in the Beresford's situation, duty had very little to do with it?

'Dreadfully anxious,' Lydia Beresford agreed. 'But,'

she added, brightening, 'that is all behind us now. William is improving every day, and in the summer Giles will have a little playmate. Which reminds me. I fear I did not thank you properly for your kindness, Miss Lynley. It was very good of you to come to my assistance. But what of yourself? Are *you* alone? May we escort you somewhere when William—?'

'No, no,' Sarah interrupted hastily. 'My friends are still in the haberdashery. I am to meet them here, so you see I am not put out in the least.'

Lydia smiled again in her friendly fashion. 'Oh, I am so glad. Well, we must let you return to your shopping. Do you ever attend the Assemblies here? Not that either William or I are in any condition to *dance*,' she tacked on drolly, 'but the suppers are very good, and there are cards. Perhaps we shall meet again. Come, Giles, dearest. Make your bow to Miss Lynley and then you may give me your arm across the road.'

Feeling somewhat responsible for the little family, Sarah waited until they had crossed to the other side and Giles had seated his mama on the bench outside the entrance to the gardens. She waved farewell and had half-turned to brave the hazards of the haberdashery again, when a tall gentleman in hussar's uniform strode around the corner. Even from a distance and with the noise of the traffic, Sarah could hear Giles's shrill cry of 'Papa! Papa!'

The little boy rushed forward to be swept up in his father's arms and carried back to the bench. Sarah could see him talking nineteen to the dozen and knew he was relating the tale of their adventure. Suddenly unable to move, she stayed where she was, all thought of Lady Wribbonhall, Julia and shopping gone from her mind.

It was like watching a play, she thought vaguely. But

this was real. The look of tender concern on Major
Beresford's lined but handsome face as he bent over
his wife, was real. The expression of love, wholly
returned, shining in her eyes, was real.

They exchanged a few words and she saw the Major
shake his head and smile. Lydia laughed up at him and
he took her hand and kissed it. Sarah knew what they
were saying as surely as if she was standing right beside
them. Knew that he was chiding his wife, but gently,
and that she was reassuring him that nothing was
wrong.

Then he put Giles back on his feet, drew Lydia up
beside him and they all turned towards the gardens,
and just for an instant Sarah saw the expression on the
Major's face as he gazed down at his wife unbeknownst
to her. Adoration, total and unwavering, was there,
plain to see.

She looked away, shaken and embarrassed, feeling
as if she had intruded on something very private, and
then, unwillingly fascinated, unable to resist, she looked
back.

They had entered the gardens, young Giles running
ahead and leaping into the air with childish exuberance
every few steps. Without stopping to think, drawn by a
compulsion beyond reason, Sarah glanced up and down
the street, crossed over when the way was clear and
followed the Beresfords through the gate.

She didn't hurry. She might have been moving in a
strange sort of daze, but she retained enough wit to
know that she would look very foolish if she was
caught.

The Beresfords didn't hurry either, but strolled
along, pausing now and then to admire an early spring
bloom or a tree bursting into blossom, while Giles ran
all over the place, returning every so often to show his

parents some new treasure he had found on the grass. There was an odd familiarity about the scene, but she had no memories of any similar outings with her own family.

She puzzled over the small point for a few seconds before the answer came to her with stunning clarity. The Major walked with a slight limp and his tall frame was thinner than it should have been, evidence of a long illness, but he moved with the same controlled power she had seen in Ravensdene. Beside him, Lydia looked small and dainty, and yet she had entrusted herself to her much larger husband, had borne him a child and was carrying another.

Sarah stopped dead in the middle of the path. It was as well she did so, because a second later the Beresfords stopped also. The Major passed his arm about Lydia's waist, leaned closer and said something to her that made her smile. She stood on tip-toe and brushed her lips across his, only to have them captured in a swift response. Then, as if recollecting their public surroundings, the Major broke the embrace, turned his wife's steps towards a gate in the distance and called to Giles.

Frozen where she stood, Sarah watched the Beresfords leave the gardens and vanish from sight, the memory of their brief kiss imprinted on her mind as if etched there.

Eventually, without really being conscious of moving, she started to walk again. Time passed. She tried to reason, to sort out the jumbled images in her mind, but the only thing she knew with any certainty was that a world that had once seemed very familiar to her was now very, very different.

And so were her surroundings.

'Oh, no!' Sarah stopped short and looked around her

in dismay. She was still in the gardens, but in her abstraction she had wandered far off the path and was in some sort of leafy glade, surrounded by rhododendron bushes. It was pretty enough, but the bushes were too tall for her to see very far. Somewhere in the distance she could hear voices, but they came to her on the wind and she couldn't tell from which direction.

'Oh, you *idiot*!' Wheeling about, she began to retrace her path, castigating herself every step of the way. For some reason the sound of her own voice was comforting, even if she was running through every synonym for fool that occurred to her. She had just reached mooncalf and was about to go on to numskull when a faint sound behind her pulled her up short.

She glanced back at the glade. There was nothing there of course. But even as she turned to start walking again, she felt the hair at her nape stir ever so slightly. The feeling that she was being watched swept over her like the brushing of icy fingers across her flesh.

Sarah's stomach clenched in a spasm of fear. She fought it back at once. This was ridiculous. She was taking her recent folly to new heights. Mouth set in a determined line she turned again to confront whoever was there.

No one. Except an increasing awareness of a presence. Invisible, but there.

It was enough. Fleeing from nothing might be silly, but since there was no one around to see her foolishness, she didn't care. Sarah broke into a run. In seconds she was clear of the bushes and on a wide, curving path that did not look in the least familiar. It didn't matter. Picking up speed, she raced along the path, went hurtling around the corner and ran straight into the Earl of Ravensdene.

CHAPTER SIX

'Oh! My lord!'

Sara scarcely had time to recognise the other victim of the collision before she found herself locked in an embrace that threatened to crush her ribs.

At her startled exclamation he released her as if she had burned him. 'Miss Lynley! What in God's name are you doing alone in these gardens? Are you insensible to the dangers in such a situation?'

As a first reaction from a gallant rescuer, this thundered interrogation left a lot to be desired. Sarah could only stare up at him in confusion while her senses still reeled from the impact of his hard body against hers.

'Why were you running like that?' Ravensdene looked past her, his eyes narrowing on the corner behind her, but when no one appeared, his gaze returned to pin hers with glittering intensity. 'Did someone accost you?'

'No! No.'

Clutching her bandboxes, Sarah tried to put her crazily whirling thoughts in some sort of order. It had been difficult before; it was impossible now. As well as Amy and the Beresfords, her mind had been so filled with her previous meetings with Ravensdene, with every instance of his gentleness, with that last heart-shaking smile, that the sudden re-emergence of the dangerous, cold-eyed predator was simply too much.

This was the man who had rendered her helpless in seconds, who had brought back her memories of Amy's screams, of harsh, laboured breathing, and the terrible silence that had followed.

'I didn't. . . I just remembered Lady Wribbonhall. . . and I was hurrying. . .'

'You just *remembered*? Miss Lynley, what possessed you to be so imprudent as to leave Lady Wribbonhall's protection in the first place? Why are you wandering around in here? Are you lost to all sense of propriety?'

She winced as the questions were hurled at her like thunderbolts.

'No, of course not. I—'

'Lady Wribbonhall is beside herself with worry. You have used her very badly.'

'I'm sorry. I didn't mean. . . I wasn't thinking. . .at least I *was*. That was why—'

'Thinking! Obviously not with any noticeable degree of reason.'

Sarah began to lose her temper. 'I don't know why I am standing here trying to justify myself to you, sir,' she declared, drawing herself up to her full height. It was all of ten inches below Ravensdene's but she was too incensed to care. 'If you will let me pass, I shall return to Lady Wribbonhall and make my apology to one who will accept it in the manner in which it is offered.'

Sarah didn't flatter herself that this speech went any way towards mollifying her rescuer, although why he should be so furious was beyond her, but it did put an end to his lecturing.

'By all means, Miss Lynley,' he said with more than a suggestion of gritted teeth. 'Let us go.'

'I don't recall asking for your escort,' Sarah informed him. 'Kindly stand aside, sir.'

She might as well have been talking to a rhododendron bush. Ravensdene took her arm in a grip just short of punishing, turned about and began marching her down the path. 'Don't be an idiot,' he muttered. 'And give me those bandboxes.'

'I said I don't need your—'

'And *I* said give me the damned bandboxes!' The bandboxes were yanked out of her grasp with a force that nearly took her hand with them.

Sarah ground her own teeth. Insufferable, arrogant male! How could she ever have thought him kind merely because of one or two peculiar instances when he had obviously been acting completely out of character?

'There is no need to use such deplorable language,' she stated, nose in the air. She was about to continue along the same lines when he interrupted her.

'Be grateful it's only my language that's deplorable. At the moment it's either that or I strangle you. Little fool! I'm beginning to think you need a keeper.'

'A keeper! How dare—?'

'What in Hades did you think you were about? There are soldiers all over this town. What if you had been accosted?' His mouth twisted into a mocking line. 'Or have you armed yourself with another pistol?'

Sarah glared up at him with heavy meaning. 'Unfortunately, no.'

A muscle clenched in his jaw but he didn't answer. Which was just as well, Sarah reflected, because those two words were about all she had breath for. Ravensdene was hauling her through the gardens so fast she would not have been surprised to find herself achieving the miracle of flight.

They reached the gate by which she had entered and she was bundled through it with scant ceremony. Knowing her face was unbecomingly flushed, and conscious of an uncomfortable twinge in her side that presaged pain if she had to walk much farther, she was somewhat relieved to see a curricle and pair waiting near the corner.

Then dismay engulfed her. Surely Lady Wribbonhall had not abandoned her to Ravensdene's mercy? Would she have to endure his disapproving company all the way back to Wribbonhall Lacy?

'I am not getting into that curricle until I know where—' she began, only to swallow the rest on a startled squeak as Ravensdene tossed her bandboxes into the curricle, then picked her up and tossed her in after them as if she weighed no more than their contents.

Sarah landed on the padded seat and bounced. Grabbing hold of the hood to steady herself, she sat up and glared at him. It didn't seem to have much effect. Impervious to the mental daggers being hurled his way, he walked around the curricle, climbed in beside her and flicked a coin to the urchin who was holding the heads of the two black horses in the traces.

For some reason the sight of the glossy pair annoyed her intensely. Why couldn't he have had grey horses, or chestnuts, or even bays?

'I suppose all your horses are black,' she accused irrationally. 'I'm not surprised. I daresay it comes in handy when you have to kidnap ladies at night. However, this is broad daylight, my lord, and if you think I am going to tamely sit here while you—'

'Don't put yourself to the trouble of screaming for help,' he advised, guiding his pair into a neat U-turn and setting off up the street at a smart pace. 'Lady Wribbonhall is waiting for you at the Lamb Inn, so you will have to endure being kidnapped for only five minutes. But you're right, Miss Lynley. All my horses are black.'

Sarah was too incensed to notice the calmer tone in which this last remark was delivered. 'Just what I would have expected,' she retorted, as if owning black horses was a crime worthy of the highest condemnation. 'And how, pray, did you come to be in those gardens at that particular moment, my lord?'

He followed this abrupt turn in the conversation without a blink.

'Lord Devenham and I met Lady Wribbonhall and Miss Wribbonhall as we drove into the yard at the Lamb. They had just discovered that you had not returned to the inn after you had apparently become separated, and both were extremely worried. Naturally I offered to search for you while Devenham remained to allay their anxiety.'

'Naturally,' Sarah muttered.

'And while we're on the subject of that particuiar moment,' he continued with grim purpose, 'what was it you were running from, Miss Lynley? And don't give me any more whiskers about suddenly remembering Lady Wribbonhall, or even forgetting her in the first place.'

'But I did!' she exclaimed indignantly. Then subsided abruptly into silence as she recalled what had caused her most uncharacteristic lapse in memory. She could never explain *that*. Nor could she tell him she had been fleeing from something unseen, but sensed. It was entirely too much like Averilla Smisby's invisible foot-pads. Goodness knew what he would make of such a weak story.

'I told you. I was thinking,' she said at last with more than a touch of defiance.

This response remained unanswered for a few seconds while he was forced to negotiate a tricky path through several other vehicles. Sarah glanced down and could have sworn there was less than an inch of space between her side of the curricle and a barouche drawn up at the side of the road.

She had a strong urge to shut her eyes until they were safely past, then inspiration dawned. Here was a heaven-sent opportunity to lead the conversation into less nerve-racking channels. Compared to that, Ravensdene's terrifying style of driving was a mere bagatelle.

'A neat piece of driving, my lord,' she remarked with hideous brightness. She winced inwardly and tried to paste a suitably admiring expression on her face. Either she wasn't very talented at dissimulation, or Ravensdene had been complimented too many times before on his handling of the reins.

'Thank you, Miss Lynley,' he said dryly. Then before she could rally for another attempt at casual conversation, his voice dropped to the soft, dangerous purr that set her insides quivering. 'Now, tell me what you were thinking about.'

Sarah swallowed. Her mind went completely blank. It was quite a shock, because a second ago it had been busily preparing a lecture on horses she had driven. 'I . . .my sister,' she blurted out, and felt her heart stand still.

He sent her a quick, rapier-sharp glance. 'Your sister? I didn't know you had one.'

'No,' she whispered. 'I don't. Not any more.'

She felt him glance at her again before he had to return his attention to the busy street. She was grateful he didn't speak. Expressions of sympathy or, worse, questions from him under the present circumstances would have dangerously threatened her control, already teetering on the brink. What on earth had possessed her to come out with such an ill-considered statement?

She was still trying to find the answer to that puzzle when Ravensdene turned the curricle into the yard at the Lamb Inn.

Sarah went limp with relief. The Lamb was often reputed to be the haunt of smugglers—indeed, there were even rumours that a secret tunnel led from the inn to St Mary's Church for the convenience of these ruthless persons—but Sarah wouldn't have cared if a deputation of murderous free-traders was waiting for them in the yard. She had never been so glad to reach her destination in her life.

Unfortunately, her relief was premature. As an ostler came running to take the horses, Ravensdene sprang down from the curricle and walked around to assist her to alight. Not with a politely outstretched hand, Sarah saw to her dismay. He meant to lift her down.

And in that same nerve-racking moment, as she gazed down into those crystalline green eyes, she found herself remembering in minute and accurate detail how it had felt to be held against him when they had collided; the crushing strength of his arms, the size and warmth of him.

Like being enveloped by heat and steel.

Sarah's mouth went dry as she got shakily to her feet. For some unfathomable reason her legs seemed to have turned to jelly. Various methods of leaping to the ground without his assistance darted through her brain, but before she could act on one he took the decision out of her hands.

Grasping her firmly by the waist, he swung her down and released her the moment her feet touched the ground.

Eyes wide, Sarah looked up at him, shaken to find

that she had instinctively gripped his arms for support
and now couldn't seem to let go.

Her gaze fell to her tightly clinging hands. She
ordered herself to loosen her grip, to step back, but the
command seemed to be lost beneath a haze of sensation that began in her palms, tingling against the feel
of hard, muscled strength, and flowed all the way to
her toes. Quite suddenly, she couldn't even breathe.

'You see how simple things can be if you would only
trust yourself to me, Miss Lynley,' he murmured.

The words succeeded in snapping Sarah out of her
daze. She gasped, snatched her hands away, and fled
into the inn before he could enlarge on the theme.

She found Lady Wribbonhall alone in a private
parlour and at once launched into a breathless, incoherent apology. It was several seconds before she realised
that her explanation, in which Lydia Beresford, her
little boy and the gardens had become quite incompre-
hensibly muddled, was totally unnecessary. Far from
being beside herself with worry, Lady Wribbonhall
merely looked up from her contemplation of their
purchases with an expression of pleased, if weary,
satisfaction.

Sarah halted in mid-sentence, her already disordered
mind seething with wild conjecture, as a small commotion behind her heralded the arrival of Julia in
company with Lord Devenham. Ravensdene followed
them through the doorway in time to hear Julia's bright
greeting.

'There you are, Sarah. Mama said she had seen you
leave the haberdashery with another lady. We thought
you must have met up with an acquaintance, but we
were too far away to call out to you. Wasn't it a
frightful crush?'

'Well, I don't wonder at you escaping, Sarah, dear,'

Lady Wribbonhall added indulgently. 'I know how you dislike crowds, but it was very naughty of you to desert us like that. However, there is no harm done, and I see Lord Ravensdene has brought you safely back.'

'Yes, ma'am. And I am very sorry to have deserted you, but Mrs Beresford was not well and. . .'

Sarah let the sentence trail into the mists of oblivion while she wondered what in the world was going on. Where was the distraught chaperon of Ravensdene's description? Lady Wribbonhall looked perfectly happy, and was now launched on a lively discussion with her daughter and Lord Devenham. Sarah's brain reeled anew. Was *nothing* what it seemed today?

'Oh, Sarah, you will be delighted with the scheme we have hatched.' Julia, bright-eyed with excitement, broke into her chaotic thoughts. 'You, too, my lord. At east—' she hesitated, flushing, as she caught sight of Ravensdene's expression '—I hope you will join us.'

'Of course he will,' Devenham said, coming swiftly to Julia's rescue. 'Won't you, Nick?'

'Delighted,' Ravensdene agreed dryly. 'Where, precisely, am I to join you?'

'Why, at the ruins of the old Priory,' Julia informed him, all animation again. 'Oh, do say we may go, Mama. You see, Lord Devenham and I met Eliza Langdon and her brother, and Harry and Sophie, when we went to buy Sarah's bonnet, and Eliza suggested we have a picnic. Everyone says the weather will hold and the ruins are the perfect place. There are reputed to be several ghosts haunting it, you know. Think of the fun we'll have hunting for them.'

Sarah thought of it and shuddered. She had had enough of invisible spectres to last her a lifetime. But she was not proof against Julia's pleading eyes when they were turned on her. She summoned up a smile of agreement and was rewarded with an impulsive hug.

'Well, as the party will be a large one, I daresay it will be quite acceptable,' Lady Wribbonhall approved. 'How will you get there, my love?'

'Oh, there is not the least difficulty,' Julia assured her. 'Everyone will meet at Wribbonhall Lacy on Thursday morning, and we ladies shall travel by carriage while the gentlemen ride. I know you would rather go on horseback, Sarah, but you know what Sophie Sherington is like. She would insist on riding also and her horse plods along at such a pace it would take us forever to get there. The carriage will be much easier, and I shall drive.'

Lady Wribbonhall and Devenham spoke as one.

'No!'

'But—'

'If Miss Lynley would prefer to ride,' Devenham added with the smooth address for which he was noted, 'I shall take her place in the carriage and handle the ribbons. Miss Sherington will not be in riding gear so there will be no argument from that quarter. How will that suit you, Miss Wribbonhall? I can show you how to feather-edge a corner.'

Julia had no fault to find with this adjustment to the plan, and the innkeeper appearing at that moment to inform Lady Wribbonhall that her horses had been put to, they all adjourned to the yard.

It was unfortunate that Ravensdene and Lord Devenham felt obliged to accompany them outside, Sarah thought. Until then she had considered herself to be coping with the situation quite well, avoiding Ravensdene's gaze by assiduously helping with the bandboxes, staying in the background, and in short trying to behave as if she wasn't there.

That was before Ravensdene stepped forward as she was about to mount into Lady Wribbonhall's barouche. Desperate to get away from him, she placed her foot on the step before she had lifted her skirt sufficiently and promptly tripped on the hem of her carriage dress. Only Ravensdene's swift action in catching her elbow prevented Sarah from landing face-down on the floor of the carriage.

'Thank you, my lord,' she gasped in an unnaturally high voice. She felt ready to sink into the ground.

He immediately took advantage of the situation to lean closer.

'Do I really alarm you so very much, Miss Lynley?' he murmured.

The hint of amusement in his tone had her spine stiffening. 'No, you do not!' she declared, looking him in the eye for precisely one second. 'Consider my clumsiness merely another example of a female losing her wits over you. Good day, sir.'

He laughed, a soft sound that sent shivers rippling through every limb, and taking her hand, raised it to his lips for the most fleeting of caresses. 'I'll remember that,' he said. 'Good day, Miss Lynley.'

Sarah's heart gave a violent leap. At the same time heat broke out all over her body. Really! Kissing her hand! What did Ravensdene think he was about? Didn't he recognise sarcasm when he heard it? Did he think she had *meant*—?

Her thoughts disintegrating into a maelstrom of shock, outrage and a shivery feeling that she told herself was fear, Sarah scrambled into the carriage and sat back against the squabs. She was not going to say another word. *Not one more word!* Until she was sure her brain was in control of her mouth.

And she was *not* going to look at him! Not this time.

Never mind that he was watching her. Oh, yes, she could feel the touch of those glittering eyes, like emerald fire burning through her defences, could feel him waiting, compelling her to look at him.

When had it become so difficult to control her own senses, she wondered hysterically. Why was it so difficult to resist him? It should be easy. *Easy!*

Except. . .the resolve that had been forged into unbreakable steel in a sudden conflagration of brutality eight years ago was in danger of crumbling like so much dust. Everything around her had taken on a strange, frighteningly new face.

There was Julia, blushing at something Lord Devenham was saying to her as he held her hand for far too long. There had been Lydia Beresford, not only accepting her husband's touch, Sarah recalled, stunned anew by the knowledge, but actively, lovingly, seeking it.

Was that what Julia wanted of life, she wondered, painfully aware of the shy glow on her friend's countenance? She had known, of course, that Julia expected to marry one day, but she hadn't thought her friend would be so *eager*.

But then neither Julia nor Lydia had seen Amy lying broken and bloody and lifeless; they had not heard the dreadful sounds preceding her sister's death.

And as if to remind her, there was Ravensdene, dark and powerful and intense, standing by the barouche, positively *willing* her to look at him. She wished he would not watch her so. She wished she knew why he had exaggerated Lady Wribbonhall's concern for her. She wished she knew which man he really was: the frightening stranger she had encountered in the woods, or the friend who had treated with gentle understanding what must have seemed to him to be very puzzling behaviour two days ago?

It would be easier if he was never kind, Sarah decided suddenly, as the barouche began to move. Because you could not reconcile brutality and tenderness. The two simply did not go together.

Nick eyed the besotted smile on his friend's face as the barouche turned out of the yard and disappeared down the road. 'Should I congratulate you, Dev?'

Devenham turned from waving farewell and grinned at him. 'Not yet,' he said. 'But I'm addressing the situation.'

'Ah. That explains why you're willing to indulge Miss Wribbonhall's quest for ghosts. The bonnet is a bit of a puzzle, however.'

'Bonnet? What the devil— Oh!' Devenham shook his head and laughed. 'You mean when I escorted Miss Wribbonhall to the milliner while we were waiting for you to find Miss Lynley. I tell you what, Nick. That shop was a nightmare. Ghost-hunting will be nothing to it. Never seen so many militant females in all my life. And it seemed to me that the less there was to the hats, the more the damned things cost.'

Nick's answering smile was a touch cynical. 'One of the pitfalls of the attached male,' he warned. 'Wives can be expensive.'

'Well, I daresay it depends on the wife,' Devenham remarked sapiently. 'And speaking of matters marital, you're not exactly being discreet yourself, old boy. Are you hoping to throw the local ladies off the scent by pretending an interest in Miss Lynley?'

'Hmm. An interesting thought. But to answer your question: no, not at all. It would be most unfair to her.'

'Oh, I don't know. Perhaps she wouldn't care. After

all, she's the only female, apart from Miss Wribbonhall, who hasn't been hunting you.'

'Very true.' Nick narrowed his eyes thoughtfully at the now empty road. 'And I'm beginning to suspect why,' he added, more to himself than to Devenham.

'Good God! You're not piqued by her disinterest, are you, Nick?'

'I ought to stuff that remark down your throat, my friend.'

Neither voice nor expression had altered, but Devenham appeared gratifyingly alarmed. 'No, of course you're not,' he apologised hastily. 'Sorry, old fellow, but the way you said that. . .for a minute I thought. . . Well, it wouldn't be surprising if you did wonder why Miss Lynley seems to be immune. I mean, I know you've been out of England for twelve years, but you must know how eligible you are.'

'Good Lord.' Snapping out of his preoccupation, Nick seized the Viscount by the arm and began steering him down the street. 'You've been talking to my mother again.'

'Well, it's true,' argued Devenham, still apologetic but persistent. He began ticking off points on his fingers. 'There's the title, you're wealthy, you've been fighting in the Peninsula—'

'What the devil has that got to do with anything?'

'Gives you an air of glamour—or danger. Take your pick.'

'Bloody hell!'

'Actually—' Devenham ground to a halt with the air of a man who has just thought of something brilliant '—marrying Miss Lynley might not be such a bad idea after all. You'd be able to get on with the job of trapping your spy in peace.'

'I would certainly like to do so,' Nick said with heavy meaning.

A guilty look replaced the pleased smile on the Viscount's face. 'Yes, I know. Sorry about setting you up for this picnic on Thursday, Nick, but I couldn't disappoint Miss Wribbonhall. She had her heart set on it and. . . Well, you know how it is.'

'Only too well,' Nick murmured. For an instant his eyes were cold with memories, then he shrugged them off. He'd been young. Young and ignorant and blind. But not any more. Now he knew precisely what he wanted. Had known the instant he'd been informed that Sarah was missing.

His eyes narrowed again as he remembered the rapid succession of emotions that had jolted through him at that moment. The quite irrational thought that she had no business getting lost without him. The chilling fear that, alone in a town full of soldiers, she might be afraid or in danger. And overriding all, the sudden blinding knowledge that he might lose something incomparable if he didn't make her his.

His frown deepened. Obviously tightly leashed physical desire was affecting his cool, logical brain. There was no need to think in such melodramatic terms. It had been quite natural to worry about Sarah's safety, but all he had to do was make it very clear to her that she was to restrain her somewhat reckless tendency to place herself in potentially hazardous situations. He did not foresee a problem in the matter. He had seen enough of Sarah to form a fairly accurate opinion of her nature and character. When she forgot to be afraid of him—and he was going to get to the bottom of that before he was much older—she was a responsible, sensible young woman. Exactly as the Reverend Butterlow had described her, in fact.

And if he had to marry for expediency, exactly what he wanted.

'Uh. . . Nick? '

Devenham's voice pulled him out of his reverie. He wondered briefly what had been in his eyes to make his friend sound so unusually tentative, before he recalled where the conversation had left off.

'Don't worry about it,' he advised the Viscount. 'Unless there's something waiting for me at the receiving-office today, we might as well kick our heels at a picnic as anywhere.'

'You're expecting a message from London?'

'Or closer to home.' He smiled slightly at the Viscount's startled expression. 'I'm not entirely alone in this,' he said as they started off again. 'Figgins is helping me, of course, but I have one or two other contacts along the coast.'

'Well, that's a relief,' retorted Devenham. 'Considering there's several miles of beach to watch. But what if nothing happens? You said something about a trap being laid, but if you think it's some local bigwig. . .' He paused, brows drawn together in puzzlement. 'Can you be sure of that?'

'Beyond reasonable doubt. God knows, in cases like this anything can happen, but no one from that particular department of the Foreign Office has ever travelled down this way, so the information has to be passed to someone living nearby, and I can't see our traitor in town forwarding it to a village tapkeeper or an illiterate fisherman.'

'Forwarding. . . Good God! Don't tell me they use the penny-post?'

Nick sent him an amused glance. 'Why not? Nothing safer. Or more unobtrusive.'

'I suppose not, but. . .' Devenham apparently

decided to take his word for that. 'What about the French side of things? You said your agent there discovered where the information entered France. From the real French agent whose place he has taken, I presume.'

'You presume correctly.'

'Hmm. And is this Frenchman now languishing in prison?'

'He's been eliminated.'

Devenham grimaced. 'I won't ask how. By the by, how does the information travel to France?'

'As far as we can ascertain,' Nick said slowly, 'a message is sent to France via fishermen who clearly have few scruples, that a certain cargo will be ready for shipment in a week or so. The French agent then crosses the Channel himself to take personal delivery.'

'Dangerous.'

'Yes, but necessary, I think. The people we're looking for on this side wouldn't have been able to travel to France regularly without their absence being remarked.'

'You're convinced they have to be persons in such notable positions?'

A wry smile curved Nick's mouth. 'I'm afraid so, Dev. The information that's been stolen in the past was available at only the highest level. It stands to reason it would be passed to someone similarly placed, who then, we assume, meets with the French agent somewhere near the beach.'

'Quite a chain.'

'And effective. The only weak link would be whoever runs the boat, and I daresay the fellow could be easily replaced should his conscience ever get the better of him.'

'My God! Murder?'

Nick shrugged. 'This might not be a battlefield, Dev, but it's the same war.'

'I know, but one doesn't realise— Hell, Nick, and here I've been ribbing you about all the distractions you've had to put up with lately. Damn it, there's the Assembly tomorrow night, too, and now Thursday. . .' Devenham shook his head. 'I hope you know that if you have to cry-off, I'll smooth things over for you.'

'Thank you, but I fully intend to be present at the Assembly, and on Thursday. Our ghost-hunt may give me an opportunity to retrieve my position.' He grimaced, remembering Sarah in full retreat. 'Such as it was.'

'Eh?' said Devenham, startled. 'What have ghosts to do with catching your spy?'

'Nothing. I'm talking about catching a wife.'

The Viscount's jaw dropped. He stopped dead once again—this time outside the receiving office. '*Wife*? What in the— Do you mean. . . *Miss Lynley*?'

'Why are you surprised? It was your suggestion that I marry her.'

'But you objected to it!'

'No. I said it would be unfair to *pretend* an interest.'

Devenham was struck speechless.

Nick grinned at his friend's dumbfounded countenance and turned into the receiving-office.

He ascertained that there were no messages awaiting him and returned to the street to find the Viscount standing exactly where he had left him two minutes ago. A quite unaccountable flash of irritation went through him.

'You know, Dev, you are giving an excellent imitation of a stuffed and mounted trophy. I should think you'd approve. Apart from my task here, weren't you enumerating all the reasons why I should remarry the other day?'

The Viscount came to life with a start. 'Well, yes, but I didn't mean. . . I thought you'd choose. . .'

Nick turned his friend's footsteps in the direction of the Lamb. 'I seem to be spending a great deal of time today steering people in the direction in which I want them to go,' he muttered, marching the Viscount along rather forcibly.

'It's the direction you're going in that worries me,' Devenham retorted, undeterred.

'You don't consider Miss Lynley to be a suitable match?'

'Damn it, there's no need to go all quiet and dangerous on me, Nick. I daresay Miss Lynley is perfectly eligible. It's just that after Marianne. . . Well, surely some degree of attachment. . .' He looked at his friend and encountered a politely raised eyebrow.

'Oh, devil take it, I'm sure Miss Lynley is a very good sort of girl, but I find it hard to believe she's your sort. She's so timid for one thing. Take the last half-hour—she scarcely opened her mouth. And she practically has a fit of the vapours every time you go near her.'

'Oh, not every time,' Nick said thoughtfully. In fact, he mused, until that moment when Sarah had almost measured her length on the floor of Lady Wribbonhall's carriage, she hadn't seemed afraid of him at all this morning.

Of course, when they'd collided and he'd found his arms full of soft, fragrant Sarah, she might have reacted rather differently if he hadn't managed to put her away from him before she'd felt the effect on his body of her nearness. He had remembered just in time that it seemed to be the potential threat in a man's physical touch that frightened her.

On the other hand, she hadn't objected to his touch when he'd marched her out of his library the other day. Obviously he'd had her too confused to notice. Perhaps there was a lesson to be learned in that.

'Well, you're the only one who knows what will suit you,' Devenham observed at last. He sounded extremely doubtful. 'I just hope you're not doing this because of some misguided notion of protecting Miss Lynley in case her uncle turns out to be your traitor.'

'I gave up such idiotic notions of romantic chivalry years ago,' Nick said very dryly. 'Don't worry, Dev, I know precisely what I'm doing.'

'If you say so,' Devenham muttered, still unconvinced. 'But I'll tell you one thing, Nick. If you really do intend to marry Miss Lynley, the tabbies will have a field-day comparing her to Marianne. They're so entirely different.'

This prospect merely elicited a faint smile.

'Yes,' Nick said very softly as the Lamb Inn came into view. 'She's as unlike Marianne as a single candle is from a blazing chandelier. That's why I'm going to marry her.'

CHAPTER SEVEN

WEDNESDAY evening's assembly had scarcely begun when Sarah realised it was going to be an evening of unmitigated disaster. She should have known.

The first intimation of what lay in store for her had occurred when Lady Wribbonhall had introduced her to the Master of Ceremonies. A very proper individual, he had no sooner provided her and Julia with cards and gold-tasselled pencils when both he and Lord Devenham, who was escorting their little party, had been nearly sent flying by a stampede of military gentlemen wishing to pencil their names in for as many dances as would be permitted.

Since Lord Devenham had taken the precaution of soliciting Julia's hand for the waltz and the first country dance, and Sarah's for the second, he had good-naturedly stepped aside to wait for the crowd to subside.

It hadn't. Anyone who could claim the slightest acquaintance with Lady Wribbonhall had done so, and in the process had reminded Sarah of how much she disliked being surrounded by large males. Or even average-sized males.

She shuddered as she recalled the scene. She had begun to feel slightly hysterical. Either that or the crush of people, the chatter, the constant requests for dances had been playing tricks with her mind, because she had suddenly found herself entertaining a wild fantasy wherein the Earl of Ravensdene appeared and whisked her out of the crowd.

This incredible flight of fancy had stunned her so

much that, as one in a trance, she had accepted the hand of the first gentleman to ask for the honour of dancing with her.

It had been a mistake. She was now imprisoned in a set with a partner who was apparently anxious to assure her that now that 'that fellow Bonaparte' had reached Paris, he would personally see to it that something was done. This heroic pose was rather diminished, however, by his unfortunate trick of tangling the gauze overskirt of her rose silk ballgown on his dress-sword whenever they went through the figures of the dance.

Sarah wondered why it was that military men felt obliged to wear weapons of violence to a ball. Perhaps he thought Bonaparte might decide to pop over from Paris for the evening. Perhaps she should have brought her pistol along. Either event would at least have given the conversation a decidedly new turn.

The absurd thoughts got her through the dance. Then, as the music ended, she happened to glance towards the doorway. That was when she knew beyond any doubt that the entire evening was destined for disaster.

Standing just inside the room, watching her, a slight smile playing about his hard mouth, was the Earl of Ravensdene. And not two paces behind him, being greeted by the Master of Ceremonies, were the Beresfords.

Sarah closed her eyes and tried to tell herself she was seeing things. She also tried to tell herself that the sudden leap her heart had given at the sight of Ravensdene was because he made her nervous.

Especially when he was smiling like that.

'I say, Miss Lynley, shall we have another go-around?' Her youthful partner looked at her hopefully.

'Thank you, Lieutenant, er, Millingham,' she

responded, groping hastily for the right name among all the others swimming about in her head. 'But my card is already full.'

He appeared downcast but unsurprised by this mendacious piece of information, and restoring her to Lady Wribbonhall, went off in search of another partner, seriously endangering the gowns of several ladies in his path, not to mention his own feet.

'Good heavens, my dear, I believe you have made quite a conquest,' Lady Wribbonhall said placidly. 'Ineligible, of course, and he seems to be incapable of walking without stumbling every few steps. Can he have been *imbibing*, do you suppose? That is the disadvantage of these country Assemblies. Almost anyone can attend. Oh, Lord Ravensdene, how very gratifying... I mean, how very pleasant to see you here, after all.'

'Good evening, ma'am. Miss Lynley. I trust Lord Devenham made my apologies for my lateness. I was unavoidably detained.'

After the briefest of greetings, Sarah became very busy straightening her overskirt.

'Dear me, we are only too happy to see you here at all,' Lady Wribbonhall fluted. 'I am sure this sort of gathering where country dances rather than waltzes are predominant is not... Oh, look, Sarah, is that the lady I saw you with yesterday? Yes, she is waving. She appears a most charming young woman. You must introduce us, my love.'

Sarah groaned inwardly and looked up. Her gaze skittered nervously past Ravensdene without actually meeting the intent green eyes focused on her face, to see Lydia Beresford waving to her from across the room.

It was impossible to tell herself she was seeing things

this time. She was trapped. There was nothing for it. As a martyr being led to the scaffold, she summoned up a brave smile and beckoned.

Mrs Beresford answered the summons with alacrity, crossing the room on her husband's arm.

'Miss Lynley,' she said with her warm smile. 'I am so glad to see you here tonight. May I present my husband? He most particularly wishes to thank you for your kindness yesterday.'

'Truly, I did very little,' Sarah disclaimed, exchanging a handshake and smile with Major Beresford.

Close to, he was seen to be several years older than his wife and of serious mien. Although perhaps it was his illness that made him appear so, Sarah thought, as his expression lightened into a charming smile and she saw again the man who had gazed at Lydia with such tenderness. Conscious that Ravensdene was watching them and listening to every word, she felt a guilty blush heat her cheeks.

However, the Major's quiet thanks, without fuss or exaggeration, soon restored some of her poise. Sending up a fervent prayer that the meeting would go off without anyone discovering that she had stooped to following people unbeknownst to them, she turned and was about to introduce the Beresfords to Lady Wribbonhall when Lord Devenham's voice smote her ears.

'Good God, Will! Is that you? My dear fellow! Where did you spring from? The last I heard—'

What Devenham had heard was destined to remain a mystery. Sarah ceased to listen, her hopes of the parties separating before anyone happened to mention that she had managed to lose herself yesterday, and precisely where Ravensdene had found her, dwindling alarmingly.

Fortunately for her jangling nerves, Lord Devenham then redeemed himself by making introductions all round. Under cover of the general conversation that ensued, Ravensdene contrived to draw her a little apart. She could only be thankful that he kept his voice down.

'Why didn't you tell me you had been with Mrs Beresford yesterday?' he demanded. 'Instead of letting me think you were wandering around alone.'

Sarah tried to pull herself together. It was no use falling apart at this point. She needed all her wits about her.

'Since I was alone when we met, would it have made any difference?' she retorted, the memory of his anger in her eyes.

He acknowledged the challenge with a rueful grin. '*Touché*, Miss Lynley.' Then as her heartbeat began to slow to a more normal pace, he added in a low growl, 'Just don't let it happen again.'

'Don't— I *beg* your—'

'Hush,' he interrupted. 'Your friend is preparing to go off to the cardroom.'

Sarah bit off her indignant protest with an almost audible snap of her teeth. He was right. With the innate good breeding that precluded them from joining a group of persons whom they had only recently met, the Beresfords were taking their leave.

'Lady Wribbonhall has invited me to bring Giles to visit her next week,' Lydia told Sarah as her husband shook hands with Ravensdene. 'What a very kind person she is. It will be such a delightful outing for him.'

'Yes, indeed,' Sarah responded warmly. 'I shall look forward to seeing you there, Mrs Beresford.'

'A most delightful couple,' pronounced Lady

Wribbonhall to no one in particular as the Beresfords made their way through the crowd to the cardroom. 'Not pushing in the least. And so comforting to know that Lord Devenham is acquainted with the Major. Where did you say you met them, Sarah dear?'

Alarm screeching once more along her nerves, Sarah tried to think. Her brain seemed singularly uncooperative, but fortunately rescue was at hand. The music began for the next dance, and, as Lord Devenham turned to her to make his claim, it was easy to pretend that Lady Wribbonhall's question had gone unheard.

'I do believe this is our dance, Miss Lynley,' Devenham began. 'Shall we—?'

'You must be mistaken, Dev,' Ravensdene murmured. 'As it happens, Miss Lynley is promised to me.' He exchanged one brief glance with the Viscount who, to Sarah's horror, very basely surrendered the field without a whimper.

She stared after his retreating form for an incredulous second, wondering what else was going to befall her that night, then, refusing to submit so tamely, ostentatiously whipped out her card and studied it.

'As it happens,' she mimicked sarcastically. 'It is you who are mistaken, my lord. You will just have to—'

He reached out, plucked the card from her fingers and coolly crossed out Devenham's name and replaced it with his own.

While Sarah was still gasping with shock at this outrageous behaviour, he then proceeded to write his name against the waltz and the supper dance.

'Are you *mad*?' she squeaked, finally getting her breath back. Abandoning any pretence at good manners, she snatched the card off him and crossed his name out with wildly agitated strokes. Her pencil promptly snapped in two.

'I do not waltz, my lord,' she informed him, continuing to wield the useless stub with enough energy to demolish that as well.

'Good,' he purred, and a slow smile lit his eyes. 'Then, since Dev has very kindly taken himself off, we can stand up for the next country dance, after all. I want to talk to you.'

'You want to— *You* want—'

Sarah's breath deserted her again. She glanced around for deliverance. There was none, of course. Her unwanted crowd of admirers had deserted her, as well, just when she needed them. Probably scared off by the predatory panther standing before her, as poor Lord Devenham had been.

'Well, *I* do not wish to talk to you, my lord,' she finally got out. 'Of all the arrogant, ill-considered actions. As if I would even dance *three* times with you! You must be—'

He took her hand without any warning and tugged her gently towards him.

'For goodness sake, my lord! What do you think you are about?'

'We don't want to miss a place in the set, Miss Lynley,' he said very politely, while dragging her most impolitely out to the centre of the room.

Sarah tried to dig her heels in and found herself skating across the floor instead. By the time she found some purchase they were at the end of the set and the music had started.

'This is intolerable,' she hissed in a furious undertone. 'It is the longest set in the room. We shall be here forever.'

'I'm afraid so,' he agreed, his eyes gleaming. 'But the alternative was to join the other set which contains all three Miss Smisbys. I know you would not wish such a fate on a hapless male.'

'*Hapless male*? You, sir, are the most *un*hapless male I have ever encountered!'

He grinned at her. 'When faced with three ladies all decked out in brilliant orange, Miss Lynley, any male is hapless.'

'Oh, my goodness!' Sarah glanced around before she could stop herself.

The three damsels behind her were indeed the Smisby sisters. And they were indeed wearing identical gowns of a glaring shade somewhere between orange and scarlet. At close range such a blast of colour was positively painful.

'That particular shade is known as "sunset red",' was all Sarah could say in weak accents. 'It is very fashionable at present.'

Ravensdene cast a quick glance beyond her shoulder and winced. 'I will take your word for it. However, I much prefer your style, Miss Lynley. You look deli. . . delightful.'

'Oh.' Feeling quite unnecessarily flustered by such a mild compliment, Sarah felt herself blush a similar hue to the garish spectacle behind her. 'Thank you, my lord.'

'But I am curious,' he went on. 'I'm sure you told me, Miss Lynley, that you neither dance nor go into society. Yet, here you are doing both.'

Sarah forgot about compliments. 'I was press-ganged into this dance if you will recall, sir,' she retorted, glaring at him. 'So if you have any complaints—'

'Oh, I'm not complaining. I merely wondered what had changed your mind.'

Hardly surprising, she allowed silently, given their previous acquaintance. She began to calm down somewhat, reminding herself that she still had the rest of the evening to get through. Really, she'd had no idea how exhausting it was maintaining an outraged demeanour.

'Lady Wribbonhall thought it would be good practice for me,' she admitted gloomily.

'Good practice?' The smile that had been lurking in his eyes all through the conversation vanished on the instant. 'For what? Have you decided to sample the pleasures of a London Season, after all?'

'Not if I have anything to say on the subject,' she muttered.

He continued to study her through slightly narrowed eyes, and Sarah felt annoyance flicker to life again. 'In fact, sir, I have as much desire for a London Season as I have to be in my present situation, which is to say none at all. I would rather be at home reading a book or playing chess with Uncle Jasper than at this stupid Assembly dancing with—'

Their arrival at the top of the set put an end to this comprehensive setdown. Nor did it seem to have the desired effect. Those ice-green eyes that could take on a dangerous glitter capable of chilling the blood in her veins were warming again with silent laughter.

'I am in entire agreement with you about the occasion, Miss Lynley,' he said as he turned into the first figure. 'But since we are here, I would much rather be waltzing with you.'

Sarah went down the set with her feet moving in one direction while her brain whirled off in quite another. She could have sworn that Ravensdene had said 'Good' when she'd informed him she didn't waltz. What was he talking about now? Was he trying to drive her insane?

And why did the thought of his arm about her waist

as he guided her into the steps of the waltz make her feel so very warm and shivery all at the same time?

It was all very unnerving. So was the slow smile he gave her as they met again at the end of the dance.

'You said you wished to talk to me, my lord,' she reminded him, taking the plunge on the general principle that attack was the best form of defence against that smile. 'I presume it was not to discuss whether or not I intend to go to London.'

He raised his brows slightly. 'No, Miss Lynley, it was not.' He offered her his arm. 'In fact, I wanted to beg your assistance in one or two small matters.'

She blinked at him. 'Beg my assistance?'

'Yes. You may have been aware that I played chess with your uncle two days ago?'

Sarah nodded before laying a cautious hand on his arm. As they began to walk around the perimeter of the room she wondered if Ravensdene suspected that she had deliberately absented herself that afternoon.

A rueful smile curved his mouth. 'You were quite correct in your estimation of your uncle, Miss Lynley. Sir Jasper routed me in no short order. I am afraid he must have been extremely disappointed at such a poor challenge as I presented.'

'Well, you did warn him that you were out of practice,' she recalled. She peered up at him warily. Something didn't feel quite right here. For one thing, that look of wry appeal Ravensdene was aiming at her did not really match the watchful gleam in his eyes, nor the dark, predatory grace with which he moved.

'That's what Sir Jasper said,' he agreed. 'However, the two of us might give him a match, Miss Lynley.'

Sarah stopped dead, frowning at him. 'You and me?' she clarified with deep suspicion.

He smiled. 'You did offer your assistance the other day.'

'I did?' She thought frantically. 'I did not!'

'It would not be such a hardship, you know. I am very quick to learn. Will next Monday be convenient?'

'Well, I—' Aware that the situation was again hurtling out of her control, she looked wildly around for rescue.

There was none. Lady Wribbonhall was still some distance away, and in any event had fallen into conversation with another matron. And although she could see Devenham making his way towards them, she knew whose side *he* was on.

Then as her gaze swept around the room in her search for Julia, Ravensdene's iniquities vanished beneath a wave of horrified disbelief. For there, standing in the entrance, resplendent in a bottle-green coat and matching pantaloons, was a sight that put the crowning touch on a series of increasingly hideous encounters.

'Oh, no!' she groaned, momentarily forgetting who she was with. 'Not the Frog.'

'Frog?'

The sharp question cut through Sarah's dismay like a sword slicing through silk. Startled, she glanced up at Ravensdene in time to intercept an extremely hard look before he switched his attention to the newcomer.

'Frog?' he repeated.

It was all too much. Even the reappearance of the Beresfords would have been preferable. Sarah began to wish for a quiet room where she could have hysterics in peace. She tried to do an abrupt about-face and immediately discovered another unpalatable fact. Ravensdene was utterly immovable. In fact, her impulsive movement nearly landed her in his arms.

'It is of no consequence, my lord,' she said, hurriedly backing away. 'Merely someone I met recently. Shall we—?'

'Too late,' he interrupted softly. 'Brace yourself, Miss Lynley. You are about to meet him again.'

Sending him a glare that she hoped plainly conveyed her opinion of this unhelpful advice, Sarah turned to confront her admirer from Tunbridge Wells.

She shuddered inwardly as he hurried towards her on short, bandy legs. A few weeks had not improved the gentleman's appearance. He was still almost as wide as he was tall, and his countenance, dominated by a pair of bulging blue eyes, still bore an unfortunate resemblance to one of the amphibian species.

These faults of person could have been forgiven, however. After all, the man couldn't help his looks, Sarah reflected, trying to be charitable. What caused her to shiver with distaste was his air of self-importance, which she knew was well-nigh impregnable and which made it impossible for him to believe his suit could be unwelcome to any lady he chose to favour with it. And this time there was no doting, possessive mama to stand in his way.

Suddenly Ravensdene's presence was elevated in her mind from disaster to godsend.

'My lord. . .'

'Don't concern yourself,' he bit out very softly. 'I have no intention of leaving you.'

There was no time to wonder at the grimness in his tone. The green-clad one was upon them. Before Sarah could prevent it, he had taken her hand and was bowing over it to the accompaniment of creaking corsets.

'Miss Lynley!' he uttered in throbbing accents,

straightening and pressing her hand clammily between both of his. 'At last! I have found you!'

She tugged unsuccessfully at her hand. 'How do you do, Sir Ponsonby?' she responded coolly, suppressing an impulse to inform him that she would rather have stayed lost.

Ravensdene had no such scruples.

'You may restore Miss Lynley's hand to her, sir, unless you wish to part with your own,' he growled.

Even forewarned as she was, Sarah nearly jumped at the menace in the low threat.

Sir Ponsonby, on the other hand, had obviously never met a panther before. He obeyed, but only so he could raise his quizzing glass to one eye in haughty enquiry. 'I don't believe I know you, sir,' he began in the pompous tones that Sarah remembered only too well.

'Ravensdene,' stated the Earl with a bluntness that bordered on incivility. He appeared singularly unintimidated by an eye thus repulsively magnified.

Sarah hurried to avert the anticipated slaughter she could see gathering in his own icy-green gaze. 'Lord Ravensdene has only recently returned to England,' she explained. 'My lord, may I present Sir Ponsonby Freem?'

'If you must,' drawled Ravensdene.

Sir Ponsonby made a noise even more reminiscent of a pond denizen than his appearance. 'Miss Lynley,' he produced after an apoplectic moment. 'I have a matter of great import to discuss with you. A very personal matter,' he elucidated, glaring at Ravensdene. 'Shall I find you at home tomorrow?'

'No, you won't, Freem,' Ravensdene stated before Sarah could answer. 'And any personal matters you wish to discuss concerning Miss Lynley may be addressed to her uncle.'

'Oh, no. . .'

'When he is improved enough in health to be receiving visitors,' Ravensdene continued as if her faint protest had not been uttered.

'I am acquainted with Sir Jasper, my lord,' snapped Sir Ponsonby, rapidly turning red. It was not a hue that suited him. 'I would not incommode him in the least, as I am sure Miss Lynley is aware. And I must say, sir, that you might let her speak for herself. Unless you have some formal claim on the lady,' he tacked on rather nastily.

'Oh, please, Sir Ponsonby, we are beginning to attract attention,' Sarah begged. She was starting to tremble. The prospect of being the cause of an unpleasant public scene, especially a scene involving angry males, made her quail.

But even as her tremors increased, Ravensdene took her hand and tucked it securely beneath his arm.

'Tell Sir Ponsonby that you are unavailable to gentlemen callers, Miss Lynley,' he instructed softly, the barest hint of a smile in his eyes as he glanced down at her. 'I fear he will be satisfied with nothing less.'

'It is perfectly true, sir,' Sarah confirmed, trying not to cling to the reassuring strength of the arm that was all but supporting her. 'Besides, I am extremely busy just now what with shopping and assemblies and picnics and one thing and another and. . .'

'You know how it is, Freem,' Ravensdene confided as Sarah's explanation faltered in a morass of unnecessary detail. 'One social whirl after another.'

'So I see.' Sir Ponsonby looked around pointedly. 'I marvel, Miss Lynley, that you would leave your—'

'Not only that,' Ravensdene interposed ruthlessly,

'but Miss Lynley is teaching me to play chess. I'm afraid the project is going to take all her spare time in the foreseeable future. Now if you will excuse us, I must restore my partner to her chaperon. Don't think it hasn't been a pleasure.'

Sir Ponsonby opened his mouth but his victims were already walking away, one of them now shaking with a mixture of relief and suppressed mirth.

'I am not going to teach you to play chess,' Sarah whispered, laughter bubbling forth as she glanced back in time to see her vanquished swain storming towards the door. 'Oh, dear, he's leaving. How could you be so rude, my lord?'

'How can you say that, Miss Lynley?' he countered. 'I was being excessively polite. And I don't want you to teach me to play chess, merely to assist me against a merciless foe.'

She giggled again. 'I doubt you need any assistance at all, sir, but what can I say? I am in your debt. Thank you. Sir Ponsonby is the most odious little man imaginable, and simply impossible to get rid of.'

He raised a brow.

'I should say impossible to get rid of using civil means,' she amended hastily. Then seeing a certain sardonic gleam in his eyes, added, 'And don't you dare say I need a keeper, sir!'

'Would I be so tactless?'

'Yes,' she said without hesitation.

He laughed. 'I'm afraid you are quite correct, Miss Lynley. But whenever I cast my mind back over our rather memorable meetings, not to mention the fact that you are still trembling like a leaf, I am forced to the conclusion that you do need a keeper. Tell me, what qualifications would you require for such a position? Would civility be necessary all the time?'

Sarah didn't know whether to laugh, scold or scream in frustration. Trembling like a leaf? So much for taking charge of her own life. She couldn't even get through a country assembly without help. This was what came of socialising with males. She should have known better.

'*All* the time,' she asserted, trying to suppress the faint tremors still rippling through her. 'Which definitely puts you out of the running, sir.'

'That's rather unfortunate,' he murmured. 'Since it is when my incivility stirs you to anger that you forget to be afraid of me.'

Sarah felt as if he had just delivered a blow to her mid-section. Her smile vanished. Her breath left her lungs in a rush. Her legs felt as if they would no longer support her.

Afraid of him?

Well, yes, sometimes he *did* frighten her, but. . .

Surely he didn't want. . .?

'You. . .you would rather have me angry with you?' she ventured on a note barely above a whisper.

He regarded her thoughtfully for a moment. 'Rather than afraid, yes. I find I have developed a considerable aversion to seeing fear in your eyes whenever you look at me, Miss Lynley.'

'Oh! I don't. . . That is. . . It isn't. . .' She faltered to a stop, shaken and confused by the overwhelming urge to reassure him that was sweeping over her. But not knowing what to say. Dear God, she could hardly *think*, let alone speak.

'Isn't it?' he pressed gravely.

'No! No, it—'

He raised his free hand to cover hers, sending heat flowing through her in a tide of sensation that made her feel shockingly weak, and yet warm, so very warm. And safe.

Their steps had slowed to a stop, but she barely noticed. A haze seemed to envelop her brain; it took several seconds before she realised he was speaking again, his voice soft and yet strangely urgent.

'Miss Lynley, I am going to ask you a question that may shock you. It will certainly startle you. Please believe that, although I may not divulge the reason for it in our present situation, I do not ask it lightly.'

When his words finally made sense, Sarah knew she had stopped breathing. The assembly rooms and their colourful, chattering occupants disappeared. She felt as if she was suspended over a precipice, unable either to retreat or step forward, the strength of Ravensdene's will the only bridge beneath her feet.

'What is it, sir?' she asked, and knew he could hear the husky, nervous quality of her voice.

He tightened his hold on her hand as if he would brace her for what was to come. 'Miss Lynley, have you ever been. . .frightened by a man?'

The obvious restraint in the question surprised her. She had expected him to be much more direct. And though she knew what he wanted to ask, somehow it seemed very important to be sure.

'Do you mean. . .?'

His eyes were grim. 'I mean,' he said roughly, 'has some man ever abused you, little one?'

The endearment shivered through her on a ripple of heat. Her lips parted, quivering, but the instinctive protest rising in her throat died unsaid.

'No,' she whispered. 'It was. . .it happened. . .to someone else.'

He studied her closely for a moment, then nodded. 'Your sister.'

It wasn't a question. He knew. Perhaps he had seen something in her face, heard something in her voice. Whatever it was, he knew.

'I'm sorry,' he said when she didn't answer. 'Come, I'll take you back to Lady Wribbonhall. I won't upset you anymore.'

'I'm not upset,' she murmured, startled to discover it was true. She was uneasy with the subject, unwilling to say more, but she was far from the overwrought female he'd had to cope with on several other conspicuous occasions.

For some reason that she did not want to examine too closely, she wanted him to know that.

'There is no need to treat me as if I'm about to fall into a swoon, my lord,' she murmured. Then, compelled by the same unknown force, added, 'Although after our previous encounters I can imagine what you must think of me.'

'No, Miss Lynley,' he said very quietly. 'You can't. I have been at considerable pains to make sure of that.'

CHAPTER EIGHT

IF ANYTHING was calculated to render her extremely nervous prior to their next encounter, it would have to be that last remark, Sarah reflected the next day as she gazed up at the fluffy white clouds sailing across the deep blue sky.

A soft spring breeze whispered through the ivy-clad stone arches of the ruined priory, ruffling the flounces of her new cambric dress and bringing a faint flush to her cheeks, but Sarah had no thoughts to spare for the dangers of exposing her complexion to the sun and spring breezes. She was too busy assuring herself that Ravensdene had not meant anything cryptic or alarming last night, and wondering why the assurance had little effect.

After all, his remark could as easily have meant that his opinion of her was far from flattering. It would hardly be surprising.

Letting the desultory snatches of conversation from her companions drift around her, she stole a glance at Ravensdene from beneath her lashes as if a surreptitious examination of the object of her disquiet might provide a few clues.

He sat beside her on one of the carriage rugs thoughtfully provided by Miss Sherington, leaning on one hand, his other arm propped across his raised knee. The position moulded his breeches to the long muscles of his thighs and pulled his coat taut across the breadth of his shoulders and back. He had opened the buttons for comfort, but the conservative waistcoat thus exposed merely emphasized the fact that there was not a single ounce of excess flesh anywhere on Ravensdene's powerful frame.

A succession of tiny tremors chased one another down her spine. Considering the nature of the outing, there was nothing improper in the way he was sitting. Indeed, everyone else had disposed themselves in similar casual poses in the sunny spot they had chosen beside the walls of the ruined priory. But the hand taking his weight was flat on the ground just behind her hip, and she felt rather... *surrounded*. Close proximity to so much raw masculine strength, even if discreetly displayed, was not conducive to rational thought.

She wondered if she was the only one who saw anything dangerous about that relaxed pose. Since no one else had seen beyond his cool, civilised exterior, it seemed safe to assume she was. Sophie Sherington and Eliza Langdon had certainly possessed no qualms about vying with each other all afternoon for his attention. For some reason, instead of amusing her, their combined antics were beginning to grate on her nerves.

Shaking off the disturbing notion, Sarah leaned away from Ravensdene under the guise of gathering up the remains of the picnic luncheon.

'Oh, Sarah, don't worry about all those baskets now.' Julia, sounding slightly sleepy, bestirred herself to protest. 'I am feeling far too lazy to help you.'

'Yes, indeed.' Miss Eliza Langdon, a blue-eyed brunette, whose soft brown tresses were quite cast in the shade when seen beside Miss Sherington's striking auburn curls, took a last sip of lemonade and set her glass down. 'Really, there is something rather decadent about lunching *al fresco*. I feel quite dreadfully lazy myself.'

Devenham's easy smile flashed out. 'Drinking lemonade while lounging about on rugs in the middle of the day,' he said, saluting Julia with his wineglass. 'That's decadent, all right. Also dashed uncomfortable when you've been sitting on a rock for the better part of an hour.'

Julia giggled. 'Well, we could have brought those stools Sophie had in her carriage, but they would have ruined the atmosphere. You can't expect ghosts to show themselves if the ruins are transformed into a dining-room.'

'What do you think, my lord?' Sophie Sherington turned a wide-eyed face of enquiry towards Ravensdene. At the sight of her auburn lashes fluttering like butterflies gone berserk, Sarah found herself stifling another intense twinge of annoyance. 'Is there not something very *abandoned* about dining outdoors on rugs?'

'No,' said Ravensdene with uncompromising brevity.

'Oh. Well,' continued Miss Sherington, faint but pursuing, 'I daresay for gentlemen such as yourself and Lord Devenham, who have experienced the excitements of battle, a picnic does seem rather tame. What heroic tales you must have to tell. I am sure we would hang upon your every word.'

Ravensdene's eyes narrowed.

'Speaking of tales, Sophie,' Sarah intervened before he could assault Miss Sherington's ears with a blistering set-down. 'Weren't you going to tell us about the gray lady who is supposed to haunt the priory?'

Out of the corner of her eye she saw Ravensdene's hard mouth relax into a faint smile, and knew he was aware of the reason for her intervention.

As well he might be, she thought, rather incensed. It wasn't the first time she'd had to rescue one of his potential victims. First it had been Harry Marsham at the Wribbonhalls' party, last night Sir Ponsonby Freem had come foolishly close to annihilation, and now Miss Sherington's bird-witted conversation was trying his patience. Couldn't any of these people see the danger they were courting in irritating a predator?

She just managed to stifle a startled gasp as another question occurred to her. Who was going to rescue her?

Sarah gave herself a mental shake. It was that wretched comment of his that had done this, she mused crossly. She didn't need rescuing from Ravensdene because she *knew* he was dangerous—even if she was beginning to think of him as a friend. All she had to do, therefore, was treat him with friendly caution. Or should that be cautious friendliness?

Oh, wonderful! Now she was thinking in circles.

'And you wake to find her staring at you from the side of the bed, her cold fingers resting on your face.'

James Langdon's sepulchral tones, followed by various squeals and gasps of horror, intruded on Sarah's mental contortions. Hoping no one had noticed her abstraction, she tried to appear interested in the discussion.

'Well, I don't know,' Devenham was saying sceptically. 'Something always puzzles me. How is it that these ladies are forever draped in gray or white? Why can't they get about in scarlet or green or—?'

'Because they're ghosts, silly.' Laughing, Julia interrupted him to start a spirited argument, but Sarah noticed that her friend had turned quite pale.

Devenham had seen it, too, she realised, and had asked the nonsensical question deliberately. He was so kind. No wonder Julia liked him. He was kind without making one feel there was more to it. Devenham's style was light; his smiling blue eyes didn't hold the disturbing depths she sensed behind Ravensdene's cool gaze.

Even when those light green eyes were gleaming with amusement, she felt it. A darkness. A locked place deep inside where he allowed no one to trespass. She knew because she had her own dark place. A place where light had not reached for eight years.

And yet, now. . . In the past few days. . .she had felt a chink of light touch that dark, secret corner of her mind. One tiny chink of light. . .and it had turned everything upside down.

'You are very quiet, Miss Lynley.' Ravensdene smiled at her, then lifted a brow slightly when she jumped at the sound of his voice. 'Are you indifferent to ghostly fashions or have you also succumbed to the decadence of the moment?'

Sarah felt herself blush as everyone ceased arguing to look at her.

'I think Lord Devenham has a valid point,' she finally managed after a nerve-racking moment in which her brain seemed to be paralysed. She wisely left the subject of decadence alone. 'Spectres do appear to be rather limited in their choice of colours. The males are usually black-robed monks or white horsemen.'

'Oh, Sarah, don't.' Sophie shivered dramatically and glanced up at the crumbling arches above them as though expecting to see a dark figure in one of the apertures. 'I am sure I shall be afraid to look around any corners in case I come face to face with a monk.'

'I think the monks left long before the priory fell into ruin,' Sarah assured her.

'Besides, he wouldn't have a face,' Harry Marsham added in the mistaken belief that he was being helpful. 'Black-cowled monks usually don't, you know.'

More feminine shrieks and shudders ensued.

Ravensdene eyed them all with some amusement.
'Well, if you're going to seek out these fascinating
spectres, you'd best be about it,' he suggested, indicating the shadows beginning to lengthen on the grass.
'The daylight will not remain forever.'

'No, indeed.' Miss Sherington jumped to her feet,
permitting the interested a glimpse of a shapely ankle,
and smiled at Ravensdene in blatant invitation. 'I cannot wait to begin. Shall we start where the crypt was
said to be, my lord?'

'Perhaps we should pack everything away first,' Julia
suggested, eyeing the wreckage in the centre of their
circle with some misgiving.

'Very true.' Devenham watched three ants march
past his booted foot to retrieve a crumb. 'The wildlife
is starting to arrive.'

'So are the curious.' Harry Marsham nodded towards
a grassy slope some distance away where a lone rider
was silhouetted against the skyline, apparently watching them. 'Dashed impolite to intrude on us like that.'

'He's probably wondering who we are,' James said,
shading his eyes as he followed his friend's gaze. 'I
don't recognise the horse. Do you, Eliza?'

'Oh, never mind him!' Sophie interrupted impatiently. 'It is public land, you know. Besides, he's
riding away now. Sarah, dearest, you won't mind clearing up, will you? I know you are much too sensible and
mature to believe in ghosts, so I daresay you will be
more comfortable here in the sun.'

'Well, really, Sophie—'

'No, I don't mind at all,' Sarah responded, calmly
overriding Julia's indignant protest. The last thing she
wanted to do was go scrambling about in a dank crypt.
'Go and find your ghosts. I shall be only too happy to
stay right here.'

'But—'

'Oh, I say—'

'Don't worry, Miss Wribbonhall.' Ravensdene's quiet tone instantly squelched the voices of protest rising on the breeze. 'I shall remain to keep Miss Lynley company and lend my assistance in clearing up. I am accounted quite good at it, you know.'

That calm air of authority was really quite marvellously effective, Sarah conceded. She could only watch in bemusement as the rest of the party meekly gathered themselves together and wandered off into the ruins. And it happened so quickly that for a minute she didn't even realise how neatly she had trapped herself. She was too occupied with the totally unexpected sense of satisfaction flowing through her that Sophie Sherington had spiked her own guns—to use one of Uncle Jasper's favourite sayings.

It was not unlike the feeling she had had last night when, after ignoring the Miss Smisbys' collective and individual attempts to attract his attention, Ravensdene had left the Assembly before supper was served and after dancing only with her.

'Tell me, Miss Lynley. Just how old are you?'

Sarah blinked at the unexpected question. 'Two-and-twenty, my lord. Why do you ask?'

His firm mouth twitched as he began collecting plates and glasses. 'The way Miss Sherington was speaking to you, one would have thought you in your dotage.'

She laughed and bent to help him. 'As Sophie is only turned seventeen, she probably considers me to be so,' she said, suddenly feeling unaccountably happy to be with him. All at once her vague fears seemed ridiculous. The others were still within earshot, and they could be seen by anyone who happened along the road.

She straightened, the thought bringing a faint frown

to her brow as she remembered the lone watcher. He had been too far distant to be recognisable, but an image of Sir Ponsonby Freem's stubborn features flitted through her mind. Surely he wouldn't have called on her uncle, discovered her whereabouts and followed her.

Sarah dismissed the notion. Sir Ponsonby might be stubborn, but he also had a high opinion of his own sense of propriety. He would not stoop to skulking about at a distance. Nor was the rider connected to her in any other way. It was foolish to be so suspicious. The man had merely been a passing traveller, curious to see picnickers at the ruins, no threat to her.

Putting the stranger out of her mind, she closed her eyes and lifted her face to the warmth of the sun, a smile curving her lips as she heard an echo of the ghost hunters' voices. Nearer, the liquid notes of a thrush rose and fell on the soft breeze that was brushing her cheeks and she could smell the sharp tang of grass and earth as the horses grazed.

It was one of those rare moments in time when everything felt perfect. In harmony. *Right.*

She opened her eyes on the thought to find Ravensdene gazing down at her. And as if it was the most natural thing in the world, she smiled at him.

Something flickered in his eyes—something so powerfully intense that she felt her heart give an odd little leap and her smile faltered. Then the green flames were banked. He smiled back; the crooked, utterly appealing smile that made her feel all warm inside, and with the warmth, the strange quivering within her was calmed and she felt at ease again.

He was probably thinking of Sophie and her wiles, she decided as she turned away and began packing baskets. She was glad he didn't spoil the precious moment by speaking. It felt good to be working together like this. As friends.

Could Ravensdene think of her in that way, she wondered, vaguely aware of a faint wistfulness tugging at her heart? He had probably never considered that a woman could be a friend, someone with whom he could share laughter, or quietness. Someone who understood about dark, locked-away corners. Someone who wouldn't expect anything more from him than friendship. She would like to be that person.

'Miss Sherington should count herself fortunate to possess your friendship, Miss Lynley,' he observed with an uncanny prescience that made Sarah wonder for a minute if he could read minds. He stowed the last of the baskets under the seat of Lady Wribbonhall's barouche and turned to indicate her dress. 'I expect it was to spare her disappointment that you elected to ride in the carriage rather than on horseback as was originally planned.'

'Oh. . .' Sarah felt herself flushing. 'Yes. Something like that.'

It hadn't been anything like that, but she would have gone to the stake before she admitted that she had worn her new cambric dress with its fashionable flounces and smartly striped Spencer because she had not wanted to appear at a disadvantage in her plain old riding habit.

'My remark was not meant as a criticism,' he murmured. 'Although when Dev allowed Miss Wribbonhall to take the reins on that sharp bend I did wonder if your decision had been rather precipitate.'

A more natural laugh escaped her. 'I must confess it took great fortitude not to grab hold of the door at that precise moment, my lord,' she confessed, dimpling up at him. 'And I hope you noticed that I did not

scream, which is more than can be said for Sophie and
Eliza.'

'Yes, those two young ladies do have a marked
tendency to give full rein to their lungs,' he said dryly,
running an eye over the chestnut pair who had kept
the barouche on all four wheels despite their over-
eager driver. 'I am only grateful that you did not feel
obliged to follow their example, Miss Lynley, or even
as placid a pair as this may have bolted. Remind me to
strangle Dev when he returns. Better yet, let us go in
search of him now and I can do it immediately.'

Sarah laughed, but obediently laid a hand lightly on
his proffered arm. He promptly tucked it more firmly
into the crook of his elbow as they began strolling
towards the priory.

'I expect Lord Devenham would have taken control
without any mishap had it been necessary,' she
remarked, trying to do some controlling of her own.
For some reason her heartbeat had become rather
uneven, and though she was again conscious of feeling
very small and defenceless this close to Ravensdene,
the faintly thrilling sensations aroused by his size and
strength now seemed more pleasurable than alarming.

Which was, she mused, vaguely alarming in itself.

'I commend your equanimity, Miss Lynley.' He
glanced down at her, his eyes warm with amusement.
'Your calm good sense gives me great hope that we
shall be able to defeat your uncle next Monday. I am
looking forward to the encounter.'

'Next Monday. Oh, yes. To be sure.'

'You had not forgotten, I trust.'

'Well. . .'

Forgotten? Of course she had. How could she be
expected to think of the future when the present was
causing her such puzzlement?

'You mean you were going to abandon me to your uncle's merciless play without compunction?' he went on, casting her a reproachful look. 'Miss Lynley, I had not thought it of you.'

'It is no use trying to look pathetic, my lord,' she said, rallying under this blatant provocation. 'I have to tell you it simply does not work.'

'Ah. What a disadvantage we males are at when dealing with an intelligent woman.'

Surprised, she looked up at him.

'What is it?' he asked at once. 'Do you find it so astounding that I consider you intelligent?'

'Well, yes, I do,' she said frankly. 'When I know you consider me to be incapable of taking care of myself.'

His gaze softened. 'Intelligence does not make you any less vulnerable, Miss Lynley. In fact, some men would see your combination of intelligence and innocence as more of a challenge.'

'Oh. Well. . .' Not sure whether or not she had just received a compliment, and valiantly trying to lighten the suddenly serious atmosphere, Sarah brandished her reticule. 'That is why I carry a pistol, sir.'

His stunned expression was quite wonderfully satisfying.

'Don't tell me you are still walking around armed?' he demanded somewhat wrathfully.

She shook her reticule more menacingly. 'The first ghost I see, I shoot.'

After a moment of startled silence, he threw back his head and laughed aloud. Sarah decided she rather liked the sound.

'Miss Lynley,' he said when he had recovered. 'You are a darling. Every ghost haunting the place must now be shivering in its shroud.'

Sarah nearly tripped over a rock half-hidden in the long grass. Good heavens! A *darling*?

She ordered herself to object at once to Ravensdene's shocking familiarity in using such an endearment, but it was difficult to protest when one was trying not to giggle at the picture of ghosts shivering in their shrouds.

Nor did it help that her heart was fluttering madly somewhere in her throat. He had managed to throw her completely off-balance again, she thought dazedly. The man was beginning to make quite a habit of it.

'Well, you will be happy to know that you are safe from my pistol today, sir,' she began in a praiseworthy attempt to rally her disordered wits. 'But though I would expect Uncle Jasper to be rather old-fashioned in his views about females and firearms, you should have less antiquated notions of what is proper.'

'Not when it comes to my—' He stopped dead.

'Your what?'

He clenched his jaw. 'Never mind. Just don't let me catch you brandishing that pistol about. In fact, I expressly forbid you to even carry the thing.'

Sarah's own jaw dropped. 'Are you out of your mind?' she demanded at last. 'The only person who has the right to issue such a veto is my uncle, and I can assure you—'

'Or your husband,' he cut in, watching her.

Sarah stopped walking so abruptly that every bone in her body felt jarred. Like an animal sensing danger but unsure of its direction, she stared at Ravensdene, aware only of the intent expression in his eyes and her own racing pulse. The breath she drew in trembled audibly in the sudden stillness.

'Since I don't have a husband and do not intend to

acquire one, my lord, that statement is completely irrelevant.'

He shifted his gaze from her face to the walls that now surrounded them, but Sarah did not make the mistake of assuming that her reply had brought the conversation to an end. Far from lightening, the atmosphere now seemed filled with a strange, brooding tension that made her feel as if the ruins themselves were waiting. When Ravensdene looked back at her, her heart began to beat so hard and so fast she thought it must surely be visible.

'You know, Miss Lynley, I had quite a long conversation with your uncle during our match the other day and—'

'Then I am not surprised you lost the encounter, my lord,' she interrupted quickly, desperate to forestall whatever was coming. 'Chess is a game that requires all one's concentration.'

'It does indeed,' he murmured. 'But it was actually your uncle who seemed rather distracted when we first began to play, and when I asked if he felt well enough to continue, he saw fit to confide the cause of his preoccupation to me.'

She was watching him now with the wariness of a small, cornered creature and for an instant Nick hesitated. Only for an instant. He was driven. Driven by the instinct to pursue that goaded him every time Sarah retreated. Driven by the need to make her his in the eyes of the world. Somehow he had to prepare her mind to be more receptive to the idea of marriage. Their marriage. And light-hearted, friendly banter seemed to be getting him nowhere.

'Sir Jasper told me,' he continued as softly and unthreateningly as possible, 'that your decision never to marry was greatly influenced by your sister's tragic

death when you were only fourteen. Miss Lynley—' he
removed her hand from his arm and held it in a firm
clasp '—I know, none better, what it is to make
decisions like that when one is very young, before
maturity brings more reasoned counsel. But don't you
think that your persistence in refusing to even consider
marriage is contributing to your uncle's ill-health? He
is extremely worried about your future.'

The sudden flash of terror in her eyes stunned him.
She snatched her hand from his grasp and backed
away.

'Uncle Jasper would never force me to marry to
ensure my future. Never!'

'We're not living in the dark ages, you know,' he
said gently. 'No one mentioned force.' All at once he
felt a gut-wrenching need to move cautiously, as though
any careless word or action on his part would hurt her
unbearably. He took a step towards her and held out
his hand. 'What frightens you so, little one?'

She drew back as if his touch might burn her.
'Nothing! Nothing frightens me!'

'If that is true, then you must surely realise that what
befell your sister is not likely to—'

'Stop!' she cried. 'Stop it!' Shaking her head, retreating so quickly she almost cannoned into the wall a few
paces at her back, she stared at him as if he was a
spectre from the blackest pit, her eyes so anguished he
barely suppressed an involuntary sound of protest.
'Whether I marry or not is none of your concern. I
won't— Don't ever speak of this to me again. Not ever!
Do you understand me? Not ever!'

Her voice breaking on the last word, she whirled,
fled through an adjacent archway and vanished from
sight.

Nick just managed to stop himself putting his fist

through the crumbling stones beside him. He cursed long and comprehensively. God, he'd really made a mull of that. Like a fool he'd thought he could appeal to Sarah's good sense and concern for her uncle's health, without even considering that the mysterious circumstances apparently surrounding her sister's death had affected her more than he knew. What the devil had made him persist when a fool could have seen how uneasy the subject made her?

But even as he asked the question, he knew what had made him act so precipitously. Her smile. That sweet, faintly wistful, innocently enquiring smile that had hit him with all the force of a fist to the solar plexus. He'd literally been unable to move.

Vaguely he recalled that he'd managed to return her smile before Sarah had turned back to the task of packing away the picnic baskets. It was as well she had, before he'd forgotten all need for restraint and given in to the fierce urge to take her in his arms and taste every sweet curve of that delectably soft mouth.

Nick's mouth compressed as the heavy throb low in his body increased. He was a long way from giving Sarah the deeply sensual, possessive kiss he was beginning to crave. Somehow he had to win her tentative trust back. It wouldn't be easy, but—

He frowned, considering possibilities. Perhaps it would not be as difficult as he anticipated. If he knew Sarah at all, she would probably stop before she had gone too far into the ruins and rally her courage in order to face the rest of the party without arousing comment.

Yes, he was on the right track, he decided, with a grim sense of purpose born of sheer necessity. When Sarah calmed down she would find the others and, using them as a shield, treat him with polite indifference until she could retreat into her home. Then she would invent an excuse to absent herself from Monday's chess match.

'Not if I can help it,' Nick muttered between his teeth. He had reinforcements that Sarah had yet to encounter; plenty of troops ranged on his side who would be willing to gently prod her towards matrimony. All *he* had to do was assure her that she had nothing to fear from him.

But first, he told himself grimly, he needed a few hard facts. He had been assuming that Sarah's sister had been seduced and abandoned by an undesirable suitor and had subsequently died, that she might even have taken her own life, but those assumptions were possibly wide of the mark. Clearly another talk with Sir Jasper Lynley was in order.

And a word with Lady Wribbonhall might not go amiss either.

Sarah stopped where a sheltered cloister adjoining the ancient scriptorium shielded her from view, a prey to so many tempestuous emotions that she felt utterly battered by the turmoil going on inside her.

Foremost among them was a sense almost of betrayal. Even the pangs of guilt reanimated by Ravensdene's mention of her uncle's anxiety paled in comparison. Betrayal that Uncle Jasper had discussed his worry over her single state with Ravensdene, but, even more devastating, the fact that Ravensdene had overstepped the bounds by probing into that dark corner of her mind. All her happy expectations of a friendship between them had been shattered on the instant.

Which was ridiculous, she told herself a little forlornly. She had no right to feel that way. Ravensdene wasn't responsible for the workings of her mind. Because she chose to see him as a friend, did not mean he felt the same way.

This eminently practical point of view did not make her feel any better. To hurt, guilt and the terrified pounding of her heart was now added a distinct feeling of foolishness.

This was the second time she had fled from Ravensdene in complete disorder. And merely because he and Uncle Jasper had been discussing her in relation to marriage. As if the ceremony was about to be performed before she'd had any inkling of it.

Sarah pressed her cold hands to her burning face and slumped back against a convenient pillar. How *could* she have been so stupid? Ravensdene was right. They were not living in the dark ages. If he or any other man made an offer for her, all she had to do was decline.

Had she become so pampered, Sarah wondered, fighting back tears of savage self-chastisement, so spoilt by everyone's care and protection that she flew into hysterics at the first mention of the forbidden subject?

She let her hands fall and stared unseeingly down at them while she forced herself to contemplate that unpleasant possibility. Unless she wished to think of herself as possessing the sort of highly-strung, over-delicate sensibilities she despised, she had better pull herself together and brace herself to face Ravensdene again.

For a moment she quailed at the prospect. Then she remembered where she was. Brushing her cheeks quickly to erase any signs of tears, she straightened. First she would find the others. Courage was all very well, but sometimes one needed reinforcements.

In somewhat calmer fashion than the way she had dashed into the cloisters several minutes earlier, Sarah glanced around, trying to pinpoint her location in the ruins. She had been here before, but many years ago, and her memories of the place were vague.

Behind her, the colonnade opened onto a small quadrangle that allowed the afternoon light to pour into the stalls where the long-departed monks had once laboured over their illuminations and manuscripts. The westering sun cast her shadow before her in an elongated slant across the ancient flagstones. It was growing late.

Sarah turned her head to the right, the way she had come, listening over the faint breeze for the sound of voices that might lead her to the rest of the party. Several seconds passed before she realised that she was staring at another human shadow only a few yards away.

Her heart stopped. Shock sent ice flowing through her body until even her fingers and toes tingled. Like herself, whoever was standing there was hidden from direct view by the pillar beside him. Sarah had no doubt at all that it was a man who remained concealed so close to her, so motionless. She could see the clear outline of her bonnet in her own shadowy image, but the second image had no such distinction. He was bareheaded.

When her mind shuddered back into action a second later her first thought was that Ravensdene had followed her. It was more comforting than the possibility of an apparition, but she dismissed it instantly. The shadow was not much longer than her own, and in any event Ravensdene would not lurk behind pillars—even if he knew she was upset. She had first-hand knowledge of how he dealt with hysterical females, and it involved warmth and strength and comfort, not tactics that were eerie in the extreme.

Nor did she think that Lord Devenham would indulge in such pranks. No. The shadow probably belonged to James or Harry. One of them was lying in wait to convince the ladies that the place was haunted. It would be just like them.

So why didn't she call out and unmask the would-be ghost, Sarah asked herself, shivering? Why, at this inauspicious moment, were images of the unknown horseman flitting through her mind? And why was she experiencing the same chilling awareness that had overcome her in the gardens the other day?

One thing was certain. She was not going in *that* direction.

For a moment it looked as if she was not going in any direction. Her legs felt like tissue and her feet refused to move. Then, finally unglueing her feet from the ground, she began to make her way very quietly down the cloister.

She had not gone more than a few paces when an ear-splitting scream rent the air.

CHAPTER NINE

SARAH did not wait to see if the owner of the shadow reacted to the scream as she did. She gathered up her skirts and tore down the colonnade to emerge into the open at the entrance to what had once been the priory herb garden.

The cause of the commotion was not hard to find. Everyone was clustered about Sophie Sherington who was lying in a crumpled heap on the grass, nursing her ankle.

Everyone, that was, except Julia and Devenham.

But even as she registered their absence, Sarah saw the pair hurrying towards the small crowd from the direction of the crypt. Ravensdene was there also. He must have appeared about the same time as herself, Sarah thought, but from the opposite side of the garden, not far from where she had left him.

All were present and accounted for, and she alone had come from the cloisters.

She glanced back, half-expecting to see a concerned or startled stranger emerge from the corridor. The archway behind her remained empty.

Puzzled and still a little shivery inside, she joined the group, avoiding the long, searching look Ravensdene gave her by kneeling down beside Sophie, who was gasping out an explanation in which ghosts and hidden rocks figured largely.

'I tripped over this stupid stone,' she finished on a wail. 'When Eliza and I ran away.'

'Ran away from what?' Harry Marsham demanded

with scant sympathy. He grinned. 'A ghost? *I* don't see one.'

Sophie glared at him. 'Something moved,' she insisted, pointing. 'Up there.'

Everyone turned to look at the partially ruined wall above them. As they did so, a bird flew into a crevice in the rough stone. It carried a twig in its beak. Clearly, domicilary construction was in progress.

'There's your ghost, Sophie,' Eliza said, laughing. 'I told you it was nothing.'

A chagrined frown crossed Miss Sherington's face, but Sarah noticed that her mouth was tight with real discomfort.

'Where does your leg pain you, Sophie?' she asked, taking the younger girl's hand.

Sophie's lip trembled. 'My ankle,' she quavered, reminded of her injury. 'I twisted it when I fell.'

Momentarily forgetting her altercation with Ravensdene, Sarah sent a fleeting glance up at him, fully expecting to see a hard look of disbelief on his face. Given Sophie's past performances, not to mention the activities of several other ladies, she would not have been surprised to find herself confronting a coldly furious male whose patience with female strategems was at an end.

But confounding her again, he hunkered down on Sophie's other side, his expression conveying nothing more than grave concern.

'Then I suggest you do not walk on it on this uneven ground, Miss Sherington,' he said gently. 'If Lord Devenham brings the carriage around to this side of the ruins, would you permit Mr Langdon to carry you to it? You will be very much more comfortable there, I assure you.'

'Yes, thank you.' Obviously feeling more shaken

than she appeared, Sophie turned from Ravensdene to the childhood friend who had always been there to mend her hurts. 'Oh, James, I'm so sorry. I've ruined everyone's day.'

'Nonsense,' he said at once. 'It is time we were starting for home anyway. Don't worry, Sophie. I'm sure you'll be all right and tight again for your waltzing party next month.'

This sally drew a small, watery smile from her. Sarah smiled, too, and gave him an approving look. 'To be sure she will,' she agreed, taking a rather shaky breath. 'Sophie, while the gentlemen fetch the horses, why don't you let me take your boot off? I am sure it must be hurting you.'

The two younger gentlemen, taking this hint that they were in the way, departed on their errand. Sarah glanced up, every nerve quivering with apprehension when Ravensdene did not immediately follow their example.

Their eyes met. He smiled faintly, rose to his feet, and taking Devenham's arm, followed the others without a word.

Sarah did not know what his silence forebode, but two days later she was wishing Julia would follow his example.

'But, Sarah, you can't refuse an invitation from Lady Ravensdene. It would be most impolite when you have no previous engagement.'

Setting her lips in a mutinous line, Sarah moved down the garden path to select another bloom destined for her uncle's library. 'How do you know I have no previous engagement?' she asked, parting an early rosebud from its bush with a rather agitated snip of her shears.

Julia frowned. 'Because I would be similarly engaged. We do move in the same circles, you know.'

Sarah sent her a reproachful look which had absolutely no effect. Her friend returned to the attack with all the uncompromising tenacity of a bull-terrier.

'As it happens, Mama and I have also been invited to Comberford tomorrow, so you will not be alone. Lady Ravensdene's note said that if the day is fine, we'll partake of tea by the lake. Nothing could be more charming.'

Or more reminiscent of the picnic, Sarah thought, wincing inwardly. She still felt like hiding somewhere whenever she recalled her hysterical flight from Ravensdene. And then to have him treat Sophie with such kindness. . .

She had not been able to think of anything else all the way home or since. Not even the memory of the shadow in the cloisters had distracted her for long. No doubt the man had been an innocent visitor to the ruins, as startled by mysterious shadows and blood-curdling screams as she had been herself. He had probably exited at top speed in the other direction.

Having thus explained the matter to her satisfaction, Sarah had spent the past two days brooding over the thought that every time she decided that Ravensdene was best kept at a safe distance, he had turned around and behaved in a way that aroused the strangest feelings inside her. Wistful yearnings unlike anything she had ever known. And the only way she had been able to cope with them was to deny their existence.

Unfortunately, denial had not been effective. In fact she had been feeling quite inexplicably bereft, as if something of immeasurable value had been taken from her.

And as if that was not worrying enough, she was now

wondering why Ravensdene's mother had sent her a
very personally worded invitation. A large formal gathering she might have coped with, but her ladyship's
note had sounded alarmingly friendly.

'Wait a minute,' she squeaked, abruptly jolted out of
her reverie as Julia whisked her basket out of her
hands and began propelling her towards the house.
'Where are we going? I haven't finished—'

'You are going to write a polite note of acceptance
to Lady Ravensdene,' Julia responded with a steely-
eyed determination that Sarah hadn't known her gentle
friend possessed. 'And I am going to stand over you
until you do it. My whole future is at stake.'

'What!' Sarah tried to halt and was dragged
ruthlessly onward, through the hall and into the
drawing-room.

'What do you mean, your whole future is at stake?'
she demanded, finally catching her breath when Julia
stopped beside a small writing table and indicated the
quill reposing thereupon. She eyed her friend's flushed
and agitated countenance and momentarily forgot her
own problems. 'Julia, what are you talking about?'

Julia abandoned her terrier tactics and wrung her
hands. 'Oh, Sarah, I haven't seen Bar—that is to say,
Lord Devenham, since the picnic, even though he came
to call on Papa yesterday, because Mama and I were
out for hours visiting tenants and when we got back
Papa had gone up to town on some stupid matter of
business—as if he couldn't have waited... But never
mind that. So I don't know what was said, but why
would Bar—that is, Lord Devenham, call to see Papa
and then not come to call today—although I've been
here all afternoon—but, you see, if it's only me and
Mama at Comberford tomorrow, Ravensdene might
not feel obliged to stay in, and Bar—I mean, Lord

Devenham, might go with Ravensdene to wherever it is gentlemen go when their mothers entertain ladies and I won't see him for *another* whole day and by then I will have died of anxiety!'

Her brain reeling from this spate of verbiage, Sarah fixed on the one word that seemed to have stayed in her head.

'Bar—?' she queried, fixing her friend with a look of heavy meaning.

Julia's flushed face took on an even rosier hue. 'Well, I did tell you that I had become quite well acquainted with Lord Devenham,' she said with an attempt at airy dismissal. 'His name is Barney.'

'Barney,' Sarah repeated. Several startlingly detailed pictures suddenly sprang into her mind, racing through her memory with a speed that made her dizzy: Julia and Devenham hurrying from the crypt at the ruins, the slightly dazed expression in Julia's eyes, the soft rosiness of her mouth, the faint look of tension on Devenham's face.

'Good heavens!' she exclaimed, stunned into voicing the realisation aloud. 'At the ruins. . . You were. . . He was. . .'

'Yes, we were and he most definitely was,' Julia confirmed defiantly, clearly having no trouble in interpreting this stammered attempt at speech. Then, apparently overcome by her own memories, her hands clasped and such a glow came into her eyes that Sarah stared, hardly able to recognise her girlhood friend in the blushing, tremulous young woman standing before her.

'Oh, Sarah, when he kissed me. . .it was beyond anything.'

'Beyond anything,' echoed Sarah weakly.

'Yes. But there's more. When I said that, Barney just

smiled at me and. . . Sarah, I swear to you, that smile positively turned my knees to water.'

'Knees to water.' She knew precisely what Julia meant. She seemed to have lost control of her own knees. An image of Ravensdene's hard, beautifully etched mouth had imprinted itself behind her eyes and would not be dismissed. She felt an abrupt need to sit down. It was almost beyond her control not to raise her hand and touch her own mouth, suddenly warm and soft and tingling.

'And I simply have to see him again as soon as possible, so you are going to pick up that pen and write to Lady Ravensdene.'

'Write to Lady Ravensdene.'

'Yes. Now!'

Oh, thank goodness. At last. An excuse to sit down.

She had been temporarily unhinged, of course. It was the only possible explanation.

'Another cup of tea, Miss Lynley?'

'Oh, no. . . That is, yes, thank you, my lord.'

Sarah winced at her incoherence, tore her gaze away from Ravensdene's mouth, and took cover behind her tea. Unfortunately her hinges didn't appear to have returned since her conversation with Julia yesterday. She still felt distinctly rattled. And all because her heart had given the strangest leap when she had seen Ravensdene and Lord Devenham coming across the lawn a few minutes ago to join the teaparty.

She had told herself it was uneasiness, or at least embarrassment at having to face him again, but when Ravensdene had greeted everyone without paying her any extraordinary degree of attention, her unruly heart had promptly plummeted straight to the pit of her stomach. She had been so distracted by the odd sensation that, since then, she had contributed not one word to the conversation.

Fortunately no one seemed to have noticed. Julia and Devenham were talking quietly together, while the two older ladies chattered away with all the comfortable familiarity of old friends. She hoped Ravensdene was equally oblivious to her inner turmoil, but when she risked a glance at him from beneath her lashes she saw him watching her intently.

'Have you heard how Miss Sherington does, Miss Lynley?' he asked at once, as if he had only been waiting for her attention before speaking.

Placing his cup on the table, he came to stand beside her chair. Beyond him the sun shimmered on the silvery waters of the lake, throwing his profile into sharp relief. Unable to see his face clearly, Sarah told herself he looked big and dangerous towering over her, but then he turned slightly as though wondering why she hadn't answered, and the expression in his light green eyes held nothing more threatening than polite enquiry.

Again that odd sense of loss tugged at her heart.

'I believe. . .yes. . .that is, I rode over to Sherington Court the other day, my lord,' she stammered, wishing she could stop sounding like a chit just out of the schoolroom. 'Sophie had only twisted her ankle slightly. Dr Salcott says a day or two of rest will set it to rights.'

'I am happy to hear,' he replied gravely, 'that an epidemic of sprained ankles is not about to be unleashed among us.'

Sarah's lips parted, confusion flitted across her face, but the smile he had hoped to draw from her didn't materialise. Instead, after a sidelong, half-wary glance at him, she turned away as his mother addressed some remark to her.

Nick gritted his teeth against a surge of impatience. He would have liked to hurl tea-tray, plates and delicacies into the lake. Unfortunately he had to restrain his natural instincts and accept the fact that he was not going to have the opportunity today to recover the ground he had lost.

But at least Sarah was here. He grimaced inwardly as he recalled his visit to the Grange on the day after the picnic. He already knew that Sarah had visited Sophie Sherington that afternoon. Sir Jasper had let it fall that, not five minutes after being informed of his imminent arrival, Sarah had decided to pay the call and to drop in on the Reverend Butterlow's ailing housekeeper on her way home for good measure. Since he had seen said housekeeper out and about, in perfect health, that very morning, he had promptly returned home himself and enlisted his mother's support. She had been positively delighted to oblige.

Of course, now he had to make sure his matchmaking parent didn't go too far in pursuit of the cause.

Shaking off the various schemes to get Sarah alone that were floating about in his head, he pulled his attention back to the conversation going on over the tea cups. It was as well he did.

'Naturally I will move back to town when everything is settled,' his mother was saying to the company at large. 'Nothing is more tiresome than a parent on the premises when one is trying to establish—'

'What you mean, Mama, is that you are missing all your friends and cannot wait to hear the latest gossip,' Nick corrected her in quelling accents.

'Do I, dearest? Well, if you say so. Not that dear Papa was ever precisely interfering,' she went on, turning to

Sarah with a charming smile. 'He was an exceptionally indulgent parent. And grandparent, too. Why, when Nicholas hit a cricket ball through the breakfast parlour window he roared for only five minutes. Of course, the window was closed at the time which—'

'Mama, I don't think Miss Lynley wishes to hear—'

'Unfortunately, his tolerance did seem to disappear as he grew older,' Lady Ravensdene continued with gentle inexorability. 'My mother was used to be the only person who could coax him into a better temper whenever anything tried his patience. From what Winwick tells me, you possessed the same talent, Miss Lynley. So useful.' She cast a glance at her scowling son and muttered cryptically, 'Two of a kind, you know.'

'Er, yes, ma'am. That is. . .' Sarah faltered, not quite sure what she was supposed to be responding to. It was difficult to attend to such a rambling conversation when her disordered mind was torn between her growing conviction that she had lost any chance of Ravensdene's friendship, and an awareness of him that was so acute she could practically feel him breathe. 'I have noticed that poor health does tend to irritate gentlemen somewhat.'

'Dear me, yes,' agreed her hostess. 'But I have every confidence in you. Such a pleasant part of the country, too. Nicholas always liked spending the summers at Comberford when he was a boy. An ideal location. So close to your uncle. So convenient.'

Sarah frowned. Had she missed something else in her distraction? She was already living with her uncle. How much closer did she need to be?

'I am sure dear Sir Jasper would agree,' Lady Ravensdene mused in her vague way. 'You have cared for him for some time, I take it?'

'Yes, ma'am.' Grateful that at last there was a defi-nite question she could answer, Sarah found herself elaborating. 'My parents died when I was quite young, you see, and my sis. . .' She hesitated, took a deep breath and continued. 'My sister, Amy, and I came to live at the Grange.'

Lady Ravensdene nodded. 'Poor child,' she mur-mured. Although precisely which child she meant was rather obscure. 'Your devotion to your uncle does you credit, my dear. I daresay that is why I have not seen you in town any time these past few years.'

'Miss Lynley will tell you, Mama, that she has no taste for town life,' Ravensdene said before she could reply.

'Is that so?' Lady Ravensdene appeared inordinately thrilled by the news. She beamed. 'Excellent. And you play chess, too. Nothing could be more delightful.'

Sarah decided to abandon any attempt at keeping up with her hostess's conversational leaps and bounds. She suspected that such a feat was impossible. One needed one's wits about one, and hers had taken a leave of absence. Not only that, she had the uneasy feeling that Lady Ravensdene's style of conversation could not entirely be dismissed as the vagaries of a vague mind. The look in her ladyship's eye was unexpectedly shrewd.

She was just beginning to wonder when Lady Wribbonhall would put an end to the visit so she could go home and be miserable in peace, when a rather odd cacophony of noise sounded in the distance. Everyone else heard it at the same time. A shrill yapping, growing nearer, and rising above a chorus of high-pitched shrieks.

'What the deuce—?' demanded Devenham, begin-ning to rise to his feet.

The answer burst onto the scene before he had
finished. Around the corner of the house scampered a
small puppy with three ladies in hot pursuit. Yelping
with excitement, the puppy careered across the lawn,
dashed straight between the legs of the light wooden
table and vanished into the bushes growing at the side
of the lake, leaving mayhem in his wake.

Cups, plates and macaroons went flying as the table
teetered and fell. Lady Wribbonhall let out a faint
scream as tea cascaded into her lap. Julia sprang out of
her chair to avoid the same fate and promptly collided
with the foremost puppy pursuer. Both ladies sat down
rather abruptly on the grass just as the other two
intruders reached them. One managed to stop in time.
The other swerved wildly and, still shrieking, arms
flailing, plunged headlong towards the lake. There was
a loud splash.

Sarah, who had also leapt out of the way with
perilous haste as the table crashed to the ground,
suddenly found herself clasped securely against
Ravensdene's side, held there by an arm that felt like
iron about her waist. She didn't remember how she'd
got there or seeing him move, but at her startled gasp
he released her at once.

'Well,' he murmured for her ears alone. 'At least we
know the puppy really exists. Now if only the footpads
would put in an appearance. . .'

She didn't have time to reply to this frivolous utter-
ance, or to wonder about her varied and shocking
responses to his quick action. Everyone started talking
at once as they sorted themselves out.

'My best maroon silk!' wailed Lady Wribbonhall,
tottering from her chair and flapping uselessly at the
damage.

'Miss Wribbonhall! Are you hurt?' Devenham bent

to help Julia to her feet, ignoring the other two damsels who were now gazing, eyes starting with horror, at the lake.

'Good heavens above!' Lady Ravensdene, still seated in solitary splendour, cup in hand, amid the wreckage, placed her tea carefully on Sarah's abandoned chair and raised her eyeglass. It was purely an affectation. She stared over it at the young lady who was extricating herself from the loving embrace of the reedy shallows.

It was Averilla Smisby, clad in a muslin gown that, wringing wet, did absolutely nothing to disguise the fact that she was wearing not a stitch of clothing underneath it.

'Oh, no!' she exclaimed, holding handfuls of dripping muslin away from her body. The material promptly clung to various other places. 'Oh, my! Oh—' with a sidelong glance at Ravensdene '—just look at me!'

Only the ladies obliged. Turning his back, Ravensdene gazed at the house as if suddenly struck by an architectural muse, while Devenham sank into a chair and put his head in his hands.

'Oh, good gracious me!' Lady Wribbonhall, clucking like a demented hen, rushed forward. 'Miss Smisby! You can't just stand there. Come out at once! Dear me! What is to be done? How could you be so *immodest*, so lost to all sense of decorum?'

As if her exhortations had released them from their shocked paralysis, the other Smisby girls hurried to their sister's aid. Sarah didn't dare catch Julia's eye as instructions and reproaches filled the air, rendering the scene more reminiscent of a hen-house in an uproar than before. She was already in dire straits trying to suppress the laughter threatening to overtake her.

Fortunately, Lady Ravensdene was made of sterner stuff. She had been right, Sarah reflected, watching her ladyship's face as Averilla Smisby splashed towards the bank. Ravensdene's mother was no more vague than her son.

Rising majestically, her gaze still fixed in frigid disapproval on the apparition in the lake, she held out an imperious hand. 'Your coat, Ravensdene, if you please.'

He shrugged out of it and handed it over without a word.

Despite her struggle for composure, Sarah felt her eyes widen as she took in the solid proportions of his chest and shoulders, clad in fine white lawn. Before she could wrench her gaze away, he looked straight at her and winked.

She nearly choked. And he knew it, the wretch. It was all she could do to control herself long enough for Lady Ravensdene and Lady Wribbonhall to lead three very chastened Miss Smisbys away, one of them wrapped in Ravensdene's coat, her sandals squelching miserably with every step.

Only Euphemia looked back briefly. 'My puppy. . .' she began.

'Don't worry, Miss Smisby,' Lady Ravensdene interposed firmly. 'He shall be found and returned.'

'Is it safe to look?' Devenham got out in a strangled voice as the group reached the terrace and vanished into the house. He was still bent over, his head clutched between his hands.

But not for any reasons of discretion, Sarah discovered, studying him more closely. His lordship had been rendered utterly helpless with laughter.

She looked at Julia, then at Ravensdene. As one they all burst into similar paroxysms and collapsed onto the nearest chairs.

'Oh, dear,' said Julia when she could speak. 'How

very dreadful it is to laugh at such a want of conduct, but how can one help it? When I think of Mama's face when Averilla Smisby stood up in the water and asked everyone to look at her—' She broke off, overcome by another fit of giggles.

Sarah eyed her friend with mock solemnity. 'You would be amazed,' she said, 'at what some females will do.'

The abrupt cessation of mirth beside her made her turn her head. Ravensdene was regarding her, one midnight dark brow raised, a slightly quizzical look in his eyes. Sarah suddenly realised what she had said.

'Oh!' she exclaimed softly, but there was no real distress in the sound. In fact, distress was the furthest thing from her mind. On the contrary. She felt light, floating, as if a weight she had been dragging behind her had just been cut loose. It was the feeling of awkwardness that had plagued her in his presence, she thought. Her embarrassment at her idiotic behaviour the other day. In their shared hilarity it had vanished completely.

'You never said a truer word, Miss Lynley,' he murmured, and smiled at her.

'That's all very well,' said Devenham, distracting Sarah from the quick rush of happiness welling up inside her. 'But that young lady needs a good talking-to. Are you sure you're not hurt, Miss Wribbonhall?'

While Julia reassured him, Ravensdene rose to his feet, reaching out to set the table to rights in the same fluid movement. 'I think Miss Smisby will receive all the talking-to you would wish on her,' he observed. 'And if I know my mother, by the time she's finished with those three, they won't come near the Place again.'

'I should think not.' Julia giggled. 'But I suspect

Leopoldina and Euphemia were as shocked as Mama.
And Averilla could not have known you would be near
the lake, my lord, so perhaps we should not be too
harsh.'

'You are too generous, Miss Wribbonhall.'
Ravensdene's tone was dry. 'Especially if, as I suspect,
that dog was deliberately turned loose inside the gates
and—'

'Good God! The puppy. I suppose we should go and
look for it.' Devenham sprang up and made a great
show of peering into the nearest bushes. 'Did you
happen to notice which way the little devil went, Nick?'

An amused smile crossed Ravensdene's face. 'No.
But feel free to search the place, by all means.'

'Least we can do, if it will get those harp—uh,
females off the premises betimes,' Devenham declared
purposefully. 'Miss Wribbonhall, you and I shall take
the woods.' He took Julia's hand in his before anyone
could suggest an alternative plan. 'Nick, why don't you
and Miss Lynley search the gardens?'

'An excellent idea,' Ravensdene murmured, manag-
ing not to grin.

Sarah, whose gaze had been going from one man to
the other all through the exchange, suddenly heard the
unspoken dialogue going on between them. She looked
at the lightly covered, powerful physique of her host
and felt a frisson of doubt slide down her spine. She
might be feeling more at ease with Ravensdene, but
being alone with him again was another thing entirely.

It was too late to protest, however. Devenham was
already leading an equally flummoxed but willing Julia
across the lawn towards the home wood. When they
disappeared into the leafy bower, Sarah swallowed
against the strange tightness in her throat.

'It is quite all right, Miss Lynley.' Ravensdene

studied her face for a moment, then said deliberately, 'Miss Wribbonhall will be perfectly safe with Lord Devenham, I assure you.'

'Oh. . .' Flustered, she clasped her hands. 'I am sure she will be. That isn't what. . .'

'Is it your own safety that concerns you?'

'No! Good heavens, no. What could happen in a garden? I—'

'Then shall we go?'

The calm question acted like a particularly effective dampener. Sarah ordered herself to stop babbling, unclenched her fingers and laid her hand on Ravensdene's proffered arm. The heat and hardness beneath her fingers immediately turned her limbs to water. The fine lawn of his shirt was no covering at all. She might as well have been touching his bare flesh.

She almost collapsed at the thought. The garden seemed miles away, but once they were enclosed by the tall, green hedges surrounding the formal arrangement of paths and flower beds, Ravensdene halted. It was a fortunate thing, Sarah reflected vaguely. She didn't think she could trust her legs to go any further.

'Miss Lynley,' he said gravely, covering her hand with his. 'May I speak plainly with you?'

Doubt and apprehension immediately suspended every faculty. He was going to mention her strange behaviour. She just knew it. Unable to speak herself, she gestured slightly with her free hand.

'I wanted to thank you for coming here today,' he began, his voice very deep and soft. 'After my unchivalrous insistence on raising an obviously delicate subject with you in such public surroundings the other day, I was not sure you would accept my mother's invitation. Thank you. You have made her very happy.'

Sarah could only stare at him while surprise con-

tinued to render her speechless. Having steeled herself
for anything from reproaches to a demand for an
explanation, the only response that sprang to her mind
was a wild impulse to ask if her presence had made
him happy, too. The highly improper question was so
ready to tumble off her tongue that she was thoroughly
distracted from her niggling sense that something was
missing from Ravensdene's contrite speech.

'Please think nothing more of it, my lord,' she finally
managed. 'My. . .my own behaviour was not precisely
exemplary on that occasion. No doubt you have been
wondering. . .that is. . .'

'I doubt if the reason is far to seek,' he said dryly.
'You've been nervous around me ever since our first
meeting. I can hardly blame you. I was extremely rough
with you; an action I now deeply regret. I can only
assure you, Miss Lynley, that I will do everything
within my power to erase such an appalling first
impression, which is why I agreed to let Dev and Miss
Wribbonhall search the woods while we tackle the
garden. I hoped—'

He paused, looking down at her averted face, before
adding in a voice so low she had to strain to hear the
words, 'Please don't be afraid of me, Sarah.'

Oh, who could resist the sincerity in *that* plea? Certainly not she, Sarah thought, shaken unutterably by
the knowledge that Ravensdene still regretted his violence in the woods and assumed she still feared him
because of it.

'It is not precisely that I am afraid of you, my lord,'
she whispered hesitantly. She kept her gaze lowered,
almost unbearably conscious of the quietness of the
garden, of how alone they were, of the growing intimacy of the moment. The chance to erase the
impression she must have left him with at the picnic, to

recapture that sweet sense of harmony, beckoned irresistibly, and yet she still felt a need to pull back, to
protect herself in some way.

'There is no need to search for explanations, Miss
Lynley.' He tipped her face up with a hand beneath
her chin and met her troubled gaze. 'Given your usual
good sense, I am sure you consider your reasons for
avoiding marriage to be sound and sufficient.'

'Oh. Thank you.' Sarah returned his look doubtfully.
'I think.'

He smiled and, releasing her, began walking again,
leading her towards a fountain that stood at the junc-
tion of several paths in the centre of the garden.

Sarah followed blindly, her thoughts quite uncharacteristically at sea. Having been told that an explanation
was unnecessary, she now found herself overwhelm-
ingly anxious to give him one. But what was she to
say? The dreams that plagued her sleep were terrifying
enough without reliving the nightmare during the day.
Even the thought of relating the story behind her
decision never to marry caused a roiling nausea to
churn in the pit of her stomach. She couldn't do it.
She needed something else. Something he would
understand.

Sarah's eyes widened as an idea flashed into her
mind. It would involve another discussion on the subject of matrimony, but what better way to eradicate the
memory of her hysterical rantings of two days ago?
And this time she was prepared. This time she could
control the conversation.

'Marriage is, as you say, a delicate subject,' she
remarked, feeling rather like a bather testing the
waters, one cautious toe at a time. 'And one about
which my views were fixed at quite a young age, my
lord. While my parents were still alive, in fact.'

'Oh?' She felt him glance down at her as they strolled past a fragrant lavendar bush. 'From your tone, Miss Lynley, I deduce that theirs was not a felicitous match.'

'Far from it, sir. My father married late in life when he was extremely fixed in his ways and not inclined to tolerate the, er, flightiness of a much younger wife. Even though his own behaviour was far from acceptable.'

'Hmm. Let me tell you, Miss Lynley, that if flightiness is a euphemism for what I suspect, then a husband's age or behaviour has nothing whatever to do with it.'

Sarah blushed. 'Yes, I am fully aware that there are two sets of rules pertaining in society, my lord. A woman may look forward to comporting herself in an exemplary fashion while her husband does what he pleases, regardless of her feelings in the matter. Or she can seek a match in which the partners agree to lead separate lives once the wife has fulfilled her duty in producing an heir.

'Where no such agreement exists, however, constant arguments and acrimony are not very pleasant for the other members of a household, sir. In fact, it was during the course of one such altercation that my father was distracted from his driving, causing his curricle to swing wide on a bend and collide with a tree. Both my parents were killed instantly.'

'I'm sorry,' he murmured rather thoughtfully. 'It must have been most distressing for you. . .'

The silent 'but' hanging on the end of that sentence jangled loudly in Sarah's head.

'Yes, well, I daresay my reasons for avoiding either of those situations might be considered foolish, my lord, but I would rather remain single than—'

'Miss Lynley!' He halted with startling abruptness and turned her to face him, his hands resting lightly on her shoulders. 'I would *never* consider you foolish.' Both voice and expression gentled. 'Merely very sheltered and inexperienced.'

'Not so sheltered that I don't know what goes on in polite society,' Sarah retorted, feeling unaccountably annoyed by that remark. She promptly forgot how very big Ravensdene's hands felt wrapped around her more fragile frame. 'Just because your own marriage was an unusually happy one, does not mean—'

His grip tightened with a force that brought her awareness of danger rushing back with dizzying speed. Sarah gasped, fully expecting to hear her bones crack at any moment. 'I'm sorry,' she stammered. 'I—'

'Hush.' He released her immediately, silencing her by the simple expedient of brushing his fingers lightly across her lips. Then, taking her hand, he led her up to the fountain a few steps away and indicated the stone coping.

Sarah sank onto the makeshift seat with a willingness that had nothing to do with compliance, her dazed mind grappling with the puzzle of how such a fleeting touch of Ravensdene's fingers could cause a shimmering ripple of sensation to flow from her lips to her throat, and from thence to spread a tingling heat across her breasts—and all this while her heart was pounding with alarm.

The puzzle was destined to remain unsolved. Ravensdene seated himself beside her and fixed her with an unnervingly steady regard.

'Who told you I'd once been married?' he asked.

His calm tone did absolutely nothing to soothe her frazzled nerves. 'Lady Wribbonhall,' she owned faintly. 'But it was not. . .not in any *gossiping* way, my lord.'

When he raised a brow in quizzical disbelief, Sarah

felt a guilty blush suffuse her cheeks. Oh, why hadn't she been struck dumb before she'd come out with that statement about his marriage? So much for taking control of the conversation. It seemed to be drifting into rather perilous channels again, and far from being struck dumb, her tongue appeared to be taking on a will of its own, aided and abetted by a question that was suddenly dancing tantalisingly about in her brain. A question, she realised with a start of surprise, that had been hovering in the back of her mind for a very long time. Ever since Lady Wribbonhall had mentioned the subject, in fact.

'Yes,' she heard herself saying in earnest tones. 'Lady Wribbonhall quite understood why you might not wish to be pursued, my lord. Indeed, she seemed to have been greatly impressed by your wife's beauty and... and general demeanour. Angelic was the word she used, if I recall, and...'

Sheer disbelief at her own temerity at last had her clamping her lips shut on the rest. She looked into Ravensdene's frowning eyes and could not believe what she had done. Now it was she who was trespassing beyond the boundaries of friendship. As if some demon of curiosity had been released from the shackles of polite behaviour, and not even the memory of where curiosity had led her before had had the power to stop her.

Then as Ravensdene looked away, guilt and remorse swept over her in a swamping wave, the force of it almost drowning her. She had hurt him. She had behaved no better than Sophie Sherington. And now, when she needed to speak, to beg his forgiveness, her mind had ceased to function, her throat had seized up...

Oh, if only Julia and Devenham would return. The puppy appear. *Anything*.

'Yes, Marianne was incomparably beautiful.'

Sarah froze. Even her heart seemed to stand still. The words were spoken so quietly that for a minute she wasn't sure if she'd actually heard them. Hardly daring to breathe, she stared wide-eyed at Ravensdene, thankful that he continued to gaze down into the water hushing gently beside them.

'She was somewhat taller than you, Miss Lynley, and very fair. Her hair was that rare shade that shines almost silver in some lights; her face and figure were deemed to be perfection. Yes, an angel was exactly what she looked like.'

If someone had just dashed the chilly waters of the fountain over her, Sarah couldn't have felt more shattered. The shock made it almost impossible to breathe. It could not have been more obvious to her that Ravensdene's heart had been buried in the grave with his beautiful angel of a wife.

She found herself blinking back a sudden rush of tears and was horrified at her loss of control. What was happening to her lately? Why was she acting so unlike herself? Why did she *feel* so unlike herself? Panicked one moment, incredibly happy the next, only to be cast down into this trough of despondency. She should be grateful that Ravensdene was still conversing with her instead of delivering the set-down she deserved. The least she could do was respond with sympathy for his loss without embarrassing them both by turning into a watering-pot.

This stern, if silent, rebuke had her floundering under another tidal wave of guilt. She fought it back, determined that, this time, she would not leave Ravensdene thinking her prone to uncontrollable outbursts.

'I'm sorry,' she ventured, forcing a tentative smile. It wavered somewhat at the edges, but at least the exercise served to push her seesawing emotions to the back of her mind. 'I know what it's like to lose someone you love.'

He looked at her then, his eyes grave. 'Your sister?'

Sarah nodded, and in that moment she decided that whatever the cost to herself, Ravensdene deserved the truth. Or at least part of it. She had intruded, unforgivably, driven by her sudden incomprehensible curiosity about his wife, whereas he had demanded nothing. No explanations, no reasons, nothing. Because he thought she was afraid of him.

'Goodness!' she managed on a nervous little laugh. 'I do not know how we came to be so side-tracked, my lord, when I believe I was trying to explain that you do not frighten me.'

'Don't I?' he asked gently.

'Certainly not.' She sat up straighter, gaining confidence with her resolve to make amends. 'If I have seemed to you to have been dwelling on an episode to which I freely admit I contributed my share, sir, it is because those woods hold very disturbing memories for me. Memories that have nothing to do with what happened between you and I.' She hesitated, then finished baldly. 'My sister was assaulted and killed there.'

'I see.'

'Yes. And, unfortunately, the day we met was the first time I had ventured there alone.'

'Is that why you were armed that day?' he asked. 'Were you afraid something of the kind might occur again?'

Conscious of the searching quality of his gaze, Sarah glanced down and began trailing her fingers idly through the water. 'Not exactly,' she said slowly. 'It was not a...a random attack.'

When he didn't ask for clarification but just waited, she drew in a deep breath. 'Amy was murdered. By one of our grooms.'

Silence. She could almost hear his brain sifting through the scant information.

'What happened to the murderer?' he asked after a moment.

Sarah sighed and withdrew her fingers from the water. She folded her hands in her lap and contemplated the garden beds in front of her. 'He drowned. When his body was discovered washed up on the beach a day or so later, everyone thought he had been trying to escape by swimming out to one of the ships anchored in the Downs.'

This time the silence threatened to stretch into infinity. She wished she knew what Ravensdene was thinking, but a quick, sidelong glance at him revealed nothing more than a slight narrowing of his eyes as he, too, stared thoughtfully at the garden.

She did not need to read his mind, however, to know what the next logical question would be, and an explanation as to why a groom would want to attack and kill his employer's niece threatened to drag her down once more into the murky depths of her nightmares. She had said enough.

'Miss Lynley—'

'Dear me, we seem to have been sitting here talking forever, my lord!' She sprang to her feet, bracing knees that felt distinctly wobbly. 'Julia and Lord Devenham will be wondering what has become of us.'

'I doubt it,' he said very dryly, rising also. His unwavering gaze remained on her face a moment longer, causing her heart to beat uncomfortably fast as she waited to see if he would follow her lead. Then the unnervingly contemplative expression vanished from his eyes and he smiled at her.

'In fact Dev is probably proposing to Miss Wribbonhall even as we speak. I know he intended to do so at his first opportunity, and like any good strategist he seized it.' He grinned suddenly, the wicked, boyish grin she found so endearing. 'Why do you think he was so anxious to go hunting for that wretched hound?'

'Oh.' Sarah laughed at the memory of Devenham peering under bushes that clearly contained no recalcitrant puppies. A second later her brain rocked under the impact of Ravensdene's meaning.

'Good heavens! That means Julia will be betrothed. And then married. And then—' She stopped right there.

'Yes, we do seem to be forever running up against the institution of matrimony, don't we, Miss Lynley? However, I can assure you that Dev will handle the matter with a great deal more address than I did. Nor are all marriages like those you described earlier. You need have no fears for Miss Wribbonhall's future happiness.'

'Oh, I don't,' she stammered, thrown immediately back into confusion by this assurance. She wasn't sure if Ravensdene was referring to proposals or marriage. Either option held uncountable dangers as far as she was concerned. 'I am sure Lord Devenham is everything that is gentlemanly, but. . .'

The line of his mouth seemed to harden. 'Whereas I am not.'

'I did not say that, my lord.' *Well, not precisely*. Sarah blushed selfconsciously. 'And you *are* a gentleman.'

She looked down and added after a painful pause, 'I, more than anyone, should know that.'

He reached out and took her hand, his long fingers closing firmly about hers. 'Thank you, Miss Lynley,' he murmured, and waiting until she raised her eyes to his, he brought her hand to his lips and held it there.

Sarah felt her breath stop. Was this what she had feared? This liquid, melting warmth rushing through her. His lips were firm and yet gentle against her fingers. She thought once again of the lethal power beneath his civilised clothing, felt the heat emanating from his big body, and wanted only to step closer. In his shirt, breeches and topboots he was overwhelming in his masculinity, but she remembered how swiftly he had moved to stop her from falling, how securely he had held her, she remembered Lydia's trust in her husband and Julia's anxious wait for Devenham to declare himself, and for the first time in her adult life, she thought of safety, of protection, in the arms of a man.

The notion was enough to stun her into utter immobility, her gaze caught and held by the glittering green eyes that watched the myriad expressions flitting across her face with all the piercing intensity of a hunting cat.

Several excited yips from only a few feet away broke the spell.

Completely unnerved, trembling inside, Sarah jumped as though she'd been struck.

'I think we've discovered our quarry, Miss Lynley,' Ravensdene observed softly, releasing her hand. His deep voice was rougher than usual, the purr more of a low growl, but Sarah scarcely noticed. She was still trying to cope with the knowledge that, in the moments before the barrage of barking started, she hadn't wanted to flee, screaming, from the garden.

Shaking her head in an effort to restore her scrambled wits, she scurried around the fountain after Ravensdene, her speed due more to rattled nerves than any great desire to find the cause of the disturbance, and skidded to a halt beside her host, who was calmly surveying the scene in front of them.

A large ginger cat sat atop the stone wall at the end of the path, diligently washing one paw, while totally ignoring the hysterical antics of the puppy below.

'Heavens, what a fuss!' Thankful for the chance to hide her flushed countenance, Sarah hurried forward to scoop up the excited puppy. 'No, you are not another cat to be running up walls,' she informed her captive, who promptly started licking her face in a frenzy of affection. She cuddled the little creature closer, not at all disturbed by the enthusiastic greeting. 'Yes, I know it is all very exciting, but you have been a very naughty dog. Stop that, sir. I do not need a bath at this moment.'

'You will if you allow him to kiss you all over like that.'

Ravensdene strode up to her and plucked the squirming bundle of fur from Sarah's unresisting arms. Alarm bells jangled once more in her head. His voice still held that slightly rough note and he had sounded almost abrupt. As if. . .

She must be going mad. Surely he couldn't have meant that he wanted to. . .

Oh, if only there was not a regiment of butterflies dancing a quadrille in her stomach she would be able to *think*.

'Miss Lynley?'

'What? Oh, I beg your pardon, my lord. Were you saying something?'

His mouth curved in a wry smile as she glanced

distractedly up at him, but behind the rueful amusement in his eyes was a hint of something so tender it made her breath catch.

'Merely that I'm glad you still consider me to be a gentleman. Your opinion means a great deal to me.'

'Oh.' Sarah focused her eyes on her feet. 'As does yours. To me, I mean.'

She shivered, suddenly conscious of a yielding sensation deep inside her. As though by saying the words, something, some part of herself that had once been very closely guarded, had softened, leaving her as vulnerable and trembling as a baby fawn gazing upon the world for the first time.

'What is it?' he asked quietly.

'I... I was just thinking...' She looked up, bewildered, only to have her gaze caught by the sight of the puppy, now peacefully asleep in the crook of Ravensdene's arm. She stared in wonder at the sight. The puppy, too, was frail and vulnerable, and yet there it lay, so tiny and trusting, in the hold of a man who could be either predator or protector. But which? How did the puppy know? How could she tell? 'I was thinking of trust.'

'A gift I would treasure always,' he said very softly.

There was a heartbeat of silence. He was waiting, Sarah realised. But for what? *Her* trust? She had not been speaking so particularly. And yet, he waited. It was like being poised on the brink of discovery, she thought, without knowing precisely what it was she was about to discover.

Then, as frissons of alarm began rippling along her nerves again, Ravensdene's free hand appeared in her line of vision. 'Friends, Miss Lynley?'

Oh-h-h. Every tightly wound muscle in Sarah's body

went limp with relief. *Friends.* Oh, yes! She wanted that more than anything, and if Ravensdene did also. . .

Her spirits, so low only minutes ago, soared to dizzy heights. She raised her eyes to his. 'Yes, of course, my lord,' she breathed. And, a brilliant smile lighting her face, she put her hand in his.

'Friends.'

CHAPTER TEN

'ARE you quite certain, my lord, that Uncle Jasper was the white?' Sarah levelled her brows at the chessboard in front of her and contemplated the fast-approaching conclusion to Monday's chess match and her imminent defeat. 'It seems to me that since I took his place, I have been losing pieces with unprecedented speed.'

As if to prove her point, Ravensdene removed a bishop with a deceptively simple strategy that she suspected had been planned at least three moves ago. She glared at him. 'I thought you said you were out of practice.'

He grinned unrepentantly. 'It's all coming back to me.'

'Is it?' she muttered. 'It all seems to be leaving me.'

She bent over to examine the board more closely before shifting a pawn a cautious square forward.

'At least you still have your queen, Miss Lynley. Which is more than can be said for me.'

'Since it was not I who relieved you of it, sir, that is poor comfort indeed. I could wish Uncle Jasper had not felt the need to retire, and not merely for his own sake.'

A soft laugh was her only answer. Ravensdene leaned back in his chair, one hand toying idly with her captured bishop while he considered his next move.

Sarah found herself studying the strong, elegant fingers curled around the carved ivory chess piece. The two very different qualities intrigued her. Like the rest of him, his hand was big, its strength obvious. Indeed, she had felt the power in those long fingers herself. On more than one occasion.

But there was a fascinating masculine elegance, also, in the fine shape of his hands and the length of his fingers. An elegance that told of restraint, and a self-control that would not easily be surrendered. It made her wonder just how gentle those powerful hands could be.

'Your move, Miss Lynley.'

'Oh!' Blushing hotly, Sarah jumped and peered with what she hoped passed for intense concentration at her few remaining troops. What on earth had possessed her to entertain such a thought? No wonder she was being wiped from the board.

'Hmm. I see you have moved your king, my lord.' Now that was a truly intelligent observation. Especially since she was supposed to have been watching.

'He was in grave danger of being threatened, Miss Lynley. By your queen.'

'Permit me to tell you, sir, that you look to be in an invincible position,' Sarah contradicted, finally getting her colour back under control. She could do nothing about the odd little shiver travelling up and down her spine. The strange phenomenon still seemed to occur whenever Ravensdene's voice lowered to that soft, gentle purr.

'Not entirely invincible,' he murmured. 'Actually the king is relatively helpless. He can only wait for the queen to come close enough for him to capture her.'

'If she doesn't capture him first.' Sarah met his eyes for an infinitesimal second. Why did she feel so breathless all of a sudden when they were merely discussing chess strategies?

At least, she thought that was what they were discussing. With Ravensdene she wasn't always sure. Since yesterday she had recalled too many occasions when a commonplace remark on his part seemed to have held some deeper meaning.

'Ah, but that is one of the risks of the game,' he said, watching with great interest as she made a reckless diagonal dash across the board with the queen in question. 'Dear me. An unusual move, Miss Lynley. Did you happen to notice this knight lurking over here?'

'Oh, no!' Sarah squeaked in dismay as she watched an undefended rook carried off. 'How very unfriendly of you, sir.'

'Yes, I know,' he admitted without the least sign of compunction. 'And after our pact yesterday, too.' His green eyes glinted devilishly. 'What now, Miss Lynley?'

She had to laugh at his unabashed air of triumph. 'I'm afraid white will have to concede, my lord. That was my last major piece apart from the queen, and you will soon have that surrounded. Oh, dear. How will I ever break the news of such a rout to Uncle Jasper?'

The wicked laughter faded from his eyes as he carefully put the white queen down on the board next to his king. 'Perhaps you were playing under the disadvantage of worrying about your uncle,' he suggested. 'Is it uncommon for him to rest during the afternoon?'

'Not uncommon, no.' Sarah frowned as she considered the question. She was glad Ravensdene had put such an interpretation on her absent-minded play, but now that she came to think of it, her uncle had appeared to be in reasonably good point when he had claimed weariness after a disturbed night and had retired to his chamber an hour ago.

Her frown deepened as she took in Ravensdene's casual pose. He didn't appear to be in any hurry to leave, despite the absence of either host or female

chaperon. And now that she came to think about something else, she recalled her belated discovery in the
middle of the night, of what had puzzled her about their
conversation yesterday. Ravensdene had certainly
admitted to raising a delicate subject in public surroundings, but he hadn't actually apologised for mentioning
the subject in the first place. Or for interfering in what
was essentially none of his business.

He was rather good at that, Sarah mused, sending
him a quick, covert glance. Seeming to say something
without saying it at all. It was a talent that made her
somewhat nervous, despite his avowal of friendship.
After all, she might not have been friends with a man
before, but it was safe to say that such a relationship
would be rather different to the one she had with Julia,
for instance. Perhaps a still greater degree of clarity on
a certain subject was in order.

'Uncle Jasper often has disturbed nights,' she
explained, gathering her thoughts. 'And I must confess,
my lord, that until recently, it did not occur to me that
my future might be one of the matters keeping him
awake.' She shook her head, genuinely remorseful. 'I
don't know why I didn't see. . .'

Ravensdene spoke slowly, as though choosing his
words, his gaze on the black king and white queen
standing side by side in front of him. 'Sometimes, Miss
Lynley, when one has nurtured an idea in one's mind
for a long time, one cannot see the wood for the trees,
so to speak. Sometimes a. . .considerable jolt is necessary, to make one aware of the possible alternatives.'

A jolt? Well, she had certainly received several of
those lately.

'Yes, well, it has recently been brought home to me,
my lord, that Uncle Jasper needs reassuring.' She
paused half-expectantly, but the only change in

Ravensdene's expression was the faintly amused curve
to his hard mouth.

So much for a more specific apology, Sarah reflected
wryly. She resigned herself to the inevitable, and got
the rest out in a little rush. 'So I think I had better
confess the truth about my reasons for entering
Society.'

'The truth?' He looked up at that, clearly startled.

Sarah felt a quite illogical burst of satisfaction when
his black brows drew together. At least she wasn't the
only one experiencing jolts.

'That would certainly be interesting,' he stated rather
forcibly. 'What, pray, *is* your real motive in entering
Society?'

'I intend to make as many contacts as possible in
order to apply for a position as a governess or housekeeper when—' she faltered momentarily '—when the
time comes.'

'A *governess*? A *housekeeper*?' Nick mentally ran
through the more probable fates that awaited a housekeeper who looked like Sarah. The pictures forming in
his mind were not reassuring. In fact, given time and
his suddenly fertile imagination, they threatened to
grow to nightmarish proportions.

He cast a lowering glance at Sarah's incensed
expression. The trouble was, of course, that the little
innocent had no idea of just how damned alluring she
was. Even when she was scowling at him, as she was
now, his body was tense and throbbing with the fierce
male urge to drag her into his arms and change her
scowl to soft female surrender. As for what happened
to him whenever she smiled—

'Is there anything wrong with that?' she demanded,
pulling his thoughts back to the present discussion.
'They are respectable professions, you know.'

'Believe me,' he stated with undiplomatic frankness, 'no woman in her right mind would hire you as a governess.' Her mouth fell open but he swept on regardless. 'And what would you do if your male employer turned out to be not so respectable? Pull a pistol on him?'

Sarah had managed to close her mouth, but this was too much. She rose from her chair and turned an intimidatingly haughty glare on him. Unfortunately, Ravensdene chose to remain annoyingly unintimidated. He stood up also.

'There would be no need for such an action,' she retorted, hurriedly backing away a few steps so he couldn't tower over her. 'If I were to seek a post where a man was my employer, naturally it would be an older gentleman. As your mother observed yesterday, I am well able to cope with such persons.'

A smile crept into his eyes, startling her. 'Sarah, you sweet little idiot, how very innocent you are if you think a man's age would ensure your safety.'

'O-h-h!' Flushed and floundering, she didn't know which statement to attack first. 'I am *not*. . . How. . . Well, if you have a better idea, my lord, I would be more than happy to hear it!'

He eyed her heightened colour for a moment, then strolled across the library to prop himself negligently against her uncle's desk. His hands curled around the edge on either side of his thighs.

'As a matter of fact, I do,' he said quietly. 'A better idea that will benefit all of us. It is, in fact, the second matter in which I was going to beg your assistance.'

Sarah took in the distance between them and the careless way he was leaning against the desk, and began to calm down. Perhaps he had a companion for his mother in mind; in which case it would not hurt to listen. She took a deep breath and resumed her seat, folding her hands primly in her lap. This time she would behave with dignity—no matter what he said.

'I am listening, my lord.'

He decided to ignore the exaggerated sweetness in her tone. 'It would involve a position much like the one you mentioned, Miss Lynley. You would be in charge of several establishments, you would be a most suitable companion to their owner, and your presence would also ensure the gentleman's, er, protection.'

'Protection?' she repeated, startled. 'I am not some sort of guard, sir.'

'That was not precisely what I meant.' He thought about it, then added with a grin, 'Pistols wouldn't be necessary. At least, I hope not.'

She ground her teeth. 'My lord, I believe you are making game of me. It is not at all—'

'Oh, *hell*!'

The exclamation was so explosive that Sarah broke off to stare. Ravensdene straightened and took a couple of steps towards the window, raking his fingers through his dark hair. Stunned at such uncharacteristic behaviour on his part, she was totally unprepared when he swung about, crossed the room in three quick strides and hunkered down before her, covering her hands with one of his.

'I'm making the most awful mull of this,' he murmured, a rueful smile in his eyes. 'Miss Lynley—Sarah. . .' His voice went deep and soft on her name. 'I am asking you to do me the very great honour of becoming my wife.'

Everything in the room went still. Including her heart. She couldn't answer, couldn't think. Her voice, her mind, her every faculty remained suspended in the moment when Ravensdene had asked her to marry him. Then tiny tremors began coursing through her, making her shiver imperceptibly.

His hand tightened over hers. 'I know you have set your mind against marriage,' he continued very gently. 'But would you consider it just for a moment? There are several advantages to both of us.'

'S. . .sev. . .'

'Yes.' He went on as if she had asked a perfectly intelligible question. 'I have already mentioned the benefits to me. For yourself, you would have the comfort of securing your uncle's peace of mind, and I can assure you that *you* would be a great deal more comfortable and secure as my wife than as a housekeeper or a governess.'

'What you say is perfectly true, my lord.' Her voice sounded terrifyingly faint but at least it was working again. If only her brain would do likewise. It was like groping about in a thick, swirling fog, Sarah thought. She couldn't see properly, couldn't reason, couldn't marshal any arguments to refute his logic. She wondered vaguely why she didn't just say no. No arguments. No reason. Thank you for the honour, my lord, but no.

The words floated about in her dazed mind, but somehow they couldn't seem to get past the locked muscles of her throat. It was very strange, because several other words were having no trouble whatsoever.

'You mentioned that I would be in charge of several establishments, that I would be a companion. . . To you?' she clarified.

He nodded, smiling faintly.

Not his mother. Sarah dismissed the notion and tried to complete the list he had given her, but her mind boggled anew at the notion of Ravensdene needing protection. If he did, then she was Prinny and the entire Carlton House Set rolled into one.

'What you have described, my lord, sounds rather like a marriage of convenience,' she ventured at last, conscious of a need to tread very warily.

'Yes, Miss Lynley, what I have described does sound rather like a marriage of convenience.'

She considered the statement, frowning slightly. As if sensing that his touch might be adding to her confusion, Ravensdene removed his hand, rose to his feet and sat down opposite her. His watchful gaze never left her face.

'A marriage of convenience, sir, usually means that a wife. . .or. . .or husband, of course. . .is not required to meet certain. . . That is to say, there are, I believe, certain marital—' she searched frantically for the right term '—*obligations*, that. . .'

'Miss Lynley,' he interposed softly. 'If you accept my offer, I promise you our marriage will have nothing to do with obligations.'

'Oh.' She blushed hotly and looked down. 'That is very reassuring, of course, but have you considered fully? I mean, we discussed such arrangements yesterday, if you recall. You have a title and titled gentlemen usually require an heir or. . .or something.' Oh heavens, if a benign providence was listening, she would sink through the floor and vanish.

Benign providence was apparently short of hearing that day. She stayed where she was, aware that Ravensdene was watching every flow and ebb of colour, every nuance of expression that crossed her face.

'It's true that I haven't considered the need for an heir,' he agreed after a long silence. 'Probably because, being the second son, I never expected to inherit the title. However, the necessity still doesn't arise, Miss

Lynley. Fortunately, I'm possessed of two younger brothers, one of whom is already married and the father of several offspring.'

The familiar gleam of amusement came into his eyes when Sarah risked a quick glance upwards. 'I can assure you that the line of Daltons is in no immediate danger of extinction.'

She had to smile at that, but she believed him. If Ravensdene's brothers were anything like him, they were probably exceptionally virile men. She blinked in startled reaction to a thought that was so utterly alien to her.

'Miss Lynley.' Ravensdene leaned forward, drawing her gaze back to him. He linked his fingers loosely on the chessboard between them and fixed her with a steady regard. 'Sarah, yesterday you denied you were afraid of me, but you still seem to have serious doubts. Please tell me how I may further reassure you that you will have nothing to fear from me.'

'Oh, it's not. . .' Searching her mind for a way to explain her hesitation, she thought again of Ravensdene's first wife. Why would a man who had once insisted on following his heart, now be equally determined on a marriage in name only?

Or perhaps that *was* why, Sarah reflected, conscious of a sharp little pang in the region of her heart. Because Marianne could not be replaced in quite the same way. After all, who could follow an angel?

The realisation was unexpectedly lowering.

'We have established your duties as chatelaine and companion,' he murmured, cutting through her confusion at the sudden direction of her thoughts. 'And disposed of my need for an heir. What else is there?'

Sarah could only look at him. His expression was polite, calm, almost remote, the brilliant intensity of his light green eyes shuttered by half-lowered lashes as he waited for her answer. At that moment she might have convinced herself that he posed not the slightest threat to her; but she had the very powerful impression of a hunter—waiting.

'I think you could be dangerous,' she blurted out.

'Not to you,' he denied at once. 'Never to you. Besides—' the wickedly boyish smile flashed out '—didn't you hear me say it was *I* who needed protection? How can you doubt it after yesterday's episode with the Smisbys?'

From a deep well of feminine pride that she had never suspected she possessed, Sarah managed to summon up a severe frown. It was no use trying to explain her misgivings. She would never be able to sort out such a jumbled mishmash of conflicting doubts and emotions, even if she could bring herself to mention Ravensdene's former marriage again, which was impossible.

Being made fun of, however, was a different matter.

'I daresay being pursued so relentlessly is vastly irritating, my lord,' she agreed tartly. 'But you are not exactly helpless. I cannot imagine why you would want to go to the trouble of marrying a female you don't— In short, sir, I can think of no one in *less* need of protection—from anyone!'

She waited, half-prepared for an ironic or humorous rejoinder, but to her surprise Ravensdene studied her broodingly for a second, then rose and moved a few paces away to stand in front of the small fire burning in the fireplace beside the chess table. He leaned one hand on the mantlepiece and gazed down into the flames as if fascinated, but Sarah suspected his thoughts were quite divorced from firelight.

'If I'd come to Comberford merely to spend the

summer,' he said, starting to speak so abruptly that she jumped, 'being pursued by ambitious females wouldn't matter. But—'

'But?' she prompted in a suspenseful whisper.

He turned to look at her. 'Sarah, whether or not you accept my offer, what I'm about to tell you must go no further than this room.'

'Of course not,' she breathed, eyes wide and fixed on his. 'But you don't have to...'

'I want to,' he said, and smiled fleetingly. 'You see, little one, I trust you.'

Was that supposed to mean he expected her trust in return?

She didn't have time to ponder the point. Ravensdene was speaking again, his gaze once more on the fire, his voice low.

'Did you ever hear anything of the Battle of Badajoz, Sarah?'

She frowned, not expecting such a seemingly unrelated question. 'Yes, a little. I read the reports in the papers at the time. There was a terrible loss of life.'

He nodded. 'Almost two thousand men fell in the first two hours in a space less than a hundred yards square. I saw it.'

He was seeing it now, Sarah thought. In his mind. Reliving that day almost three years ago. To her it had been printing on a page, tragic, but distant. He had been part of it, perhaps part of an unsuccessful attempt to prevent it.

Something throbbed again, sharp and painful near her heart. She wanted to go to him, to offer comfort, to relieve the memory somehow, but didn't know what to say. An experience like that would be years in the healing. She knew.

'But it needn't have happened like that if the men in

charge hadn't received the wrong information,' he went on after a moment. 'Or rather, the correct information in time.'

'Information? You said something of the kind once before.'

'Yes.' He glanced at her briefly. 'The two incidents are years apart and unrelated, but I want you to understand that any sort of information in the wrong hands can make the difference between life and death for hundreds of men. And it's my job to make sure that military plans or correspondence between Wellington and the Foreign Office don't fall into those hands.'

'Your job?'

'Well, up until six months ago it was.' He gave a short laugh and looked directly at her, his eyes hard. 'I was very good at acquiring information as well. Perhaps you should know, Miss Lynley, that the gentleman whose offer you're contemplating was a spy.'

Did he think she would be repelled by the admission? On the contrary, Sarah realised with a small sense of shock. She already knew he was dangerous. Now she knew he had probably done things to get information from the other side that would likely give her nightmares, but she also knew, suddenly and without any doubt, that he had never indulged in any mindless, senseless violence. He was a man of honour, with a sense of integrity so deeply ingrained he would always be marked somewhere inside by what he had done, despite the lives he might have saved.

'That must have been very lonely,' she said softly. 'Dangerous, too.'

There was a flicker of surprise in his eyes before they went cool and watchful again. 'When you're young, danger has a seduction all its own,' he said evenly. 'But to return to the point, although Napoleon's capture last year put an end to the war, it didn't necessarily mean that other activities came to a halt. I was still on the continent myself until six months after my brother's death.'

Sarah nodded. 'And now that Napoleon has landed in France?'

'There's a possibility that someone who was passing information across the Channel from here will do so again.'

'A traitor,' she murmured, understanding instantly. 'That's what you meant the other day.' Then the rest sank in. 'Here! You're at Comberford to stop him?'

'Once I know who it is, yes.'

'O-h-h. No wonder you didn't want all the attention and. . .'

'Precisely. I have to admit, however, that some of the blame for it can be laid at my door. I shouldn't have brought my mother with me, but as I told Dev, I thought it would lend a touch of realism.'

'Lord Devenham knows?'

'Yes, and Figgins, my groom. And now you, Miss Lynley.'

She had a fleeting wish that he would call her Sarah again. 'Well, be assured, my lord, that I will not repeat anything of what you have told me. As for your offer. . .'

She thought he moved but wasn't sure. No, not movement, she amended. It was as if he was suddenly alert, every muscle taut as he waited for her answer. She realised her hands were gripped tightly together in her lap and tried to relax them. 'I have decided to accept.'

He watched her for an instant then said with a faintly harsh intonation, 'For England?'

'Isn't that why you offered for me?' she countered,

unwilling to delve too deeply into her reasons for accepting his proposal.

'I can't deny that I had no thought of marriage before I came to Comberford,' he admitted. 'But there are other reasons, Sarah. My estates do need a mistress, but I don't look forward to the prospect of fending off matchmaking mamas or the like every time I have to set foot in town. A marriage between friends seems a much pleasanter solution to the problem.'

A marriage between friends.

Sarah waited for the quick rush of relief she had felt yesterday. It didn't come. Instead she was conscious of a sensation that felt perilously close to a let-down. She hurriedly told herself it was a normal reaction to the worry of making such a life-altering decision.

'Well, I, too, would never marry simply for reasons of patriotism,' she said, rallying herself to respond in kind. 'If you do truly wish for a chatelaine who is also a friend, sir, I would be happy to fill the position.' She looked up at him somewhat doubtfully. 'There is just. . .'

'Tell me.'

'I was thinking of Uncle Jasper, sir. I don't wish to leave him at this time, but I can see that your need for a wife is somewhat immediate. However, I suppose an *engagement*. . .if it was puffed off in the papers. . .'

'Sarah—' He broke off, a rueful smile curving his mouth as he came to sit at the table again. 'I have a confession to make,' he said, the smile reaching his eyes as he studied her increasingly wary expression. 'Your uncle gave me permission to address you some days ago and—'

'Oh! I knew it!' she exclaimed. 'I thought something was going on when Uncle Jasper— But I interrupt you, my lord. I'm sorry. Please go on.' Sarah subsided in her chair and waited for the rest.

His green eyes were alight with devilment. 'I was going to say that Sir Jasper is eager for our marriage to take place once the banns are read. In three weeks, to be precise.'

'*Three weeks*!' Sarah's voice soared. Visions of announcements, visits, shopping, fittings and packing, all danced giddily about in her head. 'But I can't. . .'

'Nothing elaborate, of course,' Ravensdene went on as if this feeble protest had not been uttered. 'Our families and immediate friends only. The ceremony would take place in the village church, and we could then partake of a simple luncheon here before returning to Comberford. Naturally a honeymoon is out of the question, but under the circumstances it would not be a requirement in any case.'

'But—'

'And you need have no fear that I will remove you any great distance from your uncle. No matter how my task here falls out, I am quite content to spend the summer at the Place. If any business should arise at Ravensdene Hall that needs my attention, I would be gone for only a few days at a time.'

'That is very understanding of you, my lord,' Sarah managed in even fainter accents. 'But. . .three *weeks*!'

He looked at her, his eyes very clear and intent. 'Sarah, may I be frank?'

'You always are, my lord.'

A faint echo of his smile appeared then vanished. 'I find it saves time. But the fact is that time is something Sir Jasper may be short of, and he knows it. He is very anxious to see you wed, but in proper form, and without the comment that must arise if we were to procure a special licence.'

'I see.' Sarah mulled that over and knew he was right. And though the blunt assessment of her uncle's health could not but distress her, Ravensdene had given her the means to make sure that Uncle Jasper's last months would be free of worry. It all seemed very civilised and efficient. No wild displays of emotion. No mad outbursts of passion. No need, therefore, to fear an assault upon her person.

She wondered why she still wasn't feeling any wild outbursts of relief.

'Very well, my lord,' she agreed briskly, shaking off her strange mood. 'Three weeks it is.'

'Good.' He smiled and held out his hand. 'That should give you just enough time to practise calling me Nick.'

Sarah's lips parted. No sound emerged, however. Instead she found herself suddenly short of breath. And since she had put her hand in Ravensdene's before he had finished, she suspected he knew as much.

She swallowed and tried again. 'Yes, of course, my lord. I mean. . .that is. . . N. . . Nick.'

'Nearly perfect,' he growled softly, and, raising her hand to his lips, he kissed her fingers.

CHAPTER ELEVEN

HER short engagement might have been considered by some to be enough time to practise calling her husband by his given name, Sarah reflected three weeks later as the door closed behind her maid, but it was difficult to practise when the person you were supposed to be practising on was hardly ever present.

Nor did it appear that the situation was likely to change, despite the wedding that had taken place only that morning. Ravensdene had certainly been attentive enough during the ceremony and the luncheon that had followed, but his gallantry had ended when they had arrived at Comberford Place some hours ago. After greeting the servants, lined up in a vast array to welcome their new mistress, the master of the house had retired to his library, only reappearing, briefly, to dine with her before wishing her a very polite goodnight.

Sarah had suddenly found herself feeling very much alone. She no longer had the daily care of her uncle; tomorrow Lord Devenham was escorting the Wribbonhalls and Julia to his ancestral home for a visit with his family; even the Dowager Lady Ravensdene had driven back to town that very afternoon.

And considering that Ravensdene wanted a companion, she found his behaviour rather odd and not a little disappointing. Her wedding night was not what she had expected.

On the other hand, since she had not wanted a wedding night in the first place, she could hardly complain that her husband was treating her with proper, if rather distant, courtesy. There was, in fact, no cause for complaint at all, she told herself as she turned to survey her new bedchamber.

The room, with its heavy, old-fashioned furniture, was too large to be described as cosy, but with a welcoming fire crackling in the grate and the wine-red velvet drapes curtaining the windows and high, four-poster bed, it looked warm and comfortable. The walls had recently been covered with an elegant rose and cream flowered paper, the design of which had been repeated in silk on the daybed and dressing-table stool. Branches of silver candelabra provided plenty of light and the bed was made up with a feather-down quilt and a small mountain of plump pillows.

Every consideration for her comfort had been provided. And given the circumstances, her wedding day had been all she had expected. She had been cossetted and fussed over as much as a bride could wish, surrounded by family and friends and familiar minions all day, and now the quiet of her bedchamber was exactly what she wanted. No doubt Ravensdene had assumed as much, except. . .

Frowning slightly, she crossed the room to stand before one of the windows that looked out over the woods and a corner of the lake. It was dark outside. Her reflection stared back at her, an ethereal, ghost-like figure in a negligee of shimmering pearl silk and lace.

She was feeling quite strange, Sarah thought broodingly. Slightly let down, and yet nervous, on edge—although she had no fears that Ravensdene would open the door connecting their rooms and demand his husbandly rights.

That was the problem.

The totally unexpected thought literally sent her reeling. Her legs tottered and she was leaning against the windowsill for support before she knew it. Good heavens! Had she run *mad*? What was she *thinking*? She didn't want to find herself fighting off unwanted advances from her new husband. Of course she didn't. It was just. . .

She had *missed* him.

Sarah shook her head and told herself not to be ridiculous. Just because she had rarely seen Ravensdene, except in company, during their brief engagement, did not mean she had any reason to feel so unaccountably low in spirits. No doubt he had been busy hunting for his traitor. She, herself, had been constantly occupied; it was probably exhaustion that was responsible for her odd mood.

In an effort to boost her spirits Sarah thought back over the past three weeks, reminding herself that she had coped exceedingly well with all the myriad tasks of arranging a wedding at such short notice. Why, she had even routed Sir Ponsonby Freem who, when news of the engagement had reached his ears, had had the objectionable gall to follow her home from the village, where he'd been staying at the inn, in order to object to a state of affairs of which he did not approve.

Sarah shivered slightly and wrapped her arms about herself as she recalled the unpleasant incident. After a lengthy consultation about the wedding ceremony with the Reverend Butterlow, she had steeled herself to take the shortcut home through the woods—without a pistol—only to become aware, before she had gone half a mile, that someone was following her. The very softest rustle of bushes behind her had been singularly unnerving, reminding her far too vividly of the two previous occasions when she had thought someone was watching her.

It had also, however, made her angry. Scowling furiously, she had wheeled about, hands on hips, one small foot tapping on the ground while she waited. A minute later Sir Ponsonby had plodded around the corner, mopping his brow with a large handkerchief, his bulk clearly not suited to hiking through woods.

She had had the fleeting thought that her shadow had sounded much closer, but had been so incensed by then that the notion was completely forgotten as she had launched into a diatribe that shredded Sir Ponsonby's character and morals beyond recognition, before concluding with a scathing condemnation of gentlemen who spied upon and harrassed ladies who had made it clear they wanted nothing whatever to do with them.

Sir Ponsonby had retired positively crushed, unable to get a word in edgewise to defend himself. And she had done it all herself, she recalled, suddenly more cheerful. Despite the fact that, when he had been informed of the encounter, Ravensdene had had several pithy words to say on the subject of her confronting importunate suitors while quite alone, the truth remained that she had rid herself of a nuisance male without any help from her panther.

Her pleased smile promptly vanished. When had she started thinking of Ravensdene as *her* panther? That sort of reasoning could become very dangerous indeed. She would do better to remind herself that panthers did not make particularly suitable domestic pets. One could not tame them.

The thought was depressing. Now she was back to feeling lonely again. Yes, that was it. She felt. . .lonely. She *had* missed Ravensdene's company. Had missed the sense of companionship they had shared, the gleam

of amusement that could warm his eyes and soften the
stern line of his mouth. Had even missed the way he
issued her with orders and instructions.

A tiny sigh whispered past her lips. No doubt now
that they were married that sense of companionship
would return, but. . .

She wondered what he was doing right now; if he
was alone, too, and thinking as she was.

She was finally alone. He heard the faint click as the
outer door to Sarah's bedchamber closed behind her
maid.

Nick stood at his window, staring out at the glimmer
of moonlight that cut a swathe across one corner of the
lake and tried to remind himself that more than a
plaster wall separated him from Sarah. The reminder
did nothing to alleviate the rigid tension invading every
muscle in his body.

Just as well, he thought grimly. That tension was the
only thing holding him in check. He didn't dare release
it. Used to moving at blinding speed when his quarry
was in sight, he now had to summon every ounce of
patience he possessed so as not to frighten Sarah away.

He cursed softly, remembering that three weeks ago
he had not anticipated any problem with control. Damn
it, he'd never had a problem with control. But this
afternoon, when it had finally struck him that Sarah
was under his roof, within his reach, *his wife*, he'd had
to lock himself in his library, prey to a totally unexpected, unrelenting, grinding *need*.

Not that a contemplation of his grandfather's collection of ancient tomes had done any good. Need had
since coalesced into an equally unrelenting, agonising
ache. God knew how he was going to get any sleep
knowing Sarah was snuggled up in bed right next door.

A bitten-off groan escaped him at the image. He had to think of something else. It shouldn't be too difficult. After all, it wasn't as if Sarah was Marianne, and he was blindly in—

His thoughts skidded to an abrupt halt. Nick narrowed his eyes at the moonlit view in front of him. Funny where a man's mind could take him when he was strung out on a rack of frustration. He wanted Sarah. So badly he hadn't trusted himself to do more than dine with her tonight. He also felt a fierce need to protect her, to shield her from harm. But that was because she was his wife. A sweet, desirable, and very suitable wife. There was nothing else involved.

In fact, if he was going to stand here brooding, he would be more profitably engaged in pondering his spectacular lack of success in discovering more details about Amy Lynley's murder. His instincts told him there was more to the story than perhaps even Sarah realised, and he never ignored those instincts. However, Sir Jasper had been too distressed by the subject to discuss it at length, and when subtly questioned, Lady Wribbonhall had told him with unsubtle bluntness that the story would be better coming from Sarah if he would only be patient and gentle.

Patient and gentle. Right. He wondered what Sarah would say if he turned around this minute, strolled into the adjoining room and told her he'd come for a chat.

The idea had some merit—until he looked at the grim purpose in the hard face reflected in the window. She would never believe it. He didn't believe it himself. And if he didn't find a way of releasing some of his more primitive instincts, success would be as elusive as his sweet, desirable and very suitable wife.

* * *

'Good heavens, Winwick!' Sarah paused in the act of raising a slice of toast to her lips and stared towards the open window. After a night during which some very disturbing dreams had invaded her slumber, she had looked forward to a peaceful breakfast in company with her husband. Both husband and peace, however, were conspicuously absent. 'What on earth is that dreadful racket? It sounds like. . .'

'Shots,' supplied Winwick imperturbably, continuing to pour coffee as if hearing shots fired at the uncivilised hour of eight in the morning was a perfectly commonplace occurrence. 'His lordship has been practising for some time.'

'Practising! Whatever for? A siege?'

'Not that I know of, my lady. His lordship likes to keep his eye in, so he says, but while her ladyship was staying here she banned the habit.'

'I can readily understand why.' Sarah put her toast down and rose, the purposeful light of battle in her eye. 'Obviously his lordship is unused to having gently bred females in the house.'

Winwick permitted himself a tiny, satisfied smile. 'You will find the target set up in the garden furthest from the stables, my lady,' he instructed as she marched out of the room. 'His lordship didn't want the horses upset.'

'Didn't want the horses upset,' Sarah muttered, stalking towards the garden where she and Ravensdene had found the puppy. 'Are horses supposed to be more delicately—?'

Two more blasts in quick succession drowned her out as she reached her destination, but it hardly mattered. The sight that met her eyes had temporarily deprived her of speech anyway.

A target had been set up against the wall at the end

of the long path, and standing an impressive number of
yards from it, his back to her, was Ravensdene, a pistol
in each hand.

Sarah's eyes widened as he brought both weapons
up and fired them almost simultaneously. She had often
watched her uncle try his marksmanship with the guns
in his collection, but in the way Ravensdene was standing there, methodically sending ball after ball into the
centre of the target, she saw a cold, deadly efficiency
that chilled her to the bone.

When silence fell again she couldn't think of a thing
to say.

'I'm sorry if the noise disturbed you, little one,' he
said, turning to face her. 'How are you this morning?'

The polite enquiry, coming after such a demon-
stration of lethal skill, was strangely shocking. Sarah
had to struggle for a full minute to regain her sense of
outrage, not to mention her voice. She didn't bother
asking how he'd known she was there.

'What do you think you are doing, my lord?'

'Testing these new double-barrelled pistols,' he
replied casually, squinting down the barrels of the gun
in his left hand. 'You have to shift the aim slightly for
the second shot or it tends to fire low.'

Her blood was still running cold and he was discussing the merits of double-barrelled pistols? She glared
at him. 'How very inconvenient.'

'Yes, I knew you'd understand, being such a crack
shot yourself.' He looked up and grinned. 'Come and
try it. I'll reload for you.'

'Uh. . . I don't think. . .'

'We can move a bit closer to the target if you like. I
wouldn't want to have you at a disadvantage.'

'Have me at— Give me the gun!' Sarah was marching forward before she thought better of it, but if her

eyesight was keen enough to glue pieces of shell together, she reasoned defiantly, then she could hit a much larger target with a gun.

'Here you are. I've loaded only one barrel, but that should be enough for you.'

'Thank you, my lord. Good heavens, it weighs a ton!' The pistol dangling from her hand felt more like a cannon.

'They are heavier than your usual weapon,' Ravensdene observed, with what she considered to be a diabolical smile. A hideous suspicion began to dawn on her, but he spoke again before she could put it into words. 'Here, use both hands—like this.'

He moved to stand directly behind her, reaching around to put his hands under her wrists to brace them. Gritting her teeth, Sarah managed to raise the pistol to chest height.

'I'll take some of the weight,' he murmured in her ear. 'You just aim and pull the trigger.'

Just aim and pull the trigger? How had she ever managed to get herself into this situation? She couldn't even get her fingers to move; the muscles of her arms were too busy melting beneath the warmth of Ravensdene's hands. The rest of her was not faring any better. He felt huge behind her. Huge and solid, as unyielding as the high brick wall behind the target; and she was caged within his arms, surrounded, his sheer size alone enough to send all her senses into a turmoil.

'Do you need any help?' he asked.

Help? Of course she needed help! That dark purr, so close to her ear, turned every limb to water. If he wasn't virtually supporting her, she would collapse in a heap right there at his feet.

The image was positively humiliating. Bracing herself, Sarah squeezed her eyes shut and jerked her fingers convulsively on the trigger. There was a deafening roar, followed by a small startled shriek as she was sent staggering back by the recoil.

Dropping the pistol, she whirled and clutched at Ravensdene's coat in an effort to steady herself. And was immediately stunned by an intense longing to nestle closer as his arms came around her, to have him hold her more securely. There was strength here. Strength and safety. Here in his arms she was sheltered, protected.

'You missed,' he said.

Something in his satisfied tone got through the reverberations still ringing in her ears. Sarah stiffened as a blush rose from her toes to her brow. Here she was thinking about being cuddled by Ravensdene when all *he* was interested in was—

'Revenge!' she exclaimed, raising her head to glare up at him. 'Oh, you wretch! You knew I'd never fired a gun in my life, didn't you? Don't you dare laugh at me like that.'

His mouth twitched. 'You may have noticed, my sweet, that a laugh has not crossed my lips.'

'You're laughing with your eyes.'

He seemed to go very still, his eyes darkening even as she watched. Sarah stared, fascinated. She hadn't known a man's eyes could do that, go from glittering ice-green to a jade so dark it was almost black. His voice was darker, too. Deeper, rougher, it stroked over her heightened senses like a gentle hand, leaving a shivery kind of heat in its wake.

'Am I, Sarah?'

Sarah suddenly remembered how close they were, how she had wanted to be closer. But even as she felt her heart begin to flutter wildly, her colour fluctuate, Ravensdene released her and stepped back a pace.

'I'm afraid I couldn't resist seeing if you'd go through with it,' he confessed, turning away to retrieve his pistol. 'But I should have known. You don't lack for courage, Sarah.'

The words were uttered lightly, but she felt a distinct sensation of tension. As if the air surrounding him was vibrating slightly. Or perhaps it was her, still trembling.

'I don't?'

'No. It gives me great hope.'

'For what?'

He didn't answer or even glance her way, but his smile was slow, almost lazy, as he concentrated on pushing a ball into the chamber of the weapon he held. The sight of that smile caused something to stir deep inside her. Something that was not lazy at all.

'How. . .how did you know I had never fired a pistol, sir?' she stammered .

'It wasn't difficult. No experienced markswoman would take a pistol from someone and stuff it into her reticule without first checking to see if it was loaded.'

'Oh. Uncle Jasper's pistol.' She remembered the episode in his library. 'Very clever, my lord. Dear me, how long ago that seems.'

'An age.'

'Well, I wouldn't put it quite like that, but— What are you doing? I have to tell you, my lord, that if you are loading those pistols again with a view to firing them, I shall object most strongly. I do not intend to eat my breakfast to the accompaniment of shots. You will cease and desist at once.'

'I will?'

'Yes. I do not approve of violent pastimes.'

'Very wifely. But the exercise serves to release some rather, er, primitive instincts, you know.'

'Exercise? You were just standing there.' She shivered faintly at the remembered impression of a lethal, unstoppable force. 'If you feel the need for exercise, my lord, you will have to do something else.'

'Something else?' he murmured. The lazy smile came back. 'Do you have any suggestions, my love?'

'Winwick, from now on, when his lordship is practising his shots, we shall have the windows closed.'

'Yes, my lady.'

'No doubt we shall all grow accustomed to the noise.'

'If you say so, my lady.'

'Perhaps I could persuade him to take up cricket instead, if he feels the need to hit something.'

'I would not recommend it, my lady.'

'Well, I know his lordship once broke a window in here, but—'

'Worse, my lady. The ball also shattered his late lordship's coffee cup. He had been about to take a sip from it at the time.'

'Oh. No cricket.'

'I thought you said there were fish in this lake, my lord.'

'There are, but you have to cultivate a little patience. Stop complaining. It was you who wanted me to take up something quiet, remember? And you called me my lord again.'

'Oh. Well, sitting about in a boat for hours, while not being allowed to utter a word for fear of scaring the fish, is going to the other extreme, sir. . . I mean, Nick.'

'Hmm. There's definitely room for improvement.'

'No, Sarah. You have to hold the horseshoe like this.'

'But it feels so awkward.'

'Not as awkward as it's going to be if you hit me instead of the spike.'

'Really, Nicholas, how can I hit you when you're standing right behind me?'

'Don't call me Nicholas.'

'Your mother does.'

'Only when she wants to annoy me.'

'Oh. Well, Nick, then.'

'Better, but I think there's still a little way to go. Tell me, my love, have you ever driven a high-perch phaeton?'

'I don't think this is the proper way to drive a high-perch phaeton and pair, sir.'

'Probably not, but at least we won't end up in the ditch.'

'But what will people think if they see us driving about with your arms around me?'

'They'll think we're happily married.'

'Oh. Are you happy, Nick?'

'Yes, little one. That was excellent, by the way. I think we're ready to try a variation on the theme.'

'What? But I didn't do anything.'

'Patience, my love, patience.'

'Patience?'

'Trust me. These past few days I've become an expert on the subject.'

'Nick, what *are* you talking about?'

'Later.'

But the trouble was, Nick decided the day after the driving lesson, it was 'later' that was going to take his self-control to the very edge.

He sat back in his corner of the carriage and watched Sarah arrange the skirts of her antique-gold, braided

and frogged pelisse neatly about her ankles. A matching antique-gold bonnet framed her face, its jaunty
sable plume curling forward to mingle with her curls.
The sight of the feather almost caressing her soft cheek
made him want to wrench the whole thing off and do
some mingling himself.

He managed to cage his instincts. By dint of long
midnight walks through the woods and cold, early
morning dips in the lake he had so far kept his desire
for Sarah under some semblance of control, and he
wasn't going to ruin everything now because of a
provocative feather. Unfortunately, his restraint, not to
mention the more physical exertions he had inflicted
upon himself, had also succeeded in honing his body to
an even harder, more painful edge. Before another
week was out he was probably going to be driven
insane.

But he would do it, Nick swore silently. He had been
given a taste of success in the knowledge that Sarah no
longer retreated from his touch. The next step was
to awaken her to the possibility of a deeper intimacy
than friendship. To awaken her slowly, carefully, with
all the gentleness she needed before she could give
herself to him completely, no matter what it cost him
in willpower. Because this past week had shown him
something else.

The marriage he now wanted with her had become
too necessary for him to even contemplate failure.

'Do you know something, Nick?' Sarah stopped fussing with her skirts and bent a severe frown upon him.
'When you said "later" I thought you were going to
teach me an exciting new skill such as taking a fly off
the leader's ear with my whip, but instead we're driving
sedately along in a closed carriage.'

'Mmm-hmm.'

'That is not an answer. Why could we not have ridden over to visit Uncle Jasper?'

'Have I told you that you make a very charming countess, Sarah? Dictatorial, of course, but charming.'

'Dictatorial! I wish you will not go off at a tangent when I am talking to you, my lord. It is most distracting.'

He grinned. He didn't even mind her calling him 'my lord' now, he realised, when she said it in that delightfully disapproving tone. 'I am very sorry, my sweet, but to tell you the truth, I have a rather tricky question on my mind.'

Sarah was promptly distracted. She blinked at him in surprise, having no trouble, even in the muted light of the carriage, in seeing the devilish gleam in her husband's eyes. 'You do? Good heavens, whatever can it be?'

His grin became another of those slow, lazy smiles. 'I was trying to decide whether or not to kiss you. And if I do, whether that extremely fetching bonnet would be in danger of coming loose and striking me.'

Sarah was quite sure her mouth had fallen open. 'You were trying to decide. . .'

She could go no further. Her mind was quite unequal to the task of expressing the utter confusion of her thoughts.

'Yes.' Ravensdene reached out and took one of her hands in his. Still stunned, she let it lie limply in his grasp, even when he slipped his thumb beneath her glove and began stroking the inside of her wrist.

'It is quite permissable to kiss one's wife, you know. In a friendly, affectionate kind of way, of course.'

'Of. . .of course,' she echoed faintly. It was amazing how the light stroking of his thumb against her flesh could play such havoc with her thought processes. She should be feeling at least a little alarmed at the thought of Nick kissing her. Her heart was, indeed, beating rapidly somewhere in her throat, but all she could think of was the past week, in which she had known nothing but gentleness from him, and that sweet sense of companionship that drew her closer to him with every day they spent together.

And now he wanted to kiss her.

'Um. . .well, if you would like. . .that is to say, my bonnet is really quite secure, Nick.'

'In that case. . .' he murmured. And leaning closer, he brushed his lips over hers in a caress so light she barely felt it.

'Oh.' The tiny sound of disappointment escaped her before she realised he had moved back only a few inches. Blushing, tremulous, suddenly more uncertain than she had ever been in her life, she waited.

'Close your eyes,' he ordered huskily.

She obeyed. For an instant a feeling of defenceless-ness threatened to overwhelm her, but then she felt Nick's mouth on hers again and warmth banished the sudden attack of nerves. This time he lingered, letting her absorb the sensations of his lips pressed lightly to hers, the gentle caress of his breath across her mouth, the shimmering heat rippling upwards from the touch of his fingers on her wrist.

When he drew back again she was feeling quite inexplicably witless. Her eyes flew open to find him watching her.

'That was. . .very friendly,' she managed to utter in a voice completely unlike her own.

'Did you like it?'

'Well. . .yes. . .that is. . .'

'You don't sound very certain.'

'I suppose that is because I'm not used to such activities, my lord.'

'Oh, no,' he growled. 'You're not going to retreat behind "my lord" this time, sweet Sarah.' His glittering eyes, deepest emerald in the shadowy carriage, looked straight into hers. 'I see I shall have to kiss you again so you can make up your mind.'

Her gaze held by his, Sarah could only manage a small nod of agreement. 'That would be very helpful,' she whispered, just before his mouth covered hers.

His lips were slightly parted. She felt the difference immediately, and was as instantly shaken by an impulse to part her own. She trembled, torn between shyness and the delicious feeling of his mouth moving gently on hers. Somewhere in the back of her mind she doubted if any amount of kisses would clear the confused mists from her brain, because each kiss was so much more than the last. Sweeter. Warmer. Oh, the warmth, seeping through her bloodstream until she felt as if she might melt.

Then just before he drew back, she felt the tip of his tongue trace the line between her lips and the warmth became a sharp little explosion of heat striking deep inside her.

'I believe we have arrived,' Nick murmured, releasing her wrist and reaching for the door.

Sarah blinked. His voice held the intriguingly rough note she had heard once before, but the words were so commonplace that for several seconds her whirling mind could hardly make sense of them. 'Arrived?' She gazed blankly at the portico of the Grange. 'Oh dear, I do hope Uncle Jasper doesn't wish to play chess.'

Uncle Jasper did wish to play chess, but, to Sarah's relief, he was happy to challenge Ravensdene to a match. It was just as well, she reflected, watching them from her seat by the fire, because when she made an observation on the game that immediately caused her husband to grin and her uncle to stare at her as if he'd never seen her before, it became perfectly obvious that she was still in a fuzz-brained trance.

Matters had not improved two hours later when she mounted into the carriage for the ride home. Fortunately, her uncle had not seemed unduly worried by her distracted state. In fact, when she leaned forward to wave farewell, she decided he was looking particularly pleased with himself.

'Sir Jasper seemed quite well,' Nick observed, echoing her thoughts as the landau swept through the gates.

'Positively beaming,' Sarah agreed absently. She supposed she should feel rather more concerned that her voice still sounded as if she wasn't quite there, but she had just discovered something else even more astonishing. Being alone again with Nick in the close confines of the carriage was giving her some very unfamiliar, not to say shocking, ideas.

'Nick?'

'Hmm?'

She studied the reticule on her lap with rapt attention while twisting the ribbons around and around her fingers. 'Now that you have kissed me in a friendly, affectionate kind of way, do you suppose we shall exchange many more...um...?'

'Many more such kisses?' he concluded for her. She could feel his gaze on her face. 'Do you dislike the notion?'

'Oh, no! I would be very happy to... That is, such kisses do not have anything to do with...with those obligations we spoke of. Do they?'

He reached across the small space between them and covered her restless hands with one of his. 'Sarah, I

made this promise to you once before. Nothing of what
we share will have anything obligatory about it.'

'Oh.' She sent him a shy glance from beneath her
bonnet. 'What we share. That sounds so very agreeable,
Nick.'

'Does it, little one? Does that mean you would like
to share another kiss before we arrive home?'

'Yes, I would,' she breathed, her gaze now locked
with his. 'I would like that very much indeed.'

'So would I,' he murmured in a soft rasp that was
like a cat's tongue stroking down her spine. Or a
panther's tongue, she thought, quivering at the memory
of his tongue lightly tracing the seam of her lips.

'But this time—' he moved closer, studying the elaborate gold bow holding the ribbons of her bonnet in
place under one ear '—we'll dispense with this.'

Sarah couldn't stop the breathless little gasp that
escaped her lips as his fingers brushed the side of her
throat. Nick's expression didn't change, but she felt a
hard tension invade the hand still covering hers, an
almost violent restraint, as though he had been about
to tighten his grip at the small sound and had stopped
himself in time.

Was he so wary of frightening her, she wondered,
awed by the notion? Then the question vanished from
her mind when he removed her bonnet and placed it
on the opposite seat.

'You won't need this either,' he said softly, taking
the reticule from between her clenched fingers and
tossing it after her bonnet.

She trembled, suddenly feeling defenceless again. As
if a bonnet and a reticule were any sort of protection,
she thought, raising eyes wide with uncertainty to his.

'It's all right, little one,' he murmured. He touched
the side of her face, his fingers incredibly gentle as he

traced the curve of her ear, the delicate line of her jaw, the sensitive flesh just beneath.

Sarah's eyes half-closed, her lips parting on a tiny sigh of pleasure. She felt as if she was melting, all her limbs turning to warm honey.

'Sarah,' he whispered, making her look up at him.

He nearly groaned aloud when he saw the first signs of awakening desire in her eyes. And she didn't even know it, he thought. Didn't know what she was doing to him. Didn't know what she herself was feeling.

'I'm barely touching you,' he ground out, shaken by the sweet innocence of her response to the light caresses. 'Barely touching. . .'

'Nick?' It was a soft cry of nervousness and need.

'Yes,' he murmured against her lips. 'Like this, sweetheart.'

He brushed his mouth over hers again very gently, waiting for the tension to leave her body. Slowly her lashes closed, silky soft against his lips when he kissed them. He kissed her brows, her cheeks, the delicious curve of her upper lip and with every undemanding caress he felt her soften, felt her give more of her trust, until he drew her closer and she was in his arms, willingly, at last.

'You're so sweet,' he breathed. 'Sweet Sarah.'

'Nick?' she cried again. She sounded dazed, but the nervousness was gone. Her lashes fluttered open. 'You said you would kiss me.'

Despite the raging need pounding in his veins, he smiled down at her.

'I am kissing you.'

'No.' A faint blush tinted her cheeks. 'Like you did before.'

Good heavens, she thought weakly. What had he done to her? But she was too enthralled by the promise of feeling that exciting little sunburst of heat again to be shocked by her boldness.

He lowered his mouth until their lips were just touching. 'With my tongue?' he asked in the softest whisper.

She shivered convulsively, the words alone enough to cause tiny arrows of fire to dart about inside her, and without warning the pressure of his mouth increased as he tasted her lips with a gentle probing touch that made her limbs go weak. This time the tingling explosion of heat had her clinging to him. Her lips parted, seemingly of their own volition and he was inside her mouth, touching, stroking, possessing.

Sarah gave a muffled cry of shock, feeling the impact of the invasion with every part of her being.

He withdrew at once, soothing her with fleeting little kisses that feathered over her eyes and cheeks before returning to her mouth.

'It's all right, sweetheart,' he murmured. 'Don't be afraid. I'm only kissing you. Only kissing you, little one. You'll like it, I promise.'

'Nick, I—'

'Yes. Just like that. Let me taste you, Sarah. I won't hurt you. Let me—'

No, he wouldn't hurt her. She didn't know why she was so sure of that. He could be violent, deadly, but in the urgent, husky tone of his voice she heard a plea she responded to instinctively. A plea that reached everything that was intensely feminine in her.

She trembled as he drew back far enough to look down into her face. She raised dazed eyes to his, wondering what she would see there.

Darkness. His eyes were so dark, blazing with a green fire that in one searing second had touched her senses, reached into the closed place in her mind,

awakened something so deeply buried she hadn't
known it existed.

'Do you want me to stop?' he asked, his voice low
and tense with restraint.

Yes, restraint, she thought wonderingly. He was in
control. He hadn't hurt her. Had not even frightened
her, apart from that one moment in which she had felt
more startled than truly afraid.

'No.' Her lips framed the word. No sound came out,
but he understood. The fire in his eyes seemed to flare
higher, reaching out to enfold her as he bent to kiss
her again.

And then she couldn't see his eyes at all, because
her lashes fluttered down as his mouth closed gently
over hers.

CHAPTER TWELVE

THOSE kisses on the way home had really been quite extraordinary, Sarah reflected two days later as she arranged her collection of shells on the window ledges in the library. Not only had they taken over a large portion of her mind, rendering her prone to fits of abstraction at rather inconvenient moments, but just thinking about them stirred faint echoes of the deliciously thrilling sensations they had aroused.

Unfortunately, echoes were all she had. Since the interesting excursion to the Grange the other day, Nick had kissed her several times. Light good-morning kisses when they met at the breakfast table. Friendly good-night kisses when she left him in his library on her way to bed. And brief, affectionate kisses at various times in between. They were not, however, anything like the kisses on the way home.

She was very much afraid that those particular kisses were addictive. She wanted more. But Nick hadn't given her more. Despite the fact that she had done everything possible to tempt him, from shifting subtly closer whenever they were together, to touching him with shy, fleeting little forays of her hands at every opportunity. Neither method had worked. As far as she could see, he hadn't even noticed her tentative encouragement.

On the other hand, she could hardly blame him. She, herself, didn't fully understand why she should want to encourage him in the first place.

Sarah stepped back to see the effect of two large

spiralled shells on the ledge behind Nick's desk, while
her mind continued along a path that was far removed
from shells.

She should have felt threatened, afraid, uneasy at the
very least, at the thought of further intimacy with her
husband. After all, it was not as if she wasn't aware of
the dangers inherent in the subtle change in their
relationship.

But she was changing, too. Something was happening
to her. Something that had started weeks ago when she
had encountered a man of brutal strength and lethal
speed, and even through her almost mindless terror,
had believed him when he said he wouldn't hurt her.

Was that the difference? she wondered, struggling to
follow her line of reasoning to some sort of logical
conclusion. Was the relationship between a man and a
woman a simple matter of trust? She thought of all the
married women of her acquaintance, and realised with
rather startled bewilderment at not having seen it
before, that they all seemed to have survived the
experience. And in the case of Lydia Beresford, whom
she had met again during her engagement, rather more
than survived.

But then what of Amy? Had her sister trusted and
been betrayed? Or had Amy's flirtation with a man
who was bigger and stronger than her been nothing
more than the poor judgement of a wilful, headstrong
girl; a moment of foolishness that had cost her her life?

'You are looking very solemn, my love. What has
put such a frown on your brow?'

Sarah glanced up, her breath coming a little faster at
the familiar deep tones, as Nick strode into the library,
closed the door behind him and walked over to join
her at the desk. His green eyes narrowed on the newly
adorned ledge.

'Ah, I see you've found a home for more of your shells,' he observed blandly. 'What a good thing we have plenty of window ledges at the Place. I feared I would be obliged to resort to smashing some of the collection, accidentally of course, before we were overrun.'

Despite her unnervingly uneven pulse, Sarah had to laugh. Her amusement promptly vanished, however, when Nick bent to kiss the tip of her nose. A quick, friendly kiss. She had a sudden, insane impulse to demand to know why a man who was clearly at the peak of his masculine strength and power was content with a marriage of convenience.

Then she wasn't at all sure she wanted to hear the answer.

'There will be no more smashing of shells,' she said severely, taking refuge in raillery. 'Really, Nick, I had no idea that males were prey to such constant violent impulses. It must be extremely wear—'

She stopped dead, abruptly aware of what she had said.

He looked down at her, eyes narrowed again, searching. 'Indeed? I thought you were of the opinion that males were nothing else but violent.'

Sarah felt herself blush. She knew he was watching her with the waiting intensity that always reminded her of a big hunting cat, but she couldn't prevent her gaze going to his mouth. 'I know better now,' she whispered, conscious of her heart beating wildly in her breast. Something akin to panic fled down her spine. She hadn't intended to say that! At least not until she'd done a great deal more thinking. Those four little words could hold a myriad of meanings and she wasn't sure how Nick would take them. How could she be? She didn't know precisely how she had *meant* them.

Blushing more hotly than ever, she rushed into speech once more. 'I see you have some letters, my lord. Is there a note from Julia, or Lydia Beresford perhaps? She was going to write when they were all settled at Devenham Court. How very kind it was of Lord Devenham to invite the Beresfords to join his party. Especially as the purpose of the visit is for Julia and the Wribbonhalls to meet his mama and sisters.'

Nick didn't answer. He was too engrossed with the delicate tide of colour sweeping from Sarah's brow to the neckline of her dainty muslin dress, and in tormenting himself with images of his mouth following the same path. He wondered if the blush went as far as her breasts and nearly groaned aloud at the swift stab of desire that tightened his loins.

He wasn't used to restraint, damn it. These past few days had been sheer torture. He had forced himself to respond only casually to Sarah's shy, innocent advances in the hope of winning more of her trust, but he had discovered a rather fatal flaw in his scheme. The feel of her small hands on him played havoc with his already over-strained senses. His self-control was shot to pieces. Sarah now only had to brush past him and his entire body would clench in a spasm of need. But if he allowed himself to start making love to her in his present state and she called a halt, which was all too likely in *her* present state, he wasn't at all certain he would be able to stop.

Then he looked down into her clear amber eyes, their expression doubtful, half-wary, questioning his long silence, and knew he would always stop if she wished it. If it tore him apart he would stop.

'No, there's nothing from Devenham Court,' he forced himself to say, dragging his reluctant gaze back to the mail in his hand. The long-term picture, he reminded himself again. He also had a job to do. He'd never had any trouble concentrating on a job before. Why was it so damned difficult now? 'Only a letter from London, some correspondence from my agent at Ravensdene Hall and a note from the Sheringtons reminding us of their waltzing party later this week.'

'The Sheringtons' waltzing party?' she repeated, sounding so dismayed that the urge to toss the mail aside, take her in his arms and savour the sweet taste of her deliciously soft mouth again before he went out of his mind, was effectively doused. For the moment, at least.

'Nick, I think I should tell you—'

She broke off, overcome by a fit of coughing as Nick produced a heavily scented, gilt-edged invitation card and held it at arm's length. 'Here it is,' he murmured, grimacing. 'Reeks of jasmine.'

'Sophie's favourite perfume,' Sarah managed weakly, catching her breath at last. 'Nick, about the waltzing party—'

'We don't need to attend if you would truly dislike it. No one expects us to engage on a social whirl at this time. I'm sure Miss Sherington merely sent the reminder as a courtesy.'

'But you wish to go,' she murmured, seeing the truth in the faint frown drawing his brows together as he perused the note. And she knew he didn't wish to attend the party out of any desire to socialise; it was part of his job. The sudden intrusive reminder came as an unpleasant jolt. She was startled at the twinge of resentment she felt that his attention was so obviously elsewhere.

'Sherington Chase is the only estate of any size that I've yet to visit,' he explained almost absently. Then, as if suddenly recalling her presence, 'Not that I suspect

Lord Sherington particularly, but they live near the coast and our presence will give Figgins an opportunity to listen to any stable talk that may prove useful.'

'Especially as all the coachmen and grooms on the neighbouring estates have families who make their living from the sea,' Sarah added, forcing herself to match his cool tone. 'But you misunderstood me, Nick. It is not that I don't wish to go, precisely, but...the problem is that I do not waltz.'

'Good God, is that all? Don't concern yourself over the matter. The only man you'll be permitted to waltz with will be me.'

This unexpected but comprehensive edict had the totally predictable effect of once more robbing Sarah of breath. Especially as it was issued while its instigator was now glancing through the accounts from Ravensdene Hall.

'Well, I do not know how I am supposed to take that, my lord, but you still do not—'

The glittering intensity of his eyes when he turned his gaze on her was enough to make her forget the rest. All at once she had his undivided, utterly focused attention.

'It's called possessiveness,' he growled very softly. 'Get accustomed to it.'

Sarah's jaw dropped. Her mind reeled. *Possessiveness*? From a man who had been treating her like a *sister* for the past two days? Her vague feeling of irritation exploded into fully fledged outrage.

'Please do not put yourself to the trouble of exerting so much emotion on my behalf, my lord,' she stated haughtily, turning on her heel and beginning to stalk out of the room. 'If you had let me finish a moment ago, you would have heard me say that I do not waltz because I have never learned the steps, not because I wish to reserve the dance for my husband. Now, if you will excuse me, I will— *Nick*!'

Her startled cry was drowned out by the slamming of the door she had just opened. Sarah blinked at the sight of her husband, his large hand flat on the oak panels, barring her way, when she had left him at the other end of the library. He must have moved like lightning, she thought dazedly.

For a second his eyes held an expression that sent shivers racing all the way down her spine. She knew she had nothing to fear from him, but she had a sudden chilling vision of what was likely to happen to the traitor when Nick caught up with him. Then his face relaxed into a crooked, rueful smile that held its own particular dangers.

'Oh, sweetheart, don't look at me as if I'm about to attack you. I'm sorry. I'm afraid I've been guilty of venting my frustrations on you.' He removed his hand from the door and cupped the side of her face. 'Sarah, don't you know by now that I wouldn't hurt you for the world?'

'Frustrations?' she queried cautiously, not committing herself to answering that last loaded question until she knew just what frustrations he was referring to.

'Yes.' He seemed to hesitate, then glanced past her, indicating his abandoned correspondence with a quick movement of his head. 'I've just had word from London that, so far, no one has taken the bait they so optimistically left dangling in the files at the Foreign Office.'

'Oh.'

'Yes, "oh" is about all one can say on the subject. And since none of the local inhabitants have behaved in a suspicious manner, things have ground to an extremely irritating halt. It's a poor excuse for growling at you, I know, but—' the fingers against her cheek curled inwards, stroking her before he let his hand fall '—will you forgive me?'

'Well. . .' Sarah watched the hand that had touched her so gently clench into a tight fist at his side, and felt her pulse start to race as a rather daring idea occurred to her. 'Perhaps we could make a bargain, my lord?'

One black brow went up. He tilted his head, the glance he slanted down at her full of amused speculation. 'Bargain away, little one.'

Sarah swallowed the sudden knot in her throat. 'I'll forgive you, if you teach me to waltz,' she said, feeling quite uncharacteristically reckless. The slow smile he gave her made her wonder if she had just lost her normally sensible wits.

'Done,' he murmured before she could retract the offer. He held out his hand and bowed.

'*Now*?' she squeaked.

'Why not? Will you do me the honour, my lady?'

Well, when he put it like that. . .

Sarah smiled quite brilliantly and, remembering her observations at the Assembly, extended her left hand to his right. 'I should be delighted, my lord.'

Her formal manner and brilliant smile were then immediately shattered when Nick passed his left arm around her waist, drew her close and raised their clasped hands above their heads. Since he was so much taller than her the position had her arm stretching quite high. A feeling of intense vulnerability swept over her. His hand was warm and large, curved against her waist. He would only have to move it a little higher, she thought, shivering inwardly, for his thumb to brush the underside of her breast. And she would be unable to do anything to stop him.

She wished she knew if her shivers were shivers of alarm or excitement.

'Do you wish to hum a refrain?' he asked, with what she considered to be quite heartless ignorance of the fraught state of her nerves. 'Or shall we just go through the steps?'

'I think. . .just the steps,' Sarah managed through dry lips. She knew she was blushing hotly, but whether it was the relative helplessness of her position, her embarrassingly heated thoughts, or the feel of his hard body pressed to her side, she wasn't sure.

'It will be easier if you relax and let me guide you,' he murmured. 'I won't lead you into anything you're not ready for.' Then before she could search for any deeper implications in that remark, his hand tightened on her waist. 'Ready?'

She didn't get a chance to answer. Which was a good thing, Sarah mused in the hazy corner of her mind that was still capable of thought. Before she had so much as taken a decent breath, she was whisked into a whirling, twirling series of manoeuvres that had her stumbling blindly through the first steps while she listened to a spate of instructions that made her dizzy.

Fortunately for her reeling senses, sheer necessity had her pulling herself together before she tripped over her own feet. Embarrassment spun away as the book-lined walls whipped past her bemused gaze. She discovered, in fact, that it was impossible to feel embarrassed when one was being whirled about the room by a husband issuing commands such as 'Two to the left!' 'Right!' 'Turn!' in the voice of a parade-ground sergeant.

When they came to a halt several minutes later, Sarah felt quite breathless and her head was still spinning, but the basic steps of the waltz were indelibly imprinted upon her brain.

'There, how did you like that?' Nick asked, sounding as if he had not exerted himself in the least. There was a smile in his voice, but Sarah didn't have enough energy left to take affront at it.

'Most. . .most exhilarating,' she gasped, unconsciously leaning against him while the library walls gradually returned to their proper places.

'Of course, that is only one way of dancing the waltz,' he went on. His arm tightened with a slow but inexorable pressure about her waist and he drew her around to face him. 'In Vienna, a few people are starting to waltz like this.'

Sarah looked up. There was less than an inch of space between them. Her hand, released from its position aloft, rested against his chest. Against her palm his heartbeat was strong and steady. He wasn't even breathing hard, she realised.

'How. . .how very shocking,' she whispered.

His wicked smile made something warm and tingling uncurl in the pit of her stomach. Suddenly the library felt far too small. She felt far too flushed. And Nick felt far too big, too strong, too close.

'Not for us,' he reminded her. 'We're married.' His lashes lowered, half-shielding the intent expression in his eyes, and he murmured, 'How do you feel?'

Sarah swallowed and thought about it. 'Small,' she produced in a similar-sounding voice.

The curve of his mouth was inexpressibly tender as he gazed down at her. 'You are small,' he said, his tone the deepest, darkest purr she had ever heard it. 'Very small. Very soft. Very delicate.' He lifted his free hand to lightly trace the fullness of her lower lip with his thumb before lowering his mouth to hers. 'That's why I'm going to be very, very gentle with you.'

Every nerve in Sarah's body sprang into quivering life as Nick's mouth brushed hers. He was going to kiss her. Oh, at last. Already a heart-shaking excitement was racing through her, causing the echoes of his previous kisses to fade into insignificance. She gave a small yearning murmur, her lips parting beneath his in instinctive invitation, her hands clinging to the powerful breadth of his shoulders.

His arms closed around her, steel bands holding her tightly against him, so tightly that the low sound he made as his tongue stroked into her mouth vibrated through her entire body. She trembled uncontrollably, all the strength going out of her limbs as Nick took her mouth with a slow, deep possession that made her feel weak and languid and yet more intensely alive that she had ever felt before.

And she was kissing him back. Unknowing, unthinking, drowning in sensation, seduced by the intimate penetration and retreat of his tongue until she was kissing him as hotly, was holding him as tightly, until every hard muscled contour of his body was imprinted on her softer curves.

Every hard muscled contour. . .

The stunning awareness of rampant masculine desire hit her with a force that made her gasp. But even as she tensed, Nick broke the kiss, swung her up into his arms and strode across the room to sit down in an armchair large enough to accommodate both of them. He cradled her on his lap, pressing her head against his shoulder.

'Hush, little one.' His voice was soft and husky, in stark contrast to the coiled steel of muscles held under rigid control. 'Is that better?'

Sarah nodded. She couldn't stop shaking, but nor could she stop clinging to him. He was danger, safety, terror, excitement. The blatant evidence of his arousal brought all her doubts and fears rushing back, and yet she wanted. . .

Dear God, she didn't know what she wanted. She was being seduced all over again even as he held her. The violently leashed power beneath her hands was an enticement she couldn't resist when he cradled her so carefully. Her fingers were moving almost of their own accord, kneading iron-hard muscles, pressing closer to the heat burning through the layers of clothing he wore.

'It's all right, sweetheart. Don't tremble so. I know you felt what kissing you does to me.' He made a sound that was not quite a laugh and brushed his mouth across her curls. 'Impossible not to feel it. But you don't have to be afraid. I only want to kiss you. . . touch you. . . Will you let me do that, Sarah?'

'That's all?' she whispered, anticipation and apprehension all but stealing her voice. She should be saying no and running from the library. He would let her go. She knew it as surely as she could feel his heart thudding against her breast. Was it that knowledge alone that kept her there in his arms?

'That's all,' he echoed, holding her closer. 'It'll be better this way, you'll see. You won't feel— I won't frighten you.'

'Nick, I don't know if I am frightened. At least. . .' She gave a confused little laugh that was as ragged as his had been and hid her face against his shoulder. 'I don't know what I'm feeling anymore. I don't know *anything*.'

He touched her chin with the edge of his hand, gently raising her face to his. She trembled again at the heat blazing in his eyes when he looked at her mouth.

'Do you want to find out?' he asked very low.

Sarah tried to speak and couldn't. Nervousness held her utterly still, but awakening desire and something more, something she couldn't name, called to her on a deeper level. She lifted a hand to his face, letting her fingers touch his mouth as if the answer lay there. Perhaps it did, she thought vaguely, feeling him tense even more beneath her caress. Strength and gentleness. Brutality and tenderness. She had thought they could never merge in the one man, but now. . .

'Yes,' she whispered.

The sigh had scarcely passed her lips when she felt his arms flex. With a groan that sounded as if it had been torn from deep within him, he pulled her closer and touched his mouth to the soft flesh beneath her ear.

Surprise held Sarah motionless. Half-anticipating another deep possession of her mouth, the tender caress took her completely unawares. She softened against him, her eyes closing, as he trailed lingering kisses along the line of her jaw and down to her throat, warming her, tasting, cherishing. Her head fell back and she felt his muscles bunch and shift beneath her as he turned slightly so she lay back against the high curved arm of the chair.

Dimly she realised that the position made her more vulnerable to him, but the waves of heat flowing through her swept all rational thought aside. He touched his tongue to the pulse beating wildly at the base of her throat and she shuddered in helpless, sensuous response. He traced the delicate bones beneath her flesh while his mouth went lower, and weakness invaded her whole body. Every muscle softened, went limp. She whimpered and didn't know if it was in protest or pleasure.

'Yes,' he whispered, raising his head to look down at her. 'Just relax, my little Sarah. Let me love you.'

He began to kiss her again. Long, slow kisses that went on and on until she had no awareness of anything save his mouth on hers, the warmth of his fingers stroking her throat, and a need that was growing more urgent with every second.

She shifted, suddenly hot and restless. Her breasts felt full, the nipples tingling. In some distant part of her mind she thought she ought to be shocked at her own response. There was a reason why she shouldn't be doing this, but she couldn't think, couldn't remember it. Needs she had never known before were overwhelming her. She wanted Nick to touch her there, where the tingling was becoming a sweet torment, knew without knowing that he could satisfy the strange yearning within her. Oh, if he would only touch her. . .only touch her. . .

Then her breath unravelled in a broken cry of pleasure as he stroked his fingers across her breasts.

The sound of her own voice startled her. Her eyes flew open to find his gaze on her, narrowed, glittering, utterly focused.

'Nick?' she whispered, her voice shaking. She didn't know if he even heard her, so absorbed was he.

'Again,' he murmured, and it was not a question. His hand brushed the tips of her breasts once more, but lightly so that she arched, instinctively seeking a firmer touch.

'Is this what you want, little one?' He bent to kiss her, so swiftly that Sarah didn't have time to answer, even had she been capable of coherent speech. For a moment the kiss distracted her, then she tensed, gasping, as she felt Nick slide his hand beneath the neckline of her gown and chemise and cup the soft flesh he had been tormenting.

'It's all right,' he said hoarsely, the arm beneath her back tightening as if he was afraid she might struggle. 'I only want to touch you. I have to... Oh, God, Sarah... Sarah...'

Her lips parted on his name but no sound came out. When had it become impossible to speak, to see, to breathe? She could only feel, feel the heavy warmth of his big hand surrounding her breast, the exquisite arrows of pleasure darting through her with every stroke of his thumb over her nipple.

'Am I hurting you, sweetheart?'

His voice, low and rough, penetrated the hazy clouds surrounding her consciousness, making Sarah aware of the tiny sounds coming from her throat. Shameless, she thought vaguely. She couldn't even remember when he had loosened her clothes. She should stop him, open her eyes and say something, but it was too much trouble, easier just to murmur, to let the pleasure and warmth enfold her.

'No,' she whispered, and shivered, wondering if that was really the truth. He wasn't hurting her, and yet the strangest ache pulsed deep inside her. The chair was suddenly too small, too confining. She felt an urgent need to lie down, to have him stretch out beside her, to have him touch the ache, satisfy it... *somehow*. 'Oh, Nick...'

'This?' he murmured, and, lowering his head, he took the rosy, pouting tip of her breast into his mouth and gently tasted her.

Sarah almost fainted beneath the onslaught of sensations. She cried out, her lower body moving in a helpless rhythm that echoed every hot caress of Nick's tongue on her sensitive flesh. She felt his arms tighten, felt him move against her, and suddenly he was touching her in a way that wrenched a very different cry from her. A high, panicked sound that held shock, pleasure and terrified memory in equal measure.

Nick heard the shock, and the fear, and her cry went through him like a dagger plunging straight to his heart.

He stopped instantly, cursing himself savagely for a fool while he held Sarah against him, murmuring words he didn't even hear. God, what was he doing? He hadn't meant to take her this far; had intended to arouse her only gently, to awaken her gradually to his touch. Not to drive her into panic-stricken flight because his blood was pounding in his veins, his entire body was one vicious, grinding ache and he'd been only seconds away from taking her right there on the library floor.

The library floor, for God's sake! He must have been mad to start anything here. He hadn't even locked the door.

'It's all right,' he groaned. 'It's all right. Don't be frightened, darling. It's finished, right here, right now. You're safe. You're safe with me, Sarah.' If he repeated it often enough, maybe he'd believe it. Maybe she would.

'I know,' she half-sobbed into his shoulder. 'I know I'm safe. I'm sorry. Nick, I didn't know. . . I couldn't . . .it felt. . .'

'Sshh,' he murmured, rocking her gently. 'It's all right.'

She shook her head almost fiercely and clung to him as if she wanted to crawl beneath his clothes to the underlying warmth of his body. 'I feel so strange. Scared, but. . .not really. . . Oh, I don't *know*!'

It took Nick a full minute to realise what she was saying. When his mind finally grasped the fact that, far

from succumbing to panic-stricken flight, Sarah was
being torn apart inside by a battle between fear and
her own awakening senses, he had to clench his teeth
against the torrent of desire that swept over him. He
surfaced to find her struggling to right her clothing
without exposing any more of herself to his gaze.

Too late, he thought, stifling a groan as she managed
to pull the lace-trimmed strap of her chemise over one
shoulder, hiding the flushed curves of her breasts. The
sweet, hot taste of her still lingered on his tongue,
making him crave more, but this wasn't the place—or
the time—to ease the turmoil inside her by finishing
what he'd started.

'Here,' he said, grimacing at the low, hoarse sound
that emerged from his throat. 'Let me.'

She flinched away from his hand, shaking her head,
not looking at him. 'No. I can do it. Let me go, Nick.
Please.'

One glance at her averted face had him complying,
but as he set her on her feet he stood also, keeping a
steadying arm about her waist. Her hands were shaking
so much she had to abandon the attempt to tie the
laces of her chemise; when she reached for the tiny
buttons at the back of her gown, he couldn't stand it
any longer.

'Damn it, let me help you,' he rasped, brushing her
hands away and moving to stand behind her. He could
tell by the way she was trembling that she was having
to fight not to flinch away from him again.

And he couldn't think of one damned thing to say.
He wanted to comfort her, but sensed that comfort
would overset her precarious control. He wanted to
snatch her up into his arms and carry her upstairs to
bed, but that was out of the question. He wanted to

put his fist through the nearest available object, but knew only too well what that would do to her.

In any event Sarah didn't give him a chance to do anything. As soon as the buttons of her gown were securely fastened she flew to the door and yanked it open.

'I have to go,' she stammered, looking everywhere but straight at him. 'Mrs Winwick. . .menus. . .'

The door slammed behind her as she fled.

'*God damn it to bloody hell!*'

Nick wheeled and lashed out with his clenched fist, sweeping everything on the mantelpiece to the floor. Candelabra, vases and various small ornaments flew across the room and hit the side of his desk with a resounding crash. The action served to release a totally insignificant fraction of the emotions raging within him.

He slammed both fists down on the denuded ledge and stared at the floor. God in heaven, what had Sarah done to him? He had never lost control of himself like that. *Never*!

Behind him the door opened again.

Nick turned so swiftly that the newcomer froze in the doorway. Then his gaze went to the wreckage on the floor. He frowned in disapproval.

'Never mind that,' Nick snapped. 'What the devil do you want, Figgins?'

The groom stepped into the library with all the cautious approach of a deer who knows a predator is nearby. He closed the door carefully behind him, an action that immediately drew his master's brows together.

'Thought you might be interested in seeing some hoofprints, me lord,' he murmured. 'But if I've come at an inconvenient time. . .'

'No.' Nick walked over to a small table near the door

and reached for the brandy decanter thereon, fully
aware that he had never resorted to finding answers in
a bottle of brandy in his life. Not even when—

He replaced the decanter with a thump and turned.
He might as well be distracted by Figgins as anyone.
Sarah needed some time. And so did he.

'What hoofprints?' he demanded. 'There are
hoofprints all over the place. At least there should be
if my grooms are doing their job exercising my horses.'

Figgins ignored this growled aside with magnificent
disdain. 'Not those sort of hoofprints, me lord,' he said.
'Actually, 'twere young Peake who found 'em. As nice
a set as you would like to see, in that marshy bit o'
ground beyond the lake. Lucky for us he took it upon
himself to show me the spot and explain that it ain't
healthy to tether horses in that kind of place.'

'He must know you would not do so.'

'Well, *you* know it, sir, but there's no getting away
from it. A horse stood there for some considerable
time, I'd judge. There's a few old trees about that
would give cover. Nice place to watch the house—if'n
someone wanted to. O' course, Peake didn't think of
that. Blind as a bat, poor lad.'

Knowing of the rivalry that existed between Figgins
and the Peakes, father, son and grandson, who had
ruled the stables for decades, Nick merely narrowed
his eyes. 'Go on.'

'Well, it looked to me like whoever it was tried to
brush the prints away, but you know how it is in that
type of ground, me lord. Unless you do a good job of
marks that deep, as soon as the moisture seeps up
again there you have it. Four nice little horseshoe-
shaped puddles.'

'Any tracks leading away?'

'Not so's you'd notice,' Figgins answered. 'The

ground dries out again fairly close by and the rides are full of tracks, coming and going. I think he went south.' He frowned meaningfully. 'Towards the Grange.'

'Or the coast.'

Figgins shrugged.

'All right, Figgins, we'll take a ride along the coast and then backtrack. See what we can find. You've done well, although I can't see why anyone would be watching this place if the bait in London hasn't been taken.'

'Something from an old job?' Figgins suggested.

Nick considered then shook his head. 'I doubt it. Up until six months ago I hadn't been in England for twelve years. Only a very few highly placed men knew of me and—'

He stopped, remembering that he had said much the same thing to Devenham some weeks ago. 'On the other hand, the men we're looking for *are* highly placed, and astute enough to smell a trap and leave it untouched while they remove any obstacles. I warned them of that possibility, but you might as well speak to a stone wall as government ministers. Let's go, Figgins.'

'Aye, sir, but are you sure it ain't inconvenient? I couldn't help but notice—'

'Figgins, shut up.'

'Aye, sir. But it ain't as if he's out there now in broad daylight, and the little lady looked a mite upset when I passed her in the hall and—'

'*Figgins*!'

'Eh? Oh, aye. I forgot. I *should* have said, her little ladyship. Sorry, me lord.'

Nick raised his eyes to the heavens and gave up.

Arms wrapped around her waist as though to hold herself together, Sarah paced across her bedchamber to the window, turned and paced back to the door. She repeated the sequence several more times, her feet moving faster and faster with each lap.

It didn't help. Her pacing was doing nothing for the heated restlessness quivering inside her and no amount of arm-gripping was banishing the feeling that she was about to fall apart.

How *could* she have behaved like that?

Abandoned. Shameless. In broad daylight! In the *library*! She was horrified!

At least, she amended with rather despairing honesty, her mind was properly horrified, but her traitorous body persisted in remembering the incredible sensations aroused by Nick's hands and mouth. Nervous, yes even frightened though she was, she hadn't wanted him to stop. She had *liked* it.

Sarah stopped pacing, sat down on the nearest chair and put her face in her hands. Unfortunately, her fevered brain continued to roll pictures past her closed eyes. He had looked at her half-naked body, touched her, oh, heavens, kissed her. . .

She sprang up and resumed her pacing, back and forth, back and forth, faster and faster, until her skirts were flying out behind her. If their marriage had not been one of convenience she thought she might not feel so dreadful. But it was. At least. . .

She fetched up short beside the bed. Across the room her startled reflection stared back at her from the dressing-table mirror.

If their marriage was one of convenience, why had Nick started kissing her in a manner that had about as much resemblance to a friendly affectionate peck as a mild summer breeze to a raging tempest? Why, for that matter, had he continued to kiss her and touch her when he knew her views on the subject?

Not that she'd been raising her voice in support of

those views at the time, Sarah reminded herself, trying to be fair. But had Nick merely lost control for a moment, or did he want to change the terms of their marriage?

She continued to stare straight ahead as she considered the question, conscious that her heart was beginning to race again. Had this past week shown him that friendship was not enough? After all, he was physically at the peak of his strength, and if Lady Wribbonhall was to be believed, had once loved passionately. Given that, did he truly want her? Could he want a real marriage? Could he even...oh, was it possible? Could he even be falling in love with her—as she was with him?

Sarah gasped in shock. She staggered against the bed, one hand grabbing for a bedpost as her knees gave way. Clutching the polished oak, trembling as if she had a fever, she lowered herself to the quilt, her stunned gaze still fixed on her ashen-faced image in the mirror.

She loved him.

She watched her eyes widen in astonishment, saw her lips part as though she would say the words aloud. No sound emerged, but it didn't matter. Her love for Nick was *there*. Deep in her heart. Had been there for a long time, blossoming, growing, waiting to be acknowledged. If she hadn't been so afraid, so cowardly, she would have recognised what was happening to her weeks ago. She wasn't *falling* in love. She had fallen. She was helplessly, irrevocably, utterly in love with a man who might never want anything more than friendship from her, and who thought she wanted the same thing.

But then, if she had changed...

Could he?

The question crept into her mind, tentative, silent, terrifying in its tremulous hope. She did not have an answer. She thought Nick enjoyed her company, he was kind to her, gentle with her. . .

'Oh-h-h.' The soft exclamation whispered through the quiet room like a sigh. Sarah leaned her forehead against the bedpost and trembled anew. Yes, so gentle with her, as if he knew how afraid she was of male passions. How could she not have fallen in love with him?

And for a few brief, shockingly exciting minutes there in the library, he had at least desired her.

Until he had remembered who she was.

The thought came out of nowhere, threatening to bury her fragile hope beneath a pall of blackest gloom. Not even the reminder that Marianne had been dead for over ten years eased the painful fist squeezing her heart. One indisputable fact remained. Nick had stopped making love to her. She had all but thrown herself at him and he had stopped.

Sarah made a small sound of pain and bent over, rocking herself until the first sharp pangs abated. The moment of despair didn't last long. She didn't let it. Didn't dare. Better to remind herself that she had suffered worse than this and survived—and not by languishing about on beds.

But what was she to do? How did one go about fighting the ghost of an angel?

She sat there for a while, thinking over the past several weeks, searching for clues that might give her some hint of her husband's feelings. That was one thing in her favour, she thought, a little cheered. Nick *was* her husband. And he was very much a man. Men had rather primitive impulses. It stood to reason, therefore, that even the most controlled male would sometimes yield to those impulses.

Sarah stared at the mirror, considering that logical point of view. A second later she blinked, startled to see a very thoughtful, determined expression come over her countenance. It was rather similar to the expression Julia had worn when she'd made her write that note to the dowager Lady Ravensdene.

Then her eyes went wide again with astonishment. Good heavens! Surely she wasn't contemplating. . .

It was impossible. She couldn't do it. She didn't know the first thing about tempting a man. At this moment the very thought of what had transpired in the library was enough to make her wonder how she was even going to face Nick again without blushing from her brow to the soles of her feet.

And she was still afraid. That hadn't changed. She loved Nick, she trusted him, but the images of Amy were still there in her mind, fainter perhaps by day, but ripping apart the veils of sleep at night so that she woke often, sobbing and shaking with a terror that never went away.

Sarah jumped to her feet and stood shaking, fiercely resisting the urge to pace again. Pacing would not help her escape from the nightmare that was always at her heels, that had sprung to her mind the instant she'd considered a real marriage. Nor could she think rationally while in the grip of fear. She needed to do something quiet, something that would keep her from reliving those heated moments in Nick's arms and wondering if it had been like that for Amy before everything had been destroyed because she had pushed a man too far.

Sarah shuddered and tried to push the memories aside. Her restless gaze caught the corner of a box visible through the open door of her dressing room. It was one of the many chests brought from the Grange, and had yet to be unpacked, but she knew what it contained.

Her gaze sharpened. Yes, the very thing. Her sketching equipment. She would take her table and stool and sketchbook down to the lake and draw. She would empty her mind of fiercely passionate, green-eyed panthers and fill it instead with images of trees and lake and sky.

She suddenly realised that, until that instant of shock when Nick had touched her so intimately, her mind had not been filled with images of her sister.

The knowledge sent her scurrying for her pencils. She wouldn't think about it. At least not right now. She was too confused. There was too much she didn't know. About Nick, his intentions, his feelings. . . And her own love was too new, too painfully vulnerable; a butterfly just emerged from its chrysallis, unable to fly, fragile and defenceless.

She needed time. She needed to restore the calm balance of her mind. And then she would be able to think about marriages of convenience, and what exactly Nick had meant when he'd offered for her, and what she was going to do if the answer was not the one she wanted.

There hadn't been anything unusual about the tracks beyond the lake. Nothing that would make it easy to recognise a particular horse or to follow it. The entire afternoon had been a waste of time, Nick concluded grimly as he and Figgins returned from an inspection of the woods to the north of Comberford.

They had ridden for some distance, circling the grounds without finding any further signs that a rider had been watching the house. Whoever it was had obviously done so under cover of darkness, and had been careful to go to ground some distance away where the appearance of a stranger would not occasion comment that might reach the wrong ears.

He frowned at the thought, unable to rid himself of the notion that he had missed something rather vital in his observations on the case. But foremost on his mind at that moment was finding Sarah and setting things to rights.

Patting his horse absently, Nick dismounted and with a quick word to Figgins, strode towards the house. He shouldn't have left Sarah alone. All afternoon he'd been haunted by her distress, her flushed, averted face, the way she had trembled and shrunk from him.

Damn it, she hadn't even been able to look at him. He should have followed her, taken her in his arms no matter how she protested, and admitted that he'd intended to seduce her from the start because he wanted their marriage to be real.

That was what he was going to do right now, Nick promised himself, bounding up the front steps. He flung open the door and strode down the hallway. Then when she forgave him for deceiving her—and he wouldn't let her go until she did—he was going to set out to seduce her all over again.

His plan received a slight set-back when he discovered a minute later that Sarah wasn't in her bedchamber. But she had been. An empty box lay in the middle of the room. It looked as if its contents had been removed in something of a hurry.

Nick strode to the window and glanced out. He saw Sarah immediately. She was seated on a low stool beside the lake, a folding drawing-table set up before her, and she was sketching.

Sketching! As if nothing untoward had happened!

A volatile mixture of rage, frustration and desire surged through him at the peaceful scene. He turned on his heel and retraced his steps, meeting Winwick halfway down the stairs. The butler took one look at his face and flattened himself against the stair-rail. Nick scarcely noticed him. He crossed the hall in two strides, slammed open the library door and stalked towards one of the french windows that opened onto the gardens.

He had just stepped onto the terrace when the shot rang out.

CHAPTER THIRTEEN

SARAH heard the explosion from the woods less than twenty yards away and half-rose from her seat. Her hand was outstretched, about to put down her pencil when she saw a blur of movement from the corner of her eye. Before she could turn her head she was hurled from her stool, through the air and onto the ground.

She landed, unhurt but winded, on top of her assailant. 'Nick!' she gasped, stunned recognition restoring her voice.

It was all she had time for. He rolled, covering her with his body. 'Are you all right?' he asked very softly.

'Well, I was until—'

'Shhh.' His hand covered her mouth lightly and he raised his head, seeming to listen.

His warning was unnecessary. Sarah had ceased to speak the moment she registered the overwhelming sensations aroused by the feel of his weight on her. There was no time to be afraid. Warmth and weakness invaded every limb. Then she heard someone running along the path from the stables and tensed again.

'It's all right,' Nick murmured, releasing her mouth. 'It's Figgins. Stay down. Stay right here and don't move until I come back for you.'

'But—'

His green eyes blazed down into hers. 'Don't move!' Each word was enunciated with a savage clarity that silenced her instantly, then he was gone.

Sarah contemplated the greyish, lowering sky above her and wondered if she had managed to fall off her stool by herself, hit her head and become delirious. Hurrying footsteps and anxious voices reassured her that she was awake and lying flat on the lawn while waiting for her husband to return from who knew where.

'My lady! Lawks a'mercy! What happened? We heard a shot and that there Figgins goes rushing off, though I told him 'twas only his lordship firing at the target he's got set up in the garden—'

'I'm all right, Peake. Oh, heavens! Why is everyone running out of the house? Winwick, too. Have you all gone as mad as— Ouch!' Sarah sat up gingerly, rubbing a bruised knee. She assumed that since she was now surrounded by loyal retainers, Nick would not object to her moving. It was a mistake.

'Damn it, Sarah—'

She glanced over her shoulder to see Nick striding from the woods towards her. His face was a mask of controlled fury and something else she didn't recognise, and in that precise instant, as their eyes met, the significance of the shot hit her with stunning force.

She sprang to her feet and ran to meet him, everything else forgotten in the terrible fear seizing her heart. Seconds later, sudden memory had her halting as if she had run headlong into a wall. Her voice was barely audible, as if all the air had been knocked out of her body.

'Nick.' She extended a hand, saw it shake, withdrew it. 'You're safe.'

He caught her by the shoulders. 'Of course I'm safe, you little idiot. I thought I told you to stay down.'

Her laugh was a ragged sound of shock and confusion. 'It upset the servants. I think they thought I was dead, just lying there.'

'Oh, God, don't—' Ignoring the crowd behind her,

he pulled her into his arms. 'Come on, let's get you into the house.'

'But, Nick, what happened? Where did Figgins go? Who. . .?'

'Hush. Later.' He laid a finger over her lips, the gesture silencing her more surely than his words. Fear lanced through Sarah again, settling like a sickening, ice-cold lump in her stomach, as she thought of traps and traitors, and that while panthers were predators they could also be hunted.

She pushed the thought away in sheer self-defence, listening only vaguely as Nick questioned the servants and gave orders. Someone picked up her scattered pencils and the small wooden stool. Winwick, looking pale and worried, retrieved her sketchbook. Nick let her go long enough to fold her drawing-table. She saw him run a finger around one corner of the wood before he tucked it under his arm and reached for her.

'You're going straight upstairs to your room and have your maid prepare you a warm bath,' he said, as the little procession started for the house. 'Then you're having dinner on a tray in bed.'

'But—'

'No arguments. You've had a shock.' His eyes met hers. 'Several shocks.'

Sarah felt the blush she had anticipated earlier suffuse her face. She looked away, praying he wouldn't mention what had happened earlier, hoping desperately that he would.

'There's nothing to worry about,' he murmured. 'I'll join you upstairs after dinner and then we're going to talk.'

Talk? That should prove interesting, she thought, beginning to feel slightly light-headed. What would they talk about? His precise definition of a marriage of convenience? Her conviction that he had found it so easy to stop making love to her because she was not the woman he loved?

Perhaps a discussion on those two points would be helpful after all. She might then be able to put into better perspective the mind-shattering revelation that had just burst upon her. That she would do anything, risk anything, to hold onto whatever Nick had left to give her. Because the past few minutes had shown her, with devastating clarity, what it would do to her to lose him.

Nick stood in the quiet, dimly lit bedchamber, looking down at his sleeping wife.

She appeared very small and vulnerable, curled up beneath the covers of the big four-poster. Her hair was a swathe of sable silk spilling across the pillows, her lashes soft fans of the same hue against her cheeks. One little hand was tucked under her chin, the fingers curling inwards.

The muscles in his gut clenched hard as fierce desire and tender protectiveness surged through him on a tide of emotion that nearly brought him to his knees. She was so innocent, and so sweetly seductive in her innocence. And if that shot had been an inch closer he could have lost her.

The part of him that was sheer, primitive savagery stirred restlessly, but his mind was ice-cold and steady. Had been from the moment he had seen the damage done to Sarah's drawing-table and had known that the intended victim had not been himself, but her. Since then he had examined and discarded theories with grim, relentless logic, searching for the one fact that eluded him until he was left with the only thing that made sense.

There were still two questions hanging over his theory. He had sent Figgins off to London for one answer; the other...

He gazed down at Sarah again and for the first time in years felt more than fleeting regret for what he had to do. She stirred, as though sensing the bitter emotion within him, but didn't wake.

Stifling a rough sound, Nick took off his coat and tossed it over a chair near the fireplace, then pulled another chair closer to the bed and sat down. He yanked off his boots and stretched his legs out. He might as well make himself as comfortable as possible; it was going to be a long night. But he couldn't bring himself to waken Sarah just yet. Let her sleep before he had to force her into the dark memories that lay trapped inside her—and that without any certainty of success. Let her sleep before he had to tear her apart to keep her safe.

Savage rage stirred again when he thought of the man who had threatened her life, and this time he let it prowl closer to the surface. It was necessary. Because something else lay beyond the savagery. Something crouched, waiting, beneath the rage; something as powerful, as predatory and, he knew, as ultimately destructive. Rage was preferable. He could control rage, he could use it. He needed it if he was to keep Sarah alive.

The other was something he would not even acknowledge.

Sounds filled her head, beating, pounding, drowning out the terrified throbbing of her heart. Choked screams. Harsh curses. Ripping cloth. The sounds of beasts locked in a struggle that could have only one end.

And she couldn't stop them. Somewhere in the depths of her nightmare she was sobbing, screaming at them to stop, but they wouldn't listen to her. Then the sounds stopped. The dream changed. She was running into darkness that had no end. Behind her danger stalked, coming closer no matter how fast she ran, no matter how far. But she had to keep running. She had to get help. Had to save Amy... Amy...'*Amy—*'

Sarah came awake with the scream still filling her throat. She sat bolt upright in bed, gasping for the air that always eluded her in the dream.

Strong arms came around her immediately, holding her against a large male body that was powerful and warm and infinitely safe.

'It's all right, sweetheart. I'm here. You're safe. It was only a dream.'

For a moment she was a terrified fourteen-year-old girl again, being comforted by her uncle. Then she heard the dark velvet voice of her panther and knew she was safer than she'd ever been before in her life. She turned into his embrace with a shuddering little sigh.

'Nick. You're here.'

'Yes, little one. I'll always be here.'

For immeasurable precious minutes she was content to nestle in his arms, savouring the feeling of his fingers threading through her hair, stroking damp tendrils from her face while the shadows of terror receded.

But thought and reality intruded all too soon. He must have come to her room to talk and found her asleep, and since he'd been there to comfort her before the echoes of her scream had faded, he had clearly stayed.

She blinked, slowly taking in the sight of his discarded raiment, the chair close by, illuminated by a single candle, the fire still burning in the hearth. She didn't know how long she'd slept, but sensed the hour was now quite late. Why was he sitting here on her bed dressed only in shirt and breeches? Why had he stayed?

'Better now?' he asked, bending his head over hers.

She nodded and made a move to be free, remembering the turbulent see-saw of determination and uncertainty that had eventually driven her into an exhausted slumber. The feel of his arms around her was heaven, but was it only kindness? Oh, why had he stayed?

His arms tightened, stilling her. 'You were dreaming of your sister, weren't you, Sarah? Tell me about it.'

The gentle command stole her breath. 'I. . .can't.'

'Yes, you can.' His voice was so soft and persuasive that she almost believed him. 'Tell me about it and it will start to go away. While it's locked inside you, you can't be free to—' His hand flexed suddenly in her hair, then relaxed and resumed its stroking. 'You can't be free.'

After a moment's reflection, she looked up at him. 'I never thought of it like that. Everyone kept telling me to forget it, but. . .' Tears stung her eyes and she lowered her head quickly before he saw them. 'It didn't work.'

'Tell me what happened to Amy,' he said again. 'How did it start?'

'We had been to the beach.' The first words came hesitantly and she felt Nick tense.

'We?' he said sharply. 'You were with her?'

She nodded against his shoulder. 'Yes. There was a storm coming, like the day you and I met, so we were hurrying. I saw a man beside the path. If he hadn't moved I would have walked right past him because it was getting so dark. But he moved, and I saw him.'

'The groom?'

'No.' Sarah took a long, quivering breath. 'But he was there. Amy looked past me and I heard her cry out, "Hal, what are you doing?" I wondered what she meant, then something hit me and I fell.'

'That's all you remember?' he asked when she fell silent. 'The groom, another man and being hit?'

She started to shake. 'No. I. . . I. . .'

'It's all right, sweetheart. It's all right.' God, he hated this. He held her closer, his mouth pressed to the soft curls at her temple. 'You're safe. It happened a long time ago. They can't hurt you now, Sarah.'

'I know.' She clung to him, instinctively seeking his male heat to counteract the bone-deep chill of remembered horror. 'It was Amy.' Her voice cracked on the name. 'Crane hurt her.'

'Hal Crane? That was the groom?'

'Yes. I could hear her screaming that he'd killed me and he kept shouting at her to be quiet. Then. . .it got worse. There were sounds. . .awful sounds. . . He was cursing her, telling her she'd made a fool of him and he was going to take what she owed. I tried to help her, but I couldn't move. I couldn't see. It was so dark and I couldn't see.'

She raised her head, unaware of the tears pouring down her cheeks. 'It was like some sort of horrible dream. Sometimes I thought I *was* dreaming. I'd be asleep and then wake and hear terrible things. And then. . .it seemed a long time later. . . I woke up again and there was nothing, just silence except for him breathing.'

'The other man, the one you saw, did he do nothing while Amy was attacked?'

His deep, gentling tone brought her back from the brink of her nightmare. For the first time Sarah realised she couldn't see Nick's face through the haze of tears blurring her vision, but she could feel his thumb against her cheek, brushing the wetness away. He bent his head and kissed her lashes, catching more tears on his lips.

'I don't know.' Her voice was husky and she swallowed, looking away again to stare at the glowing log in the fireplace. 'I couldn't see. Whenever I tried to open my eyes everything got blacker. But I heard his voice. He was angry, but his voice was so precise, so cold. I've never forgotten it. He called Crane a lustful fool and ordered him to kill me. . .if he hadn't already done it—'

He made a hoarse sound and she stopped. 'What?'

'Nothing, little one. Go on.'

Sarah shook her head. 'That's all I remember until I heard Uncle Jasper calling my name. It was raining but there were lights, and so many people. I didn't understand why. Someone turned me over and. . . Oh, Nick, I saw her.' Her voice broke again, shattering into silent tears that made her shudder convulsively. 'I saw Amy. . .'

'God Almighty!'

He held her to him, rocking her gently as she struggled against the wave of memory. When she could speak, it was in a whisper. 'The next time I woke up I really was in bed, and it was daylight. A few days later Uncle Jasper told me that Crane's body had been found and I didn't have to worry about giving evidence to the magistrate, that I should forget everything. I tried to tell him, but. . .' She drew back a little, eyes wet and anguished. 'Nick, do you believe there was another man?'

He frowned down at her. 'Yes, of course. Didn't your uncle?'

'Everyone said I was confused. Dr Salcott told me

I'd taken a brutal blow to the head and had lost so much blood that I must have fallen into a delirium. But I didn't. I *didn't*!' she whispered insistently. 'But there was no evidence to prove there had been a second man and they wouldn't listen. They wouldn't talk about it at all, except to say it was a miracle I'd survived.' She shook her head and stared into the fire again. 'I didn't think it was such a miracle when it was my fault that she died. I knew. . . I should have stopped it.'

No, Nick thought, not bothering to correct that last remark. He knew that sort of guilt could only be lessened when time and healing brought the realisation that she'd been physically unable to save her sister. The real miracle was that Sarah had survived with enough inner strength beneath her gentle innocence to trust a man as much as she had trusted him earlier that day.

He stifled a savage curse as he thought of what she had suffered. Violently assaulted, drifting helplessly in and out of consciousness, but not mercifully out of it enough to be spared the knowledge of her sister's rape and murder and the cold-blooded threat to her own life. And then to be disbelieved, to be told to forget it. No wonder she had nightmares. He could willingly have consigned all her well-meaning but misguided relatives and friends to a collective hell, except that by their unwitting interference he'd been able to justify his questions.

It didn't help much. He would have questioned her anyway, which would, he decided, have sent him into a hell of his own making.

She sighed and seemed to relax against him. 'You were right,' she murmured. 'I do feel better now.' She pressed her cheek closer, rubbing her head against his shirt in an unknowingly sensual gesture that tightened his body. 'How did you know?'

Ignoring the growing ache in his loins, he tipped her face up to his with a gentle finger beneath her chin. 'We all have nightmares, Sarah.'

Her lovely eyes, unshadowed now and soft in the candlelight, gazed into his. 'Yes,' she breathed. 'Even you.'

Nick looked down into her face, more shaken by her words than he wanted to admit. It seemed to him that she was seeing straight into the soul he thought he had lost. He remembered other faces, friends, enemies, places he'd known, dreams where he couldn't find himself, and knew that with her he was whole again.

He bent until their lips were less than an inch apart. 'Not any more,' he said.

The kiss was gentle, demanding nothing, giving comfort. He was being kind, Sarah told herself as her eyes fluttered closed. But the warm touch of Nick's mouth on hers sent the sweetest ripples coursing through her.

Her lips parted, her arms crept around his waist, and so slowly that she couldn't have said when it changed, their mouths fused in a joining so long and deep she had no memory of when they hadn't been kissing. When Nick drew back, his breathing ragged, his face taut with the desire she had seen in him that afternoon, hope flared inside her with a force that was frightening.

'Sarah, we have to stop. You're not ready. . .'

The hoarse tone of his voice brought her gaze up to his as he put her away from him, his hands sliding from her shoulders to her wrists. The emerald flames in his eyes had been banked, but she could feel tension humming through him in the fine tremor of his hands as they lay over hers on the bed. Then he broke that slight contact also, and she knew suddenly that what happened between them from that moment on was to be her decision alone.

The realisation made something inside her tremble once, violently, as if she had been abruptly abandoned in the midst of a thick fog, unable to see which way to go. Dimly she was aware that there might be a terrible price to pay if their relationship changed. She knew that he'd loved another woman whose place she could never take. But *she* loved *him*, with every fibre of her being; with her heart, her mind, her soul. Given that, there really was no choice.

'Ready?' she asked with an uncertain little laugh. 'I'm not sure I know what you mean by ready. But. . .' She looked up at him, quivering wildly inside with nerves and trepidation. 'I know I don't want you to leave, Nick.'

His smile was infinitely tender. 'I don't intend to leave. You're going to sleep in my arms every night from now on.'

'I. . .am?'

'Yes,' he said very softly. 'And one night, when you trust me again, I'm going to touch you the way I did this afternoon.'

She thought about that. 'Those obligations we—'

'*No. God damn it!*'

She jumped, her eyes going wide and startled. Then as her gaze flashed to his, she saw his control shatter in an explosion of raw need that stunned every sense she possessed. His face went hard, his eyes fierce, blazing, almost savage in their passionate hunger. He looked primitive, as if polite society had barely touched him.

Fear, sheer primal female fear, streaked through her, urging flight, but at the same time she was paralysed, completely and helplessly fascinated.

'I don't want any damned *obligations*,' he ground out

through clenched teeth. 'I want to touch you and have you touch me. I want to look at you lying naked in my arms, kiss you in places you haven't even dreamed about. I want to make love to you until we don't know where you end and I begin, until we can't damn well breathe without the other feeling it. And then I'll want to start all over again. *That*'s what I want, Sarah. It's what I've always wanted.'

She swallowed into a silence that was deafening. 'That,' she managed with an incredible effort, 'was quite a list.'

His eyes closed and he turned away, breathing deeply in an obvious effort at control. When he looked back at her it was like gazing into the fathomless depths of the sea. Tension had put a white line about his mouth and his big body was utterly still, as if he didn't dare move.

'Which scares the life out of you,' he said, and the aching regret in his voice made her cry out in protest.

'No, that's not true!'

He raised his brows in disbelief and she flushed. 'Well, not the life out of me,' she amended. 'But—' a shy smile curved her mouth and her lashes lowered, hiding her expression from him. 'I expect most brides are a little nervous.'

'Sarah. . .'

It was a raw whisper. She felt him watching her and trembled with anticipation and longing and love. He reached out and touched her cheek fleetingly with the tips of his fingers, but didn't make her look at him. She was glad of it. She wouldn't have been able to hide the desperate hope burning fiercely in her heart at his words.

'Sarah,' he murmured again. 'Will you be my wife in more than name?'

'Yes,' she whispered without hesitation.

He dragged in a shuddering breath, then reached for her and drew her into his arms as if she was made of the finest, most delicate porcelain.

'I won't hurt you,' he vowed, and though the words sounded as if they were engraved in solid rock, it was the shaking of his voice that brought her gaze up to his. His eyes had gone dark with desire but this time she could feel the fierce hold he had over himself in the tension of the muscles beneath her hands.

'I know,' she whispered. 'I trust you, Nick.'

He gazed down at her. 'Enough?'

'What do you mean?'

'I might shock you, frighten you.'

She thought of the way he'd startled her that afternoon and shivered with remembered pleasure.

'Yes, like that,' he murmured, watching the colour bloom beneath her skin. He bent and kissed her gently. 'If I do something that shocks you, little one, will you trust me enough not to stop me?'

What could she say? The decision had been made. Yes, she was unsure, nervous, still afraid of the unknown, but she had given her heart, would give her life for him if it was ever asked of her. How could she withhold the one gift he desired? Loving him, she would give whatever he asked, without demanding more than he could give in return.

She couldn't speak for the emotions tightening her throat, but she leaned closer and, hiding the love in her eyes beneath lowered lashes, touched her lips shyly to his.

It was enough. With a hoarse sound that was vow and plea combined, Nick wrapped his arms around her, parted her lips with the gentle pressure of his tongue, and took her mouth with his.

Weakness flowed through her instantly. She thought she had known what to expect of his kisses, but this was different. Deliciously slow. Deeply possessive. He kissed her as if they had all the time in the world, as if he was prepared to spend the entire night teaching her how heart-shakingly intimate a kiss could be.

And he touched her, stroking her through the shifting silk of her nightgown, tracing the delicate bones beneath her heated skin, cupping the aching fullness of her breasts, shaping his palms to the indentation of her waist and the gently rounded contours of her hips and thighs.

He was so gentle. The contrast between the gentleness of his touch and the size and power of his hands made her shiver in an uncontrollable response that could have been fear or excitement or both. She didn't know and no longer cared. All she wanted was for him to go on touching her, kissing her.

'Sweetheart, do you want me to blow out the candle?'

The husky question against her lips made her feel as if she was surfacing from some deep place where thought had vanished, leaving only sensation. She opened dazed eyes and felt heat wash over her in a searing tide at the burning, focused intensity of his gaze. His eyes were narrowed, glittering, watching his hand as, one by one, he undid the tiny buttons that fastened the bodice of her nightgown.

She gave a soundless gasp and went still, scarcely breathing.

'I don't. . . I don't want darkness.'

'I won't rush you,' he murmured. And held her close, understanding. 'I know you'll be shy.'

Still holding her, he smoothed the garment over her shoulders and down to her waist. For an instant her hands were trapped in the long sleeves, but her small sound of protest faded as he swiftly freed her. Sarah shivered as the cooler air in the room touched her naked flesh and instinctively brought her arms up to cover herself. He didn't try to stop her, didn't make any attempt to remove the frail shield. He could have, easily, she thought wonderingly. But he merely smiled into her eyes and released her.

'Wait,' he said, and, standing, he stripped off his shirt in one swift movement before sitting down on the bed again.

Sarah's mouth went dry. Her eyes widened as she looked at him. She forgot to be shy about the fact that she was sitting there half-naked, exposed to his gaze. Clothed, he looked big and immensely strong, but now she could see his strength in the sleek, beautifully defined muscles that rippled beneath his skin as he moved.

A panther, she thought, utterly captivated. Lean and dangerous and powerful, with a kind of masculine grace that was riveting.

'You're beautiful,' she breathed, reaching out a hand to touch him. The feel of the black pelt covering his chest startled her. It was soft against her palm, but with an intriguing abrasiveness that was very male and strangely exciting. She curled her fingers into its thickness, then straightened them again to test the underlying layer of muscle. There was no give in him at all.

'You're the beautiful one,' he said huskily. 'And you're playing absolute havoc with my good intentions, sweet Sarah.'

She scarcely heard him, so enthralled was she by his overwhelming masculinity, but when he circled her other wrist with his fingers and slowly drew her arm away from her body, she went still again as he looked at her.

'So beautiful,' he whispered. 'Dear God, Sarah, I have to hold you.'

The expression of naked desire on his face made her tremble, but before she had time to be afraid, Nick wrapped his arm around her waist and drew her up against him and all thought was suspended. She felt their flesh pressed together for the first time and cried out in wonder.

He murmured reassurance against her lips, but her shock had been one of intense pleasure and she pressed closer, her arms curling around his neck as he began kissing her. And so gently that she felt as if he was peeling away the layers of her uncertainty and fear one by one, he laid her back on the bed and led her into a world of sensation she had never dreamed existed, easing her into passion, pulling back when it became too overwhelming, calming her with soft words and slow, tender caresses before taking her higher.

It was like flying, Sarah thought in some distant part of her mind. Flying into the heart of the sun. Heat surrounded her. Heat from his mouth on hers, on her throat, her breasts. Heat from his hands, those strong, beautiful hands, touching her in places that made her melt and shiver, until he caressed her with such devastating intimacy that when he left her for the few seconds it took him to remove his remaining garments, Sarah whimpered softly in protest.

Then he was back, gathering her into his arms, parting her legs as he lowered himself over her. Sarah's breath caught; she gripped his shoulders. Her trembling body stilled as she felt his weight, felt the intimidating strength of him against her softest, most vulnerable flesh. Just for a moment she felt smothered, overwhelmed, his sheer size and the sudden dimming of the light as his body seemed to engulf hers bringing panic bubbling to the surface again.

He knew, sensed it at once, for he went still also, his heart thudding violently against her breast, shudders racking the powerful muscles beneath her hands. And those betraying shudders were enough to ease her own tense limbs. She moved slightly and found that their bodies aligned as if made especially for the other, that the feel of his weight on her was a delicious excitement, sheltering and warm.

She moved again and heard the harsh breath he drew in.

'Oh, God, Sarah, don't. Be still, little one. I can't. . . I've wanted you for so long. Don't let me frighten you.'

'I'm not afraid,' she whispered.

But in her shaking voice he thought he heard the last remnants of fear and it leashed the raging hunger inside him as nothing else could. She was so small and delicate beneath him, offering him the gift of her innocence, that to hurt or frighten her would be to destroy whatever he had left of tenderness.

'Sweetheart. . .' He cradled her face in one hand, tilting her chin up until he could see into her eyes. 'Look at me.'

She didn't know if she could. The stark intimacy of meeting his gaze as he eased into her body was almost more than she could bear. She gasped once at a tiny, stinging pain that was gone before she even thought to flinch, and he caught the small sound in his mouth.

Then she lost her breath entirely, lost all sense of self, as Nick became part of her in a joining so absolute, so perfect, she felt as if her very soul had merged with his.

'Mine.' He groaned the word against her lips. 'Mine. Until we don't know where you end and I begin.'

'Yes.' She could only breathe the word, clinging to him, flushed and feverish, wondering how he could make her feel so much, so intensely. All her senses seemed to go wild as he began to move with heart-shattering care. She could feel him everywhere. Inside her, over her, around her. Fear was vanquished. In the dark, heated passion of his embrace the nightmare of the past was a distant memory, stripped of its power over her future. Instincts older than time were guiding her, urging her to move with him until she could no longer be still.

She heard him say her name, his voice desperate, driven; felt his arms tighten with almost crushing force, and realised in vague wonder that he was as helpless in this moment of complete and utter unity as she, taking pleasure from her body even as he gave it.

And then a sweet, wild fire began suffusing every quivering nerve she possessed, sweeping her beyond thought into a maelstrom of exquisite sensation until, with a sob of mindless surrender, she gave herself into his keeping, trusting him to keep her safe, while the deep, secret pulses of ecstasy throbbed through her body with every shuddering beat of her heart, bonding her to him for all time.

CHAPTER FOURTEEN

SHE awoke to sunshine and an absence of shadows. Somewhere nearby she heard the sound of water being poured and then the quiet closing of a door. Nick must have ordered a bath for her, she thought drowsily. How had he known when she would wake?

Sarah turned her head on the pillow and sleepily surveyed the thoroughly rumpled bed in which she was lying. The bed wasn't the only object in that condition. She was feeling thoroughly rumpled herself. Deliciously rumpled. In fact, her state of rumpledness would have been quite complete except that she wasn't wearing anything.

A beatific smile spread across her face. She was alone but no longer lonely. Nick had become so much a part of her, had made her so completely his, that even without his presence she felt linked to him in some vital way.

She smiled again and hugged the pillow to herself as happiness welled in her heart. Oh, if she had ever let herself dream of such a night the reality would have far surpassed any maidenly imaginings. To fall asleep in her husband's arms after he had tenderly cared for her after her initiation into womanhood had been almost sweeter than what had gone before. He might not love her and yet she had felt loved; infinitely cherished, infinitely safe.

She had thought there couldn't be more, but he had woken her twice during the night, teaching her the joys of sharing as well as surrender, making love to her until nothing existed except the dark, tender world of physical intimacy that he created for them. And though each time had been as the first, as gentle, the pleasure he had given her became so intense that at the end she thought she might die of it.

And then just after dawn he had left her. She remembered stirring, a murmured protest on her lips when the warmth of his arms was withdrawn. He had hesitated, one hand clenching on the curve of her thigh. Then, with a gruff command to go back to sleep he had gone. She had obeyed, sinking back dreamlessly into slumber, both mind and body in a state of blissful satiation.

She laughed suddenly, feeling quite unaccountably giddy, and hugged the pillow again. The future beckoned, bright and full of promise. She would heal the pain in Nick's heart and then set about winning his love. In her euphoric state she had no doubt that such a feat was entirely possible. After all, he had healed her, and she loved him so much.

A sudden vision came to her, of a predator prowling through darkness, always in shadow, hunting by night. He had lived in the shadows of war and loss too long, but she would make sure his future was full of life and laughter and love. The way her own life had been before tragedy had overtaken her.

Sarah glanced towards her dressing-room as memory stirred—of one thing still remaining. Somewhere in her wardrobe there was a small bandbox containing a bundle of clothes. The clothes she had been wearing on that last day with Amy. She had never worn them again but, racked by grief and guilt had been unable to destroy them.

But now everything had changed. Her love for Nick had made her whole again. Before she left her room she would hunt out those old clothes and have them taken away. Then she would be free of the past, free to coax her panther into the light.

Flinging back the covers with a sudden burst of energy, Sarah hurried into her dressing-room and rang for her maid. The task of bathing and donning a chemise, petticoat and figured muslin gown didn't take long. As soon as her hair was pinned up in a simple knot from which tendrils hung in natural curls, she dismissed the girl, then, taking a deep breath, she opened her wardrobe and rummaged for the bandbox.

Her hands shook slightly as she drew it forth and knelt on the floor to open it. There was still a lingering trace of fear, but it seemed different. She wasn't sure if it was caused by the mystery surrounding yesterday's shooting or because she was confronting her nightmares alone. She frowned as she lifted out the reticule she had been carrying that day, remembering that she hadn't told Nick about the part of the dream that had not actually happened—where she'd been running from danger.

A shiver raised the flesh on her arms at the thought, and deciding there was no need to go through every article of clothing, she lay the reticule down again. As she did so something rustled inside. Strange. She tilted her head, trying to remember. Had she been collecting shells that day?

Curious now, Sarah retrieved the small bag and pulled at the drawstrings. A few grains of sand lay at the bottom, along with a cambric handkerchief, a length of sea-green ribbon and something that had definitely not been there eight years ago. A crumpled ball of paper. Extracting it, she smoothed out the creases.

A quick glance at the writing thereon did not

immediately solve the mystery. The note was in French. Scrambling to her feet, she carried the paper into her bedchamber and over to the window, and was about to bend her mind to the task of translating the faded missive when the door opened and Nick strode into the room.

All Sarah's faculties immediately seized up. It was ridiculous after the night they had shared, but suddenly she was overwhelmed by a wave of paralysing shyness. It didn't help that the expression in his eyes as he looked at her seemed to her rattled nerves to be rather guarded. All her plans and resolutions were abruptly shaken by a quite hideous tremor of doubt.

'Oh! Good. . .morning, my lord.'

She expected a chiding comment, a smile—even the flicker of a smile would have been reassuring—but though the guarded expression faded as he crossed the room towards her, the intent searching look that took its place was equally as unnerving. He stopped only a yard or two away, but made no move to touch her.

'Are you all right?' he asked, his voice very low.

Even in her flustered state, Sarah recognised concern when she heard it. Her disordered brain promptly swerved in another direction. Had he taken her helpless response for distress? She remembered almost sobbing with ecstasy at one stage, remembered how tightly he had held her, remembered that although his muttered words had been of reassurance, his voice had been ragged, as driven as the powerful movements of his body.

She blushed to the roots of her hair and forced her throat to unlock. 'Yes, of course. Why would I not be? That is. . .' Her hand clenched, crumpling the note still clutched between her fingers.

Nick glanced down at once. 'I didn't mean to make

you nervous, little one,' he said quite gently. 'Let me rescue that before you crush it beyond recognition.'

'Oh! No!' Sarah whipped the letter out of reach. 'It is nothing, my lord, I assure you. Merely. . .' Oh, good heavens, merely what? She couldn't think. Her action had been prompted by sheer instinct, a silent warning that she should read the missive herself, try to comprehend how it had come to be secreted with her belongings, before Nick saw it.

She should have known, however, that he would not be fobbed off with incoherent stutterings. He reached out, removed the letter from her frozen fingers and straightened it with a sharp flick of his wrist.

It took him only a second to see that it was written in French. He sent her one hard, very penetrating stare, then turned away and walked over to the fireplace to read it.

Sarah stared at his rigid back and felt her stomach start to churn. The tension emanating from him was so great she could almost see it humming in the air between them.

'Nick?'

He wheeled at the sound of her voice, stunned incredulity in his eyes. '*You*, Sarah? *You*?'

Completely at sea, abruptly terrified and not knowing why, she could only stand there, struggling to meet his gaze. The effort took every ounce of resolution she possessed. Incredulity was giving way to rage barely suppressed, but, far more devastating, behind the anger in his eyes she saw a bitter mockery that sliced into her heart with the savagery of a double-edged sword.

'Nick, I don't understand. What does it say?'

'You don't know, of course.'

She paled at the harsh sarcasm, but, somehow, it was that bitterness that gave her the strength to draw a semblance of dignity about herself, to lift her chin, to answer him, her eyes steady.

'No, I don't know. I found it only a few minutes ago among...among some old clothes and I haven't had a chance to read it.'

'Indeed? Then permit me to enlighten you, madam. I have not as yet perused the whole, myself, but a cursory glance is quite sufficient to establish to the meanest intelligence that this is a communication between spies!'

Her lips parted in shock. 'Spies? But how...? Oh, dear God, you don't think that *I*...?' She gazed at him in horror, unable to believe he would contemplate such a thing even for a moment.

He hardly seemed to hear her faint protest. 'Who else has access to your clothes, Sarah? Who else ventures to the beach armed? Or is found alone in a public garden, no doubt after meeting your accomplice. Oh, yes, you gulled me so easily, didn't you, my lady? With your shy innocence, your maidenly reluctance, your—'

'It wasn't *maidenly!*' She was suddenly rocked by a surge of anger so great it made her tremble violently. 'You *know* I was innocent! You know that, Nick. And you know why!'

He looked shaken out of his rage for a moment and she hurried on. 'What I told you last night was *true*. You must believe me! I would never betray—' But there she stopped, appalled, unable to continue as a dreadful suspicion flashed through her mind.

'Then you're shielding someone close to you. Or helping him. Is that it, Sarah? Your uncle? Or was it your sister? Is that what you meant last night when you said you should have stopped it?' He gave a laugh, short and hard. 'By God, I thought I had learned my lesson years ago after Marianne— But apparently not.'

'I know I can never be like her,' she began, her voice low and shaking. 'But it is not right to condemn me without—'

'Oh, you are more like her than you know,' he interrupted savagely. 'More talented, in fact. Let it console you that you made me forget for a few weeks how devious a woman can be.'

'Devious? No.' Stunned by this new charge, she could only flounder in utter confusion and hurt. 'Your wife was. . .'

'An angel?' His harsh laughter flayed her senses, mercilessly mocking. 'Yes, she even managed to look like an angel while she sat sobbing out a tale of abduction and rape when I caught her at an inn with the first of her many lovers. It was unfortunate from her point of view that the room contained a cheval mirror.'

'A. . .mirror? '

'I could see her face, my lady. The expression she thought she had hidden from me behind her hand while she wept. The performance was flawless—until I saw her secret smile. But that does not concern us now. Tell me, Sarah, were your nightmares caused by guilt, because you turned a blind eye to your sister's activities?'

She flinched at that but the pain of his accusations was becoming blurred. It hurt her that he would so instantly misjudge her, but a strange numbness was creeping over her. She was trying to think. There was something else Nick was telling her, something deeper than his words, but it was buried beneath the tangled weight of fact and surmise and suspicion buffeting her mind.

'*Answer me damn it!*'

She started, so lost in thought she hadn't realised he had come closer.

'Was Amy working with Crane?' he snarled. His hand flashed out before she could move and he circled her throat with his fingers. 'Or were you both in it up to your pretty necks?'

'I was only fourteen,' she whispered. 'Amy had been ...flirting with Crane. That's what I meant. I should have told Uncle Jasper so he could put a stop to it, but it had happened before and she had always tired... I didn't know Crane would consider her promised to him. Nick, I didn't know he would kill her.'

Her voice broke, unconsciously pleading, and he stepped back, letting his hand fall.

Sarah scarcely noticed the frowning look in his eyes. He had not been hurting her, indeed his hand had been warm on her throat, his touch light. He might be enraged beyond reason, but somehow that gentle clasp had kept her from outright panic. But now desperation gripped her, setting her thoughts to scurrying back and forth like terrified mice.

'I don't know what Crane might have been doing,' she cried. 'But I can't believe that Amy... Nick, she was foolish and heedless and...and...like our mother in many ways, but she would not have turned traitor.'

'Could Crane speak French?'

'I...' Bewildered, she shook her head. 'No, of course not. He could scarcely read or write English. I couldn't understand why Amy—'

'Then how the bloody hell could he have acted alone?' he roared. 'Damn it, Sarah, we're left with you and your uncle. The proof is here in a letter you admit was in your possession and in language no servant would use.' He gestured furiously with the paper and started to translate aloud, biting the words off one by one. "Imperative we know the precise strength of the forces commanded by Well—"'

He stopped, so abruptly that Sarah blinked. Eyes narrowed, he scanned the rest in silence and then he went utterly white.

The change was so rapid that she did not immediately comprehend what was happening. Indeed, she had scarcely heard him for her mind and senses had been so battered she couldn't cope with anything more. Her only thought now was to escape. To find somewhere quiet and still so that, like a small wounded animal, she could hide while she tried to protect a heart in danger of shattering beyond repair.

Her nervous gaze darted from Nick to the door and she took a trembling step in that direction.

'No! Sarah. . . God, what have I done? Sarah, I didn't mean—'

A discreet tap on the door cut him off. Before he could stop her, Sarah darted forward and opened it. Winwick was standing on the other side, looking faintly outraged at having to intrude on the lady of the house before she had left her bedchamber.

'I beg your pardon, my lady, but his lordship wished to be informed immediately should anyone ask for him, and there is an individual below who—'

'Yes, thank you, Winwick.' Nick strode across the room and into the butler's line of vision. 'I'll see him in a minute.'

'Yes, my lord, but that is not all—'

Seeing Winwick determined to continue, Sarah seized her opportunity. She slipped through the open doorway, ignoring Nick's fierce command to stop, and sped along the passage to the main staircase. Halfway down the stairs, knowing she was out of sight, she halted, clutching the bannister with one hand while the other tried to prevent her heart from splintering against her ribs. There was a terrible ache in her chest and she couldn't see, couldn't seem to focus properly.

The agony was not so much for the hurt Nick had dealt her—the shocking truth about Marianne, bewildering though it was, had somehow brought a measure of understanding, an instinctive knowledge that his accusations had not been wholly rational. No, the ache was for the pain Nick had suffered, and the enormity, the sheer impossibility, of the task she had set herself. A man who had once loved could perhaps be taught to love again, but a man who had been betrayed? A man who had then deliberately chosen to live among shadows, where betrayal was constant and a way of life?

Sarah clutched the bannister more tightly as a crushing weight of despair threatened to descend on her. Even Nick's trust seemed as beyond her reach as the stars, and yet how could she not try to win it, no matter how long it took?

Dear God, *this* was love, she thought, almost staggering under the realisation. Not just the pleasure and closeness of the night, nor the giddy happiness of this morning, but this emotion that filled her entire being, that forgave, that understood, that was stronger than resentment or anguish or doubt. An emotion that could, she discovered, still cling to hope in the face of seemingly insurmountable odds.

Shaken and trembling, she continued down the stairs, driven by the need to find a place where she could think. There was so much to consider. Nick's accusations for a start, and the horrifying conclusion that since she was innocent, the next likely suspect was her uncle. And yet she could not believe Uncle Jasper had lied to her all these years. He was too kind, too honourable. Somehow she had to make Nick believe that. He had not meant those terrible things. If she could just stay calm and explain. . .

She reached the hall and remembering that Winwick had interrupted to announce a caller, turned towards the library. Whoever the 'individual' was, he was probably waiting in the small room where Nick conducted estate business. The library would be empty and quiet.

She opened the door and stepped into the room—and remembered an instant too late that Winwick had been about to say something else.

'Oh! Excuse me, I. . .'

The gentleman who had been standing before the fireplace, studying the portrait above him, turned at the sound of her voice. He was tall and lean, with pale brown hair and eyes that rather matched his buff-coloured coat. Sarah had the strangest feeling that she had seen him somewhere before, but then she looked again at his eyes and forgot the notion. They were very bright, almost expectant, as though their owner was anticipating some excitement.

She wasn't sure if this was the 'individual' or another visitor, but for some reason that avid stare made her uneasy.

'I beg your pardon, sir,' she murmured, reaching back for the door knob. 'No doubt you're waiting for my husband. He will be down directly.'

The man turned more fully towards her. 'Oh, no need to run off, my dear Lady Ravensdene,' he said in a very precise, very polite tone. 'Your presence will save us all some considerable time and trouble. Do come in and sit down.'

Instead of complying, Sarah stood rooted to the spot. Every drop of blood drained from her face. There was a roaring in her ears. It drowned out his last words, but she had heard enough. She would never forget that voice. Never.

'*You!*' Her horrified whisper echoed through the room seconds before the door was slammed open with a force that propelled her forward in an automatic move to avoid being trampled.

Nick strode into the library, his gaze lighting on her immediately. 'Sarah? Oh, my darling, thank God you haven't left the house! I didn't mean it, sweetheart! I—'

'Dear me, how very touching. And most convenient, I do declare. Yes, Ravensdene, it is I. Please close and lock the door behind you. If you need an incentive, you may notice that this small pistol in my hand is pointed at your wife. A toy, but it fires quite accurately over short distances.'

Nick froze, his eyes going very light and narrow. For a moment as his gaze flashed to the man in front of him, Sarah thought he was going to attack, then he seemed to relax, to go still and watchful.

'You won't shoot anyone in here, Catsby,' he said calmly. But he closed the door nevertheless.

Sarah jolted as the key turned in the lock. She hadn't taken her eyes off Nick, as if the sight of his face, hard and alert, would hold the recurrence of her nightmare at bay. He had not looked at her after that first searing glance, but she sensed he was aware of every breath she drew.

'Nick.' She could barely whisper. 'He was there. . . that day. He was the other man.'

'Ah. You do recognise me,' Catsby said before Nick could answer. 'I wondered if you had seen me the day your sister died, my lady, but when there was no investigation I thought I was safe. All these years. Such a shame that you had to give up your retiring life,

Sarah. Really, you know, I could not take the chance that our paths might cross after you were so ill-advised as to marry Wellington's top agent.'

'You know. . .' Her brain reeling, Sarah glanced from one man to the other. 'You know each other?'

'He's my contact's secretary,' Nick said without shifting his gaze from the man whose hand was clenched around the pistol. He moved slightly, drawing Catsby's attention away from Sarah. 'So you tried to kill her yesterday, Catsby. Why not me? I was the one set to catch you and your accomplice, as you clearly know.'

'Quite correct, Ravensdene. You see, our esteemed superior has a habit of mumbling to himself whenever he is worried. One can hardly blame him for such an indiscretion—who notices a mere secretary, after all? I knew all about his little trap, baited with false information, but I could hardly shoot you out of hand. Think of the fuss. I couldn't risk that while true information continues to net me a tidy sum.'

'Money?' Nick scorned. 'Is that all the war means to you, Catsby?'

'Easy to be contemptuous when you're not obliged to live on a meagre salary,' Catsby spat, an ugly look momentarily twisting his features. He seemed to regain control of himself with an effort. 'A gentleman's pleasures are expensive, as I'm sure you'll understand. As for yesterday, well I confess that bungled shot was the result of temper. Your wife must have as many lives as a cat.'

He turned to Sarah, a chilling smile on his lips. 'I nearly had you in those gardens at Eastbourne, you know. But Ravensdene always did have a habit of being where one would most wish him not to be.'

'The man in the street,' Sarah murmured, remembering. 'You nearly collided with us.'

'Yes, a fortuitous coincidence, was it not? I was in Eastbourne ostensibly to check on Ravensdene's progress, but, having seen you, decided to follow you instead. What I heard of your conversation was enough to cause me grave concern. You hadn't appeared to recognise me, but I couldn't take any chances once I knew Ravensdene had made your acquaintance. I followed you to the ruins, also, and later in the woods. It was most annoying to be so constantly interrupted by a succession of fools.'

'You've been stalking her?'

Nick's voice was so gentle that for a moment Sarah wondered why she went so cold inside at the sound of it. Then she saw his eyes and knew instantly that, though she had never seen that look before, others had. It was the utterly emotionless, ice-cold deadly stare of the predator, waiting for the right moment to kill.

'Dear me, you seem to think this is personal, my lord. Please disabuse your mind of the notion. Violence is most abhorrent to me, but my creditors are becoming rather insistent. Quite threatening, in fact. If violence is to be done, therefore, I would rather—'

'Abhorrent!' Sarah stared at him, hardly aware of having spoken. 'How can you say that when you stood by and watched while Amy—?'

'Sarah. Don't, sweetheart.'

'Oh, it's quite all right, Ravensdene. No, no, my dear, you must acquit me of condoning the assault on your sister.'

'Acquit you! I saw—'

Catsby made a deprecating noise. 'You saw my French accomplice, Henri, my lady. And Crane, of course. He was our go-between. Yes, I can see you've already worked out that there were three of us,

Ravensdene. Your mistake was in assuming that since no one from the Foreign Office travelled to this part of the coast regularly, the information was posted to an accomplice. A logical assumption, but erroneous. A go-between was necessary to let me know when Henri arrived, since I could not loiter about Comberford without being noticed. Much safer to stay at an inn several hours away. Whenever I rode out everyone assumed I was visiting a mistress somewhere nearby, an impression I was always careful to impart. Amazing what people will swallow if one follows a regular routine.'

'However, to return to my story: useful though he was, Crane was becoming a problem. Really, that entire afternoon was a series of the most irritating setbacks. I was delayed by my horse throwing a shoe, and Henri, no doubt in a Gallic frenzy at the thought of missing the tide, decided to write me a note and leave it with Crane. There was absolutely no need for Crane to accompany Henri back to the beach, and no need to panic when they chanced upon two heedless girls. Henri, of course, fled directly to the beach after Sarah was struck, but then that fool Crane argued with Miss Lynley and one thing led to another. *I* had no knowledge of what had occurred until I came upon the scene after Crane had, er, finished with Miss Lynley. She was almost insensible with shock, but naturally I had to kill her.'

'Naturally?' Sarah's voice trembled and she saw Nick move abruptly before going still again when Catsby shifted to aim the gun at him.

'She knew too much,' he went on, watching Nick but still addressing her. 'I assure you I did not enjoy the task. Murder is such an unpleasant business, and then there was Crane to dispose of as well.'

'A fool but also a convenient scapegoat,' Nick said dryly.

'Precisely. It took little persuasion to convince Crane that he was in grave danger of being hanged for rape and murder. We joined Henri on the beach where Crane was, er, permanently silenced. Unfortunately, we then discovered that he had mislaid the letter Henri had left for me—we assumed during his contretemps with the lady, since it was not on him when we searched his body. That gave me a few nasty moments, I can tell you, but the woods were full of Sir Jasper's men by then and we couldn't chance going back to look for it. We had already been forced to flee the scene before ascertaining whether Sarah was still alive.'

Sarah shuddered at this cold-blooded recitation of events, but her mind was now strangely clear and very calm. The spectre that had haunted her for years had finally materialised, and now that she faced the reality fear had gone, replaced by an grim determination to see him pay for his crimes.

'You killed Amy,' she said very softly as though making it clear.

She felt Nick glance at her. 'Easy, love. He won't get away with it.'

'Oh, you think not, Ravensdene?' Catsby's polite tone slipped a little. 'You may be rash enough to try disarming me on your own, but you won't risk Sarah's life. It didn't take me more than a minute to see you're besotted with the girl.'

Nick's eyes met hers for the merest second but Sarah felt her heart shake. 'Yes, I love her,' he said calmly. 'And I'm not prepared to see you or anyone else take her from me, Catsby.'

'Oh, Nick. . .'

'Yes, yes, very touching, as I observed before,'

Catsby interposed testily. 'However, let me assure you, Ravensdene, that I intend you to go together.'

'Don't be an idiot, Catsby. Who do you think is going to be your scapegoat for murder this time? One of the servants? As soon as you fire a shot they'll be breaking down the door. You wouldn't get beyond the terrace.'

Catsby smiled coldly. 'I am not quite the fool you believe me to be, Ravensdene. We shall go out to the garden where your servants have heard you firing guns at targets for several days, and there you will have a most tragic lovers' quarrel.'

He turned to Sarah. 'Brought on, of course, by your husband's investigation into Sir Jasper's affairs, my dear Sarah. You see, it is all perfectly logical. Distraught, you plead with Ravensdene to desist, becoming quite hysterical in the process and taking no heed of the fact that he is armed. In the ensuing struggle, he is accidentally shot. What else is there to do but put a period to your own existence? By the time the servants realise something is amiss, I will have returned to Eastbourne, where I have been staying, quite innocently, under orders to assist Ravensdene. Brilliant, as I'm sure you'll agree.'

'Not quite, Catsby,' Nick contradicted, much to Sarah's relief. She had been racking her brains to find a flaw in Catsby's scheme, but short of refusing to be marched at gunpoint out to the garden, she could find none.

'You see, I sent Figgins to London last night to discover if anyone from the Foreign Office was in the habit of travelling to *any* location a few hours' ride from here. Once he knows where, it will be a simple matter to bring the innkeeper to London to identify you. It's over. I suggest you leave the country immediately.'

'What!' Sarah gaped at him. 'You're going to let him—'

'*No*!' It was Catsby who interrupted her, his eyes wild. 'I won't leave the country and live in squalor. Don't you understand, Ravensdene? I'm in debt. Facing complete ruin. I can't let you stop me.' He jerked the pistol at Sarah, his polite façade cracking. 'Get over to the window and open it!'

When she hesitated, he lifted the pistol and pointed it straight at her heart.

'Sarah! Do as he says!'

Nick's sharp command jolted her into moving. She cast him a pleading look over her shoulder and he smiled faintly, softening his tone. 'Don't be afraid, my darling. I won't let him hurt you.'

It wasn't herself she was worried about. Catsby was clearly beyond reason, desperate enough to kill them here if he was pushed too far. Trying frantically to think of a way out of their predicament, she walked over to one of the long windows and unlatched it. Her gaze fell on the large shell she had placed on the adjoining ledge. She went very still.

'Good.' Following her, Catsby motioned Nick closer, matching him step for step. 'Now, we'll go outside as if for a stroll. Push the window open, Sarah.'

She lifted her hand as if to obey, moving very slowly.

Her hesitation was too much for Catsby. He began to swing the pistol towards her again, and in the split second when it was pointing harmlessly at air, she bent, grabbed the shell and hurled it straight at him.

He cursed viciously, flinging up his hand to protect his face. The gun went off with a deafening roar at the same time that Nick went past her in a deadly lunge that took Catsby down to the floor with him. The two men rolled, sending a chair toppling, then Nick came up on one knee, his arm hooked around his enemy's throat. Sarah saw the muscles bunch beneath his coat an instant before a sharp crack rent the air.

Everything seemed to go very quiet. Letting Catsby slide to the floor, Nick got to his feet and looked at her.

Sarah could only stare back at him across the few feet that separated them, unable to believe it was over. 'Do you think you should search him?' she finally asked, trying to sound perfectly calm. 'He might have another pistol.'

'Sweetheart—' The cold, deadly glitter left his eyes, leaving something dark and hurting. 'He's dead, Sarah.'

'Dead? Oh. Yes, of course he is.' Somewhere in the distance she could hear the servants hammering on the door. The noise was vaguely annoying. 'For a minute I thought you were going to let him escape.'

'Only while you were in danger. Sarah. . .'

'It's quite all right, you know.' She smiled at him. At least she hoped it was a smile because Nick seemed rather worried about something, but her face felt so stiff it was difficult to be sure. 'Thank you,' she added in a very polite voice.

'*Thank you*?'

She nodded. And her control crumpled. With a strangled sob of relief and reaction she flung herself into his arms. 'Oh, Nick, I thought he had killed you . . .when the pistol went off.'

'No.' His arms closed about her at once, strong and protective. 'Oh, God, Sarah, I'm sorry. I'm so sorry!'

She raised brimming eyes to his face. 'For what?'

'Yes, there are quite a few things for which I have to beg your forgiveness,' he said grimly. The line of his mouth hardened. 'Not least of which is the way I endangered your life and then caused you to witness. . . Oh, Sarah, little one—' his hand came up to brush away her tears '—you've had to live with such violent memories. I didn't want you to see me kill someone, to know what I've been, what I am.'

'You're the man I love,' she sobbed, clinging closer. 'Of course you're capable of killing someone, but only to protect others, not for your own gain. I'm *glad* he's dead. Why do you think I threw that shell?'

His laugh was ragged, and laced with wonder. 'My brave little love. Fortunately your aim is better with shells than with pistols. Oh, sweetheart, say that again. About loving me.'

She tried to obey but found that she was crying too hard. And Nick was holding her too tightly, her cheek pressed to his racing heart, his face buried in her curls. His arms were like steel about her, but he was shaking.

Abandoning the impossible task of trying to sound coherent, she let their embrace speak for her, drawing warmth and strength from him while giving of her own.

A minute passed before he gently tipped her face up and kissed her. There was still a faint tremor in his hands and she gazed up at him wonderingly, awed that this controlled, powerful man could be rendered so vulnerable. And for love of her. She was almost afraid to believe it.

Then he smiled at her, and the tender concern burning through the amusement in his eyes removed every shadow of doubt from her horizon.

'Can you be brave for a little while longer, my darling?' he murmured. 'I think Winwick has found another key to the door. And I know he is going to disapprove most vehemently of shots fired inside a gentleman's house.'

Two hours later, Sarah was precisely where she most wanted to be. Ensconced on her husband's lap in her bedchamber, secure in his embrace, and engaged in the agreeable task of reassuring him that she was perfectly recovered from the vissicitudes of the morning.

'Would the innkeeper's evidence really have been sufficient to convict Catsby of treason?' she asked, having been doubtful on that point ever since Figgins had returned with confirmation of Nick's theory.

'Probably not sufficient for a conviction,' he admitted. 'But the suspicion alone, had it come to the ears of the cents-per-cents, would have made his life extremely unpleasant. Besides, he was in no condition to reason with any clarity of intellect this morning. The mere knowledge that I had exposed his methods was enough to tip him over the edge into panic.'

He drew her closer, his head bent protectively over hers. 'And once I knew he was the cause of the nightmare you've lived with all these years, I never intended to let the matter go to court.'

Sarah nodded and decided not to mention the small fact that she would have liked to have known of his intention. She had already scolded him for omitting to inform her that he'd been armed all along—to which he had replied, unarguably, that they could hardly have conducted a conversation on the subject at the time. And her panther was still looking rather tense and dangerous. It was time to turn the discussion into more interesting channels. Such as when he had first come to love her.

'Hmm. I think it was that night at the Wribbonhalls' when you laughed at the notion of carrying a pistol to a party,' he mused, pretending to consider when she put this crucial question to him.

Then he added with a rueful smile, 'Not that I was admitting any such thing *then*. I knew I wanted you, my darling, and had done from the moment I had you pinned to that tree, but even last night when I realised how close you'd come to being killed, I wouldn't let myself think in terms of love. The fear of losing you was too great.'

Sarah nestled closer. 'You won't lose me, Nick. Not ever.'

'I don't deserve that,' he said, his voice husky. 'Not after this morning.' He brought his hands up to frame her face, gazing into her eyes, his own dark and anguished. 'God forgive me, Sarah, when I saw that letter I tried to tell myself it couldn't be love tearing me apart, but I was lying. I knew then that I loved you no matter what you might have done, that I'd do anything to keep you from prison or execution, and that knowledge made me blind with rage. It's no excuse, but that's why I lashed out at you, why I was so damned unreasonable.'

'It's all right,' she murmured. 'I knew, somewhere inside me, that you weren't really saying those things to me.'

'When I started reading that cursed letter aloud and saw that it referred to *Wellesley*, as the Duke was once known, everything you'd been saying suddenly made sense. Apart from your own honour, you would have been too young to have been involved. My God, if you knew what I felt then. I couldn't think beyond the fear that I had driven you away forever. Even now I don't know how you can forgive me. I don't deserve you, Sarah, but I swear to God I'll spend the rest of my life trying to.'

'Oh, Nick, hush. I can hardly blame you for suspecting me when *I* suspected poor Uncle Jasper for a few horrible minutes, and with even less evidence. I suppose that letter was shoved into my reticule by the servants who found me that day. Being unable to read French, they would have thought it was mine if it lay nearby. Later I directed one of the maids to pack everything away, never dreaming something so damning existed. If I hadn't known Uncle Jasper so well. . .'

'Yes, you've had years to build your faith in your uncle, whereas I. . .'

'Whereas your faith had been destroyed,' she finished softly. 'I understand, Nick. Truly I do. You must—' She faltered and glanced away, sitting up straighter so he held her only lightly. 'You must have loved her very much.'

'Is that what you've been thinking?' he asked. And when she only nodded, he drew her close again, turning her face up for his kiss. 'I thought it was only your fear of men, or, rather, of intimacy with a man.'

She blushed and shook her head. 'Not with you.'

'Oh, love, if ever I heard an invitation. . .'

Smiling, he let the sentence trail off, but as she shyly returned his smile his expression changed, turning fiercely intent. 'Sarah, you don't know how rare and precious you are. Your innocence, your sweetness, your truth and courage. Yes, twelve years ago I fell in love with a pretty face. A boy's love that couldn't see past the surface to the vanity and shallowness beyond. And Marianne's betrayal did hurt for a while, but by the time she'd conceived another man's child and died, I didn't love her at all. There was nothing there to love.'

'I'm sorry,' she whispered, aching for the boy whose heart must at least have been bruised, his illusions shattered.

He kissed her again. 'I'm not. Because when I did find the woman I could love, my heart knew her instantly—even if my mind took a while to catch up.'

'Oh, Nick. . .' She couldn't help but laugh, even through the tears of happiness filling her eyes. 'I would rather have a man's love than a boy's.'

'You have both,' he said very softly. 'You've given me back a part of myself I thought was lost forever, Sarah. You've given me back a belief in honour, in goodness.' He bent and kissed her with devastating gentleness. 'You've given me back tenderness.'

'I don't think it was ever truly lost,' she said, touching his cheek with loving fingers. 'Just buried for a while. So you could survive in the world you lived in.'

'Oh, Sarah. . .my own sweetheart. . .' His arms closed around her in fierce possession. Sarah felt the surge of power in his body as he lifted her and rose from the chair to carry her over to the bed.

'I shouldn't do this,' he muttered hoarsely, laying her down as if she might break. 'Not after last night. It's still new to you. But I need you, darling. I need you more than you'll ever know. I'll be so gentle with you, I swear it.'

'I know,' she whispered, drawing him down to her. 'I'm not afraid, Nick. I was before because of Amy, but also. . .it wasn't *finished*. I always sensed danger somewhere, waiting. I think that's why I started walking and riding alone. I had some vague notion of drawing the danger out so I could be free. But now you've taken it away, and. . . I want you, too.'

A sound of raw need tore from his throat as he took her in his arms, sweeping her beneath him with a barely restrained urgency that made her go weak all over. She quivered with excitement at the feel of his weight on her, loving his strength, feeling deliciously helpless, but safe. So incredibly safe.

Their lips met. Clothing fell away. Whispered words of love, of need, of desire, drifted in the warm, golden light filtering through the half-drawn bed curtains. And this time their love was given freely, openly. Nothing was held back. Love so ardent, pleasure so intense, they reached the heights of ecstasy together and hovered there, their souls touching for one rare, timeless moment, before they rested, entwined, still one, so close they could not tell one heartbeat from the other.

A long time passed before Sarah stirred and looked up at her husband. She melted all over again when she saw the expression in his glittering green eyes. No longer hard or cold or dangerous, but warm and tender, and filled with so much love she felt her lips tremble with the quick rush of emotion filling her heart.

'I never imagined a man could be so gentle,' she whispered.

He smiled lazily and glanced down at their entwined limbs. 'You're not ready for anything else yet, my little love, but when you're used to me, when you feel completely safe, sometimes it'll be so wild you'll think we're soaring. But I'll never hurt you, Sarah. Not ever.'

Sarah thought about that and felt a distinctly wicked, distinctly female smile curve her lips. She raised herself on one elbow, crossed her arms on Nick's chest and propped her chin on her hands. 'How long do you think it will take me to grow accustomed to you, my lord?'

He grinned. 'Well, you're already showing an unusual aptitude for driving me out of my mind, so. . .' He cupped her head in one large hand and drew her closer to take her lower lip lightly between his teeth. 'Not long at all,' he growled.

Sarah had a sudden thought that it might be dangerous to arouse a panther. The notion didn't bother her
at all.

'Would tomorrow be too long?' she enquired
innocently.

'Why hurry?' he murmured, and gave her another of
those biting little kisses. She felt his body tense against
hers. 'First I'm going to taste every inch of you, sweet
Sarah, and I intend to take my time over the process.'

Her arms wreathed around his neck. 'You do?'

'Yes.' Holding her lambent gaze with his, he turned
slowly until she was beneath him. His hand cradled her
face, gently holding her still for a kiss that was not
gentle at all, but deep and possessive. When he lifted
his head a long time later and Sarah saw the intense
glitter in his eyes, she shivered in tingling anticipation.

'Sarah,' he said very softly. 'You know, I once told
Dev that Marianne was like a blazing chandelier; the
flames burn so hotly they swiftly die. But you, my
Sarah, are the single candle flame that will burn in my
heart for evermore.'

'Oh, Nick, I love you so. . .'

He didn't let her finish, but it hardly mattered, Sarah
mused happily as Nick swept her once more into their
private world of love and desire. It had all been said
anyway. Her panther would never be entirely tamed,
but she had won his heart. He would walk by her side.

For evermore.

HIDDEN FLAME

by

Elizabeth Bailey

Dear Reader

My own early introduction to Georgette Heyer gave me so much pleasure that it is always a tremendous thrill to me to write historical romance for others to enjoy. This imagined world becomes all too real to me, and yes – sometimes the characters do take over! Writing is akin to directing a play: one creates the whole image, and controls everything living within it – rhythms, emotions, motivations, the very stuff of human endeavour. Both disciplines demand a sense of the dramatic – and, let's face it, an addiction to fantasy and fairytale: one tends to live, eat and breathe the story during the creative process. I have in recent years become both a playwright and director, often directing my own plays – both adaptations of classics, and original material. This has been an exciting development, and in future I will be concentrating on these pursuits – alongside writing novels. I could never abandon the delight of creating romantic fiction. I am definitely one of the 'incurables'. If, as I suspect, you are too, then this story is written for you.

With best wishes.

Elizabeth Hawksley

Elizabeth Bailey grew up in Malawi, returning to England to plunge into the theatre. After many happy years 'tatting around the reps', she finally turned from 'dabbling' to serious writing. She finds it more satisfying for she is in control of everything; scripts, design, direction, and the portrayal of every character! Elizabeth lives in Surrey.

Other titles by the same author:

CHAPTER ONE

THUNDER crackled over the dark, empty street. One of the horses whiffled a protest and shuffled a hoof, dragging slightly at the tether that held it and its fellow securely fastened to the single lamp-post, which imperfectly lit the inn yard, its small flame dancing as the glass about it shook in the uncertain weather. Behind the horses, the curricle, its hood up against the piercing March wind and the oncoming rain, shifted on the cobbles, and settled again.

The gentleman did not even turn his head. Outlined against the dim glow from outside, his tall silhouette filled the open doorway. A towering, greatcoated apparition, its face shadowed by a low-brimmed beaver. A dark figure, seemingly at one with the angry elements at his back.

Involuntarily the landlord of the Feathers shivered, peering uncertainly up at this late wayfarer, whose peremptory summons on the front door had recalled him to undo the bolts he had only just shot to.

The gentleman's pose seemed negligent enough. One gloved hand rested casually against the door-jamb, drawing the folds of his greatcoat wide. Which was why, Mr Pigdon told himself firmly, he looked so all-fired *big*. The landlord drew a breath.

'And what might you be wanting this time o' night?' he demanded belligerently.

'What the devil do you think I want, fellow?' came the irritable reply. 'Do you take me for a highwayman?'

Mr Pigdon relaxed a little. Not only was the gentle-

315

man's intonation unmistakably genteel, but he was
slurring his words very slightly. Furthermore, decided
the experienced landlord, if that wasn't the fumes of
brandy on his breath he didn't know his own business.
A question, it was, whether he was propping up the
door, or the door was propping him!

A streak of lightning forked across the sky behind,
and the gentleman grew impatient. 'Do you mean to
keep me standing here all night, man?'

Mr Pigdon started, his attention drawn back from
the threatening sky. He stood aside to let the gentleman pass. 'Come you in, sir, come you in.'

'I am obliged to you,' the gentleman returned, a
satirical inflexion in the light voice. 'I will be still more
so if you will have someone look to my horses.'

'Aye, sir, that I will,' the landlord agreed, thankfully
shutting the front door as another burst of thunder
erupted overhead.

'Immediately!'

'Aye, sir.' Mr Pigdon picked up the candle which had
been ready to light him to bed from a shelf in an alcove
by the door, and bustled past the visitor down the hall.
He threw open another door. 'If you'd care to wait in
the coffee-room, sir, I'll fetch the ostler.'

The gentleman nodded briefly, and, as the landlord
left, stepped into the dimness of a dark room lit only
by a single candle on the mantel above the hearth, and
the glowing embers of a dying fire below. He halted
before it, looking about at the relentless blackness with
an expression of distaste, pursing the fine lips that were
visible below the hat. A sudden glare from outside lit
up the windows briefly. There was a muted refrain of
the crackle of doom, and he heard the rain start.

A miserable night! Appropriate. A night on which
witches roamed, and the gods were angry. A night to

bring any man to contemplate the dogged scourge of Lady Fortune's whip with a jaundiced eye. Lady Fortune? Lady *Ill*-fortune more like! Had she got him marked out for her vicious games for life?

The landlord came back into the room just then, interrupting his gloomy thoughts.

'Now, sir. The lad'll bed down your cattle. I take it you'll be needing the same yourself?'

'Certainly. Though I trust you may have something slightly better than a stall,' suggested the gentleman wryly.

Mr Pigdon bristled. 'True it is that we ain't in the habit of entertaining the likes of you, sir, most of the gentry as stops here in Newark preferring to bait down Saracen's Head with that there Mr Thompson, but——'

'My good fool, I am perfectly aware of that. But the plain fact is that I have had a devilish run of ill luck, and I do not care for Thompson's tariff. In a word, my pockets are damnably to let. Now, have you a bed, or have you not?'

Such a ready admission of his circumstances startled the landlord. Furthermore, if the gentleman had no money——

'Don't put yourself about!' recommended the visitor, stripping off his gloves. He added with uncanny perspicacity, 'I have enough to cover my shot *here*.'

The slight, disparaging inflexion on the last word annoyed Mr Pigdon, but he gruffly assured the gentleman that he should have the best spare bedroom and all the comforts his poor house might afford.

'I trust that includes brandy? Bring me a bottle, if you please. And——' with another unfavourable glance around the room '—perhaps some more light?'

'Aye, sir. At once,' said the landlord, hastily bending

to put a couple of logs on the fire and poke it back to life.

When he rose, he discovered that the gentleman had removed his hat. The light from the candle on the mantel fell on a countenance so classically pleasing, topped by a quantity of gold, curling locks that brushed the high-caped collar of his greatcoat, that the landlord was startled. The changed look at once dissipated the sinister aspect that the gentleman had generated thus far.

He seemed to recognise the effect he was creating, for he suddenly smiled. It was a smile of great charm, causing even the toughness of Mr Pigdon to crack.

The landlord found himself returning the smile with a grin of his own. 'You wouldn't care for a bite to eat afore you takes to your bed?'

'Now that,' the gentleman said in a more friendly tone, 'is an excellent suggestion. Nothing troublesome, mind.'

'It's no trouble, sir,' the landlord told him cheerfully, and went out.

Left to himself, the gentleman let his smile fade.

'Let's hope the fool hurries with those candles,' he muttered. The atmosphere in this dark room was oddly disquieting, giving him the distinct impression that he was not alone. Or was it the heavy rain slapping against the windows, the wind's eerie message as it whistled down the chimney and flickered at the flames that had begun to lick about the new-laid logs?

Shrugging off the thoughts with his greatcoat, he threw the latter over one of the two big tables and turned back to the fire.

'Cleaned out again, confound it!' he said aloud, kicking moodily at one of the logs, and sending a shower of sparks up the chimney. He had enough for his day-to-day needs, of course, but he would be hard-pressed to see himself through another month if he was to live in the style befitting a gentleman. Unless he were to pay his godmother a second visit in as many weeks? Or would that make her suspicious? He should have remained with her for the hunting, devil take it, instead of going to his friend Woolacombe! The man had always a pack of gamesters about him. Useless to have imagined he might resist temptation! Now what the devil was he to do?

The opening door recalled him to the present situation. A stout woman entered, bearing a candelabrum and a tray, and on her plump face, under the nightcap that concealed the rags curling her hair, was an expression of the gravest displeasure. The gentleman took due note of it in a single glance, decided that nothing was to be gained by ill temper, and, reassembling his smile, he turned it upon her full-force.

'Good evening. I am afraid I am giving you a great deal of trouble.'

Mrs Pigdon was in no very amiable humour. The late arrival had necessitated her getting out of bed and throwing on a voluminous dressing-robe in order to prepare suitable accommodation—on a night such as this, moreover, when all a body wanted was to curl up under the quilt and hide from the horrors outside. She was not impressed when her spouse informed her there was a member of the gentry below, for the only visitors of that sort to frequent her humble hostelry were those who had fallen on evil times. Like that hoity-toity voiced little madam earlier in the evening. She'd seen through *her* in a twinkling, she had! But she'd at least enough to pay her board. *This* party had the nerve to announce his shameful embarrassments to all the world!

But Mrs Pigdon was a sharp-eyed dame for all that. No sooner did she set eyes on the gentleman than she recognised his pecuniary position to be merely temporary. There was nothing shabby or worn about the close-fitting blue coat or the buckskin breeches; and the starched neckcloth—no longer as neat as it might have been—and the ruffles to his shirt-sleeves were of the finest linen.

Her first concern laid to rest, Mrs Pigdon examined the gentleman's comely countenance, and, like her husband, visibly thawed at the onslaught of the smile.

'No trouble, sir, I assure you,' she answered, unconsciously echoing her spouse. She set the candelabrum and the tray down on one of the tables, removing his greatcoat and placing it carefully over the back of a chair so that she might lay out a cloth and utensils. 'We'll have a supper of sorts ready in a twinkling, sir.'

'You are very good,' the gentleman said.

She bustled to the door and her voice took on a repressive note. She had not been pleased to hear that the gentleman was a little the worse for drink!

'Pigdon's bringing the other, sir.'

He merely nodded. Perfectly aware of the veiled disapproval, his kindlier feelings abated, to be replaced by a resurgence of ill humour. Devil take it! Was it for this common servitor to censure his habits? When the brandy arrived, he filled a glass and tossed it off, in a gesture of childish defiance. But when the landlord had left the room he reached into a pocket of his greatcoat and brought out a flat silver flask. This he carefully filled from the bottle and then replaced in the greatcoat.

Mrs Pigdon, returning with his meal, noted the disgracefully lowered level of the liquor in the brandy bottle and gave him a look that spoke volumes. It was productive of a sudden gleam in the gentleman's eyes, of unholy amusement.

'Don't trouble yourself,' he said, gently sardonic. 'I have a hard head.'

The landlady was not amused. Her face pinched in disapproval, she laid out a dish of sliced cold beef, a platter of bread and butter, the remains of a pigeon pie and some cheeses. Also a jug of water and another of sobering porter, thoughtfully provided by the landlord. A parting sniff as she left the room gave the gentleman to understand that he had disappointed her.

Mr Beckenham felt a perverse satisfaction. To hell with the woman! Who was she to censure him? With a liberal hand, he poured himself another glass. But as he raised it to his lips the windows flashed bright again, and the heavens gave forth another stream of rumbling abuse.

'God, what an accursed night!' mumbled Mr Beckenham, and, sipping his liquor, he looked over the makeshift meal with revulsion. 'To what am I reduced? Hell and damnation!'

As if in response to his cursing, the wild night struck back at him, flaring a double blow of brilliant whiteness that seemed to tear at him through the windows.

His head turned, eyes narrowing against the glare. As the room lit, an image crossed his vision—of a thin black figure seated in a corner, crouching witch-like in the gloom.

His heart lurched sickeningly. The devil! He was seeing things. Too much brandy!

But as the dark closed in again and his eyes began to adjust, the glimmering outline of a pale face encroached upon his senses.

The thunder rolled away as Mr Beckenham stared, leaving the place eerily silent, and his heart still. Was it a ghost? Or merely his imagination playing tricks? Cursing briefly, he closed his eyes, looking away.

As he opened them again, they flicked, almost out of his own control, to check. *It was still there.*

Mr Beckenham froze. His fingers about the stem of his glass tightened. There was a sharp crack, and the broken glass fell from his hand, tinkling on to the table and spilling its golden liquid on to the pristine white cloth.

'Hell and the devil!' swore the gentleman, starting forward.

There was a frightened gasp and the ghost rose, too, staring at him out of the two hollows that were its eyes.

'I—I beg your pardon,' faltered the ghost. 'I think I startled you.'

'Dear God in heaven!' ejaculated Mr Beckenham on a tide of relief. 'You're *real*.'

A flicker at the window and a faint cackling echo of thunder laughed at him. The gods were enjoying their own cruel joke! Mr Beckenham decided savagely. Well, he would have his revenge!

He seized the candelabrum, and, lifting it high, moved towards the pale face. It shrank back against the wall, edging towards the door. As he neared, he could see that it belonged to a slight female form encased in dark garments, its hair entirely concealed by a white cap. Small wonder she looked like a ghost! No. A witch! A black witch, casting spells from her hiding-place in the corner.

Abruptly the woman speeded up, making a dash for the door. He strode forward to intercept her, grabbing one wrist as he reached her.

'Come here, witch! You don't escape me so easily.'

'Let me go!' came in a harsh whisper from the pale face.

'By no means.'

Tugging her away from the door, Mr Beckenham pulled her close, holding the candelabrum high. In its light was revealed a thin face, with skin so pale that it was almost translucent, whose high cheekbones emphasised the hollows below and under her brows. From within these, a pair of deep grey eyes looked up at him. There was fear in them, but more than fear—defiance, a little, and challenge.

'Why were you hiding there?' he demanded compellingly. 'Spying on me!'

She shrank a little, the eyes dilating. Her voice was pitched low, the fear overlaid with edgy defiance.

'I didn't mean to *spy*. I couldn't help it. I came down for the fire, for it was cold in my room. Then I heard the door, and you came in, and—and I did not dare to reveal myself because——'

'Because I am a man, and because I am drunk?' he guessed.

'Yes,' she agreed, and a little of the fear seemed to leave her.

'My good girl, I am not in the least drunk,' he told her, his brows lifting haughtily. He saw her glance across at the table and followed her gaze to the brandy bottle. 'Oh, well. Perhaps a trifle foxed, but that is all.'

Then he recognised that her eyes had strayed to the food, glistening a little. The pink tip of a tongue touched her pale lips.

Mr Beckenham had hold of her wrist still, and all at once he felt how slim it was. His hand was closed loosely over it. Like a bracelet! he thought. God, but the girl was a stick! Sudden pity softened him towards her, and he forgot his urge for revenge.

'Are you hungry?' he asked abruptly.

Her eyes flew back to his and she swallowed painfully. 'Oh, no, I—I was just—I did not mean. . .'

Mr Beckenham let go her wrist and stepped back with a little bow, gesturing to the table. 'Pray share my supper, ma'am.'

She shook her head. 'Oh, no, I could not. I should leave you now.'

'Should', not 'shall', he noted. She *was* hungry. He smiled, charmingly, and saw the grey eyes widen. But she did not smile in return.

'It would be a kindness on your part, ma'am,' he said persuasively. 'These good people have been to an enormous amount of trouble on my behalf, and I am sure I shall be quite unable to do justice to their generous provision.' Forgetting his earlier disgust at the food that had been set for him, he thought only that this girl would appreciate it, whatever its quality.

She hesitated, glancing again at the food, longing in her eyes, and back to him, uncertain. 'I don't think—it would be seemly.'

'Who is to know?' he countered, and, setting a firm hand to her back, he began gently to propel her towards the table. 'You need not fear me, ma'am. As you have so sapiently observed, I have consumed far too much brandy to be capable of any amatory advances.'

'Yes, that *is* what I feared,' she said, glancing up at him as they reached the table. 'Not that you might attempt anything, perhaps, but. . .but in my situation, one is vulnerable to—to certain *propositions*.'

He held the chair for her to sit. 'You mean, I dare say, that, having given you supper, I might expect payment in kind.'

There was no trace of a blush on her pallid cheek.

Her attention was on the food. Her voice was vague as she responded. 'Yes, that is usually the way of it.'

She drew a breath as he offered her the platter of bread, and her fingers shook as she lifted a slice from among the pile. He sat down and watched her, fascinated, as she put the bread to her mouth, her eyes closing in a kind of ecstasy when she bit into it. It must be many hours since she had eaten.

The shock of her discovery and his malevolent thoughts of her were gone with the lessening of the storm. Only the sound of the rain, pattering more gently against the window, disturbed the quiet now. It was like coming to harbour after a rough passage — with an armful of comfort to hand. Only there could be no comfort from *this* bosom. His glance travelled over the girl's face and the visible parts of her upper body, and with another pang of compassion he saw that she was woefully thin.

Suddenly urgent to feed her, he looked about the table and discovered that there was only the one plate and set of utensils. He stood up. 'I had better ring for another cover to be laid.'

'Oh, no, *pray*,' she begged, dropping the bread and rising also, and casting an apprehensive glance over her shoulder at the closed door. 'No, no, don't. It would not do to be discovered in so — intimate a situation.'

'What the devil do you care for the opinion of such persons as these?'

She looked away. Low-voiced, she answered, 'I *have* to care.'

He was silent, moved a little by the underlying pain he detected in her voice.

Her eyes came back to meet his, and a tentative smile glimmered on her lips. 'May we not share your things?'

Mr Beckenham found himself quite unable to withstand the plea. An idea occurred. 'I know! We will take the gamester's way, and follow Lord Sandwich.'

'I don't understand,' she said, sinking back into her chair and gathering up the hastily discarded slice of bread.

'Watch.'

The gentleman laid several pieces of beef between two slices of bread, and, putting it on his own plate, placed it before the lady. She put down the slice she already had, and looked at the plate. Abruptly she broke into a delicious laugh, her thin face lighting up. Then she seized the offering in her hands and began to eat.

She tried at first to do so in a properly genteel way, nibbling daintily. But gradually, her appetite quickening, she ate faster and faster, stuffing the food ravenously into her mouth and bolting it down.

In a very short space of time, she had demolished two more such beef sandwiches supplied by Mr Beckenham, with the addition of a large slice of pie, the whole washed down with gulps of water in between, only so that she might clear her mouth for more food.

Mr Beckenham, at once amused and touched, watched her, eating little himself. He preferred to drink—ignoring the landlord's porter—from his silver flask, which he had substituted for the broken glass of brandy. It was only when at last the girl sat back with a sigh of satisfaction, apparently replete, that he ventured to address her, his tone unwontedly gentle.

'How long is it since you had a square meal?'

She closed her eyes briefly and shrugged. 'I do not remember.'

He gave a soft laugh. 'You ate that as if it was to be your last meal on earth.'

A gleam of humour appeared in her eye. 'It may well be. Oh, not on earth, perhaps.'

'I am relieved to hear it.'

She smiled at him. 'I have to thank you. That was— oh, like finding an oasis in the desert!' She glanced at the windows, where the rain had almost ceased. 'Quite the wrong simile at such a time. But I feel exceedingly warm and cosy, as if the storm is over—for now.'

His grin was rueful. 'I fear it is merely a lull. Listen!'

The girl's eyes lost their sparkle as the faintest of rumbles came to her ears, and Mr Beckenham was sorry he had drawn her attention to it. He saw her shoulders shift, and she unconsciously raised a hand to undo the buttons of the bodice of the dark pelisse she still wore over an equally dark gown, the top of which was now revealed, made high to the throat.

He glanced up at her face again, and discovered that she was looking at him with some interest, and it struck him that until now starvation had held her attention to the exclusion of all else.

'What?' he demanded, disconcerted by the direct gaze, framed by the small white frill of her otherwise severe cap. 'Why do you look at me so?'

'You do not appear to be foxed at all,' she explained.

He laughed. 'Is that all? The truth is, I have had only enough to permit me to drown my sorrows.'

She nodded, as if she understood. 'You mentioned something of the sort when you first came in. You are short of money?'

Taken aback by her frankness, he gave a self-conscious laugh. 'Devil take it, ma'am, is that a question to ask a stranger?'

'Perhaps not in the ordinary way.' She smiled, and a glow entered the deep grey eyes. 'But when the stranger has done one a signal service——'

'None of that! You have done *me* a favour, I told you so.'

'It is kind in you to make such a pretence, but I saw the compassion in your face, and I am grateful for it. If I may make a return by listening to your troubles, I am very willing to do so.'

'My good girl,' Mr Beckenham said in some embarrassment, 'I can assure you my troubles are vastly inferior to your own. What in the world is a girl of your quality doing at such an inn? And alone?'

Her face closed in and she eyed him with a return of the defiance and challenge he had seen in her eyes at first. A glimmer of lightning lit the window again, and the thunder could be heard, distant and muted. The gods were displeased again! he thought facetiously and held up a hand, as if he read her thought.

'No, very well; it is none of my concern.'

She looked down at the table, and then raised her eyes to meet his again, the challenge gone.

'That was ungracious of me, when you have been so kind. The fact is, sir, that I have been alone for several years now. And when I. . .' She hesitated, as if seeking the appropriate words.

Mr Beckenham did not interrupt. He was thinking how unconscious she seemed now to be of the awkwardness of their encounter. Or had her initial fears been merely a result of the disorder of mind induced by her very apparent hunger? One could never think straight when the body's ills took all one's attention.

She continued, breaking his train of thought. 'When I spoke of your circumstances, it was only in the belief that I might understand your plight. For I am at such an inn because it is all I can afford—and *you* would not be here had you better means.'

'True enough,' he admitted.

She inclined her head. 'I am on my way to take up a situation as companion and had to put up here to catch the cross stage tomorrow.' She bowed her head a little, and began to falter. 'It is—it is many months since my last situation, and. . .and I have had to eke out my remaining funds. That is why——' raising her head to give him a grateful look '—I had none to spare for a meal at this place.'

Mr Beckenham took a long pull at his flask, and then carefully topped it up from the bottle. He did not look at her as he spoke.

'Your frankness does you credit, ma'am. If I was not similarly open, it is merely because my embarrassments can only be laid at the door of my own folly, and not to the workings of chance.'

'Sir,' said the lady, looking him straight in the eye as he paused in his task to glance at her, so that his hand stilled and his gaze remained on her serious face, 'I am no more the victim of circumstance than are you. I am as I am through the choices I have made, and I will not whine at fate.'

There was a silence. Complete silence, for the rain had ceased and for the moment the storm seemed to have moved away. Mr Beckenham continued to stare at her, an odd sense of unreality invading his mind. Such steadfast determination in her voice! And what pride she had, that transcended her meagre purse and the threadbare pelisse that so little kept out the winter cold that she still wore it inside the house, and had been obliged to come down from her room to seek a little warmth from the dying fire.

'May I know your name?' he asked quietly, laying down his flask and the brandy bottle.

She shrank into herself, and then gave a tiny shrug. 'You may think of me as "Theda".' Almost as an afterthought, her eyes clouding, she added, 'No one has called me that for years.'

Before he could answer, the door opened. They both looked round, and met the startled eyes of Mrs Pigdon, the landlady.

'*Miss*!' she gasped. 'Why, miss, I thought you was long abed!'

'No,' Theda said quietly, but Mr Beckenham could hear a quiver in the voice. 'I came down to be warmed by the fire.'

The landlady's eyes narrowed. 'Oh, you did, did you?'

She glanced from one to the other, at the remains of the food on the table, and wrath entered her face. Arms akimbo, she made herself ready for battle.

Ranging on her side, a flare from the window lit up the coarse, reddening features, followed immediately by the uncouth clatter of the skies, echoing her strident voice.

'And what might be the meaning of all this, may I ask? I'll have you know this is a respectable house, and "goings on" I will not put up with!'

Mr Beckenham was on his feet. 'Now listen to me, my good woman——'

'Don't you "good woman" me!' snorted the outraged dame. 'I know what my eyes are telling me. And as for you, miss,' she said, rounding on Theda, 'you're no better than you should be, just as I suspected at the outset.'

'Just one moment——' began the gentleman.

But Mrs Pigdon was not in a mood to listen. 'Come down to be warm by the fire, indeed! Heard the gentleman's voice, more like, and come down to see what you might get out of him.'

'I *beg* your pardon?' gasped Theda, rising from her

chair. Even she had not bargained for such an insult as this!

'You may well!'

'How dare you speak to me so?' Theda demanded, her voice husky with distress.

'Dare? *Dare*? How dare *you*, miss, turn the Feathers into little better than a bawdy-house? Out you'll go, this minute!'

Theda blanched even paler, a wicked flash and an ominous rumble preventing her from hearing the curse that issued from Mr Beckenham's lips. All outrage fled before the hideous prospect of being thrown into the streets on such a night.

'You are quite mistaken,' she said desperately, but she might as well have spared her breath.

'Mistaken, am I? We'll see that. I won't have it! Not in my house. I'm a respectable woman, and I won't have no "goings on", not if you were ever so high and mighty, the pair of you. Which you ain't, not by a long chalk!' she averred, descending rapidly from outraged virtue to mere verbal abuse.

'You are being quite ridiculous, my good woman,' began Mr Beckenham loftily, trying again to stem the flow.

But this time, Theda interrupted him. 'Pray don't, sir. The blame is mine.'

'To be sure it is!' concurred Mrs Pigdon aggressively. 'And you'll pay for it, my girl. You can get your things, such as they are, and clear off out of my establishment.'

'*What*? Don't be a fool, woman!' The gentleman flung out an accusing finger at the window, through which the flickering and crackling still lingered on. 'Send her into *that*? Besides, you can't turn the girl out at this hour.'

'Pray, sir,' begged Theda, white to the lips and trembling. 'Say nothing more! I am quite ready to go.'

'Wait!' called out the gentleman, as she moved swiftly towards the door.

But Theda heard only the landlady's vicious tone following her. 'Aye, and so you should be. Think shame to yourself! Calling yourself a gentlewoman and all!'

At the door, Theda almost bumped into the landlord, who was standing in amazement at the acrimonious scene within the room. As the girl disappeared through the door, Mr Beckenham seized Pigdon's arm and turned to confront his wife.

'You are come in a very good hour, sir! For mercy's sake, persuade your good woman here to allow the lady to stay. What she proposes is positively inhuman! Besides, the girl has done nothing wrong, and I cannot allow her to be treated this way.'

Together the landlady and her shocked spouse burst into voluble speech, which beat at Theda's ears as she fled up the stairs. Shame churned inside her, and the storm was forgotten. She was a fool not to have foreseen the outcome. Mrs Pigdon had shown herself to be anything but sympathetic when she arrived at the hostelry earlier that evening.

She'd had to walk from the more expensive inn up the road which was the official halt for the northbound stagecoach. Her shabby appearance and the battered portmanteau had weighed heavily against the genteel tone of her voice. It was worse, in fact, than if she had been obviously of a more humble station, for a gentlewoman in her circumstances was instantly under suspicion of a fall from respectability. Which, lord help her, was indeed the truth! She was not, however, the common harpy for which the landlady had taken her! she reflected angrily, stepping hastily into the garret room which was all she had been able to afford. Cramming her worn, out-moded bonnet on her head, she stuffed the few belongings she had unpacked back into the portmanteau.

Taking it up, and with no very clear idea of what she meant to do—apart from escaping from the humiliations to which she had been subjected—Theda crept out of the room, down two sets of stairs, and slunk past the open door of the coffee-room, where the landlord's voice was joined to those of his wife and the gentleman.

Thankfully they were all too engrossed to notice her, and she gained the front door unmolested and slipped through it, closing it softly behind her.

The chill of the March night struck at once through her thin pelisse. It was no longer raining, but the sky was pitch-black with cloud, as she saw when the unremitting storm sent flittering light across it. It must be past twelve, for the gentleman, she knew, had arrived after the clock on the coffee-room mantel had struck eleven. The lamp-post that welcomed travellers to the inn had long lost its cursory flame, and she had neither candle nor lantern to light her way through the darkened streets.

In mounting dismay she peered into the gloom, the invidious nature of her position coming home to her with a vengeance.

CHAPTER TWO

THERE was not a soul in sight as Theda began resolutely to trudge down the street, looking for a lane that might lead her off the main road, which, being only of packed dirt, was already a hasty-pudding of mud which churned under her mercifully booted feet. She tried to hold up her long skirts with her free hand, grateful for the moment to the intermittent lightning which showed up the worst of the puddles ahead.

The only idea she had was of discovering some sort of shelter for the night, for she must catch the stage to her destination early in the morning. The eerie stillness of a town asleep caught at the edges of her already stretched nerves, and she shivered with apprehension as well as from the biting wind.

Come now! she encouraged herself. There was no one about. And even if there were, what had she to fear from some sturdy citizen?

Then she found a lane and turned down it, thankfully feeling cobbles under her feet. She let go of her skirts, but immediately felt a prickle of fear at putting herself out of reach of the inn. For a craven moment she was tempted to go back and throw herself on the mercy of the landlady. But the woman's insults rankled, as did her earlier insolence—for her contemptuous glance had raked Theda's person when she had dared to ask at the Feathers for a room for the night.

Theda thought she had learned to subdue the spirit of rebellion that threw her into defiance on the receipt of such slights. But she had not. Storm or no storm, she could no more have returned to the inn than she had been able to return penitent to the bosom of her family six long years ago, when the same stigma would have been laid to her then as had been laid to her now.

The thought gave her courage, and she stepped out more boldly, coming into another road that ran parallel to the main one. Her eyes had become accustomed to the dark, and she could see, as she peered down it either way, that to the left this road opened out. A square, perhaps?

Another horrible crackle overhead pushed her into decision. Changing direction, she hurried towards the place, and found it to be a large open space, surrounded by little shops, their shutters closed now, but by the legends she could just see painted above their doors they were given over to trade. The whole area was saturated with water, which still trickled in little rivulets through the uneven cobble stones, and down the walls from the tiled roofs.

It must be the market square, Theda decided, glancing about and finding odd shapes that looked like empty barrows. And that thin stump of a thing, that must surely be the pump.

She checked about for a likely place of shelter. There was a small colonnade to one side before a large building. The Corn Exchange? She would investigate that. At least it would be out of the wind, and hopefully dry. Although the miserable cold was likely to keep her awake all night—if one could sleep at all in the open air, with a raging storm about one and the fear all the time that someone might find one camped out like a vagrant!

She was just crossing the square, and wondering where in her portmanteau she had placed her woollen shawl, when she became aware of footsteps that were not her own.

She froze momentarily. They were coming down one of the streets that led to the square. In her fright, she could not judge which one, and looked fearfully this way and that. One thing only was certain. *They were coming this way.*

Unreasoning panic blanked out her thoughts, and, grasping her portmanteau, she flew for the colonnade of the Corn Exchange. Just as she reached it, the light from a lantern spilled on to the square, and she saw a man enter the place behind it.

Holding her breath, Theda crept behind one of the wide pillars, carefully put down her portmanteau, and crouched down, trying to make herself visible only as an unidentifiable hump.

The footsteps halted, and she could see the beam of the lantern swing from side to side. Her heart was thumping so hard that she could feel the breath catch in her chest. Not even hearing the rolling crackle above, she was conscious only of the moving light, as the footsteps began again and it swung this way and that, searching something out.

Instinct told her that she was being hunted. Panic kept her from wondering why. She crouched there, her eyes, enormous in her white features, fixed on the light that came steadily closer.

A sudden explosion of brightness lit up the whole sky. Unable to help herself, she looked up, and knew at once that her movement was seen, as in the instant gloom that succeeded it the lesser light of the lantern swept an arc and found her face.

The beam stopped there, and Theda remained a moment, blinking in its glare, like an animal's prey, frozen with fright. Then, as the thunder roared, startling her out of immobility, she leapt up and ran, blindly, as for her life.

At once the footsteps started after her, and she heard a voice calling out. But the words were meaningless to her, and she ran on, her breath ragged. She was not watching the uneven cobbled ground beneath her racing feet, and an unexpectedly large stone tripped her progress, bringing her to a stumbling halt.

The running steps behind her closed, and a hand grasped her shoulder, swinging her round.

'You little fool!' scolded a voice—muted, but blessedly familiar. 'What the devil do you mean by running from me?'

Theda stared up at Mr Beckenham's handsome features under the shadowing beaver hat, her mouth open on gasping breaths, her eyes dilating in fear.

'I—I don't *know*. I thought—I *couldn't* think!'

His face softened. 'You poor girl! I'm sorry I frightened you.'

She shook her head a little, and found that her hands were grasping at his coat. A warm, large one closed over them, reassuringly.

'Come, now, it is all over. There is nothing more to fear.'

'It—it was f-foolish of me, I know,' she managed, her teeth chattering.

'Your hands are like ice!' he said in concern, and placed an arm quickly about her, his thought only to warm her. 'Have you no gloves?'

She nodded. 'Y-yes, but in my anxiety to be gone I f-forgot them.' Her voice trembled on a laugh. 'Just, I suspect, as you did!'

His light laugh sounded above her. 'Quite right. I did.'

As she hunted for a worn pair of leather gloves in

the pocket of her pelisse, she did not appear to notice that she had been pulled closely in to the gentleman for a few brief seconds. Recollecting herself suddenly, she jerked away sharply. But not before he had felt the painful thinness of her upper arm, the jutting of her hip against him.

'The devil!' he muttered, almost to himself. 'The girl is skin and bone! Small wonder you are so cold. Here, hold this a moment.' He gave the lantern into her now gloved hands, and proceeded to strip off his greatcoat.

'I have always b-been thin, you kn-know,' Theda told him, but with a tremor still in her voice.

'You are positively skeletal, girl!' In a moment, the huge greatcoat was placed about her shoulders, drowning her, and as he retrieved the lantern he began to scold. 'You are an irresponsible little fool! The storm may break again at any moment and you will be drenched. You should know better than to walk out into strange streets alone.'

'What else was I to do?' she protested with spirit, hugging his warm coat gratefully about herself. 'Would you expect me to remain after what that woman said of me?'

'Better to endure her insults than to die of exposure.'

A bleak look flitted over her face. 'I don't know that. Sometimes it seems that death might be. . .' She faltered to a halt as her eyes met his again. As if she was ashamed of her momentary weakness, her chin came up. 'In any event, she threw me out.'

'To be sure she did,' agreed Mr Beckenham impatiently. 'But that was in her first rage. You had only to ride out the storm—*inside* preferably——' with a flash of humour as the heavens reminded him of their still present threat '—and the dust would soon have settled. And I had the situation well in hand.'

'Oh, indeed? It seemed to me that you could not edge in a word!' retorted Theda.

'I did so after you left, and would have done so had you stayed.' He grinned engagingly. 'I am a specialist at handling irascible women.'

A tiny choke of laughter escaped her. 'So I perceive.'

His eyes roved the pale features, a stirring in his breast that was not quite compassion. On impulse, he put out a hand, and touched the back of it to her cheek. 'Still so frozen! You are like to die in any event, if you will not look after yourself better!'

'I am much more resilient than you suppose,' Theda said, a faint smile on her lips.

'Well, I am not! I am growing cold.' He took hold of her arm. 'Let us go at once.'

Theda held back, urgency in her voice. 'You cannot ask me to go back there!'

'Yes, I can. If you had not so stupidly bade me keep quiet, I should have done the trick long since, and you would not have had to leave the place at all. It is all settled now, so you may be easy.'

'No! No, I will not go back.' But she sounded unsure now.

'Most certainly you will,' stated the gentleman, urging her irresistibly forward. 'I am not making this sacrifice for nothing.'

She halted, staring up at him. 'Sacrifice?'

'Yes, sacrifice. The good lady has agreed that you may return for the night only if I remove,' he explained.

In the light of the lantern, her eyes were pools of deep distress. 'Oh, you should not have done that! What will you do?'

He was touched by her concern, but he smiled. 'I shall go on to the Saracen's Head.'

'But you cannot afford it!'

'Don't fear for me. I know Thompson very well. He will chalk up my shot for another day.'

Theda continued to look at him uncertainly for a moment. Then she sighed. 'I have only to thank you. Such chivalry is rarely met with by such as I, and although I know I should refuse it, for it will put you in debt, I confess I *cannot*.'

'What a pother you make!' he laughed. 'It is nothing at all to me. I am forever in debt, you must know. One grows accustomed to it.'

She said no more, but went to pick up her portmanteau from the Corn Exchange colonnade.

'That you will give to me,' said Mr Beckenham firmly, taking it from her.

'But it is not heavy, and the inn is no great distance,' she protested.

'You may carry the lantern, then,' he conceded, and handed it over.

The sky above them lit again, and the next rumble produced the first spattering of rain.

'Quickly!' urged Mr Beckenham, stepping up his pace.

Theda had almost to run to keep up with his long strides, and had much ado both to keep hold of the lantern and prevent the mass of the gentleman's greatcoat from falling off her shoulders. She had no breath left to speak, and, beyond recommending her to beware of puddles, her companion wasted no words either.

Arrived at the inn, he hammered on the door. It was opened immediately by Pigdon, who had evidently been on the watch for them.

'Found her, then,' he observed, moving back to allow them to enter.

Mr Beckenham looked down upon him from his

superior height and handed to him the lady's portmanteau. 'Take this. And mind you see to her comfort!'
Without waiting for a reply, he turned to Theda, who
was slipping off his greatcoat. He stayed her hands.
'No, keep it.'

Theda shook her head and his fingers fell away. She
held it out. 'I could not possibly do so.'

He hesitated before taking it. 'I have another.'

'But not with you,' she objected gently. 'You have
already done too much. My conscience would not
suffer me to accept any more.'

Reluctantly he received the greatcoat back.

Theda smiled at him out of her thin, pale face.
'Besides, you look so well in it, and it is far too large
for me.'

Mr Beckenham laughed, and took the hand she held
out to him. 'Take good care of yourself. . .witch.'

He said it only because he had forgotten the name
she had told him, but the delicious little gurgle of
laughter she gave coincided so precisely with another
crackle of thunder that it seemed suddenly apt.

Then, disappearing up the stairs in the wake of the
landlord's candle, like the ghost he had first thought
her, she vanished out of his life.

Theda's eyes remained closed as the lumbering stage-
coach rumbled its way from Newark, where she had
caught it outside the Saracen's Head, to Ashby-de-la-
Zouch, where it would remain for the night before
proceeding to Stafford. But Theda was not asleep.
Even if one could have slept, with the incessant lurching over the mired ruts that the storm had left behind,
she was not tired.

On the contrary, she had slept remarkably well, in a
large bed over the sheets of which the grudging Mrs

Pigdon had passed a warming-pan before Theda slipped between them. She could not remember when she had last enjoyed such comfort. On a full stomach, too. Oh, the bliss of it! And she did not even know the name of the kind benefactor to whom she owed so much. It was not merely that he had paid her shot. He had paid it as if it were his own. For it was *his* room and *his* bed in which she had lain so snugly. Replete with his food, too.

He had not bought Mrs Pigdon's approval, but honour had been assuaged and she had done her duty as, she said, befitted a Christian.

'It's not what I hold with, nor yet what I'm accustomed to,' the matron had said virtuously, as she'd brought a laden tray to the best spare bedchamber in the morning, 'but I'm an honest woman, and I don't cheat nobody, be they never so undeserving! A breakfast he paid for, and a breakfast you shall have.'

Theda had gazed with awe upon the dish of ham and eggs, the lavishly buttered bread and the pot of tea, bereft of words. Having discharged her duty, Mrs Pigdon had left the room, with a parting injunction to the unwanted guest to be sure and hurry.

'For the coach won't stay for you, and I don't want you begging back here, that I don't!'

Theda had hardly heard her, overwhelmed as she had been by the thoughtfulness of the unknown gentleman. She had set to with a will, but had been dismayed to discover that her appetite did not match it. She had only been daunted for a moment, however. She might be proud, but she had learned to be provident! Remembering her host's clever trick of the night before, she had made a sandwich of the remaining ham and wrapped it carefully in one of her pocket handkerchiefs, placing it securely in the pocket of her pelisse. At least she would not be hungry today!

For who could tell what might await her at journey's end? Her history was not such as had ever permitted her to procure any but the meanest of genteel occupations. No high-born dames, no wealthy patroness for Miss Theodosia Kyte! Her employers had been in general the aspiring mothers of young daughters of tradesmen—the honest working citizens whom her father would have disparagingly stigmatised as 'cits'— hoping that a little of Theda's quality might rub off on their uncouth girls to help them to an advantageous marriage.

Miss Kyte considered herself fortunate to have finally been offered a post in a better class of household, for Sir John Merchiston's widow sounded a much more promising prospect than Mrs Mugglesby, to whom she had last been in service. Moreover, an older lady should need a companion for a much longer period than a girl on the catch for a husband.

Lord, how she longed for some such measure of security! Only to know each day that tomorrow one would still have a roof over one's head, a bed to lie in and food to put on the table. In six years she had never been able to cultivate that devil-may-care attitude that seemed to characterise the gentleman at the Feathers.

His face came into her mind as she thought of him. A comely countenance, with a degree of charm in that useful smile of his that should not be permitted to any one man. A fine figure, too—broad in the shoulder and muscled in the leg. And what was it about golden hair? Novelty, perhaps. It was not so long since that the fashionable had discarded their wigs and taken to cultivating natural heads. Yes, she had to concede that the gentleman's exterior qualities were uniformly pleasing.

Not that *she* was susceptible. Oh, no. She had long ago closed her heart against all invasion. Men—especially handsome men—were not *safe*.

She thrust her eyes open, as if she would banish the image from them. They fell upon the grey drizzle that followed the storm, and her spirits unaccountably sank. She discovered that she was hungry, and, having enquired the time of her neighbour in the coach, a thick-set farmer, decided it was safe to consume her sandwich. She would be in Mountsorrel, where she had been told to leave the coach, by three.

But the long haul through the muddy roads slowed the horses' progress almost to a walk, and it was not until after five in the evening that the vehicle finally came to a halt outside the George inn in Mountsorrel, a little place some distance before the larger town of Ashby-de-la-Zouch.

Weary to her bones, and once more cold to the marrow, Theda stepped down and requested the guard to unstrap her portmanteau from the back. She stood with it in her hand, looking about for some signs of a waiting servant. The George was busy with the stage-coach passengers, two of whom had gone in to bait, the others walking about to stretch their limbs while the ostlers led the exhausted cattle away and brought out a fresh team. But there seemed no one about who was not already occupied with his own legitimate business.

The air struck dank and chill, and the overcast sky pre-empted the onset of dusk. Apprehension began to filter into Theda's breast as she waited. Heaven send they had not given up on her! She shivered. The letter had definitely stated that she was to be met. But if they thought the coach was not coming. . .

Before she had quite given in to despair, however, from out of the doorway of the inn came a dour old man in ancient, shabby livery, with shiny elbows and tarnished braid. Back bent, he twisted this way and that, peering in a short-sighted way at the newcomers wandering around the yard.

This must be her guide! Theda decided, so relieved that she barely took in the poor quality of his attire, thinking only that the delay must have been made more acceptable to him by a lengthy sojourn in the tap-room. She hefted her portmanteau, and was about to cross to him when he spied her, and shuffled up, a trifle unsteady on his legs.

Squinting up at her out of a pair of rheumy eyes, he addressed her, his voice cracked and senile. 'Be the name Kyte?'

Theda sighed thankfully. 'Yes, I am Miss Kyte. Are you from the Merchiston house?'

The old man nodded briefly, chewing on something at the side of his mouth. Then he spat in the road, and delivered himself of a surly condemnation. 'Late you be.'

It was not an encouraging start.

There was little conversation exhanged on the journey to Merchiston Lodge, which was accomplished in a battered gig, drawn by a shuffling cob, long past its prime. The ancient servitor, who drove with a slack rein and a sublime disregard of the pot-holes, seemed to take it as a personal affront that Miss Kyte had kept him waiting for more than two hours. After animadverting bitterly on the demands made on his old bones, as he had heaved the lady's portmanteau into the boot, he had climbed laboriously into the gig without even offering to assist her to do the same.

Theda's lips had tightened, but she had made no

complaint. She was used to insolent treatment from
fellow servants—for she had long learned that a companion, be she never so genteel, was regarded as little
more than that. Her tiredness fled before the immediate prospect of encountering her new employer.
Despite the disrespectful non-welcome of her companion, she began to feel more hopeful as they left
Mountsorrel. They were passing through pleasant
country—hunting country, she knew, with open tracts
of undulating land among the cultivated fields, offering
a good many jumps and lengthy runs for the hardy
spirits who rode to hounds. The prospects were pleasing even on this dismal day in the gathering gloom.

But a few miles on, the country began to seem
wilder, with more clumps of trees, culminating in the
distance in what looked like a considerable forest.

'What is that?' she asked, pointing.

The aged servitor glanced along her arm and
responded shortly, 'Switham Thicket.'

'Thicket!' echoed Theda, astonished.

He seemed to understand her surprise. 'Be none so
big as looks. Lodge be just beyond. Village beyond that
again.'

'Switham village?'

But the old man had shot his bolt. He merely nodded, and Theda was left to contemplate the thicket as
they approached, the stark silhouettes of its close-
packed trees, still bare of leaves, jutting from the heavy
underbrush like so many giant goblins. The road cut a
swath through the centre of the belt of trees, and as
the gig passed between them they seemed to menace,
arms grotesquely waving, as if they resented this intru-
sion through their territory.

Theda shivered, and the old man beside her, flinging
her a sidelong look out of his rheumy eyes, smiled

sourly, as if he enjoyed the effect the place created on her. But he proved right about the size of Switham Thicket, for a bare quarter of a mile brought them to the outskirts of the other side, and almost immediately the horse was turned into a walled aperture of crumbling stone, its high, rusty iron gates wide open.

Even in the failing light, Theda could see that the drive was ill kept, and the surrounding gardens overgrown, and what must once have been a graceful line of trees bordering the rutted gravel lane now struck a flutter of apprehension in her breast. For the bald trunks with their empty branches thrusting into the blackening sky echoed the bleak and eerie threat of the thicket that ran parallel down its length, bordering the estate.

At the end of the drive, the house came into view, a low, rambling place of dark brick, crawling with ivy, with many leaded windows, some with broken panes, and gabled roofs. A long porch partially hid the squat front door, its arched cover all over tangled creepers, the grass and pavings all about it thick with weeds.

Theda's gaze ran over the shadowed building, dark but for a faint glimmer behind one or two of the myriad windows, dismay flooding her breast. To what kind of life had she come? Was this the genteel establishment she had hoped for? Even the least of her previous employers had a better-kept property than this!

The horse came to a stop before the porch, and the old servant got down and lugged her portmanteau out of the boot. Theda was more hesitant. She wished with all her heart that she could turn around and go back, depart from this unprepossessing, even *frightening* place before ever she discovered what awaited her within its mouldering walls. But there was no going back for the impoverished Miss Theodosia Kyte. Here lay her immediate future, and here she must stay.

Gathering her courage together, she descended from the gig and waited for the old man to precede her across the porch. As he reached the door, however, it was opened by a sturdy-looking dame in an old-fashioned working gown of grey wool, covered with a comprehensive apron, and a mob-cap concealing most of her greying hair but for two neat bands at the front parted in the centre. She was holding up an oil-lamp and peering out.

'At last!' she said in relieved tones. 'Miss Ara's fair spitting with impatience.'

'Weren't my fault, Taggy,' said the old man at once. 'She be late.'

The woman looked past him and caught sight of Theda. She came out on to the porch, lifting the lamp higher. 'You must be Miss Kyte. I'm Agnes Diggory, the housekeeper, and this here's my man, Adam.'

'How do you do?' Theda said, smiling a little and holding out a hand, insensibly warmed by the woman's greeting.

Mrs Diggory looked taken aback for a moment, but she took the hand and then ushered the lady inside, talking all the while.

'They stagecoaches ain't never to be trusted to keep time! I don't doubt you're in a rare hunger, miss. The mistress has had her dinner, but I've set aside a bite against your coming. I'll just take you in to Miss Ara, and when you're settled, like, I'll fetch it up to you.'

'Thank you, you are very kind,' Theda said grate-fully, glad to find Mrs Diggory a much friendlier soul than her dour spouse.

The old man had disappeared outside again without a word, having set Theda's portmanteau down in the

wide hall. As she was led towards the back of it, there
was time and light only for her to take in a number of
doors on either side, a pervasive smell of must, dark
wood panelling, and the central staircase leading to an
upper gallery that ran left and right above.

'Diggory'll take your bag up, miss,' the housekeeper
told her, opening a door to the left. She poked her
head in, raising her voice. 'It's Miss Kyte, Mum.' Then
she gestured to Theda to enter.

In a small, ill-lit parlour, with the meanest of fires in
the grate, was seated a middle-aged woman of daunting
aspect. She was as thin as was Theda herself, with a
scrawny look about the neck and chest, which were
encased in a plum-coloured poplin gown that looked
far from new, in spite of the now fashionable high
waist, and a woollen shawl huddled about the
shoulders. Her complexion was sallow, with lines of
bitterness running down to a mouth pinched in discontent, and she looked at Theda out of a pair of lacklustre
eyes, with patent contempt.

'So you're Miss Theodosia Kyte?' she said in a thin
voice whose tone matched the air of acidity that hung
about her.

Theda's heart sank. But she answered with composure. 'Yes, ma'am. You are Lady Merchiston, I
collect?'

'Do I look like a widow?' came the snappy response.
'No, I am not Lady Merchiston. I am Araminta
Merchiston, Lady Merchiston's daughter—for my sins!
You are not come to be a companion to *me*.'

Theda could barely repress a sigh of relief, although
she wondered at the strange way the woman spoke. 'I
beg your pardon. I thought, as Mrs Diggory showed
me in here——'

'My mother keeps to her bed,' Miss Merchiston

informed her 'You will meet her directly. She's been fretting herself to flinders, in case you should've changed your mind.'

'No, indeed. I'm afraid the coach was delayed considerably by the state of the roads after last night's storm.'

'Don't waste your excuses on me! It's *her* you'll have to placate—if you can.' She nodded at a chair opposite. 'For the moment you may sit down.'

'Thank you, but perhaps I might cleanse the journey's dust first?' suggested Theda.

'Presently. Sit down.'

Theda did so. Strangely, she felt more resentful of this lady's peremptory commands than she ever had of those of the merchants' wives she had previously been obliged to swallow. What would Araminta Merchiston say if she knew just how far above her in station was this obviously despised new companion?

Araminta was appraising her in a considering way. 'You don't look up to much. Purse-pinched, are you? I dare say that is why you were induced to accept so low a wage.'

Theda felt herself stiffening. 'It would appear, then, that we have both struck a satisfactory bargain.'

Miss Merchiston's eyes narrowed to slits. 'Take care, Miss Kyte! I will not tolerate insolence.'

'You misunderstand me, ma'am,' Theda said sweetly. 'I meant only to suggest that the advantages are mutual.'

'That remains to be seen,' said Araminta, relaxing again. 'You have yet to prove yourself.'

'I shall endeavour not to disappoint you, ma'am.'

If there was a barb to this speech, it passed Miss Merchiston by. She snorted.

'It is nothing to do with me. Much I care! No one

can say that it was I who insisted on having someone
in. Squandering money, I call it. Except if your coming
may release me from the necessity ever to speak to
that old hag again! That would be money well spent.'

Shocked, Theda could only stare at her.

'You need not look like that,' snapped the other
woman testily. 'You will learn soon enough how matters stand in this rat-infested refuge from hell!'

Theda hardly knew how to answer such a speech.
She had come to an unhappy house, that was clear.
Pray heaven she might find the courage to endure the
horrors that must lie in store! Pulling herself out of the
dazed state into which the woman's embittered words
had thrown her, she tried for a non-committal tone.

'Perhaps it would be best if you told me what duties
I might be expected to perform.'

'It is no use asking me. You will do what my mother
demands of you, of course.'

'I see. Then might it not be a good idea for you to
introduce me to Lady Merchiston?'

'I dare say it would,' agreed Araminta acidly, 'but I
shan't do it!'

Nonplussed, Theda said without thinking, 'How very
odd!'

'Pah! There is nothing odd in it. Why should I? I
can't abide her, nor she me! Taggy will take you up.'

The lines of bitterness seemed more pronounced
than ever as she rose from her chair and crossed to the
door. Theda, both amazed and troubled, got up to
follow her. Miss Merchiston opened the door and
called out in a piercing shriek for Mrs Diggory.

'Tag-gy! *Tag-gy!*'

Theda lifted her hands to cover her ears as the sound
echoed about the cavernous hall, seeming to go right
through her. Doubtless the bells in this house were

broken—like everything else! Her spirits drooped, and she began to dread the coming meeting with Lady Merchiston. If the mother resembled the daughter, heaven help her!

Miss Merchiston had wandered out of the room, calling out again. As Theda came out into the dark hall, she heard someone bustling down the stairs, and recognised Mrs Diggory's voice.

'I'm coming, Miss Ara!' She added as she reached the bottom of the stairs where Miss Merchiston had arrived to meet her, 'I've told the mistress as how Miss Kyte is come at last, and she said to bring her up straight.'

'Then do so, Taggy, do so!'

'Not me, Miss Ara,' said Agnes Diggory apologetically. 'She wants *you* to bring her. Insistent, she was. You know her way.'

In the light of the housekeeper's lamp, Theda saw Araminta Merchiston's face tighten into fury. Without a word, the woman began to ascend the stairs. Mrs Diggory nudged the new companion, her tone low.

'Better go after her, miss. I'll be following soon enough to make sure you get to your room and have that bite o' supper. Leave it to them two and you'd starve. Sleep in the barn, too, you could, for all of them!'

Theda threw her a grateful look, and hurried after Miss Merchiston, whose familiarity with the steep staircase enabled her to keep up a cracking pace. The upper gallery was lit only by two of the many triple candleholders in wall-sconces, one at the top of the stairs, and one down the left corridor that led back to the front of the house. Miss Merchiston went to the last door, thumped twice on it with her clenched fist as if

by such violence she announced her coming, and threw
it wide so that it bounced off the wall with a crash.

There was a screech from within and an instant
cacophony of barking and scolding broke out. Entering
behind Miss Merchiston, Theda beheld a huge four-
poster bed, its curtains fully open, the inhabitant of
which was largely obscured by a black, woolly-haired
mongrel standing astride her legs, apparently disputing
Araminta's right of entry.

'Hector, be quiet!' came a croaked command from
behind the dog, and a veined hand reached for his
scruff and tugged him back. 'Enough, I say, you foolish
beast!'

The terrier allowed himself to be dragged down to
lie on the blankets, and Theda was able to see her new
mistress in the light afforded by a lamp on her bedside
table and a set of two candelabra resting on a nearby
chest of drawers. She had a glimpse of a lined face
under straggling white locks, rising out of the bulges of
an over-large nightgown, before the dog, Hector, catching sight of the stranger, set up another protest, rising
as he did so.

'Hector! *Down*, do you hear me?'

'Dratted animal!' muttered Araminta over her
mother's imprecations and Hector's excited barks, giving him a baleful glare. 'He ought to be shot.'

It happened that the dog was silenced just as her last
remark emerged, and over his body, flattened now to
the sheet where he lay panting, the old woman sitting
up in the bed flashed her a look.

'I heard that!'

'You were meant to,' snapped Araminta instantly.

'Liar!' snarled her mother. 'You don't dare touch my
dog, not while I'm alive.'

'I never said I would.'

'You said he ought to be shot. And you never meant it for *my* ears, that's sure. You wouldn't jeopardise your chances, no, you would not.'

Araminta's face screwed into a mask of rage and she breathed deeply, as if she could barely contain herself. The old woman's mouth twisted into a smile of gleeful satisfaction, and she turned to Theda.

A pair of sharp black eyes looked her up and down out of the most wasted features Miss Kyte had ever seen. The wrinkled skin was stretched tightly over the bones, paper-thin, blue-shadowed over pink crêpe. The remnant strands of long white hair lay clumped and matted about the skull, and a stalk-like neck vanished into the white folds of her nightgown. Only the eyes, intelligent and keen, seemed to live.

'This is she, is it?' demanded Lady Merchiston in her croaking voice.

Theda dropped a curtsy. 'I am Theodosia Kyte, ma'am.'

The old woman turned back to her daughter, remarking belligerently, 'Kept her talking downstairs so you might give her a mean account of me, eh?'

'Why should I?' responded Araminta, matching her tone. 'You'll show her your true colours soon enough.'

'No doubt she's already seen yours!' retorted her mother. 'One look's enough to turn the girl's stomach. I'd wager she wishes she could turn tail and run already!' She flicked a glance at Theda. 'Don't you, eh?'

'Well, she can't,' said Araminta before Theda could reply. 'Anyone can see she'd no choice about taking the post, worse luck for her.'

Lady Merchiston's eyes snapped. 'If you'd done your duty by me, as a daughter should, the post wouldn't have been there to take.'

'Don't you begin that!' Araminta ordered shrilly.

Hector the dog growled under his breath, shifting a little and eyeing her. Lady Merchiston put out a hand and grasped his rough coat, soothing murmurs issuing from her as she gave her daughter a reproachful look.

Araminta ignored both the glare and the dog's menacing noises. 'I've been willing and able all along to do what's needful,' she went on. 'This was *your* idea, madam Mother.'

'That's as may be, but I shouldn't have to pay for what's mine by right.'

'Pah! Much you care for that. Well do I know you've gone to these lengths only to spite me. Using up as much of my inheritance as you can. Well, don't fret yourself. Diggory's on your side, as usual. He's done his best to ruin us these three hours at the ale-house in Mountsorrel, I'll be bound. And for *that* you may thank Miss Kyte.'

Theda, listening to this venomous interchange in open-mouthed shock and dismay, almost jumped at the sudden attack.

'It was not my fault!' she protested involuntarily, and thus brought herself once again under the scrutiny of those keen eyes from the bed.

'What did you call yourself?'

'I am Theodosia Kyte, Lady Merchiston,' Theda repeated patiently.

'You are, are you?' All at once she fell back against her pillows, a grim smile playing about her mouth. The dog relaxed, too, settling more comfortably under her stroking fingers and closing his eyes. 'Very well, then, Theodosia, no need to look so downcast. Unlike me, you won't be in Purgatory for long.'

'Pah!' snorted Araminta. 'Don't raise her hopes.'

'Pah to you!' riposted her mother childishly. 'And don't you go nagging at Adam, you hear me?'

'Precious Adam? As if I would!' returned her daughter sarcastically. 'Much I care for Adam! You can take him with you when you go, for all of me.'

The old lady's cheeks flew two spots of angry colour. '*Wicked*. Take yourself off, Araminta Merchiston!'

'Gladly,' said the other, making for the door.

'And send me Taggy!' called the old lady after her.

A slammed door was all the response she got. Hector's head jerked up, but was restrained by his mistress's hand.

'Steady, boy.' Turning again to Theda, she grimaced. 'Think you've strayed into a madhouse, I dare say.'

Theda was so appalled that she could barely repress a shudder, never mind summon up a smile. She tried for a neutral tone.

'I may as well begin as I mean to go on, ma'am. Is there anything I can do for you?'

To her surprise, Lady Merchiston sighed wearily and the life went out of her eyes. Her voice sank tiredly, as if in the absence of her daughter's goading all energy had left her.

'I should not think so at all. She was right, you see. Pay no mind to what she says. Might have been my idea—well, it was, but I only said it in a fit of temper!— but *she* carried it out. That's her spite, you see. She knew I didn't really want you—or anyone.'

An odd mixture of relief and apprehension made Theda's heartbeat flutter. 'Does that mean that you intend to—to send me away?'

'Don't *want* to stay, do you?'

Theda bit her lip. She did not. But she was almost penniless. To leave here now would be nothing short of disaster. The black eyes had recovered some spark of life, a question in them, as the old woman lay looking at her.

Lord, what could she say? Well, the two of them had made no bones about what they thought of her. Why should she balk at plain-speaking?

'The truth is, Lady Merchiston, that I have no alternative. I came here at the instigation of your letter, believing myself to have secured a position. I don't wish to seem importunate, but if you do intend to sever the agreement I will be obliged to ask at least for the reimbursement of the expenses of my journey.'

'Very correct, ain't you?' observed her ladyship. 'You can stay—if you can stand it.'

'But if you don't require my services——'

'I don't require a *companion*, Theodosia.' A harsh laugh escaped the almost bloodless lips, and the eyes mocked. 'What I need is an undertaker. I am a dying woman.'

CHAPTER THREE

DR SPILSBY laid down his patient's wrist and patted her hand. 'Very much better, my lady, very much better.'

'Don't lie, man!' croaked Lady Merchiston. 'We both know I'll not live out the year. Or have you of a sudden found a cure for this wasting disease?'

'I don't pretend that you are to be cured, my lady,' smiled the doctor, from under the Physical bob-wig that marked his profession. 'But your pulse is not so tumultuous and your colour has improved.'

'My spirits, too,' agreed the old lady, throwing a wry glance at Theda, who was over by the windows.

'Certainly.' Dr Spilsby rose. 'I think I may safely say that you are in a deal sounder trim these last few weeks.'

'That will be the onset of spring,' said Theda lightly, coming forward to the bed and straightening the coverlet.

'The onset of Theodosia, more like!' uttered Lady Merchiston, quizzing her. 'I declare to you, Spilsby, I was never so browbeaten! The girl is at me night and day. If she is not shovelling food down my throat, or forcing your noxious potions upon me, she is——'

'Opening the windows and changing the bedclothes,' put in Theda calmly. 'Both of which were much needed.'

'So you say! Just as you will insist on my wearing this objectionable cap,' complained her ladyship, flicking at the offending article with a bony finger. 'And I hate chess!'

'That is because you always cheat when I am not looking, instead of applying yourself to win by intelligence.'

'You see?' Lady Merchiston turned to the doctor's grinning face. 'Why can't she leave me alone to die in peace?'

'Because I need the work, Lady Merchiston,' Theda said, her eyes twinkling as she gently raised the old lady a little and placed an extra pillow at her back. 'And you know very well that once you are gone Miss Araminta will throw me out of the house.'

'I'll haunt the place if she does,' threatened the old lady.

'I've no doubt you'll do so in any event,' Theda remarked. 'To look at you one would think you were practising for it already.'

Lavinia Merchiston burst into cackling laughter, in which the doctor readily joined her.

'I begin to think that *you* are the tonic, Miss Kyte,' he said jovially.

He was quite right. Theda had been struck by an unexpected pang of compassion for Lady Merchiston. She was a cantankerous woman, but she was literally at death's door. She looked much older than her sixty-odd years, wasted as she was. Yet her household, instead of doing what they might to ease her last days, were not merely neglectful, but downright cruel.

Theda had been horrified to discover, by daylight that next day, how filthy was the condition in which the poor lady was left. Not only was the bedchamber in which she was confined dusty and cold, but her bed-linen and clothing were soiled and damp, her person unwashed, her hair uncombed.

Theda had gone down to the housekeeper, tight-lipped and curt, to ask that these things be remedied forthwith.

'All very well, Miss Kyte,' had said Agnes Diggory bluntly, 'for you to come the fine lady over me, but I've only the one pair of hands! There's only myself and Adam, you know, barring Mrs Elswick as comes in to cook of an afternoon.'

'*What*?' Theda gasped, shocked. 'Do you tell me that you are the only two servants to manage this whole barrack of a house?'

'That's right, miss. Well, most of the rooms is shut up now, so Diggory does the cleaning and makes up the fires. He can't manage more besides the garden. I dare say you've noticed, miss, as he's a good many years my senior?'

'Yes, I had noticed,' Theda agreed gently, without further comment.

'Well, he was a good fellow in his day,' the house-keeper said philosophically. 'A lifetime of this place, though, is enough to sour any man!'

Recognising the rough apology contained in this speech for the dour ill manners of her spouse, Theda smiled warmly. 'Believe me, Mrs Diggory, I have already seen enough to convince me of that!'

A grim twist came on to Taggy's lips. 'Then you can see how it is, miss. A body can't do more than it can do. What Adam doesn't see to falls to me. That means I've all the kitchen tasks and the washing to do, not to mention acting as lady's maid to both—and everything else besides!'

'But does not Miss Merchiston help at all?'

'*She*?' said Mrs Diggory witheringly. 'She'd not lift a finger in this house, she wouldn't. Not if we was to up and go. She'd starve first!'

From what she had seen of Araminta, Theda was

ready to believe it. She recalled the housekeeper's kindness to her the previous evening, when she had led her from her mistress's chamber and shown her the room that Miss Merchiston had assigned for her use. It was, as Theda had not been surprised to find, up in the attics in the servants' quarters.

Mrs Diggory had made some effort, and the little room was at least warm from a small fire in the grate, and there was a down coverlet on the narrow cot bed. But apart from a commode under the bed, and a rickety table with a cracked basin and ewer upon it, the only other furnishing the room afforded was a rail across one corner for her wardrobe, with a cotton curtain to conceal the clothes that would be hung upon it.

The housekeeper had looked about at her own handiwork with an apologetic air. 'I had thought to put you next the mistress, but Miss Ara wouldn't hear of it, I'm sorry to say.'

'I will manage, thank you,' Theda had told her, her senses by this time becoming dulled to the dreadful impressions that had battered her one after the other in this horrid house.

The food to which Agnes Diggory led her had been welcome, however, and she had chosen to consume it in the friendly housekeeper's little pantry next to the kitchen, rather than risk encountering Miss Merchiston once again tonight.

But next morning, she had woken determined to make the best of it. The house had seemed less threatening in the cold light of day, and it became obvious that a pretty establishment had been rendered hideous by neglect. The wood panelling was thick with grime, and everywhere there was a film of dust. Windows were kept closed, and their murky panes—added to the rampant ivy—kept out the light, leaving shadowed corners that would unnerve the stoutest heart.

Lady Merchiston's situation, Theda recognised, was symptomatic of the whole, and she could appreciate that the Diggorys could scarcely be expected to cope with a task that would baffle an army of servants.

'I beg your pardon, Mrs Diggory,' she said contritely. 'I had not realised. If you will be good enough to furnish me with the necessary linen, I will take it upon myself to make Lady Merchiston a degree more comfortable.'

She had done a good deal more than that. It had taken a few days to persuade her ladyship to accept change, for she had for so long been used to living in squalor that she could not at first accustom herself to an altered way of life. As Theda cleaned and swept and polished, she subjected her to a series of scoffing remarks.

'You are wasting your time, girl! What matters it if the place is a pigsty? I am as good as dead, and Araminta will not thank you. She is more like to fly out at you.'

'Then you may tell her that you ordered me to do it,' Theda suggested. 'She cannot gainsay you.'

'Yes, but I didn't order it. I don't *care* about the dirt.'

But Theda would not be deterred. At length she persuaded Lady Merchiston to allow herself to be tidied up. With infinite care and patience, Theda first cleaned the frail and malodorous body from head to toe, enduring in silence a barrage of abuse and complaint the while. Then she coaxed her employer into a fresh nightgown and placed a clean, although old-fashioned day-cap of cotton and lace upon the freshly washed and combed hair. When the old lady was helped into a newly made-up and just warmed bed, with clean sheets and blankets, and a coverlet of soft down unearthed from a trunk in the attics and hung outside to air, she sat back against the bank of lace-edged pillows and burst into a paroxysm of dry sobs.

'Ma'am, what is it?' Theda asked in quick concern. 'Did I hurt you?'

Lady Merchiston shook her head weakly, her veined hand reaching out. Seating herself on the edge of the bed, Theda took it into hers and her fingers closed strongly about the bony ones she held. Finding her own pocket handkerchief, she gave it into the old lady's other hand. In a moment her ladyship's sobs had ceased and she dried her few tears.

'What ails you, Lady Merchiston?' asked Theda gently.

The black eyes snapped at her. 'Did you never hear of killing by kindness? I dare say I shall expire without delay!'

For a moment Theda looked at her with hurt in her eyes, a little puzzled. Then she noted a curious twitching at the edge of Lady Merchiston's bloodless lips and an intensity of the creases at the corners of her eyes.

Why, the old lady was quizzing her! This was her way of thanks—the only way, perhaps, that she knew in the pitiful misery of her life.

Theda raised her brows. 'I see you are determined to prove your assertion that I have been wasting my time. In any event, you will at least not now disgrace your coffin.'

A crack of hoarse laughter was surprised out of her employer, and from that moment she began to improve in spirit. In the three weeks since, Theda had tried as far as possible to keep her so.

The one battle she lost was over the dog, Hector. He might be banished during cleaning, but he was still permitted to jump on to the bed. Compromising, Theda found a piece of old blanket to place on the coverlet so that his hairs might not spread everywhere. Occasionally, Hector gratified her by using it.

He had been ejected during the doctor's visit, and she let the dog back in to the room as she escorted Spilsby downstairs to the front door. It was almost time for her mistress's luncheon, and she went towards the back of the hall to the breakfast parlour, one of the few rooms still in use, to see if Mrs Diggory had as yet laid out the tray. As she neared the door, she heard voices within, and hesitated.

'If you imagine she does not see through your wiles,' came Araminta's shrill tone, 'then you are a great fool, Benedict.'

'Not as big a one as you, Araminta, believe me,' responded a male voice contemptuously. 'At least I have the sense to treat her with respect.'

This was not Adam Diggory, whose surly growl Theda would have recognised. It was a light voice, and it stirred a chord in her memory.

'I would scorn to display such hypocrisy as you delight in,' retorted Miss Merchiston. 'It will avail you nothing, however. But don't let me stop you. Go on up, do, and play off your airs for her benefit. Much I care!'

'I shall certainly go up, but you will announce me, Araminta, like the dutiful daughter you are,' he returned sardonically.

'Pah! I am no longer obliged to be dutiful, I thank God!' she snapped back. 'There is a servant now to attend to all that.'

The door opened as she spoke, and Theda stepped forward.

'You want me, Miss Merchiston?'

'No, I don't,' Araminta said at once, walking into the hall. 'But *he* does. Benedict, come out here!'

The gentleman stepped through the doorway, demanding testily, 'What the devil is it?'

Then he caught sight of Theda and stopped dead, staring. Her eyes widened and she felt quite faint.

In the dim light of the hall, so reminiscent of that other time, she could not mistake. It was the gentleman of the Feathers inn, her kind benefactor.

Mr Beckenham blinked. In the woman's eyes he saw a like recognition and knew his senses did not deceive him. It *was* his ghost!

He opened his mouth to greet her, a smile lighting up his features, when he caught an unmistakable signal in her face. The grey eyes were frantic, and an infinitesimal shake of her white-capped head begged his silence.

Glancing at Araminta, he espied one of her venomous looks as she eyed the girl, lips pinched together. Dear God, what the devil had his poor ghost done to excite her vicious enmity?

'Aren't you going to present me, Araminta?' he asked blandly, and saw a flicker of relief in Theda's eyes before she discreetly lowered them.

Miss Merchiston flashed him a scornful glance. 'Who do you think she is, a guest at a ball?'

'I think she is a *lady*,' said Mr Beckenham in a hard voice, 'and entitled at least to a modicum of courtesy.'

Theda's head came up swiftly, and again her eyes flashed a warning signal, as Araminta turned on him.

'Pah! If she was so genteel, she wouldn't have come *here* for the pittance she's paid. Not that I care! She's Miss Kyte, come to be *companion* to that evil hag upstairs, if you must know.'

The gentleman inclined his head. 'How do you do,

Miss Kyte? Since I am certain that my dear cousin
Araminta will neglect to inform you of it, allow me to
introduce myself. I am Benedict Beckenham, Lady
Merchiston's godson.'

'Cousin? Pah!'

'*Distant* cousin,' amended Mr Beckenham.

'How do you do, sir?' said Theda politely, sinking
into a curtsy.

'La-di-da!' snapped Araminta angrily. 'Go on, girl,
take him up. No doubt he'll beguile you, too, with his
famous charm. With what result remains to be seen—
but don't think you'll get away with any of *that* sort of
conduct in this house.'

With which she stalked across the back of the hall to
her little parlour opposite, and slammed herself into it.

'Phew!' uttered Mr Beckenham, grinning. 'What a
curst cat that woman is! How can you bear it?'

'Hush, pray!' whispered Theda. 'She has the ears of
a cat, too, and I shall suffer for it.'

'I should think you would,' agreed Mr Beckenham in
a lowered tone. 'Let us remove from this vicinity at
once.'

'You had better come up to Lady Merchiston,'
Theda said, leading the way to the stairs. 'Thank you
for not giving me away. If she had heard the circumstances of our former meeting, I am very sure she
would prove as remorseless as Mrs Pigdon at the
Feathers.'

'Undoubtedly. It is as well you stopped me.' He
grinned down at her as they ascended the stairs
together. 'But what an extraordinary thing! That *this* is
where you should have been headed. Had I had an
inkling——'

'I am glad you had not,' interrupted Theda. 'If you
had warned me *then* of the horrors in store, I should

have thrown myself *under* the stage rather than have travelled inside it.'

Mr Beckenham laughed. 'As bad as that?'

'Worse!'

'The devil it is!' He looked her over as they reached the gallery, pausing at the top of the stairs. 'At least you have gained a little flesh.' He reached out a hand to cup her chin, scanning her still thin face with its near translucent skin. 'But so pale still, poor ghost!'

Theda smiled, but pushed his hand away. 'I am always so. And I had thought you had decided I was a witch.'

His lips twisted wryly. 'If so, you are come aptly to roost. In this establishment, the broomsticks are out in force!'

She gave that infectious gurgle of laughter, and his eyes warmed. Theda found herself looking into them and became aware of a tiny flutter of the heart. She stiffened, drawing back. None of that! She turned towards the corridor.

'I had better take you in to her ladyship, Mr Beckenham.'

'Oh, not so formal,' he begged, his hand staying her as he grasped her arm.

She met his eyes again and the full charm of his smile was turned upon her. Abruptly she recalled Araminta's words. 'No doubt he'll beguile you, too.' The picture flashed into her mind of the coffee-room at the Feathers inn at Newark. The smile had come out for the landlord, and disappeared when he had left the room. Again, separately, for Mrs Pigdon. Oh, yes, he had the power all right. But *she* was not to be beguiled. Not Theodosia Kyte. Reserve entered her voice.

'I think it would be best if we remained on formal terms.'

'Why?' he asked unexpectedly. 'When we are already friends?'

'Because. . .' Nonplussed for a moment, she hesitated. But the solution was obvious. 'Because it would be inappropriate to my position here, and I have no need of further excuses to call down Miss Merchiston's reproaches upon my head.'

He nodded, releasing her arm, but Theda thought there was a shade of disappointment in his face.

'Well, I've no wish to do that. I don't doubt your life is sufficiently trying already.'

Theda continued along the gallery, towards Lady Merchiston's room, feeling ridiculously guilty, as if she had been ungracious. She did owe him something, after all. But he was dangerously attractive. She could not afford to allow her guard to slip.

There was no doubt of her employer's beguilement, she thought, as Lady Merchiston set eyes on the visitor coming into her room behind Miss Kyte.

'Benedict! My dear boy, what a lovely surprise!'

Hector, waking abruptly, looked up and set up a joyous barking, leaping to his feet and wagging a curly tail.

The gentleman's face lit as his smile came out and he went towards the bed with the intention of grasping the veined hands held out towards him. But he had first to respond to the overtures of the dog.

'Well, sir? No, don't lick my face! Down, Hector. Quiet, boy!'

This last was uttered so sharply that the dog at once lay down, uttering a whimper as he rested his head on his paws, dark eyes longingly fixed on the newcomer.

'No need to snap at him!' protested his godmother crossly.

The smile turned on and he took hold of her hands.

'Your pardon, Aunt Lavvy, but he was stopping me getting to my favourite lady. How well you look!' he declared, saluting each of her hands in turn with his lips and then leaning down to kiss her cheek.

'I may look it, but my condition remains unchanged,' the old lady told him frostily, but her bony fingers clung to his.

Mr Beckenham looked about the altered room, and seemed to take in the improvements in one swift glance. 'On the contrary, your condition appears to me to be markedly different.' He let go her hands, and made up for his earlier error by making a fuss of the dog, who was sitting on his own blanket, adding laughingly, 'Even Hector is obliged to take notice of it, I see.'

'That is all Theodosia,' Lady Merchiston said in a complaining tone, glancing at her companion. 'She is a stickler for the tiniest mote of dust. You have no idea how she fidgets me with her never-ending spit and polish.'

'Fudge!' said Theda. 'It is you who fidgets *me*, Lady Lavinia, with all your carping and criticism.'

Mr Beckenham left off patting the dog and looked quickly round at her, a frown creasing his brow. How could she dare to address her employer in such terms?

'Carping and criticism!' echoed the old lady. 'Why, I am perfectly saintly about it, as well you know!'

Theda threw her a quizzing glance. 'A trifle premature, ma'am, that adjective. But be sure I shall write to the Archbishop of Canterbury on your behalf when the time comes.'

Lady Merchiston let out a cackling guffaw, and then noticed her godson's glance going from one to the other, his face a study. She leaned forward and tapped his hand where it lay on the coverlet, supporting his weight.

'Pay no mind to us, Benedict! Theodosia and I understand each other very well.'

'So it would seem,' he agreed, sending another frowning glance Theda's way.

She met it with a puzzled look in her eyes. Did he have some objection to such bantering? Could he not see how much good it was doing his godmother? As his eyes went back to the old lady, she saw the smile turn on again, and quick suspicion kindled in her breast.

Had Araminta been right in that brief exchange she had overheard in the breakfast parlour? Was Benedict Beckenham out to 'play off his airs' on Lady Merchiston for some purpose of his own? But for what? Surely there could be no gain to him from the old lady's death? It was not as if Merchiston Lodge and its inhabitants were possessed of any intrinsic value. Were they?

Giving herself a mental shake, she threw off the thoughts. It was no concern of hers, in any event. And if he was engaged on some scheme of his own, she had better leave him to pursue it without interference. She owed him that much at least.

'I shall leave you to enjoy your godson's company, ma'am,' she said lightly, moving to the door.

'Seizing the chance of a respite, you mean,' retorted Lady Merchiston.

'Naturally. Perhaps we may even persuade him to take my place at the chess-board.'

'Certainly not,' Mr Beckenham protested. 'I am perfectly inept at the game and you always beat me to flinders, Aunt Lavvy, as expert as you are.'

'There you are, Theodosia!' cackled his godmother. 'He thinks I'm expert.'

Theda was conscious of a feeling of sad disillusionment. There could be no doubt that the gentleman was out to flatter Lady Merchiston, for no one who had played with her could fail to notice that she cheated. What was more, the old lady *knew* what he was at, for the look she shot her companion had been brimful of mischief.

'In any event,' went on her employer, black eyes teasing, 'you are not getting shot of your duties so readily. You may take Hector out for his run now.'

'As you wish, ma'am,' Theda said equably, and called to the dog from the open doorway. 'Come along, boy! You're coming out with me.'

Hector stood undecided for a moment, his eyes travelling from Theda's outstretched hand back to the gentleman who was obviously a favourite with him.

'Go on, Hector!' ordered Mr Beckenham, clicking his fingers and pointing to the door.

'Yes, go, you misbegotten hound!' added Lady Merchiston in the caressing tone she reserved only for her pet.

Thus adjured, Hector jumped off the bed with a short bark and trotted out of the room. Theda shut the door behind them both, but not before she heard Mr Beckenham begin to speak again.

'And now, dear Aunt Lavvy, I have you all to myself! Have you missed me?'

Disgust rose in Theda as she made her way along the gallery. At her lowest ebb, she would have scorned to stoop to such tactics. Her opinion of Benedict Beckenham dropped sharply. Why she should be surprised, however, she had no notion. She had witnessed the on-off charm for herself when he had thought himself alone in the Feathers' coffee-room. Well, it was none of her affair, she reminded herself again. What was it to her if he chose to conduct himself with duplicity? But she could not help reflecting that Araminta, with all her faults, was at least honest in her dealings with her mother.

As she reached the bottom of the stairs, Araminta herself waylaid her, coming out of the shadows to place herself in the companion's way.

'You have left him with her, I collect? No doubt he is oozing and oiling his way into her favour. Much good may it do him!'

Hector had run ahead to hover by the front door, whining a little. But Theda hesitated, burningly curious suddenly. 'Why should he do so?'

'Why? To get out of her more than his allowance, of course. He was run off his legs the last time and he had only just been paid for the quarter.'

Theda's jaw dropped perceptibly. 'An allowance! Lord, how can Lady Merchiston afford it?'

A thin smile creased the woman's pinched mouth. 'Simpleton! You should not judge by appearances.' Then she seemed to recollect to whom she was speaking and drew herself up. 'Get on, girl—if, as I must suppose, you are taking that brute out for exercise.'

Theda turned to go, but suddenly Araminta seized her arm in a claw-like grip and came close, almost spitting into Theda's face.

'Don't you leave him there too long, understand? Oh, he'll have his way, I don't doubt, worming it out of her. But he wants *more* than a few measly hundred— and I aim to see he does not get it!'

The grip left Theda's arm then, and Araminta hurried away down the hall, back to her eyrie. Hector whined his impatience, bringing Theda back to herself with a start. Lord above! What plague was there on this house?

She shivered as she went to the door, but all at once she recalled what she had been about to do when Benedict Beckenham had made his astonishing appearance. She put a hand on Hector's woolly black head.

'Wait, Hector. Stay!'

It took only a few minutes to run to the kitchen and request Agnes Diggory to take Lady Merchiston's luncheon tray straight upstairs when it was ready, and then Theda passed out of the house into the early warmth of a sunny April day, Hector charging ahead.

Calling out to him, she turned to the right, making for the side of the house furthest from Switham Thicket, for she had not forgotten a previous occasion when he had dashed off into the belt of trees. She had never so much resented having been made to take over responsibility for the dog from old Adam, who had been used to walk him, than on that day. Chasing him, she had rapidly lost her bearings in the heavy forest terrain and only by accident had come out again behind the house into the vegetable garden. Although the stark trees were just beginning to be in leaf, and familiarity had lessened the menacing air of the place, Theda still found herself uncomfortable within it.

The house itself no longer held so much terror for her. She had found an opportunity to creep into the large saloon at the front downstairs, where in the gloom created by the velvet curtains drawn across the windows she had seen that the large and ugly old-fashioned Queen Anne furniture was shrouded in sheets. But in the massive ballroom across the way there were only a few chairs and a sideboard or two, and even on a dismal day the light had fallen on the intricate design of a wooden parquet floor and pretty chiaroscuro frescoes painted into the panels of gracefully arched walls.

In fact, Theda thought it a beautiful old building, and felt it to be a pity that it should have been allowed to go to rack. This she had thought until this moment to be due to a shortage of funds. Now, for the first time, here was Araminta hinting that this was not the case.

For the lord's sake, then, why did they not put in some repairs? And why be so penny-pinching in the matter of service, leaving poor Agnes and Adam Diggory overburdened with their load? It could not always have been thus. Was it perhaps since Sir John Merchiston's death that things had been allowed to slide to this pass?

With frequent admonishments to Hector—who not unnaturally found enormous pleasure in exploring the overgrown gardens—to keep close, she strolled to the back of the house where a huge stable block stood almost empty. In front of it was the kitchen garden, which was the only part of the grounds to be kept in order, for Adam Diggory, although he grumbled at the necessity, was obliged to tend it as it provided most of the vegetable produce for the household table.

There had at one time, Agnes had told her, been a full complement of horses and hounds, for Sir John had been a keen sportsman. Few men living in Leicester were not, Theda reflected, for in her former life she had learned early that this was the best hunting country in England.

It crossed her mind fleetingly that perhaps this was the attraction for Benedict Beckenham. Did he want the house?

A footfall behind her made her turn, and she gasped to see the gentleman himself walking up to her. He was smiling, but the smile did not quite reach his eyes. Theda's heart began to beat rather fast, and she was conscious of a feeling of trepidation.

'So there you are!' he called in a friendly tone.

It sounded brittle, Theda thought. Unlike the way he had spoken to her earlier, or the previous time they had met. Was he wearing a mask?

'I have wasted a good many minutes hunting about the front.'

'Does Lady Merchiston want me?' Theda asked quickly.

'No, I left her to her luncheon. It is I who want you.'

He smiled again, but Theda could not respond to an overture she felt to be false. She eyed him with misgiving.

'Why do you look at me so?' he demanded, a frown descending on to his brow.

She shrugged and looked away, over to where Hector was investigating a hole in the base of the stable wall, not having noticed the new arrival.

Mr Beckenham seized her shoulders. 'Look at me, confound you!'

She did, and the sudden flare of her eyes made him let her go. He stared at her in some perplexity.

'Have I incurred your displeasure, Miss Kyte?'

'No, how should you?' she said in a light tone at variance with the sudden trembling of her fingers.

'I don't know how,' he said slowly, 'but something has changed in your manner to me.'

Theda bit her lip. 'I might say the same.'

'*Touché*.' He flung up a hand and a smile of genuine warmth lit his eyes. 'Very well, let us be frank. My godmother has been singing your praises, you see, and—you will have to forgive my suspicious mind!—it set me wondering.'

Theda's frown deepened. She felt a surge of anger. 'You are suspicious of me? For what reason, pray? What is it that you "wonder"?'

He was not noticeably discomfited by her tone. His eyes scanned her face, as if he sought there an answer to the problem perplexing his mind.

'I wonder *why* you have been so good to Aunt Lavvy. I can see for myself how much you have done, and how her spirits have improved. Yet when I first came, you tried to make me think your position here was untenable. It seems to me it cannot be as bad as you made out, if you are so well able to fascinate the old lady into thinking you indispensible to her comfort!'

Theda listened to this speech in rising indignation. Did he *dare* to impute such motives to her as he clearly had himself? What in the world had *she* to gain? In a low tone, husky with distress, she responded.

'Mr Beckenham, since I am in some sort indebted to you, I will, if you please, refrain from making you any answer, for I cannot take it upon myself to do so without speaking to you in a manner which must sound both insolent and ungrateful!'

She turned from him on the words and was aware that her tone had risen at the last. His voice followed her.

'Theodosia, wait!'

She kept on, and he was obliged to quicken his pace to catch up.

'Wait!' he repeated urgently, and, coming in front of her, grasped her arms, forcibly stopping her progress. Her smouldering eyes met the apology in his. 'I have only to beg your pardon, Miss Kyte, and confess that I entirely misread the situation. Forgive me!'

Theda eyed him uncertainly, some of the fire dying

out of her face. But she was still indignant, and she could not help the protest from leaving her lips.

'What could I have to gain, other than making the best of a bad bargain?'

'I know, I know,' he said soothingly.

'If I have a motive,' she pursued, her belligerence lessening, 'it is no different from that which led you to aid me when first we met. The poor woman was left in the wretchedest discomfort. If I feel compassion for her, it is not to be wondered at.' She found that tears were trickling from her eyes, and dashed them away with an impatient hand. 'I have only done what lay within my power to better her lot. And if it is the manner in which I address her which concerns you, let me tell you that she derives great enjoyment from such acerbic exchanges. It brightens her mood.'

'Yes,' he agreed quietly. 'I have frequently observed how she takes pleasure in goading Araminta into the worst of tempers.'

'Yes, but those quarrels upset her, too. With me it is merely a game.'

She sniffed and discovered that Mr Beckenham was offering her a pocket handkerchief. She shook her head, retrieving her own from the pocket in her petticoats.

'I don't seem to remember that the name you once gave me was "Theodosia",' he remarked as she dried her eyes. 'Though I'm afraid it slipped my memory almost immediately.'

'No, it was Theda,' she told him, replacing the handkerchief. A faint smile flickered over her lips. 'It was the pet name for me that was favoured at home.'

Mr Beckenham frowned down at her. 'You have not been "home" for some little time, I gather. I do now recall you saying no one had used the name in years.'

'Six, to be exact,' Theda said flatly.

'You must be older than you look.'

'I am almost four-and-twenty.'

'Dear God! Don't tell me you left your home at seventeen?'

Theda was silent. She looked at him with an air of apology. 'I am afraid I cannot say any more. I should not have said so much. I know it must appear churlish when I am under such an obligation to you——'

'Oh, the devil!' he snapped suddenly. 'Must you keep on throwing that up at me? For my part, there is *no* obligation. You owe me nothing.'

'But I do.'

'Oh, be quiet, girl! I don't want to hear another word on the subject.'

She said no more, although she could not herself treat the matter so lightly. Turning, she began to retrace her path towards the house. He fell into step beside her, and presently spoke again, his tone more normal.

'I am glad, at any rate, that you do not find your position here as irksome as I had supposed.'

Theda glanced up at him with an amused look. 'You are easily brought to reverse your views, are you not, Mr Beckenham?'

'What do you mean?' he asked, slightly irritated.

'I came here to be employed as a companion,' she told him. 'Instead I find myself acting also in the capacity of lady's maid and sick-nurse, for neither of which occupations have I the least experience. Your godmother is *bedridden*, Mr Beckenham. Have you any idea what that entails?'

She saw by his face that he had not, and grimaced as she thought of the gruesome tasks she was obliged to perform, degrading both for herself and for her far from easy patient. She opened her mouth again and he quickly held up a hand.

'No, don't tell me! My imagination is of an order lively enough to appreciate the invidious nature of your position without a recital of the sordid details.'

'I will spare you, then,' Theda said, with an irrepressible gurgle of mirth. 'I will remind you only that, added to all this, my employer is not likely to live very long, and I am therefore already at the necessity of seeking another post. Not, I may say, that almost *any* other post would not be preferable to this one!'

'I am sure it would,' he agreed, with a sympathetic twist of the lips.

'Well, then, I don't need to elaborate on the miserable atmosphere of this place, where everyone is at outs, and I must be always on my guard. For when one is dealing with such volatile temperaments, the slightest thing may result in my instant dismissal. Which, Mr Beckenham, I shudder to think on!'

'I wish you will address me by name!' he said in some annoyance. 'We are alone just for the moment.'

'No. If I do it in private, I may easily fall into the way of doing so in public. You must realise that Miss Merchiston loses no opportunity that offers of scolding me.'

'Of course she does,' scoffingly answered Mr Beckenham. 'Quite apart from the fact that she is regularly ill-tempered, she must be vilely jealous of you.'

'Jealous? But why?'

'My good girl, don't be a fool! You have made such a hit with Aunt Lavvy that it was inevitable she should be.'

Theda stopped still suddenly and faced him. 'Why

does she hate her mother so much? I have never seen such bitterness!'

He threw up his eyes. 'Need you ask? She was thwarted in her youth in her choice of husband. I don't recall it very well, for it happened before I came, and I was too young to be much interested, in any event.'

'You grew up here, then?'

'In this unloving family, yes. It deteriorated very much on Uncle John's death, but by then I had long left to live elsewhere. Once Aunt Lavvy became bed-ridden, Araminta had everything very much as she chose.'

Theda looked curiously at him. He had spoken in a flat, matter-of-fact way, as if all this meant nothing to him.

'Could you not have intervened?' she ventured.

He shrugged. 'I have no influence with Araminta. Besides, unless I chose to remain here, how could I see that things went on well? I have no claims upon the place, nor on Aunt Lavvy, you know.'

'But are you not related?' Theda asked, puzzled. 'And your aunt *is* your godmother.'

'She is not my aunt. I call her so only as a courtesy.' He looked at her. 'As you do with your "Lady Lavinia". She is not entitled to that, you know.'

'I know. It was agreed between us as the most suitable form of address.'

He smiled. 'You mean *you* decided it.'

'Well, yes,' she admitted, on a slight laugh. 'After I had been criticised for employing "Lady Merchiston" and "your ladyship", I finally found that compromise which she accepted. But you call cousins with Araminta, do you not?'

'Remote cousins only. Her father and my mother were distantly related—second or third cousins, I dare say. So, you see, I really have no rights here. *Most* of what Aunt Lavvy does for me, she does from choice — over and above my allowance, that is, which is held in trust.' His voice hardened. 'And she may easily choose *not* to continue to do it. Make no mistake! Araminta's selfishness and her spiteful, peevish nature are inherited.'

CHAPTER FOUR

STARTLED, Theda could only gaze at him. There was something in his voice that made her believe he was not speaking from malice himself. There was hurt behind the harsh words. What had Lavinia, Lady Merchiston done to make him speak so?

Could she have treated him to similar displays of ill will as she showed her daughter? But why? Surely Benedict had done nothing to attract her malice. Well, whatever else, this household was certainly intriguing!

As one, they turned to continue on around the side of the house, Hector racing along before them.

'A pity, perhaps, that Araminta was not permitted to marry,' Theda remarked. 'There is no doubt that they rub against each other. Why was he so ineligible?'

'Quatt? He was an apothecary in the village.'

'Oh,' said Theda blankly.

'Quite. One could scarcely blame her parents for disliking the connection.'

'What happened to him?'

Mr Beckenham grinned suddenly. 'The popular story is that he was so heartbroken he ran off to join a religious order, and has since been ordained.'

Theda had to laugh. 'How romantic! And poor Araminta. It is no pleasant thing to be crossed in love.'

He looked interested and would have spoken further. But as they came around the corner to the front of the house, they heard a familiar reedy voice hail them and, turning, found themselves confronted by Miss Merchiston herself, her pale eyes going from one to the other with the air of one who had known how it would be.

'You're wanted, Miss Kyte,' she said testily, 'and I don't see why I should have to run around after you. Why can't you keep within earshot?' She gave Mr Beckenham a nasty glare. 'Or had you other matters on your mind?'

'It happens, Araminta, that Miss Kyte was in the act of answering the summons,' her cousin lied calmly, 'for I had myself come to find her at Aunt Lavvy's request.'

'What took you so long, then?' demanded Araminta snappily, looking daggers at Theda.

'I beg your pardon, Miss Merchiston,' Theda began in the subservient tone of un underling, for there was no point in drawing Araminta's fire.

'I kept her,' Mr Beckenham interrupted in a hard voice. 'We were talking of your mother's health.'

'Pah! Much you care,' Araminta said rudely. 'You want her dead even more than I!'

'Oh, it's clear enough what *you* want,' he responded angrily.

Theda slipped quietly into the house, leaving them to their quarrel. Hector, who had been gambolling about the porch, slunk in behind her, depressed by the angry voices. Theda found Lady Merchiston in buoyant mood, very full of 'Benedict'.

'Such a loving boy to *his* mother, he was. So unlike that evil, back-biting bitch. I wish he had been my son.'

But he does not wish so, Theda thought silently. Except it might give him security. Loving, indeed! What he had said of her had hardly been the words of love. The old lady was in raptures over him, however. But she was shrewder than Theda had supposed, as she was brought to realise next day.

Mr Beckenham remained only the one night at

Merchiston Lodge, sleeping in the room next to Araminta's, which had been made ready for him. He spent most of his time with his godmother, which left Theda free to do some long-neglected tasks for herself, for her meagre wardrobe of old—and some cast-off— clothing required frequent mending, and, there being so little service, she must wash her linen herself. Theda did not see much of the gentleman, for he ate with Araminta in the breakfast parlour, while Theda always had her meals in Mrs Diggory's little pantry.

But the next morning, when Theda was on her way to her employer's room, she heard Mr Beckenham's voice within it, and hesitated.

'Be sure I shall remember it, dearest Aunt.'

'Don't bother!' came the almost snappy response. 'There's no use in storing it up. You can't repay a dying woman. Just take care you don't gamble it all away in one sitting.'

'I won't, never fear.'

'So you say. But I know you, boy. Can't keep away from the tables, can you?'

There was a tiny pause. Then Mr Beckenham said mildly, 'I'm not really a hardened gamester, you know, Godmama. If I had the wherewithal to live in comfort, I wouldn't fritter it away. I do it only to augment my income.'

'Not very successful, then, are you?' came the acid response. 'Oh, get along with you! I've no patience. I'll find a way to make you run in harness, see if I don't!'

'Goodbye, ma'am. Keep well.'

There was a cackle from the old lady. 'Ain't me you want to kiss. Think I'm blind?'

'Of course I want to kiss you. . .there. Be good, old fellow!'

There was a whiffle from Hector, and next instant

the gentleman's footsteps came swiftly to the door and Theda moved quickly away.

Mr Beckenham came out of the room, an expression of deep discontent on his features. He saw Theda and stopped short. Wrath entered his eyes and he hastily shut the door.

'Eavesdropping, Miss Kyte?' he demanded in an undervoice.

'I was waiting to come in,' Theda protested.

He grabbed her arm, hustling her down the gallery as he spoke. 'Then you should either have knocked or gone away. I trust you were sufficiently entertained!'

'Let me go!' she said in a fierce whisper. 'If Araminta were to see us. . .!'

He pulled her down the small corridor that led to the steps to the attics. 'She will not see us here. Now, then, what do you mean by it?'

'I meant *nothing*,' Theda told him urgently. 'What does it matter what I heard? I know you are dependent on your godmother.'

'And now you know how she despises me!'

'Fudge! She dotes on you.'

'Oh, yes? Besotted, is she? If she were, confound it, she'd treat me less shabbily!'

Theda's eyes narrowed. 'I thought you told me she owes you nothing.'

'She does not,' he said, adding savagely, 'but she might *care* for me a little!'

There was a brief silence. The corridor was dim and Theda could not see his face clearly. She felt unexpectedly touched by the pain she detected beneath the hot words.

'One cannot *buy* affection,' she said softly, 'any more than one can bargain with fate.'

His head turned, and although she could only just

see the shadow of his eyes she knew he was looking at
her. All of a sudden she was aware of an intensity in
the atmosphere, as if the air between them itself
became charged.

'Why can one not, Theda?' he murmured. 'Is fate so
strong? Is affection so scarce?'

Theda felt his fingers on her cheek. Her skin seemed
to burn at their touch. Into her brain came the certainty
that he was going to kiss her, and she was powerless to
stop him.

'Benedict, don't. . .please,' she whispered.

But that fatal use of his name finished it. She heard
the sharp intake of his breath, and then his lips found
hers in the darkness and the fire was lit.

They stood together, barely touching. But the searing
contact mouth to mouth set them both trembling.
Almost at the same instant, they sprang apart, ragged
in breath, staring, each at each, dim faces in the gloom.

Benedict's hoarse whisper shattered the strange
enchantment of it. 'Dear God in heaven, you *are* a
witch!'

Then he was striding away from her, his boots echoing on the wooden boards as he made for the stairs.

For a moment Theda stood motionless, watching
Benedict go. Then she turned and flew on winged feet
up the narrow stair to take refuge in her garret room.

Was she mad? Was *he*? What devil had possessed
them both?

She pressed a hand to her bosom to try to still the
wild fluttering of her heart. Her breath was short, her
lips burning hot from the touch of his. One trembling
finger traced them, as if in disbelief she sought the
source of that blistering torch that had fired her
through and through.

So light a caress to do so much! Never had Theda

experienced such a sensation. Yet she had been kissed—and more! Even at seventeen, which up to now had been the high point of her existence, the passions raised had not one tithe of the sizzling fire that had been generated by Benedict. There had been others— furtive fumblings, *not* by her design or wish, in corridors such as that. Certain men—husbands not excepted—seemed drawn like a magnet to a female in her circumstances. They must always *try*. But not one of them had made her feel as if a candle had been set to kindling within her.

A thought crept unbidden to her mind, causing a rush of liquid heat to course through her. Benedict had felt it, too! That was why he had called her a witch. Lord in heaven, what had come between them all at once? And why *now*? There had been nothing at all before. No, not even when his fingers touched her, as they had already, several times, just prior to the kiss. It had been his lips—*her* lips for him—that had sparked the sudden flame.

Her hands came up to press against her cheeks and she closed her eyes. This was *unendurable*. How could she remain here, see him again, and not die of shame at the memory? And if he *touched* her, what then? Would she erupt as she had just now?

An even worse thought came sweeping in, blotting out the first. What must he now think? Would he not read it that he might with impunity pursue her to her ruin?

Could it be worse than her present situation? whispered a treacherous small voice.

She rose abruptly from the bed. Yes. A good deal worse. She had not sunk so low as to join the ranks of *that* sisterhood! She might have renounced her family, but she had still her share of pride—in her lineage, in the family name. She would *not* disgrace it more than she had already. Certainly not for a wasteful spend-thrift, who preyed upon a gullible old woman! *No*, Benedict Beckenham. You will *not* beguile me.

Full of determination, she went down to her employer, only to have her fierce resolution instantly undermined.

'Why did you not tell me how you were placed?' demanded Lady Merchiston the moment she walked through the door.

'I beg your pardon, ma'am?' Theda said, quite at a loss.

'Benedict told me you are housed in the attics, like a common servant.'

Theda's jaw dropped perceptibly, and she was conscious of a sliver of tender warmth slipping into her heart. 'How did he know?'

'Taggy told him. Why he asked her about it I couldn't tell you. Araminta's work, I collect?'

'Miss Araminta regards me as a servant, ma'am,' Theda said, faintly smiling, and reaching a hand out to stroke Hector's woolly head where he lay on his blanket, as if to find some outlet for the feelings of gentleness running through her.

'Well, I won't have it!' snapped the old lady. 'Perfectly good dressing-room next door. My maid used to have it. You'll move in there today.'

'If it is anything like this room used to be, Lady Lavinia,' Theda said wryly, 'I fear that would be impossible.'

'Don't quibble, girl! Set it to rights as you see fit, and use it. *My* orders, and so you may tell Araminta if she makes any objection. Until I'm safe in my grave—where I long to be, let me tell you!—I am still mistress here.'

'Naturally, Lady Lavinia.' She moved away a little, patting her petticoats and looking at the dog. 'Come along, Hector. Time for your walk.'

Hector jumped off the bed eagerly, and gambolled around her. But she threw an impish look at her employer. 'I may say I am surprised to hear you express a desire to be in your grave quite yet. I am certain you have still things to settle.'

The keen eyes narrowed suspiciously, and something very like a glare marred the erstwhile good humour of Lady Merchiston's taut-stretched features.

'What are you at? Been poking and prying into what don't concern you, eh?'

Theda bit her lip. That was rash! She shrugged slightly. 'I beg your pardon, ma'am. I—I cannot help but have become aware of the—the dissension at present raging between your. . .dependants.'

'Oh, you have, have you?' repeated the old lady dangerously. 'I'll thank you to mind your business, and keep your nose out of mine!'

Folding her lips closely together, Theda dropped a curtsy and prepared to leave the room. After an uncertain glance at his mistress, Hector slunk after her. A cracked shout arrested them both.

'Come back, Theodosia!'

The dog scratched at the door, but Theda turned and looked at her. The crêpey skin of her old cheeks was flying two spots of colour. The black eyes were alight with some emotion that Theda could not fathom.

'Come here to me!' she ordered gruffly.

With some reluctance, Theda warily approached the bed. The bony fingers reached out and grasped her petticoats.

'Sit! Sit down.'

Hector, apparently under some confusion of ideas,

raced to the bed and leapt up on it. His mistress
automatically stayed him, grasping the scruff of his
neck, her eyes, their excitement mounting, fixed on
Theda as she did as she was bid. She lowered her voice
confidentially.

'Now, then. Which of them shall I favour, eh? Who
shall benefit?'

Theda's startled eyes met hers. 'Lord, ma'am how
should I know? It is not for me to say.'

'I know that, I know that,' muttered the old lady
testily. 'But you could *advise* me, at least.'

'Lady Lavinia,' Theda said firmly, 'even were I to
give you my advice, which must necessarily be based
on very little knowledge, I cannot for a moment imagine that you would take it.'

A crack of laughter left Lady Merchiston's lips.
'Think I'm more likely to run counter, do you?'

'Yes,' Theda said frankly.

'More than probable. Still, I want you to tell me
what you think.'

Theda sighed in an exasperated way. 'Very well,
then. For what it is worth, ma'am, I would recommend
an equal division of whatever it is you have to leave.'

Her ladyship nodded, eyes glowing in triumph.
'Thought you'd say that.' She reached out and seized
hold of Theda's hand, gripping it strongly. 'You're a
good girl, Theodosia. How'd you come to this pass, my
child?'

Theda looked away, although her fingers returned
the pressure. 'Excuse me on that head, if you please,
Lady Lavinia. I would not tell you, even were you to
dismiss me for it.'

The bony fingers increased their pressure, crushing
hers painfully with surprising strength. Theda gasped,

glancing down at her hurting hand and back up to find a malevolent twist in the old lady's wasted features.

'*Insolent*,' she hissed furiously. 'I should have you whipped!'

Theda's deep grey eyes grew dark with distress as she gazed into the vicious blackness of Lady Merchiston's own. Benedict's face flashed across her mind as she recalled his words. Yes, she thought wildly, this is surely the source of Araminta's inherited spite.

Then in an instant the look was gone, the painful grip relaxed, and Lady Merchiston was cackling with mirth.

'Very wise, Theodosia. You keep your own counsel, and I'll keep mine. But if either of them imagines they can force my hand, they much mistake the matter! Now go. Hector needs his exercise.'

She waved a dismissive hand and Theda rose from the bed with alacrity. She was only too anxious to get out of this room now that her employer had 'shown her true colours' as Araminta had promised she would. Hector, as eager as she for the only brief release he was allowed from confinement in the bedchamber, trotted at her heels, obedient to her call.

But Lady Merchiston called out after her, very much in her usual manner, as if nothing untoward had transpired. 'Fix up that room. I want you within call. Who knows when I may need you? I am weaker by the day!'

No one would credit it! thought Theda with an inward shudder as she went away. Later, as, with Agnes Diggory's aid, she set about putting the dressing-room to rights, a new determination began to burgeon in her breast. She would begin at once to look for another post. Let her be beforehand with the world, if she could! The thought of returning to another sparse lodging in a back-street of London, to the endless trudging back and forth to the Register Office, to the days of scant food and less warmth, filled her with dread. She had already begun, surreptitiously so as not to excite Araminta's suspicions, to scan the advertisement columns of the *Morning Post*. It was time now to begin to write letters.

Not that she dared to hope for a reference from this place! Therein lay her difficulty. If only she knew someone, even of small influence, who might put her in the way of finding something more congenial—and in a genteel home. The thought of returning to the merchant world, even after this unhappy experience, was less than welcome.

May came, and with it the return to the neighbourhood of the surrounding gentry at the close of the London season.

Mrs Rosalia Alderley, of Switham House, was the great lady of the village. She had been, before her second marriage a few years ago to Mr Alderley, Baroness to Lord Switham, who owned all the land round about, with the exception of Merchiston Lodge and other hunting boxes in the vicinity belonging to various members of the *haut ton*. Her son, Lord Switham, was still a boy, but the two Misses Switham were of marriageable age, and their mother had cleverly secured a good match for the elder in her very first season. She was, consequently, full of wedding plans when she came, as was her wont—for she considered it an inescapable part of her parish duties—to visit Lavinia Merchiston.

'Not that I am looking forward to parting with Serena, of course,' she said mournfully. 'In some ways I feel you are so lucky, Lavinia, to have kept Araminta by you all these years.'

'Don't sham it so, Rose!' snapped the old lady. 'You know perfectly well that the girl has been anything but a comfort to me.'

Mrs Alderley sighed. 'Such a pity she took to that unfortunate boy Saul Quatt, instead of that good-looking young officer that was quartered here that year.'

'I wouldn't have let her marry him if she had!' declared Lady Merchiston. 'A half-pay lieutenant, with no family connections, and nothing to recommend him but his pretty face? As well have handed her to Benedict!'

'Oh, come, Lavinia!' protested the visitor. 'Benedict's *birth* is the best of any in the district.'

'Much good may *that* do him, with the stigma of a scandalous divorce attached!'

'Well, that is not his blame.'

'No, but he has to wear it nevertheless.'

Mrs Alderley hesitated. She had a soft spot for Benedict, and his mother had been her friend. If a word from her might help him, she was not the woman to withhold it.

'You *could* make it easier for him to bear, Lavinia,' she suggested tentatively.

The dark eyes fired up in an instant. 'Yes, I could. *He* thinks I will.'

'You've let him think it,' Mrs Alderley said repressively. 'If you did not mean it so——'

'I've Araminta to think of, haven't I?' interrupted the old lady. She cackled, throwing a mischievous glance at her visitor. 'Maybe I'll make it a condition that they *do* marry each other, the two of them. What a jest that would be!'

'Oh, *no*!' uttered Rose, horrified. 'Good God, she is

his senior by more than ten years for one thing. For another——'

'They loathe each other. Yes, I know. But what a fitting punishment for both!'

'*Lavinia*,' gasped Mrs Alderley. 'That is a *wicked* thing to say.'

'Ain't it, though?' agreed Lady Merchiston cheerfully.

Rose sighed, casting up her eyes. 'I never know whether to take you at your word, Lavinia. You say the most shocking things. Benedict has done you no harm. And as for poor Araminta, what did she ever do but fall in love with the wrong man?'

The veined hands on the coverlet clenched suddenly. 'She *defied* me. As for Benedict. . .' She broke off, turning her eyes back on Mrs Alderley. 'Well, never mind that. I tell you, Rose, there are times I wish Araminta *had* married Quatt, and welcome.'

An odd look came into Rose's face, and she glanced away, shifting uncomfortably in her chair.

Lady Merchiston's eyes narrowed. 'What is it, Rose? You look like a child caught with her fingers in the jam cupboard.'

Rose looked back at her, the picture of guilt.

'Out with it, woman! What's to do?'

'Well, if you must know,' Rose burst out, 'it concerns Quatt.'

'Eh?'

Mrs Alderley drew a breath. 'You recollect the gossip that was rife at the time—that he had run away to a monastery?'

'Well, what of it?' demanded Lady Merchiston, her eyes eager.

'It seems to be true. At least, he may have begun in a monastery, but in the event he took orders and was for years a junior pastor somewhere in Worcestershire. *Now*, however, he is returning home.'

'*What*?'

'Yes. To take up a vacant living in Mountsorrel.'

Lady Merchiston's eyes seemed in danger of popping out of her gaunt head. 'He is to be a *vicar*? Saul Quatt?'

'Yes,' insisted Mrs Alderley. 'That living is not in Switham's gift, you see, so there was nothing I could do about it.' She hesitated, and then added, 'There is worse, Lavinia.'

'Go on!' ordered the other grimly.

'It seems he—he is a *widower*.'

For a moment Lady Merchiston stared. Then she burst into a paroxysm of croaking laughter, spluttering wildly, her emaciated limbs rolling about under the covers. Shrieks of mirth issued from her wide-open mouth, and flecks of foam appeared upon her lips.

Alarmed, Mrs Rosalia Alderley rose from her chair beside the bed, and fidgeted back and forth, not know-ing what to do. Fortunately, the door burst open and Theda ran into the room, accompanied by Hector.

'What is amiss?' she said quickly, coming to the bed. Hector was before her, leaping up and barking at his mistress. 'Lady Lavinia! What in the world. . .?'

Dragging at the dog, she got him off the bed, and looked up at the visitor, whom she did not know. 'What happened?'

'She began to laugh at something I told her, and. . .' Rose looked helplessly down to where the old lady still flailed against her pillows, catching her breath on each series of cackles as they left her throat.

Sitting on the bed, Theda took her by the shoulders and dragged her to sit up. 'Lady Lavinia! Pray stop this! *Stop*, I say!'

The black eyes rolled at her, and the wild laughter came to a hiccuping halt. Theda held her while she fought for breath, taking in great gasps of air. At last, her breathing still rasping a little, she was lowered gently against her pillows. Theda brought a glass of water from the bedside table to her lips and obliged her to drink. Then Lady Merchiston closed her eyes wearily.

'I'm all right,' she uttered weakly. 'I will do very well.' She half gestured with her fingers. 'Leave me now. Both of you. See to Rose, child.'

Theda looked her over, and saw with satisfaction that she was sinking into slumber. Hector, who had been whining all the while, now crept back on to the bed and pushed his nose under the veined hand resting on the coverlet. It ran once over his head and stayed there.

Quietly, Theda led the shaken visitor from the room.

'I never dreamed she would take it like that,' whispered Mrs Alderley in a shocked tone.

'Take what, ma'am?' asked Theda, leading her away down the gallery.

'The news about Quatt.' She saw the puzzlement in the other's face, and suddenly recollected that she had no notion to whom she was speaking. 'I beg your pardon, but who *are* you?'

'I am Theodosia Kyte, ma'am,' Theda replied. 'I am Lady Merchiston's companion.'

'*Companion*? Good God, when did you come?'

'In March.'

'Ah, that accounts for my knowing nothing about you. I have been in London since February.' She smiled. 'I am Mrs Alderley, you know.'

'Oh, yes, I believe Mrs Diggory mentioned you,' Theda said politely. 'I'm sorry I was not here when you arrived. I was walking Hector—Lady Merchiston's dog, you know.'

They were by this time descending the stairs, and Mrs Alderley looked about. Rather apprehensively, Theda thought. In a moment, Rose confirmed this in an anxious whisper.

'Araminta is not about, is she? I think it would be better if she does not meet me on this occasion.'

'She did not show you up, then?'

'No, Taggy did that. I only hope she did not see my carriage!'

Theda smiled. 'Well, I did not, and I must actually have been in the gardens. We could walk round to the stables, if you do not object to it—I can vouch for it that the grass is not wet—and then perhaps Miss Araminta will not hear as the horses will not come to the front door.'

'Excellent,' applauded Mrs Alderley, and amused Theda very much by tiptoeing across the hall to the front door, casting guilty glances over her shoulder as she went. Once outside, she breathed a sigh of relief, and strolled with Theda around the left of the house, next to Switham Thicket, so that Araminta would not see them from the window of her parlour.

'I have to thank you, Miss—er. . .'

'Kyte,' Theda supplied again. 'There is no need of thanks.'

She looked at Mrs Alderley as she spoke, and realised that lady was covertly observing her. She was a handsome matron, with a good figure, and a strong face topped by still glossy brown hair, untouched by grey. Theda judged her to be in the late thirties, perhaps. She was very fashionably dressed, in a morning gown of the latest sprigged muslin, the waist high, with a blue spencer over it against the spring chills.

Theda felt shabby by contrast, and was hit by a passing pang of envy. If she had not so foolishly thrown away her life, perhaps she, too, might have worn such a gown!

'Forgive me, Miss Kyte,' said the other lady softly, 'but you look quite downcast.'

Theda straightened her shoulders and quickly looked away. 'Not at all, I assure you.'

'Will you think me extremely uncivil if I say that I don't believe you?'

Theda's eyes turned to her, a question in them. Mrs Alderley smiled warmly.

'It is obvious to me that you were not born to the position you now occupy.' She threw up a hand, laughing as Theda's lips tightened. 'Have no fear! I am not going to be vulgarly inquisitive. I was rather going to ask how you come to have accepted a post which must necessarily be curtailed before too long.'

Theda shrugged. 'I did not know the circumstances.'

'You mean Araminta kept them from you,' shrewdly guessed the lady.

'Oh, no, it was Lady Merchiston herself who wrote to me.'

'Nonsense! You may be very certain Araminta arranged everthing herself, probably in her mother's name. It was an idle threat on Lavinia's part to hire a companion at all. I knew that the first time she mentioned it. That is why I was so surprised to see you here.'

In silence, Theda digested this for a moment. It was just what Lady Merchiston had said that very first night, but she had been so appalled that she had not taken it in. Araminta had wanted to escape what she regarded as an irksome duty. Yet, the original idea having come from her mother, she had been able to heap all the blame on her, even to accusing her of using up her inheritance, and continually complaining of the 'pittance' that she must *herself* have laid down in the terms of the letter she had written, purporting to come from Lady Merchiston. All to goad her mother, to punish her.

'I see that you recognise the truth of what I say,' remarked Mrs Alderley perspicaciously.

Theda's frown was turned upon her. 'Are you very well acquainted with the family, ma'am?'

'Intimately. Oh, I only pay dutiful visits now,' Rose went on, 'but I was at one time very frequently here. I was on very good terms with Isabel Beckenham, you know, poor thing.'

Blinking at her, Theda barely grasped the last little comment. '*Isabel* Beckenham?'

'Benedict's mother.' Mrs Alderley sighed. 'She died, poor soul. And I shall always believe that it was the scandal that killed her. That and. . .*other* things.'

Theda's head was whirling. Scandal? Benedict's *mother*?

They had come within sight of the stables by this time, and Mrs Alderley's coachman, seeing his mistress approaching, made haste to open the door, calling to the groom who had accompanied them to reharness the horses which had been released from the bit.

Rose Alderley held out her hand. 'Goodbye, Miss Kyte. I hope we shall meet again.'

'I hope so, too!' uttered Theda fervently, and then realised how this must sound. The woman would think she was avid for more of the background of Benedict Beckenham, which indeed she was, but it was scarcely polite to show it! 'I mean, I am sure we may, when you next come to see her ladyship.'

Mrs Alderley smiled, but made no comment. She got

into the coach, the steps were folded up, and in a moment the horses were trotting around the house towards the main drive.

Theda stood looking after them for a moment, aware of her own burning curiosity. What a house of surprises and secrets was Merchiston Lodge!

Less than a week later, an opportunity to assuage her desire for knowledge presented itself. Not, she told herself, that she was at all interested in Benedict Beckenham, except in so far as he fitted into this household. But she could not help a resurgence of the queries raised in her mind at the hint of scandal in connection with his mother as she found herself in Mrs Alderley's coach, being driven to Switham House.

'Rose wants you,' Lady Merchiston had told her succinctly. 'She needs help with the preparations for this wedding, so I said I'd lend you.'

At first, Theda did not know whether she was more angry with Lady Merchiston for loaning her out like this, or with Mrs Rosalia Alderley for making such an impertinent request. What was she, a communal slave to be passed around at their pleasure? On the other hand, it was at least a change. She rarely came out of Merchiston Lodge, except to go to the village, and it was quite a pleasure, she discovered, to be driving *away* from it. As her fury drained, she felt a surge of uplift. She had not realised how low were her spirits!

When she came to Switham House, a much larger and better-kept establishment than Merchiston Lodge, she found Rosalia Alderley to have quite another motive.

'Oh, my dear, I don't need help at all,' she declared, ushering Theda inside a spacious saloon, its windows, open to the fresh air, letting in a good deal of light.

'But I had to have some excuse, you see. I could not simply invite you to visit me, situated as you are.'

Theda gazed at her dumbly, horribly conscious of her drab, close-fitting gown of dark stuff, which was a hand-me-down from a previous employer. Its waist was in quite the wrong place about her midriff, instead of under the semi-exposed bosom where Rose Alderley's muslin petticoats began their graceful fall to the ground. Theda had followed in the *Gallery of Fashion*—which all her young charges had avidly studied—the steady rise of waists over the last three or four years, but never before had she felt quite so outdated. Her own bosom was strictly confined by the stays beneath her bodice, which was tightly hooked from her waist almost to her throat, with a neck-ruff concealing even the pale expanse between her collar bones. She must look worse than a dowd. She looked, she decided, just what she was—a servant.

'Don't look so dismayed,' begged Mrs Alderley, taking Theda's hand and obliging her to sit on an elegant Sheraton sofa. 'I just could not bear to see someone so young, and so obviously above those two cats, caught helplessly in that *bleak* place!'

Theda shifted puzzled shoulders. 'Do you mean you—you have invited me here for. . .for *myself*?'

'Yes, my dear,' smiled her hostess. 'I mean exactly that.'

Abruptly Theda rose. 'But I cannot! Oh, ma'am, don't think me ungrateful, but you don't understand. It would be quite unseemly for me to meet anyone—to *socialise*. I am not any longer of your world!'

'Sit down again, pray,' pleaded her hostess, reaching for her hand and pulling her back to the sofa. 'No one will come in. My daughters are away visiting their grandmama, for I could not have them by, making a nuisance of themselves, during all these preparations. My son is at school, and my husband in his library. You are quite safe.'

Theda relaxed a little, still biting her lip, however, her anxiety unquenched. 'I beg your pardon if I seemed ungracious. I am uncomfortable in all this elegance. I confess I feel more at home at Merchiston Lodge!'

Mrs Alderley patted her hand. 'I understand perfectly. You have grown unused to such comforts, I dare say.' Vehemently, she added, 'But that does not make it right! Good God, a companion is not a servant! I know any number of indigent dames who have found such employment, and they are treated quite as a member of the family.'

'I have never been so fortunate.' Theda said in a low tone.

Mrs Alderley leaned towards her, saying gently, 'I guessed as much. That is why I sent for you, to be truthful. I might be able to help you.'

Theda's eyes lit with sudden hope and she turned eagerly towards her. 'Oh, *will* you? How kind you are! That is the very thing I had been wishing for—someone to recommend me. For I cannot hope for a reference from Lady Merchiston, and I am afraid that. . .'

She faltered to a stop, not wishing to appear callous.

'You are right to be afraid,' Rose Alderley said bracingly. 'Poor Lavinia is certainly past hope, and whether she ends by giving the property to Araminta or Benedict you cannot possibly remain there.'

'No, indeed!' Theda concurred feelingly.

'Then it is agreed. I shall look about my acquaintance. *Something* will come up. We have perhaps a little time. Dr Spilsby thinks she will last a few weeks yet.'

'I could wish it would be sooner! Oh, not that Lady

Merchiston should go quickly, of course I don't mean that. But I would give much to get away from that house!'

Mrs Alderley nodded. 'It is an unhappy place. For my part, I think Benedict would do better if she does *not* saddle him with it.'

Theda examined the striped wallpaper in the room with apparent interest. In a light tone, she suggested, 'He does appear to be wholly dependent on his godmother.'

'For the moment, yes.'

'What will he do, then, if she leaves him nothing?'

Mrs Alderley laughed. 'Go on as always, living by his wits and cards. Many men do so in society, you know. Or he may marry money. He is handsome enough to take in any silly young girl!'

Theda felt an odd tightness across her chest, and found herself disinclined, after all, to pursue the subject of Benedict. At her request, Rosalia took her on a tour of the house and grounds. When she was leaving, there was real gratitude in her farewell.

'You have given me a breath of fresh air, Mrs Alderley!'

'Call me Rose,' smilingly requested the lady. 'And I won't forget my promise, Theodosia, don't fear.'

'You are very kind—Rose.' She returned the smile warmly. 'My close friends call me Theda.'

It was in buoyant mood that she was driven back to Merchiston Lodge, and she entered her employer's bedchamber with a smile on her lips.

'There you are!' ejaculated the old lady.

She was looking exhilarated herself, sitting up in bed with a welter of papers before her, her pen laboriously scratching over a sheet of parchment. Hector, for once restricted to the floor, gave a yelp of greeting and came to frolic about Theda's feet.

'You are come in excellent time, Theodosia!'

'Why, what is the matter, Lady Lavinia? You look to be in high gig.'

'I am,' cackled Lady Merchiston gleefully. 'I've settled my affairs to my satisfaction at last.'

'That is excellent. Have you had a luncheon?'

'Never mind luncheon! What do you say to this? I've sent for Saul Quatt.'

Theda blinked at her. 'I don't understand.'

'You'll understand soon enough. *Quatt*, girl! He's Araminta's old lover. Don't tell me you've not heard of him! You must know everything by now. Rose tells me he's back and peacocking about as a vicar.'

'Dear Lord!' uttered Theda startled. She remembered the name now. But she was even more astonished at her ladyship's next words.

'So I've decided to give him Araminta, after all. That'll take *her* off my hands.'

'But—but. . .' Theda put a hand to her cheek, trying for some coherence.

'But what?'

'Well, supposing they don't choose any longer to marry one another? He may even be married already.'

'No, he ain't. Had it from Rose he's a widower. And what if they don't want each other? He'll have her fast enough when he knows the sum of her portion.'

'And she?' Theda could not help asking.

'She'll do as she's told, or lose the lot!'

Theda gazed at her speechlessly. Was she insane, that she imagined she could force people to bend to her will in this arbitrary fashion?

'No need to look like that, miss. I've got plans for you, too.'

'*What* plans?' Theda demanded, involuntarily showing her instant indignation.

In a tone that brooked no argument, the old lady announced, 'You'll marry Benedict, and make something of him!'

CHAPTER FIVE

'WHAT?' Theda gasped.

'He can't expect to catch anything better,' went on Lady Merchiston, 'not with his history. I've decided you'll do.'

'*You've* decided!' echoed Theda in a faint voice. 'Have you taken leave of your senses?'

'Don't address me in that tone!' snapped her ladyship, eyes firing up. 'You'll do as you're ordered, I tell you! And so will Benedict, if he knows what's good for him.'

'And with what bribe is *he* to be persuaded?' flashed Theda. 'This run-down rubbish heap of a house?'

'Hold your tongue!' commanded Lady Merchiston.

'Do you imagine you can compel my silence so easily after such an announcement?' demanded Theda furiously. 'Dear lord in heaven! Am I in bondage, that you think to parcel me off as you see fit? Who do you think you are, Lady Merchiston? Even Royalty would not attempt such a thing! I will have no part in your paltry schemes, ma'am, and I utterly *forbid* you to mention my name again in connection with them.'

Lady Merchiston was listening to the diatribe with her mouth at half-cock, but at this last she revived sharply, her skeletal head coming out of her gown as on a stalk.

'*You* forbid *me*? How *dare* you speak to me in so insolent a fashion?' she growled, almost choking with rage. 'You have the temerity to refuse me, do you? You dare to *defy* me? Well, then, you may go without.

406

And go *now*. Leave this house on the instant! Never return! You are dismissed, do you hear, you ungrateful slut. Dismissed without a character, what is more. Get out! *Out*, I say!'

Theda stood appalled, all her defiance collapsing as she realised the consequences she had brought down upon herself. Turning from the ugly sight of the old woman's contorted features, she fled the room, running incontinently down the gallery to the stairs, unaware that Hector, barking excitedly, ran out after her.

Below in the hall came running all the inmates of the house to gaze up at her, their faces stunned. Hector raced down the stairs and scurried about both Diggorys, who ignored him, their attention fully on the happenings that had taken place above.

'What is it?' asked Araminta in an unprecedentedly hushed tone. 'What has occurred?'

'Your mother is out of her senses!' uttered Theda. She came running down the stairs. 'She has dismissed me, Miss Araminta. Help me, I pray you! Speak to her!'

'Why should I?' snapped the other woman.

'Because I tried to help you!' Theda told her desperately. 'She has some scheme in mind to marry you off to this man Quatt.'

Unexpectedly, Araminta's pale eyes lit up. 'But that is famous!'

'And if you don't, you will lose your portion,' Theda pursued. 'She has already taken the house from you.'

The thin, sallow features tightened and the eyes flared. 'So she wants to be rid of me! Well, she won't do it so easily, I promise you.'

'Miss Merchiston, she *has* got rid of me!'

'You!' repeated Araminta scornfully. 'What do I care about you?'

'Have some pity!' begged Theda, almost in tears. 'She means me to go without a character. And I have no money! What am I to do? Where can I go?'

'I don't care *what* you do, or where you go!' snapped Araminta. 'Get out and stay out! For my part, I'm going to tell that old hag what I think of her!'

Then she was racing up the stairs. Theda watched her go, her mind blank with panic. She became aware that Mrs Diggory was at her side.

'Don't pay no mind, miss! Wait for it all to die down, do. I'm certain sure you'll be able to stay.'

Suddenly Theda could bear no more. 'But I don't *want* to stay!' she cried, and, turning, she ran for the door, flinging it open and running through the arch of the long porch into the still sunny day.

Tears coursed down her cheeks and she ran blindly down the wild jungle of the grounds parallel to the thicket. Furious barking about her flying feet penetrated the despair in her breast, and she looked down.

'Hector! Hector, what are you doing here?' she gasped, slowing to a halt.

But the dog, excited by the preceding events, jumped around her, barking frantically. Then, apparently deciding that this was a special day, he turned and made for the thicket.

'Hector, *no!*' she shrieked automatically.

But he ignored her, rushing away to disappear among the trees. Without hesitation, she set off in pursuit, unable to think beyond the fact that he would be lost, not even considering that if she was dismissed he was no longer her responsibility.

Through the undergrowth he led her, barking at every turn to encourage her progress. Headlong she ran, heedless of the branches that caught at her, tearing at her dark stuff gown, ripping away the white cap that covered her hair.

Of a sudden Hector set up an extraordinarily excited yapping. She could not see him but he was obviously close, and must have found something unusual to seize his interest. Theda pushed through the trees and found she was coming out into the road that ran through Switham Thicket.

A curricle was in sight, its bowling progress slowing as the driver recognised the dog that was bounding straight into its path.

'Hector, stop!' he called out, bringing his horses to a plunging standstill. 'You bad dog! What are you doing there?'

Benedict. For a moment Theda stood transfixed, as everything that had passed, all Lady Merchiston's avowed plans for her and this man, came crashing in on her brain. Uttering a strangled sob, she turned back into the thicket.

She heard him call out and by the barks behind her knew that Hector followed. On she went, unable any longer to run, her chest heaving with effort, salt tears hot on her cheeks, the only thought in her mind that she must get away.

In her ears came the sound of staggering pursuit, added to the hysterical yapping of the over-excited terrier. She did not know that she gasped her sobs aloud. But as his hand grasped her arm, she recognised defeat, and, halting, she swung around.

Benedict cried out, '*Theda,*' and then fell silent, his eyes roving her, wonder in their depths.

For as she turned towards him, a great fall of bright copper hair, loosened by the wild chase, came cascading about her shoulders and fell to her waist, enveloping her in a rippling sheet of flame.

Theda opened her mouth to blister him out of the torment that consumed her...and paused, arrested by the look in his face.

She met the burning passion of his eyes, and time ceased. As one in a dream, unmoving, clogged with weighted air, she saw him shift. Above her, the sun cast dappling shadows through the waving branches, so that his handsome features seemed to flicker in her sight.

She saw his fingers come to her, dip into the fiery curtain of her hair. Slowly, so slowly, he brought up handfuls of the bright tresses, and they slid like silk through his fingers.

His face came down to her, passed by her own, and buried itself in the copper cloak. She heard a husky whisper in her ear.

'*Witch*...burning in your own flames...*take me with you.*'

Then his arms crushed her against him, and his mouth traced a path of heat across her cheek to find her lips. He struck. And time boiled back into being as the touch of his lips sent a shaft of fire down to sear her inside.

Her passion leapt to meet his, and she clung to him, her mouth dragging on his in a meeting so inflamed that she almost lost consciousness as dizziness swept through her brain. Then his face was in the hair at her throat as he sought the hollows, dragging aside the locks with urgent fingers.

'Theda...*Theda*,' he breathed hoarsely. 'My witch—my ghost—*mine*. You're mine, do you hear?'

He was bearing her down, and her limbs began to give way beneath him. Then, at the edges of her consciousness, outside the explosive heat of the passage of his lips about her neck, of his fingers reaching into some recess of her costume to make her bare flesh tingle, she heard the faint echo of Hector's bark. With it came the sense of the words Benedict's tongue had scorched into her skin: 'you're mine'.

A whirling kaleidoscope of Lady Merchiston's shrieking face, Araminta's callous mouth and Agnes Diggory's sympathetic eyes hurtled through her mind, changing the flaming heat of passion to searing fury. With strength born of the alarming change, Theda thrust the heaviness of Benedict's body from her and staggered out of reach.

'*Leave me alone!*' she screamed at the startled anger in his face. 'How dare you touch me? How dare you lay claim to me, as if I am yours for the taking?'

'What the devil. . .?' he began furiously.

'*You* are the devil!' she railed, almost beside herself. 'You and that hateful monster, that scheming wretch up there in that bed. There is a *witch*, if you want one. Go! Go and see what she has planned!'

'What are you talking about?' he demanded. 'What is the matter with you?'

'*You* are the matter, if Lady Merchiston has her way. As for me, I am dismissed, since I don't choose to be parcelled off at her pleasure!'

'*What*?'

'She has turned me off, I tell you.' Desperation lent an edge to her voice as the fury slithered away. 'And Araminta will not help me. I don't know what to do.'

Suddenly all her bravado collapsed. She stood shaking, setting the flaming tresses about her quivering so that they rippled in the shafts of light broken by the barrier of trees.

'Oh, Benedict,' she uttered brokenly, 'what shall I *do*?'

Seeing the mist that deepened the dark grey of her eyes, the pale translucent cheeks, both so beautiful now

in their glowing copper setting, it was all Benedict
could do not to snatch her back into the heat of his
embrace, and force his way to that intimate deep
caress, the thought of which now fired him with
passionate yearning. But the distress in her face held
him back. He could no more have overborne her
resistance in her present state than he could kick a
lame dog. Steadying himself with a deep breath, he
mustered control.

'Calm yourself, Theda,' he said gently, not daring to
reach out and touch her, in case his own forced calm
should desert him. 'What has occurred?'

Drawing on her own ragged breath, Theda tried to
still her shivering limbs. She did not look at him.

'I will leave Lady Lavinia to tell you her plans for
herself—if she still holds by them. I think you will care
for them even less than I.'

'You intrigue me greatly,' he said, puzzled. 'But
come. Let me drive you home.'

'Home!' she repeated on a bleak note. 'Would that
you might!'

Benedict made no reply to this, but, calling to the
dog, who was hovering near by, he started to lead the
way out of the thicket to the road. As Theda followed,
she began automatically to braid her long hair in a
loose plait, searching among the tangle at her scalp for
any pins that might have been left after the tresses had
come loose from their moorings. She had lost her cap,
and so could not again conceal the glory of her hidden
beauty, but she twisted the plait in a knot behind her
head and clipped it there as best she could with the
two pins she had found, so that it resembled the thick
queue of a man's old-fashioned wig.

In Benedict's glance, as he handed her up into his
curricle, she recognised regret, and knew that he had

fallen victim—like other men before him—to the curse
she carried with her always. That he was fully alive to
its heady effect became evident in a moment.

Having lifted Hector into the vehicle, where he sat
on the floorboards, panting with his tongue lolling out,
and wagging a satisfied tail, Benedict swung himself up
and grinned down at her as he took the reins into his
hand.

'I now understand why you persist in wearing that
very unflattering headgear. I can conceive of very few
matrons who would entrust their menfolk to such
temptation.'

Theda lifted a hand to smooth down the edges of the
fiery frame about her face. 'Yes, it—it is in my interests
to keep it hidden, I admit.'

'In mine too,' he murmured, 'if I am to keep my
hands off you!'

'Don't!' Theda begged. 'You—you must not refine
too much upon—upon what transpired between us.
Forget it, if you please.'

'Forget it! Are you *mad*, Theda? How can I possibly
forget it? I don't even want to.'

'You *must*,' she said in a stifled tone. 'There can be
no possibility of – of——'

'Hell and the devil!' he ejaculated angrily. 'What do
you take me for? Do you think I would use you like
any common slut?'

Theda could not look at him, but she said in a
subdued tone, 'It is what your godmother called me.
And—and many men in this situation would not *care*
how they used me.'

'Well, I care! I forgot myself for a moment back in
the woods, it is true,' he admitted in a goaded voice,
'but the circumstances were exceptional. I was shocked
out of my usual circumspection.'

'Your *what*?' Theda asked in a stunned tone, casting him an irresistibly amused look.

'Don't laugh at me, Theda!' he warned, catching her glance.

'I beg your pardon.' She eyed his profile in silence for a moment. Then she said, in a voice of intense interest, 'Do you always delude yourself so?'

He tried to bite back a laugh, but the grin would not be entirely suppressed. 'Confound you, Theda! Very well, then, you shall have it plain. Keep that head of yours well hidden, or I shall not be answerable for the consequences!'

'I thank you for the warning, sir,' Theda said demurely, 'and will hope to be forgiven for so wantonly playing the temptress.'

'What you're tempting me to at this moment, my good girl, has very little to do with passion!' declared Benedict roundly.

Theda gurgled. 'Very well, I shall desist, and thank you instead. For you have raised my spirits immeasurably.'

'I am happy to have afforded you amusement, ma'am,' he said ironically, and turned in at the gates of the Lodge.

'Wait!' begged Theda suddenly. 'Stop before we reach the house, if you please, and set me down.'

'Why?'

'So that I may enter alone, of course. Things are bad enough without laying more fuel to the fire.'

'Don't put yourself about,' Benedict said unconcernedly, driving on, but slowing his horses. 'I will see Aunt Lavinia. If I cannot persuade her to keep you on, I promise I shall arrange matters for you in some other way.'

'*What* way?' Theda asked sceptically.

'We won't concern ourselves over that until we know the outcome of my interview with my godmother,' he said firmly. 'Rest assured that I will not abandon you.'

Theda gave him a grateful smile, but rueful withal. 'I am causing you a deal of trouble one way and another.'

'Yes, you are,' he agreed unexpectedly, turning a grin upon her, 'and I have a strong notion that there is worse to come!'

As she laughed, his eyes travelled briefly over her features, a smile in them, and then brushed lightly over the frame of copper that had struck him with so devastating an effect.

'I should have guessed,' he said, and there was a caress in his voice. 'With that pearly skin of yours, dear ghost, that flame was inevitable!'

A warm glow invaded Theda's heart, and the grey of her eyes deepened, giving them a luminosity that lit her features. Benedict drew a hissing breath, and pulled up his horses, his eyes never leaving hers.

But Theda's face changed at once, and she pulled back. 'No, Benedict!'

His lips tightened, and he cursed under his breath, jerking the reins again. With the return of constraint she put a hand to her fluttering bosom and discovered that several hooks on her bodice had come loose—No, had been torn loose by Benedict's hand! She tried surreptitiously to refasten them, to conceal the bare expanse of flesh with the ruff that lay open, and looked away when the movement made him glance round at her. She knew he saw what she tried to do, and her embarrassment increased.

The atmosphere between them was so tense that no further words were exchanged until he stopped the curricle at the edge of the house.

'Go in,' he said curtly. 'I will drive to the stables and then go to Aunt Lavvy. Hector may come with me.'

Theda slipped unobtrusively into the house, which seemed unnaturally quiet after the hurricane that had driven her out of it. She wondered what had been the outcome of Araminta's promised confrontation with her mother, whether this Saul Quatt had answered the summons and been drawn into the inevitable altercation.

Without being seen, she managed to gain the safety of the dressing-room she now occupied, next door to Lady Merchiston's bedchamber. It was in fact a large room divided in two, one half being given over to the mistress's wardrobe and dressing stool, with the pier-glass in the corner, the other providing a small chamber with room only for a cot bed. Adam Diggory had grumblingly moved in a clothes-press and a table for Miss Kyte's personal use.

Not knowing what else to do, Theda first found a fresh cap and tucked away her dangerous locks, and then began to lay out her clothes, retrieving her portmanteau from under the bed. She was afraid to make much noise, for fear of being overheard by her employer next door, for she did not want to see her until after Benedict's promised visit.

Presently she heard footsteps coming along the gallery, and sat on the bed, waiting, her heart hammering a little.

What if she did have to go? Where would Benedict take her? Would he help her at all, after that last little exchange when her stiffness had angered him so? Suddenly she remembered Rose Alderley. Had it only been this morning that she had visited Switham House and received that kind lady's offer of help? It felt a lifetime ago! Dared she go to Mrs Alderley? It was one thing to ask for a reference, quite another to throw herself, bag and baggage, on the lady's mercy!

She could hear voices in the next room. What was Benedict saying? What *would* he say when—if!—Lady Merchiston informed him of her plan to make him marry her companion?

Presently another set of footsteps came tapping by, and Theda recognised Araminta's hasty step. The sound of a door shutting was instantly followed by raised voices. Theda's heart sank. In a moment, the door slammed and heavier footsteps passed, retreating down the stairs.

Benedict! Then he had *failed*.

But next instant came the patter of lighter feet and a fist banged on her door. 'Come out, Miss Kyte!'

Rising from the bed, Theda opened the door, apprehension in her eyes as she confronted Miss Merchiston's glare.

'Yes?'

'Go to my mother at once!' ordered Araminta sternly. Then she grasped Theda's wrist and came close, lowering her voice to a murmur. 'And afterwards, I want you in my parlour. Understand?'

Theda nodded, too heartsick to answer. Araminta released her and sped away, leaving Theda to draw a breath, square her shoulders, and make for Lady Merchiston's door.

The old lady was lying back against her bank of pillows in an attitude of exhaustion, her eyes closed. Her skin was paler than ever, her breathing shallow. On the coverlet her fingers twitched a little, but otherwise she did not move. There was no sign of her dog.

Shutting the door softly behind her, Theda tiptoed to the bed and stood looking down at the still figure in some alarm. Was she dying? Had the excitement been

too much for her? All Theda's earlier resentment faded
with the onset of pity. How pathetic a creature she was,
poor Lady Lavinia! So close to her own end, and still
trying to run other people's lives. What would any of it
avail her when once she was gone?

Lady Merchiston's eyelids fluttered, but did not fully
open. She gestured vaguely with a finger, and a weary
muttering issued from the pallid lips.

'You're there, are you? Good. . .Stay. . .Sit and stay.'

Theda sat on the bed and took the fingers gently into
her hand. They clasped hers weakly and a smile flitted
over the wasted features. For a few minutes they both
remained thus, motionless. Then the old lady pressed
Theda's hand and opened her eyes.

'My cordial,' she uttered.

Theda got up and went to the cabinet to pour a dose
of one of the mixtures prescribed by Dr Spilsby. After
it was drunk, Lady Merchiston seemed to recover a
little of her lost vitality. She sat up straighter, and
patted the bed for Theda to sit.

'I am glad you had not run away,' she said in an
unwontedly meek voice.

'I had, Lady Lavinia,' Theda said quietly, 'but
Benedict brought me back.'

'You should have known I did not mean it,' complained the old lady in a fretful tone. 'What would I do
without you? Who would care for me half as well, eh?
Ought to know my bark's worse than my bite.'

A gleam entered Theda's eye. 'Your *bite*, ma'am,
draws blood!'

Lady Merchiston's lips curved with amusement.
'Does it so? Well, well.' She shot a speculative glance
at her companion. 'Had a worthy champion, though,
didn't you?'

Theda gave her a straight look. 'Because your god-son is kind, ma'am, that does not mean——'

'That you'll take him to husband,' finished the old lady. 'Never fear. I have abandoned that scheme.' She eyed Theda narrowly. 'Now where is the sigh of relief, eh?'

A light laugh escaped Theda. 'You misunderstand me, Lady Lavinia. I have no objection to Benedict as a suitor. At least, I am sure he has enough to recommend him, should—should any female be inclined to consider him in that light.'

'But not *this* female?' interpolated her employer.

'*No*—at least, I mean...I had not *thought* of such a thing. Besides, *I* am not eligible! But that is not it.'

'Oh? Then what is "it"?'

'Lady Lavinia,' Theda began, drawing a steadying breath. 'I left my home—I *ruined* my life, except that I did not know *then* that I was doing so!—only because my par...I mean, only because *others* attempted to compel me to do as they thought fit in the matter of matrimony.' She smiled a little. 'Unlike Araminta, I was not content to bow to their decree. So you see, although I have tried since—needs must!—to subdue that dangerous spirit of rebellion, I have so little suc-ceeded that—that...'

'That when I "dared" to so compel you, you flew out at me like the spirited filly you are under that demure exterior,' stated her ladyship with a quizzing look.

'Yes, that is how it was,' Theda admitted.

Lady Merchiston snorted. 'Well, if you'd been *my* daughter, you'd have felt the rod!'

Theda looked away. 'Believe me, ma'am, the punish-ment I brought on myself was far more salutary than any thrashing could have been.'

There was a silence. Theda was aware of the keen

eyes on her, but she did not turn to confront them. She had said enough. Too much! And what had been inadvertently revealed in that last remark made by Lady Lavinia? Poor Araminta, how she must have suffered! Still, she must be grateful to Benedict, who *had* been her 'champion', and glad that the old understanding had been re-established between herself and Lady Merchiston. She would be more on her guard in future, however, now that she knew the unpredictable nature of the old lady's malevolence.

But just at that moment, she felt a tug at her scalp, and turned her head to find that the bony fingers had seized a stray strand of copper hair, pulling it from under her cap. Theda had shoved it on so hastily that she must have carelessly left a little hair visible.

'So *this* is your secret!' the old lady said in a tone of quiet satisfaction, a smile on her face. 'What a girl of surprises you are, Theodosia Kyte!'

'I am come to the right house, then,' Theda retorted.

The keen old eyes sparkled unexpectedly. 'Oh, I'm not finished yet, girl, not by a long chalk! There are more to come, don't doubt it.'

'Heaven help us all!'

'And heaven help you,' riposted Lady Merchiston swiftly, giving the lock of hair she held a sharp jerk, 'if you let Araminta know of this!' She cackled. 'Make the most of it, Theodosia.' She let the strand slide through her fingers to its full length and lay playing it between them. 'It will fade soon enough. Seen it before. Runs in my husband's family, too, you know. Araminta almost had it as a child, but it went fair—and then mouse, poor wretch!'

Taking hold of her lock, Theda pulled gently. 'If you please, Lady Lavinia.'

The old lady let it go, and watched Theda hastily

tuck it out of sight. 'Yes, keep it close. If Araminta sees it, her jealousy will be increased tenfold. She'd have killed Isabel if she could!'

Theda stared, her mind rioting. So she *knew* of Araminta's jealousy! And what did she mean about Isabel? Why should Araminta have been jealous of Benedict's mother?

Seeing that her employer's eyes were once again drooping heavily, she got up from the bed. 'Would you like anything, ma'am, or shall I leave you to rest?'

The fingers moved vaguely. 'Go, child. Bring Hector to me when next you come up. Benedict left him with Adam. . .and he don't pet him.'

Her voice was sinking, and Theda quietly left the room. She was about to return to her own chamber to put her clothes away again when an urgent hiss came at her from down the gallery.

'*Psst!*'

Turning, she beheld Araminta at the head of the stairs, and remembered that Miss Merchiston had instructed her to go down to her parlour when she had left her mother. The woman beckoned imperiously, and, sighing, Theda turned down the gallery and followed her downstairs. There had been enough emotion this day. Pray heaven Araminta was not going to vent her spleen again!

As she entered the little parlour behind her, Theda was brought up short by the sight of a stranger standing before the fireplace. He was an odd little man, peering anxiously up at her out of hunched shoulders through a pair of gold-rimmed spectacles, on his head an outdated tie-wig.

'Miss Kyte,' said Araminta, a most unusual smirk on her face, and with a note of pride in her voice, 'allow me to present the Reverend Mr Saul Quatt.'

Theda was just able to prevent her mouth falling open, but her eyes widened, and her voice trembled on the veriest hint of laughter as she held out her hand.

'H-how do you do?'

So this was Araminta's old lover! And after—what?—fifteen, twenty years, there was that in her altered manner that showed she could still regard him with affection. But what of the gentleman himself?

'I am happy to make your acquaintance,' he was saying in a very precise tone, executing a small bow.

'I have brought you here, Miss Kyte,' resumed Miss Merchiston in what was for her a pleasant tone, 'that you may tell Mr Quatt of what passed between yourself and my dear mother.'

Flicking an unconsciously amazed glance at her, Theda met in her eyes a warning. Play my game, it said, or suffer the consequences. But surely she could not wish her to reveal the matter to this poor dab of a parson?

He was looking acutely uncomfortable already, and entered upon a feeble protest. 'No, no, I beg of you, Miss Merchiston. . .*Araminta*,' he amended as the pale eyes turned upon him in gentle reproach, 'there is no need. If your good lady mother is indisposed, I would not for the world——'

'Nonsense, Saul!' said Araminta, smiling in what she evidently felt to be a winning fashion. 'She summoned you here, and it is only right that you should know the reason, albeit she is too unwell to see you herself. Go on, Miss Kyte.'

Saul Quatt turned his apprehensive gaze upon the companion, his frown shifting the spectacles upon his nose. 'I thought perhaps her ladyship, being, as I have heard, in such ill health, had need of my services as a man of God,' he ventured hopefully.

'No, sir,' Theda said, her sympathy roused. Poor man! He little knew what fate had in store. And he did not look to be equal to the formidable task of escaping the net that had been spread for him.

'Go *on*, Miss Kyte!' prompted Araminta, moving in close enough to deliver a vicious prod to Theda's ribs while she bestowed a melting look upon the hapless Reverend gentleman.

'The truth is, Mr Quatt,' Theda said in an even tone, 'that, in view of your altered circumstances, her ladyship is prepared to reconsider her decision regarding your erstwhile proposals to Miss Merchiston.'

Under the glass of his spectacles, his eyes goggled. 'My—my *proposals*? But – but——'

'You see, Saul, how opportune has been your return!' beamed Araminta, coming up to him and taking his flaccid hand between both her own.

'I—yes—um—I. . .I don't know what to say!' stuttered the stunned suitor.

'Of course nothing can be formally arranged just at this present,' went on Miss Merchiston, and Theda almost laughed out to see the burgeoning hope in the poor man's face, 'for with dear Mama in this sad condition, I could not reconcile it with my conscience to leave her in the care of other hands. But it won't be long now before all our fondest hopes will be realised.'

Looking at Saul Quatt, Theda could not help feeling that his fondest hope was likely to be that he might be struck by a thunderbolt! He looked anything but gratified, and she could only marvel at Araminta's inability to see how unwelcome was the good fortune that had come to him.

Adjuring Theda, in the prettiest way, to wait for her here, Miss Merchiston then escorted Mr Quatt to the front door, presumably bidding him a fond farewell in the sickeningly sugary tone she had chosen to adopt towards him.

It had vanished, however, when the woman returned to the parlour, the familiar peevish look once more marring her features. 'I'll have him if it kills me!'

'Does Lady Merchiston know he was here?' Theda asked, adding, 'I only wish to be adequately prepared if she should question me.'

'Don't tell her!' snapped Araminta instantly. 'I way-laid him on his arrival. I will not have her think me acquiescent in her schemes. Let her go to her grave imagining me defiant to the last. Besides, if I marry Saul now, she will think I am provided for and leave the house away from me.'

'I thought Benedict was to have the house,' Theda uttered without thinking.

'He may yet—*if* he can win back into favour.'

Theda was seized by a pang of conscience. 'You mean he is out of favour. . .because of me?'

'*You*? Pah! I knew that scheme would not hold. Benedict marry for other than money? I wish I may see it!'

The words hit Theda like a douche of cold water. Of course. Why should Benedict even have *considered* the proposal? He might desire her—he *did* desire her—but he would not *marry* her only for that! Oh, no. Just like that *other*, nameless—for she would not utter his name, even in mind—betrayer. . .

Brushing off the thoughts, she looked at Araminta. 'Has Benedict—Mr Beckenham, I should say—gone away from here, then?'

'I should imagine so, after the manner in which he stormed off. Merely because I reminded him how unlikely he was to catch an heiress.'

There was contempt in Theda's glance. 'I suppose

you told him, just as your mother did, that he might as well take me?'

The shaft glanced off the armour of Araminta's self-satisfaction. 'I said you were sunk low enough to match his sordid background, yes.'

Inwardly Theda flinched, but she replied coolly, 'Since I am unfamiliar with his background, Miss Merchiston, I am unable to comment.'

'Who wants you to?' demanded Araminta rudely. 'Go back to your duties and mind your business!'

Curtsying, Theda left the little parlour with alacrity, and went to the kitchen to find Adam Diggory and retrieve Hector from him. The dog was under the kitchen table, gobbling scraps of meat given to him by Mrs Elswick, busy at the stove.

'So you are being spoilt, are you, sir?' Theda asked of him, mock-stern.

A wagging tail was her only answer, for the woolly black head remained buried in the interesting bowl. But her voice, penetrating to the little pantry next door, brought Agnes Diggory out.

'Oh, Miss Kyte! Can you spare a moment?'

'Yes, of course, Mrs Diggory,' Theda said, coming into the little room and closing the door on the house-keeper's conspiratorial signal.

'Is all well?' Agnes asked in a whisper.

Theda shrugged, her smile awry. 'As well as anything can be in this house.'

Mrs Diggory nodded. 'True, miss. Still, you're back to your post, and that's the main thing.' She put a hand in her apron pocket and brought out a sealed billet. 'Mr Benedict asked me to give you this, miss, quiet like.'

'Thank you,' Theda said, aware as she took it that her fingers quivered. She slipped it into her pocket, smiled at Agnes, and went back into the kitchen to collect Hector. The dog safely delivered to his still sleeping mistress, who did not stir when he sneaked on to her bed, Theda sought the privacy of her own chamber and broke the seal of Benedict's note.

> Did you shrink from marriage with me, indeed, dear ghost? I assured Aunt Lavvy that it was so, and that I could never coerce an *unwilling* female. I don't know what maggot has got into her head, but I will not dance to her piping, any more than you. Yet I am so much under the spell of *your* witchery I might have viewed parson's mousetrap with a kindly eye were you the bait—and not the false promises with which I am to be lured. *Don't trust her*. And pay no heed to Araminta's spite. Confound you, Theda, you have set me afire and I *burn*!

On the day of the wedding of Mrs Alderley's daughter in early June, Merchiston Lodge was unusually quiet. Araminta had been driven to the celebrations in the gig by Adam Diggory, scorning Benedict's escort, and Mrs Diggory had been permitted to accompany them so that she might visit her mother, who lived on the Switham estates. Benedict himself, who had stayed the previous night, had driven himself over there in his phaeton, glad to be relieved of his cousin's irksome company. There was therefore left at the Lodge only Mrs Elswick in the kitchen and Theda attendant on her ladyship.

There was an air of excitement about Lady Merchiston for which her companion was quite unable to account. She was unusually alert, for her health had deteriorated in the brief time since the upset of Theda's near-dismissal. Dr Spilsby had confided to Theda his belief that the end could not now be far distant.

But today the eyes were vibrant with an anticipatory light and Lady Merchiston sat up against her pillows, her glance alternately flicking to the window and following her companion as she moved about the room, tidying up. Hector, aware of the change, sat up on the bed, following the direction of his mistress's altering gaze with his head cocking, in an air of puzzlement, from side to side.

When Theda would have left the room with a pile of soiled linen, the cracked voice stayed her. 'Wait!'

Theda turned at the door. 'Ma'am?'

'Leave that and come here a moment.'

Laying down her burden, Theda obediently approached the bed and sat as her ladyship patted the covers. 'What is it, Lady Lavinia?'

The sharp black eyes held the grey. 'What's between you and Benedict?'

Theda drew back, a frown in her eyes. 'What do you mean?'

A claw shot out and seized her wrist. 'Don't trifle with me, girl! I know you were kicking up a dust last night, the pair of you. And it ain't the first time! What's to do?'

'You are mistaken, Lady Lavinia,' Theda said firmly.

The old lady's eyes flashed. 'No, I ain't! My body may be past mending, but I've still all my wits. Answer!'

Theda paused, wondering who could have been her ladyship's informant. Mrs Diggory, perhaps? Her mind flew back to the moment last evening when Benedict had come at her out of the shadows of the hall as she had come downstairs with Lady Merchiston's empty supper tray.

'I must talk to you!' he had uttered in an urgent undervoice.

Theda had been conscious of guilt. She had deliberately kept out of his way until now, leaving the task of showing him upstairs to his godmother's room to Mrs Diggory. After the words he had written to her, it was churlish of her to avoid him, but she dreaded any interview because of what she must say.

He had been looking down into her face, lit by the candle he carried, but some sound had turned his eyes to the back of the hall. A moment later he had been dragging her, tray and all, through one of the doors into the vast ballroom.

CHAPTER SIX

'BENEDICT, for heaven's sake!' Theda whispered crossly.

He paid not the slightest attention. Shutting the door, he put his candle down on the nearest chair and drew her across to the glow that streamed in from the setting sun.

'What in the world are you doing?' Theda demanded.

'Be quiet!' he ordered, and before she knew what he was about he had snatched at her white cap and pulled it off.

Burdened with the tray, she could do nothing but back away, protesting, 'Are you mad?'

'I've been going mad,' he returned in a hoarse voice, 'thinking of this!'

Then one hand was holding her still, while the fingers of the other were busy in the folds of her hair. Theda, her heart beginning to race, acted without conscious decision. Shoving the tray into his chest, she cried out, 'Take this!'

'The devil!' he uttered, and as her hands left its edge he let her go and seized the tray before it could fall.

Theda stepped back and caught at the back of her hair just as it came tumbling down over her shoulders. Her fingers tried uselessly to stem the flow of flaming tresses, and Benedict, mesmerised, stood with the tray stupidly clasped in his hands, staring at the mass of struggling copper, bright and flickering like fire in the glow from outside.

'Lord above, Benedict!' Theda scolded. 'You must have taken leave of your senses indeed!'

'I have,' he agreed, grinning suddenly.

'Where is my cap?' she asked distractedly, as she fought with her hair.

He put down the tray on the floor, and brought out her cap from the pocket in his coat into which he had stuffed it, saying, however, 'Let go your hair or I don't return it.'

Theda had perforce to let go, for she could not contain the hair now it had sprung in so disorderly a way from its moorings. As it fell about her, she saw Benedict take a step towards her and moved quickly away.

'Don't touch me!'

His eye gleamed. 'Are you afraid I may burn my fingers?'

'No, your boats!' she retorted.

He stared. 'What the devil are you talking about?'

'I am referring to that foolish note you wrote me,' Theda said, winding her hair into a plait as she spoke, her voice deliberately cool over the tremors inside her.

'*Foolish*?' Benedict repeated. 'I meant every word.'

'Fudge! You know very well you will never marry to your own disadvantage.'

'Why to my disadvantage?' he demanded, his voice thick with passion. 'You heat my blood so greatly, I could readily give up all my hopes just to have you to myself.'

'You are talking like a green youth. It would serve you out if I chose to use the letter in an action against you for breach of promise!'

For a moment he looked taken aback. Then a short laugh escaped him. 'I know you better than that,

Theda. But I swear to God, if it was not so prejudicial to my future, I'd marry you tomorrow.'

Theda's grey eyes grew dark and her voice shook. 'Only for the opportunity to slake your desire? I am flattered!'

'And *yours*.' He seized her shoulders, but her hands came up to hold his wrists and prevent him from pulling her close. He was obedient to the pressure—for he could easily have overborne her with his superior strength—but his voice was guttural. 'You want me, too. You know you do. You never boggle at plain-speaking, so why do so now? This passion between us is not one-sided.'

Theda wrenched his hands from her shoulders, but she did not release his wrists, her grip on them tightening. 'I will say this. A woman in my situation may be vulnerable. Loneliness and a personable male are tempting seducers.'

His face changed. 'Then why hold temptation so strongly?'

She let go his wrists as if they were scalding hot, stepping smartly away. 'Give me my cap!'

He held it out. 'Yes, you had better tuck it out of the "seducer's" sight!'

Theda was busy with her hair, but at that she glanced at him and saw the hurt in his eyes. She took the cap and made herself once more respectable in silence. Then she took up the discarded tray and looked back at him where he stood now, leaning against the wall between the French windows, his silver flask of brandy open as he sipped defiantly, watching her with a black scowl on his face.

'Benedict,' she said in a kindlier tone, 'even were it possible, I would not—*could* not—marry you.'

'Oh?' His voice was hard. 'Am I that bad?'

A rueful smile flitted over her face. 'No, there is nothing at all wrong with you. It is myself who is "that bad".'

Turning from him, she made quickly for the door. He called out her name, but she did not pause. In another moment she was outside the room, her heart hollow, and the tears pricking at her eyes.

Now, as she came back to the present, Lady Merchiston's own eyes were on her in a compelling look, demanding an answer. 'What's between you two?'

Theda drew a breath. 'Benedict is dazzled by my hair, ma'am.'

'I'll warrant he is!' the old lady cackled unexpectedly. 'So he's seen it, has he? Well, well. His first experience of woman, that hair. And of love—of the most enduring kind. Even at the end, there were echoes of it still.'

Theda knew an instant of blinding, devastating hatred of the red-headed woman who had once been Benedict's love. Then the feeling was gone as Lady Merchiston claimed her attention with another acute observation.

'Not so averse to the boy as you had led me to believe, eh?'

'I like him very well, ma'am,' Theda said quickly, 'but I couldn't marry him even if I wanted to—which I *don't*.'

'Why not?'

This time Theda met the demand in her eyes without flinching away. 'Forgive me, Lady Lavinia. I would tell you if I could, I promise you, but my story involves others and—and I simply cannot in honour divulge it.'

For a moment or two Lady Merchiston continued to regard her steadily, as if she tried to read Theda's story in her face. Then she reached out a hand to clasp one of hers.

'Child, I will not press you,' she said, unwontedly gentle, 'but only tell me this. Were you in your proper station, you would, I think, take precedence even over me?'

Theda bit her lip. Then she sighed and nodded. 'Yes, ma'am. But an outcast takes *no* precedence, as you well know.'

'Ah, but you need not have been an outcast,' shrewdly guessed the old lady.

'It is true that I could have braved the scandal, brazened it out,' Theda admitted, 'but either fear or pride, perhaps——'

'A mixture of both,' interpolated Lady Merchiston.

'Probably. In any event, I chose this route and I must ever take the consequences.'

'Ah, yes, consequences.' With sudden energy, her ladyship sat up a little straighter, raising her frail body in the bed.

'If that is horses I hear on the drive, here come a purveyor of consequences.' She chuckled as Theda looked a question. 'My lawyer.'

'Your lawyer? But did you invite him, ma'am?'

'You are thinking there was no letter passed through your hands,' said Lady Merchiston gleefully. 'But it did. You recall me writing to my bankers in Ashby-de-la-Zouch?'

'A day or so ago, yes.'

'Well, I enclosed my note to Aycliffe within that, so that no one would know of his coming. You are to keep it a secret, Theodosia. Swear it now!'

'Very well, ma'am, I will say nothing if you wish it,' agreed Theda, but she was nevertheless consumed with curiosity.

The old lady saw it in her face. 'Aha! You want to know why he's coming. Can't you guess?'

'Your will, ma'am?'

'That's it. I've decided on my dispositions at last.'
She leaned towards Theda suddenly. 'And you're not
to worry over your own case. I'm taking care of you.'

'Of *me*?' uttered Theda, astonished.

'Don't you think I owe you something after employing you under false pretences? Oh, I've been aware of
your fears, child.'

'Lady Lavinia, I beg of you, don't make me any gifts!
Or if you must, let me have it *beforehand*. It would be
quite dreadful for me to benefit by your death.'

'So you say! Don't talk rubbish, girl! It will keep you
here a little so that you may have time to make your
plans.'

'Finding another post is all the plan I have, ma'am.'

'Very well, whatever it may be. I would not rest easy
knowing Araminta would see you off without so much
as a penny piece the moment I breathe my last.'

'Lady Lavinia, it is very kind of you, but——'

'Don't fidget me with prattle and thanks, Theodosia!
I *owe* it to you. And you know it! Now go down and
send Aycliffe up to me. Take Hector and don't come
back, either of you, until he has gone. Now *go*!'

Theda gave it up, calling to Hector as she left the
room. If her ladyship's mind was made up, there was
nothing she could say to change it. There was no time
to think over this latest development, for by the time
she got to the hall downstairs the doorbell was already
jangling.

Mr Aycliffe was a man in late middle age, whose
sober garments and air of portentous solemnity at once
proclaimed his calling.

'You must be Miss Kyte,' he ventured, holding out a
hand.

Theda was surprised. 'You've heard of me?'

'Everyone has, you know,' he said with an apologetic smile. 'Mountsorrel is a small place and we generally hear of all the doings round about.'

Theda frowned. 'But no one comes here! Or, wait . . .Mrs Elswick?'

The visitor's brows rose. 'Possibly, but she lives in Switham.'

'Adam!' Theda exclaimed. 'Doubtless he visits the alehouse when he goes in for supplies.'

'Extraordinary fellow, old Diggory,' remarked the lawyer, without confirming or denying Theda's suspicion. 'Devoted to her ladyship, as he was to Sir John, you know.'

All at once Theda was struck by the obvious solution to her own vexed question. It had not been Mrs Diggory who had told Lady Lavinia about herself and Benedict. Adam it was who made up the fires of a morning, when his mistress, who slept only fitfully at night, was already awake, Adam who crept noiselessly about the place, unnoticed, who must have seen them together last night outside the ballroom. Devoted indeed! She summoned a smile and nodded at Mr Aycliffe.

'Naturally you will have heard of me. Even had you not been so well acquainted with the family, I dare say. We live so isolated an existence here that to me it seems quite odd. It was foolish of me to forget how news spreads in a village.'

'Unwise, I agree, ma'am.'

'To forget? You are very right. It is something I particularly ought to remember.'

His brows rose, but he said nothing, merely appraising her out of a pair of shrewd eyes.

'You are expected, Mr Aycliffe. Will you go on up?'

Theda suggested. She smiled, adding, 'I am barred during your visit, so pray excuse me.'

He bowed and went off up the stairs. Theda took Hector to the kitchen and left him with Mrs Elswick to do what he might in the way of cajolery, for she had several morsels of interest to his ever ready stomach, and Theda was obviously not going to take him outside.

In fact the weather had not smiled on Miss Switham's wedding day, and the overcast sky did not invite a walk. Instead, Theda slipped into the ballroom to think about Lady Merchiston's determination to make her a bequest.

She could not but be gratified and relieved at the possibility of a small sum to see her through the likely lean period before she could get another post. But her mind did not dwell long on what she privately felt to be a remote contingency—Lady Merchiston was so changeable! Instead she found herself, in this room full of memories, thinking of Benedict Beckenham.

Unconsciously she put up a hand to that fatal head of hair, and her fingers, coming into contact with the enveloping white cap, brought her a sobering thought. She had hurt him. But she *had* to. It was a matter of self-preservation.

Her mind ran on the wedding celebrations as she moved to the window where a stray shaft of sunlight, escaping through the thick cloud, threw a beam across the parquet floor. Her feet began to move in the *fleuret* of a minuet. There would be dancing. For an instant, in her imagination, the ballroom was peopled with guests, and Benedict was partnering her, his gold hair gleaming in the light, his eyes on hers. . .dancing with the bride.

The sun went in and the ballroom was again shrouded in gloom—empty, but for Miss Theodosia Kyte, dreaming a foolish dream!

But as she gazed from the French windows on the tangle of weeds outside, and the now dense greenery of Switham Thicket, a plea formed in her mind as she thought of Lady Merchiston upstairs, in conference with her man of business.

Don't disappoint him, pray.

'I'm glad she waited for the wedding to be over,' whispered Mrs Alderley in Theda's ear, as she joined her by the French windows that had been opened to the terrace outside.

The ballroom had been thrown wide to accommodate the funeral guests, and Mrs Diggory was busy serving refreshments to the gentlemen who had just a short time since returned from the graveside of the deceased Lady Merchiston.

For Theda had been woken one night, a few days after Mr Aycliffe's visit, by Hector whining next door. She had risen from her bed, slipped on her dressing-robe, and lighting her bedside candle with the tinder-box on the table, she had taken it in her hand and gone into Lady Merchiston's chamber. Hector had been huddled by the door, and he had snuffed at once at her feet, whimpering. Theda had drawn the curtain about the four-poster open, and the light from her candle had fallen on the old lady's face.

Her eyes had been open in a fixed and vacant stare, and the waxen tinge to her skin had told its own tale. Theda had reached down to clasp her trembling fingers lightly about the cold wrist lying on the coverlet, but she had known already that there was no pulse to be discerned.

Oddly, Theda had found herself distressed by this long-expected demise. She had known it must come, and soon, particularly after the day of the wedding. For once the lawyer had concluded his business, having called upon both his own groom and Mrs Elswick to witness the document he had drawn up, and had been seen off the premises, Theda had gone back upstairs to find her employer in a state of near-collapse.

'All done now,' she had murmured, the once vibrant eyes quite as lifeless as the rest of her emaciated form. 'Nothing left to hang on for. Be gone soon.'

Now she had indeed gone, and her household, strangely bereft, seemed lost and forlorn all at once. Hector had clung close to Theda, and was even now shut up in her tiny bedchamber, where he had taken to sleeping. Mrs Diggory was herself but little touched, Theda believed, but she had been upset by her husband's woeful demeanour. For of them all, Adam Diggory had been the most deeply stricken by grief.

Even Araminta had been sullen and silent ever since her mother's death, and Theda had been relieved to see Mrs Alderley, who had driven over, elegant as ever in rustling black silk, to offer her condolences at a time when she knew all the men would be attending the service.

'For I wanted the opportunity to talk to you privately,' she told Theda quietly, 'although I could not see Araminta allowing it.'

She had managed, nevertheless, to seize a few moments with the erstwhile companion when the gentlemen returned, for Araminta had at once gone over to greet Mr Saul Quatt, who had, at her request, presided over the service in the local church—much to the chagrin of its incumbent, whose ruffled feathers Mrs Alderley had been obliged to smooth when she heard of the plan from him.

Miss Merchiston, who had refused to wear mourning up until today, was now correctly attired in black crêpe, but Theda had been obliged to content herself with her dark stuff gown and black ribbons to her cap. Benedict, who had arrived yesterday, was looking extremely handsome in full mourning, even to a black cravat.

Theda had been unable to exchange more than a few words with him, for she had been—on Araminta's orders—busily engaged in packing up all Lady Merchiston's things into trunks to be stored in the attics, and cleaning out her bedchamber.

'I hardly knew whether I would find you still here,' Benedict had said, catching her on the gallery as she went towards the attic stairs, burdened with a small wooden box containing the contents of Lady Merchiston's medicine cupboard, Hector at her heels.

'Araminta wanted me to clear up first,' Theda answered, trying to still the flutter that had attacked her pulses at the touch of his hand on her arm.

He acknowledged the dog's overtures, but he eyed her with a good deal of concern. 'Have you anywhere to go?'

Theda shook her head. 'No, but it is not the first time I have been in such a situation. I will come about.'

Benedict frowned. 'The devil! I wish it were possible for you to come away with me.'

'Well, it is not!' Theda said, startled.

'I know that.' His hand caressed her arm. 'If there was somewhere you might stay in the meanwhile, I may shortly be in a position to help you.'

'To *what*, Benedict?' she demanded sharply. 'A discreet establishment that you may visit from time to time?'

His eyes flashed and his fingers tightened in a vicious grip. 'You have a curst low opinion of me, by God! Why should you think I meant that?'

'Why should you suppose me any less proud than

more fortunate females?' Theda countered. 'You know very well that a lady cannot accept pecuniary assistance from a gentleman without being thought to have taken up a *carte blanche*.'

'You didn't quibble at the Feathers,' he snapped.

'I *did*, but you made it impossible for me to refuse.'

There was a silence while he eyed her smoulderingly in the light from the candles in the wall-sconces. The dog Hector, seated on his haunches beside them, glanced from one to the other in mute puzzlement. Theda sighed and gave Benedict a kinder smile.

'I am sorry. I know you mean well, and I *am* ever grateful for what you did——'

'Oh, be quiet! Do you think I want gratitude? Theda, I thought we were *friends*.'

'Well, and so we are.'

He grinned suddenly and touched her cheek lightly with his fingers. 'But no more than friends, eh?'

'You know that is impossible.'

'So you say!'

Theda laughed. 'You sound exactly like Lady Lavinia. That was one of her expressions.'

A frown came into Benedict's eyes. 'I never thought it would be so, but I miss her like the devil!'

'I, too. Odd, isn't it? I knew her so short a time.'

'What difference does that make? You've known *me* but a short time.'

For some reason the words rang in Theda's head. Had he *meant* to give them that special significance? That charge between them sparked all at once. She heard his breath hiss, and quickly drew back.

'I must take this box upstairs.'

'Running away, Theda?'

'*Yes*,' she said staunchly, and clicked her fingers to Hector, who, bored, had wandered down the gallery.

He laughed, but there was urgency in his tone nevertheless. 'Stay a moment longer! What *are* you going to do? I hate to think of you blundering about, alone and unprotected.'

She gave him a warm smile. 'Don't fear for me, Benedict. For one thing, Rose has kindly offered to help me find a place.'

'Yes, I know,' he said unexpectedly. 'She told me. If she had offered you hospitality, I would be the better pleased.'

'Lord, why should she? I will have wages to tide me over initially.'

'A pittance!' scoffed Benedict.

'Yes, I know, but. . .' She hesitated, biting her lip. Should she tell him?

But next instant, he came closer and his fingers cradled her face, the box in her hands keeping them apart. His voice was low and very tender.

'Dear ghost, I don't want you to float out of my life, to disappear without trace. Do you see?'

Yes, she did! She saw that she *must* do exactly that—run away from him as he had suggested, but as far away as she could go! But she could not say so. She summoned a light laugh. 'You are being quite absurd, you know.'

He let her go. 'Am I?' he said grimly, stepping back. 'Then do without me!'

'Don't be angry!' she begged quickly. 'I—I ought not to be telling you this, but Lady Lavinia told me she would. . .leave me something.'

Benedict's eyes snapped to attention, and his body went rigid. 'You mean she made a new will?'

Lord, now what was she to say? She had promised to keep silent. But Benedict's eyes were on her, as compelling a question in them as had been in those of his godmother.

'Theda, answer me!'

'She made a will, yes.'

'Dear *God*! What was in it? What did it say?'

'I don't *know*, Benedict. I did not see it, nor was I told. Only she said she had brought me here under false pretences and she chose to make amends this way.'

'What the devil do I care about her confounded amends?' he said harshly. 'What has she done by *me*? That is my sole interest in it!'

Hector, distressed, gave a whimper and hid himself in the skirts of his chosen protectress. Theda hardly noticed him, for hurt and disappointment flooded over her in a wave. How quickly had his attention turned from his vaunted concern over herself to his own interests!

'Does Araminta know?' he was asking urgently.

'No one knows,' Theda said, her voice shaking.

'Except you!'

There was something in his tone that brought her eyes up to his in a look of vibrant anger.

'Excuse me, Benedict,' she said with forced calm. 'I have work to do. Come, Hector.'

This time he did not try to stop her and she made her way to the attics in a seething temper, depositing the box of Lady Merchiston's effects without even thinking what she was doing. How dared he insinuate that she lied? For he had done so, if only by the manner of his speech. Now she saw the true worth of all his protestations. *Friends*? On *his* terms, she supposed. Benedict Beckenham, *you* are the liar, not I, for you caress with a false tongue for purposes of your own!

He had not sought another interview with her, and, as the ladies naturally did not attend at the graveside, the first she had seen of him since then was when the party returned from the funeral. Sighting Benedict, Theda immediately found it difficult to concentrate on what Mrs Alderley was saying.

'I have not forgotten my promise to help you find a place, although I have not done so yet.'

'You have scarcely had an opportunity, ma'am,' Theda answered with automatic politeness, 'what with the wedding and the bereavement in this house.'

'Yes, but the matter is now become of some urgency, and I feel very guilty——'

That took Theda's full attention. 'Don't say so, ma'am! Besides, it is not quite so urgent as I thought. At least, I hope that——'

She was interrupted. The lawyer, Mr Aycliffe, had come up. 'Miss Kyte, how do you do? I am about to retire to the breakfast parlour with Mr Beckenham and Miss Merchiston. Will you find the Diggorys, if you please, and join us?'

'Certainly, sir,' Theda replied, and turned as he went off to find in Mrs Alderley's face a look of blank astonishment.

'Good God! She has left you something?'

Theda grimaced. 'She said she would. It is what I was about to tell you. A little to tide me over, I gather.'

'Well, I wouldn't have believed it of Lavinia. What an extraordinary woman she was, to be sure!'

It seemed to Theda that neither Rose nor Benedict appeared pleased that she was to benefit thus. Perhaps, after all, it was only Lady Merchiston who'd truly had her interests at heart, even if only latterly. Certainly Araminta was unlikely to be gratified.

In this she was perfectly correct. She entered the

breakfast parlour, in company with Agnes and Adam Diggory, the latter red-eyed and bowed down with sorrow, to find Miss Merchiston seated on one side of the big table, opposite Benedict, while Mr Aycliffe occupied the head.

Araminta took one astonished look and jumped to her feet, pointing. 'What is *she* doing in here?'

Benedict's head snapped round and last night's frown again descended on his brow.

'Miss Kyte is here at my request,' said Mr Aycliffe in a repressive tone.

'You mean she's in the will?' demanded Araminta shrilly.

Benedict threw her a contemptuous glance. 'That would seem to be a fair inference.'

'Please sit down, everyone,' intervened the lawyer.

The Diggorys each pulled out a chair and perched on it, obviously uncomfortable. But Theda stayed where she was by the door, meeting Araminta's malevolent stare with a fast-beating heart. Did she *have* to face this?

'Miss Kyte?' said Mr Aycliffe.

She bit her lip. 'I—I would prefer to be excused.'

'I am afraid that is not possible,' returned the lawyer.

Benedict rose and came down the table. He pulled out the chair at the bottom and bowed. 'You may as well sit down.' Glancing at Araminta as Theda began to move towards it, he added, 'If she's in the will, she's in it. Dagger looks will not change that.'

As he moved back to his place, Araminta transferred her glare to his face. But she said nothing.

Benedict nodded to Mr Aycliffe. 'We are all agog, man. Do carry on.'

The lawyer rustled his papers and cleared his throat. 'This is the last will and testament of Lavinia Dorothy,

Lady Merchiston of Merchiston Lodge, Switham, Leicestershire.'

The will began in the usual way, with small bequests to several relatives of whom Theda had never heard, and a lump sum and pension for the Diggorys—at mention of which old Adam had again recourse to his handkerchief. Theda had thought her own small portion would come next, but the lawyer cleared his throat again, and read on.

'To my daughter, Araminta Dorothy Merchiston...'

Miss Merchiston's eyes glanced at Benedict, who merely raised his brows, and then passed to the paper in the lawyer's hand and there remained.

'In addition to the agreed sum of her own portion, all my jewellery, all the silver and plate, and any items of furnishing she wishes to remove from Merchiston Lodge, which property itself she may not have.'

Benedict's eyes met hers in triumph as she turned a fierce look of venom upon him.

'If my daughter Araminta requires a home,' went on Aycliffe, 'let her marry Saul Quatt, whom I am perfectly aware she has planned to entrap in any event.'

A shriek of rage and chagrin escaped Miss Merchiston's lips, and she leapt to her feet. 'The old hag! How dared she double-cross me?'

Theda could not but feel sorry for her, but Benedict's eyes were on the lawyer, who had paused.

'If you please, Miss Merchiston,' he said quietly, 'I am not finished.'

'Very well, very well, continue!' snapped Araminta, quivering with temper, and shooting killing looks at her cousin on the other side of the table.

'In addition,' resumed Aycliffe, 'and in consideration of certain advice, I leave to my daughter a further sum of ten thousand pounds.'

Theda blinked. Ten *thousand*! Lord above, she had not imagined there to be much above ten hundred to be left!

'*Advice*?' Araminta uttered, her fury ludicrously arrested by a look of blank astonishment. 'What advice?'

With uncanny certainty, Theda knew that Lady Merchiston referred to her own words. She must have decided that the house, which would go to Benedict, was worth that much above the other items she had left to Araminta.

'To my godson, Robert Benedict Beckenham, the sum of twenty thousand pounds with which to gamble his way into a debtor's prison. . .'

There was a concerted gasp of shock around the table, and Benedict himself stiffened, his frown deepening so that it cut heavy lines across his forehead and between his brows, marring his looks.

'Where I hope he will reflect on the unwisdom of employing his charm and duplicity on a woman as sharp as I.'

No one spoke as Mr Aycliffe paused. Even Araminta was too awed for words. Theda could almost hear her late employer cackling. Then Benedict, in a voice of ice, asked the question in everyone's mind.

'Is that it?'

The lawyer shook his head, and Theda saw the sudden hope flicker in Benedict's eyes. Araminta's glance left his face and returned to Aycliffe.

'Well? Does he get the house or not?'

Clearing his throat yet again, his nervousness now apparent to all, Aycliffe resumed, his tone over-loud in the suddenly still room.

'The residue of my estate, including Merchiston

Lodge and its contents other than those already speci-
fied, together with the grounds in which it is set, I
bequeath to the one person who has made my last days
worth living, Miss Theodosia Kyte.'

CHAPTER SEVEN

PARALYSIS held Theda blank of mind and body, as still and silent as everyone else in the breakfast parlour.

Then a piercing crowing shattered on their ears, and they all leapt in their seats as Araminta Merchiston broke into hysterical, shrieking laughter.

'Oh, oh, oh!' she gasped between paroxysms of mirth. 'A jest...a marvellous, cruel jest. So much for you, B-Benedict! *That* will teach you to play off your airs! Oh, oh!'

Benedict was on his feet, overturning his chair in one violent gesture, a face of livid fury turned on Theda.

'You lying, traitorous, scheming *witch*!' he snarled.

Theda's eyes met the scorching flame in his as she rose shakily to her feet to face him.

'You think *I* did this?' she whispered hoarsely, not even conscious that Agnes Diggory rushed to Araminta's side where she lay back in her chair, hiccuping on her choking laughter.

But Benedict's tongue lashed out again. 'Don't come the play-acting with me, you vicious, conniving *she-devil*. Innocent as sin, by God! May the whole accursed edifice rot about your evil little heart of stone, and *bury you*!'

Then he strode from the room, passing her chair without even glancing at her, and slamming the door with such force that the chandelier rattled above the table.

'Come, Miss Ara, come!' Agnes Diggory was saying,

dragging at Araminta's shoulders where she sat, her laughter quenched, tears streaming down her face.

'Diggory, help me!' the housekeeper called out, jerking her husband out of the stupor into which he appeared to have fallen. He hurried to her aid and between them they managed to half-carry Miss Merchiston from the room.

Theda, meanwhile, had sunk back into her chair, a stricken look in her eyes as she stared unseeingly at Aycliffe.

There was a long silence. The lawyer seemed to be studying his papers, waiting, it seemed to Theda as her brain began to function a little, for her to take the lead. She was shaking so much that she could barely speak. But she said his name.

'Mr Aycliffe?'

He glanced up, a grave look in his face. 'Yes, Miss Kyte?'

'Is there. . .?' She swallowed on a dry throat, licked burning lips, and tried again. 'Is there any way I can escape this inheritance?'

He frowned. 'Do you wish to?'

'Yes. Oh, Lord above, *yes*!'

There was another pause. Then the lawyer sighed, rose from his chair, and came down the table to take another next to hers. 'Miss Kyte, you are either a very good actress, or an innocent victim of an old lady's wiles. Which is it?'

Theda grimaced. 'Why do you ask when, like Benedict, you will take your own view?'

'Mr Beckenham is naturally upset, and therefore prejudiced. I am neither.'

'Upset?' Theda repeated with a faint smile. 'That is your word for it?'

Mr Aycliffe did not answer this. Instead, resting his

elbows on his papers, he laced his fingers together and regarded her over them. 'You see, Miss Kyte, things do not look very good for you.'

'How do you mean?' Theda asked quickly, frowning over the distress in her face.

'Look at the picture, ma'am. This will was made on the day of the wedding at Switham. No one but yourself was in the house when I came, barring the cook, who is not of the household. The letter that brought me was sent by your hand through the bankers in Ashby-de-la-Zouch. You are the person, moreover, who found Lady Merchiston dead.'

'What are you saying?' Theda demanded, indignation warring with the hurt she was experiencing from the dreadful blow that had been dealt her, the vicious attack to which she had been subjected.

'I am enumerating the items that could stand against you should the will be contested,' said Mr Aycliffe patiently.

'Contested?' Theda was suddenly eager. 'They *could* do so. Both of them!'

'They could. I doubt they would either of them succeed. But in a court of law much could be made of these things.'

'There is no need for a court of law. I neither desire this house, nor do I wish to deprive the rightful heirs of what is their own.'

For the first time, Mr Aycliffe smiled. 'Miss Kyte, there are no *rightful* heirs. Lady Merchiston was under no obligation to bestow her property except as she saw fit.'

'Oh, legal quibbling!' Theda uttered irritably. 'You know as well as I that both Benedict and Araminta have every moral right to enjoy whatever she had, while I have none at all.'

'But *you* are the beneficiary.'

'I don't *want* to be the beneficiary!'

'I am afraid it is too late for that,' Mr Aycliffe said with a faint smile. 'You cannot escape it. Once probate has been granted, which should not take many weeks, this house, and everything in it that is not chosen by Miss Merchiston——'

'Which may well be nothing!' interpolated Theda with a flash of humour.

'Everything, I say, in addition to the rest of her fortune, will be yours.'

Theda's eyes widened. 'Fortune? Lady Merchiston?'

'Fortune is what I said.'

'Oh, come, now, Mr Aycliffe,' Theda begged, a laugh of pure exasperation escaping her lips. 'After she has already left thirty thousand and more elsewhere? Don't forget, I have lived here three months, and although I know the family to be close-fisted there *cannot* have been much more than that.'

'Miss Kyte, it is often the most penny-pinching who have the most at their disposal,' the lawyer told her, his eyes twinkling.

Theda shook her head in disbelief, but said, 'Very well, sir. You may as well tell me the worst.' A glimmer of amusement twisted her mouth. 'Since I am like to be murdered for it, I had better know the tune!'

'The tune, ma'am,' said Mr Aycliffe lightly, 'is in the region of one hundred and fifty thousand pounds— safely invested in the funds.'

His face danced in Theda's sight and she sank back in her chair. 'Lord help me!' she whispered. 'Benedict will *never* forgive me.'

Mrs Rosalia Alderley looked about the library at the gleaming, polished wood, the dust-free shelves and the shining leather bindings on the many volumes stacked upon them, and brought her gaze back to Theda's face.

'You have lost no time in setting things to rights, I see,' she said in a carefully neutral tone.

It did not deceive Theda. 'You don't approve?'

Colour tinged the other woman's cheeks. 'No, no, I meant no criticism.'

'The *devil* you did not!' Theda burst out. 'You will forgive my intemperate language—culled from Mr Beckenham, I fear!—but let there be no pretence between us, if you please.'

Rose put out a hand, saying quickly, 'Forgive me! I am sure *you* are not to blame for the iniquitous nature of this wretched will.'

'Are you, ma'am?' Theda said sceptically. 'Then you are alone in that opinion.'

'Nonsense! Aycliffe himself assured me that he is convinced there was no complicity on your part.'

'Mr Aycliffe had better post an advertisement to that effect, then, before I am burned at the stake!'

'Don't be so foolish!' said Mrs Alderley quite crossly, rising from her chair.

'My dear Rose, pray sit down again,' begged Theda, softening. 'I am excessively grateful to you for *not* deserting me in this hideous pass. But there have been local whisperings, so Adam tells us. To tell the truth, I had not expected to see you again.'

'I *was* put out,' confessed Rose, sinking back into her seat. 'But it was not your fault, after all. It is just that being shown into the library, which has been shut up these many years, perhaps brought it home to me how very sad it was for. . .'

She faltered to a stop, Benedict's name hovering on her lips as she looked uncertainly into Theda's face. Miss Kyte chose not to take up the challenge.

'In fact this is the only room I have touched,' she said. 'It was a dilemma, you see. Apart from Araminta's parlour——'

'That poky little room! You cannot sit in there!'

'Exactly so. And the saloon is too full. It was only when Taggy found the key to *this* room, and I discovered it to be so beautiful, that we set to and cleaned it between us.'

The library, which had not been in use since Sir John Merchiston's death some seven years earlier, was a very pleasant room, positioned opposite the ballroom, between Araminta's parlour and the big saloon, with panelled walls, quantities of shelving, an ivory inlay desk, leather chairs before the fireplace, and a good deal of light, even on this overcast day, coming in from a glazed door leading out into a pretty walled garden.

'It *is* a nice room,' Rose agreed.

'The whole house is delightful,' Theda said decidedly. 'Or it would be if it was rendered habitable once more.'

'Is that what you intend to do? You are going to *stay* here?'

For the first time Theda's veneer of composure cracked a little. 'I would give much to be able to do so ...to have a *home*. At least Araminta has achieved that, in spite of being cut out.'

For Araminta Merchiston had become Mrs Saul Quatt within a week of her mother's funeral. It was freely said in the village that the blow to the reverend gentleman had been considerably softened by the terms of his late mother-in-law's will. In a word, Mr Quatt had scooped up Araminta's promised ten thousand with alacrity.

'You may be thankful Quatt took her,' observed Mrs

Alderley. 'Otherwise you would have had her quartered on you forever.'

Theda shuddered. 'Enough to make me run from here incontinently, as I promise you I had a mind to do!'

'Why did you not?' asked Rose in a more gentle tone than she had yet used.

'Because it would not have solved anything. The house would go more to rack than ever and serve no purpose but to make everyone concerned more miserable than they are already.'

'I *knew* you would want to set all to rights,' Rose said softly, smiling warmly at her. 'You may easily do so, you know.'

'How?' Theda demanded, eyeing her visitor with acute suspicion.

'Dear Theda, you must surely be able to see that for yourself. It is so obvious!'

'Indeed? We will have it in plain words nevertheless. How does a woman with a large inheritance commonly bestow it on a man? That is what you mean, is it not? I should marry Benedict.'

'Good God, no!' ejaculated Mrs Alderley, startled. 'I had not even thought of it.'

Theda frowned. 'You had not *thought* of it?'

'I swear not! It is Benedict who concerns me, yes, but—but *that* is not the solution I had in mind.'

There was no mistaking her sincerity, nor the obvious distaste with which she regarded the very idea of such a union.

'What, then, *did* you have in mind?' Theda asked, torn between a rather misplaced indignation, considering her own views on the subject, and curiosity.

'Well, I thought that you would take something within reason for yourself. Enough, I dare say, to—

to...' She had started with confidence, but under Theda's unnerving eye she began to falter. 'Well, to buy yourself a little house, perhaps. Something modest. Something *suitable*, as this really is *not*. And then, for the rest——'

'Yes? For the rest?'

Rose swallowed and came out with it in rather a rush. 'Make it over to Benedict by deed of gift.'

Theda blinked. 'Deed of gift? Lord! Don't you know him better than that? It would stick in his craw!'

Mrs Alderley looked quite crestfallen all of a sudden. 'Oh, dear, how right you are! I never thought of that.'

'Besides,' Theda added, her eyes flashing, 'after the way he spoke to me, I am not of a mind to hand him *gifts*.'

'He was *upset*,' Rose said pleadingly, for she had heard from Aycliffe just what Benedict had said in his black fury.

'So everyone keeps telling me,' Theda snapped. 'As if I have no right to take it amiss.'

'He must have hurt you very badly,' Rose said in a conciliatory tone, for it was no part of her scheme to antagonise Theda.

'I was not..."hurt",' Theda lied. 'It is only the injustice of it which—to which I take exception.'

'But Theda, how was he to know?'

'He *should* have known,' Theda said through her teeth.

'The—the heat of the moment,' pleaded Rose.

'Fudge!'

There was a tense silence. Theda smouldered, trying to contain her anger. That first night, after the shock had begun to abate, the vision of Benedict's snarling features, the sound of molten rage in his voice, had come back to her again and again as she lay in her

narrow cot bed, and she had wept. By this time, however, she'd had three weeks in which to move from
bitter, aching despair, to bitter, aching fury. For she
had been so sure that, once he had turned the matter
over in a cooler frame of mind, he would recognise and
acknowledge her innocence. He would return to her,
to beg her pardon for so basely misjudging her, and
they would find again the former ease of friendship,
the lack of which now gaped in her life like an open
wound.

But Benedict had not come back. He had sent no
word. He was as hot against her as ever, and would
probably remain so.

'In any event,' Theda said, speaking her thought
aloud, 'he told me himself he had no claim on Lady
Merchiston. She owed him nothing.'

'That,' said Rose Alderley flatly, 'is a matter of
opinion.'

Theda turned her head and noted the set look in the
other's face. Yes, Rose knew it all! With deliberation,
she said, 'It is a pity I cannot judge for myself.'

Rose looked struck. Slowly she spoke. 'Well, why
should you not? After all, Lavinia is dead now, and
you are no longer in her employ.'

Theda waited. How much would Rose reveal? She
had ever been curious about Benedict's background,
and now more so than ever, when everything hinged
on his moral claim to Merchiston Lodge.

Mrs Alderley sat lost in thought for a few moments.
Then she nodded with decision and rose from her chair.
'Let us walk outside. It is no longer raining, and I do
not care to talk where anyone might hear.'

They went out through a gate in the walled garden,
and encountered Hector almost at once. He was now
largely permitted to roam the grounds in freedom, and

he came gambolling up to greet Theda with a bark, and then went off exploring again, just keeping the ladies in sight, and returning now and again for a pat or an encouraging word.

'There is at least one who has adapted himself to circumstance,' observed Theda.

'Surprising,' commented Rose. 'I should think he was the only creature for whom Lavinia truly cared.'

They began to pace along the drive, for the grass was still damp from the recent rain.

'I think you are mistaken,' Theda said in an even tone. 'I think she cared for Benedict.'

'She had a strange way of showing it, then.'

'Because she left the property to me? Yet she always came to his rescue when he was in difficulties.'

'That?' scornfully responded Mrs Alderley. 'A bagatelle! Sir John died seven years ago, but in all that time Lavinia has not increased Benedict's allowance, as she might well have done, nor made any provision for his accommodation, other than saying that he might live at Merchiston Lodge if he chose.'

'Which he obviously did not choose. But why should she have done those things?' Theda demanded.

'Because Sir John wished it,' Rose told her angrily.

'Not that he trusted her. His own wife, mark you! Apart from the measly sums she doled out from time to time, the allowance was Benedict's by right, for it was left in trust for him by her husband. He would have done better to have given everything to the boy outright, but it is my belief he did not want Benedict to lose touch with his godmother.'

'You mean if he had not to come to her for money, he would not have come at all?' Theda guessed. 'I can readily believe it.'

'Yes, and I am sure it is because Sir John *meant* him

to have the house. Benedict told me he said as much to him.'

'What about his own daughter?' Theda asked.

'Oh, he was as bad as Lavinia on that count. He said she had ruined her chances by obstinacy and might count herself lucky to live on Benedict's charity.'

'But what a charming family!'

'You may well say so! And it was into *this* that Benedict was dragged, through no fault of his own, poor boy!'

Theda looked round at her. 'What precisely happened, ma'am? So far I have had only hints.'

Rose shook her head, distress in her face. 'It was all so *dreadful*. Isabel fell from grace, which is *nothing* new in our circles, let me tell you. Except that she became with child, and Robert—her husband, you must know, who was a brute with a terrible temper!—refused to acknowledge it as his own. The truth was, of course, that he was in love with someone else and chose to use poor Isabel as a scapegoat.'

'He left her?' asked Theda, disturbed by an immediate rush of fellow feeling for the unfortunate woman.

'Worse!' groaned Rose. 'He took his suit through the full panoply of law—Doctors' Commons, then a court of common law, and finally the House of Lords.'

'*Divorce*?' Theda uttered in a shocked tone.

Mrs Alderley was hunting for her pocket handkerchief. 'Yes. You may im-imagine the shocking s-scandal!' She blew her nose and wiped the tears from her eyes. 'And Isabel utterly cast off, immured in the Dower House the while.'

'Oh, how *cruel*,' Theda said. 'But how did she come here?'

'She was in such despair, poor girl,' explained Rose, having recourse to her handkerchief again. 'Pregnant, too, and without a sight of her only son. At last she wrote to Sir John Merchiston, who was a remote cousin, but whom she had known when she came as a débutante to visit here with her family for the hunting.'

Sir John, it appeared, had retained a sufficiently fond memory of his cousin, and was, besides, so moved by her plight that he went himself and fetched her back to Switham. There followed a long wrangle over Benedict's future, which Sir John Merchiston eventually won by virtue of the fact that Robert Beckenham's new wife was delivered of a boy. Benedict, at less than ten years of age, was himself delivered into the care of the mother he had not seen for almost two years.

'There was no inheritance in the case, you see, for Robert Beckenham was only a third son and chose to live at home in idleness rather than follow a profession.'

It was evident to Theda that Benedict's father could find no favour in Mrs Alderley's eyes, but she could herself perceive some echo of his father's faults in Benedict—of temper, she recalled with a tightening of the lips, and Lady Lavinia had certainly considered him idle and spendthrift.

'What happened to the baby?' she asked.

'Isabel miscarried, which was why she became so mad for Benedict's coming here.'

'But when she died? Was there no thought of sending him back to his father?' Theda asked.

'He would not have gone!' Rose declared. 'In any event, he was near fifteen by then, and looked on Sir John very much as a father. Indeed, it was reciprocal. *Unfortunately*,' she added, with a quick look round as if she thought to check whether anyone might hear, 'Sir John's partiality for Benedict extended also to his mother.'

Oddly, Theda felt no surprise. 'Thereby accounting for the jealousies of Lady Lavinia and Araminta both.'

'Yes, for Sir John was so unwise as to hold up Isabel's beauty—and she was so *very* beautiful, the image, apart from the hair, of Benedict—against poor Araminta. Comparing them, you know, and making his preference all too obvious. I heard him at it several times, pretending to joke his daughter, but in fact making her the butt of his mockery. And all this always *before* Isabel's face.'

'Small wonder the girl ended by hating her!' Theda commented. 'And Lady Merchiston? Did she know of her husband's faithlessness?'

'Oh, he was not *unfaithful*. At least, I never understood so from Isabel. But of course she knew. Wives always do, don't they? She behaved in a shocking way towards her. She was spiteful and unkind, both to Isabel and to her son—until his mother was dead, when she changed dramatically towards Benedict at least. What made it ten times worse, you see, was that Lavinia had strongly resisted Isabel's coming in the first place. It tainted them all with the scandal.'

'It would, of course,' Theda agreed, able even in the pain he had caused her to understand now why Benedict had never trusted his godmother.

'It need not have done,' Rose argued. 'But Lavinia chose to abandon her social contacts to punish Sir John. She never went to London after Isabel came here. By the time Isabel died, it was too late to alter that, for she was herself already wasting.'

'How did she die?'

'She caught a fever in the village. Benedict had it, too. But I don't think Isabel wanted to live.' Tears stood once more in Rose's eyes. 'She had suffered so much for so long. I think she welcomed the end.'

For a while they walked in silence, retracing their steps back up towards the house. Theda waited for her visitor to compose herself before speaking.

'Very well, ma'am. Now I am suitably softened up, what more can you say to persuade me to give everything up to Benedict?'

'Not *everything*,' Rose said, apparently impervious to Theda's irony. 'I would not expect that. Nor advocate it, indeed.'

'No, foolish beyond permission! And so *wasteful* of me, don't you think?'

Mrs Alderley stared at her, nonplussed. 'I don't understand you.'

'My dear Rose,' Theda said with a smile, 'you have so espoused Benedict's cause that you imagine it is enough to tell me all his unfortunate history to make me realise what I already know. *None* of this belongs to me. By rights I *should* give it up. But whether to Benedict or Araminta remains a matter for dispute.'

'Araminta! Good God, Theda, you cannot be serious!' gasped Rose.

'Certainly I am. She may be a spiteful piece, but there is no doubt that she has been very badly treated. At war both with mother and father! Her life has been quite as miserable as your Isabel's, I fear. I only hope she may find happiness with Saul Quatt.'

'Well, hope it no longer! I declare, I could shake you, Theda! She had her chances and she threw them away. She would not know *how* to be happy.'

'And I?' Theda cried. 'Am I also to have no happiness?' She saw the quick remorse in Rose's face and stretched out a hand to her. 'Never mind! Rest assured I will not buy my own happiness at the expense of. . .of another's.'

'Then you *will* give it to Benedict?' Rose said

eagerly, turning to grasp Theda's hands. Without giving
her an opportunity to reply, she went on, 'As for
yourself, I have the most splendid notion! You will
retain enough of this fortune for a decent dowry and
come to London to find a husband. And I will sponsor
you. There!'

There was no echo of her radiance in Theda's face.
She looked, if anything, paler than usual, her grey eyes
dark with some unfathomable emotion. Mrs Alderley's
own eyes dimmed.

'Theda?' she said uncertainly.

Removing her hands from Rose's grasp, Theda
responded quietly, 'That is quite impossible.'

Mrs Alderley frowned in perplexity. 'Impossible?'

'Utterly. Don't let us talk of it. Besides, until probate
is granted, all is conjecture. I shall simply remain here
until I know for certain what my situation really is.'

'I suppose you must,' Rose said reluctantly, and
Theda wondered if she had imagined all might be
settled at once. But her mind appeared not to be on
that at all. 'You can't stay here alone, Theda. You will
have to hire a companion.'

'A companion!' echoed Theda. 'For *me*?' The irony
of it struck her forcibly and her gurgling laughter broke
out. 'There is your answer. I shall hire Benedict to live
with me and leave him the place in my will!'

In late July, Mrs Rosalia Alderley, accompanied by her
husband and her son—on holiday from school—in
addition to her remaining daughter, made a belated
appearance in the seaside resort of Brighton, made
fashionable by the young Prince of Wales and his
followers.

Among the gentry residing there was to be found Mr
Benedict Beckenham, riding as hard as he could to the

devil. He responded to an imperative summons with an ill grace, and presented himself in the drawing-room of Rose's hired house in a mood of ill-concealed annoyance.

'What do you want, Rose?' he demanded truculently.

'You look terrible!' she exclaimed, taking in the blue shadows under his bloodshot eyes and the air of decadence that hung about him.

'What did you expect?' he returned. 'To find me in rollicking good humour, basking in my good fortune?'

'Oh, Benedict!' Rose sighed.

She held out a hand to him and patted the sofa beside her. Benedict looked at the hand, and pointedly took a chair on the other side of the room, lounging in a stance of deliberate contempt. The colour in Rose's cheek heightened.

'Good God, Benedict! It is not *my* fault that your godmother chose to cut you out.'

'No,' he agreed. 'But you need not expect my goodwill if you choose to consort with the enemy.'

'Enemy? Don't be foolish! Theda is nothing of the sort.'

'What, then, is she? Other than a double-dealing traitor who has chiselled me out of my dues, while throwing out lures to throw dust in my eyes!'

Rose fairly gaped at him. 'You don't know what you're talking about!'

His eyes narrowed. 'So she has beguiled you, too, has she?' He gave a short, ugly laugh. 'It was to be expected. She would fool anyone with that play of honesty, that——' his voice thickened, passion suddenly rife within it '—that damned shining *innocence*.'

He seemed to explode out of the chair, pacing to and fro as if he could not be still.

'How could she do it to me? How *could* she? Oh,

she bowled me out, all right! With that luminous cheek of hers, that flame she used to *enslave* me. Taunting me with digs at my honour, when all the time. . .'

He broke off, almost grinding his teeth, and flung over to the window to stare out.

Mrs Alderley gazed stupefied at his rigid back. Good God, there was more here than she ever dreamed! Theda, too. What *was* there between them? For Benedict had not spoken rationally, nor like a man whose hopes had been disappointed. He raged like a man betrayed, like a man whose trust had been smashed. The next thought came only to be dismissed: like a man *crossed in love*? No! Absurd. Yet if it was so. . .

'Benedict!' she said imperatively.

He turned. He had regained command over himself, for there was no trace now in his handsome features of the recent turmoil, only the too evident ravages of dissipation.

'Yes?' he said, raising his brows. He noted the determined air about her, and a cynical smile curled his fine mouth. 'Pray save the lecture, Rose. You know I am free to gamble my way into a debtor's prison. Allow me to go to perdition in my own fashion!'

'There is no necessity for you "to go to perdition",' Rose said crossly. 'You are an improvident fool, Benedict, if you cannot see the answer.'

To her surprise, the cynical look became more pronounced than ever. 'Marriage? Save your breath! She has already refused me—in no uncertain terms.'

Mrs Alderley gasped. 'You mean you *asked* her?'

'Not exactly. It was my beloved godmother's idea, but. . .' He stopped, an arrested look in his face. 'Dear *God*! So that was it. The cunning old witch!'

'What in the world. . .?' began Rose, feeling quite bewildered as he let out an amused laugh.

'I see it all now,' he said, a perfectly genuine smile crossing his suddenly lightened features. Then he frowned again. 'Yes, I see it. But will *she*?'

'Benedict!' uttered Mrs Alderley, exasperated. 'What are you talking about?'

He grinned at her. 'Just what you were talking about, Rose. Marriage. Forgive me! I must go. I have a most urgent appointment—at Merchiston Lodge.'

It was in fact more than a week later that he finally arrived in Switham. At first sight the house seemed very little changed, except that the area of grass about the porch had been scythed. It was a bright day and the early August sun picked out the myriad windows across the front, which winked at him as Benedict took his curricle down the drive. But the significance of this did not strike him at the moment.

Forgetting his altered status here, he drove around to the stables and, as he had always done before, saw to his own horses before entering the house via the kitchen premises.

'Mr Benedict!' uttered Agnes Diggory, looking up from the pastry she was rolling. 'I took you for Adam, for he's gone down Mountsorrel to fetch in some supplies.'

'Hello, Taggy,' Benedict said, smiling at her. 'Are you cook, too, now? Where's Mrs Elswick?'

The housekeeper clicked her tongue. 'Gone off to serve Miss Ara, she has—or rather, *Mrs Quatt*, I should say. Tried to get me and Adam away and all, but we wasn't to be budged!'

'I am glad to hear it,' he said, thinking how like Araminta it was to try and leave Theda totally unattended. 'Where is Miss Kyte?'

'I don't rightly know, Mr Benedict. Could be anywhere, Miss Theda could. Always busily employed.'

She wiped her floury hands on her apron. 'I'll go and find her, shall I?'

'No, don't trouble yourself,' Benedict said quickly. He came up to her and planted a kiss on her cheek, grinning. 'I'm glad to find you at least don't hold my bad temper against me!'

'Oh, go on with you, Mr Benedict! If I was to have done that in *this* house, I'd have packed my bags long ago!'

'Very true,' he agreed. 'Where's Hector, by the by?'

'Likely he'll be out roaming, if he's not with Miss Theda. Regular wanderer he's turned out, now the mistress is gone.'

'Well, his *new* mistress does not keep her bed.' He saw Agnes fold her lips together and put her attention back on her pastry. 'What is it, Taggy? Miss Theda *is* the new mistress of this house.'

'That's as may be,' Mrs Diggory said shortly.

Benedict frowned. 'You don't approve?'

'Ain't for me to say.' She paused, but the vexation would not be contained. 'But I'd be the better pleased if she'd take on and *be* the mistress!'

'What do you mean, Taggy? She can't do much with the place until probate is granted.'

Mrs Diggory shook her head. 'You don't know her, Mr Benedict. And as for not doing much, you'd hardly recognise the place!'

Benedict laughed. 'It looks much the same to me.'

'That's because you're a man, sir,' scoffed Agnes. 'And I don't know about all this "probate" flummery, because it ain't stopped Miss Ara and that there reverend husband of hers from taking all they want.'

'*What*?'

'Well may you stare, sir! I wish you could've seen them,' said the housekeeper, her arms akimbo, her plump face flushed with indignation. 'Going round the place arm in arm, the two of them, picking and choosing. *He* as bad as she, let me tell you. Twice they've been with a cart, and Miss Theda let them take it all without a word said!'

'Well, they are premature, but Araminta is entitled to it,' Benedict commented, surprisingly unmoved.

'Humph!' grumbled Agnes, by no means convinced. 'Not a stick of silver is there in this house, Mr Benedict. And if they'd a bigger place than that there little rectory, there wouldn't be a stick of furniture neither!'

'I would not bank on that, Taggy,' Benedict said cynically. 'Araminta will very likely make the wretched man stuff it all into his church.'

'Mercy, *no*,' gasped the housekeeper. 'Though I dare say Miss Theda wouldn't fret. She ain't even moved out of that there little room next the mistress, and all those lovely bedchambers up there standing empty.'

Benedict left her, armed with food for much thought, and a recommendation to try the library. As soon as he entered the hall, it was immediately apparent that there *was* a change. Sunlight streamed in from the windows above the gallery, bathing the polished panels of the walls in a warm glow. The staircase gleamed, and the banisters and railings all around the gallery gave off the same sheen. There was a new smell in the air—the fresh scent of flowers, a hint of lemon, and a drowsy aroma that reminded him of honey.

Beeswax! he realised, looking about in wonder. The place was *clean*. The windows were sparkling, the ivy stripped away to let in the light. All at once he pictured again the sun striking the glass and understood why it had done so. Moreover, the doors to the ballroom and library were open, letting in the air. So this was all it took! A little spit and polish, and a pair of determined, busy hands.

He crossed to the library and entered, assailed at once by warm memories of the man who had been to him the nearest thing to a father. He had worked at his books in here as a boy, shared port with Sir John as a stripling in his callow youth, sitting across from him before the fire in this male stronghold, deep in the leather chair. Here had he buried his face in Sir John's broad chest to weep for the loss of his mother.

Something swelled inside him. *He must have this house.* Hell and the devil confound it, this was his *home*! And it had been taken away from him.

All the resentment came flooding back. Wasn't it enough that he had been so humiliated? Must he now grind his pride in the dust and sue for the hand of she to whom he owed that indignity? For whether or no she had been instrumental in the making of that despicable will, it was her presence here that had caused it to be made. Had she not come, it would have been himself against Araminta, and he would have *won*. Even had he not, he might have supported with more equanimity *that* defeat. But *this*. . .no, by God, it was too much to expect of him!

About to leave the room with the intention of driving immediately away, he checked at a slight sound by the open door to the outside and looked around.

In an old cotton gown of striped dimity stood Theda, just outside on the shallow step, so that the bright sun glanced off the uncovered copper hair, which was piled untidily on top of her head, a few strands breaking loose and waving into the bare expanse of pale, glowing flesh above her bosom. With her back against the sun, her face was shadowed so that he could not see her eyes. But he knew that she stared at him, and felt rather than saw the hostility there.

CHAPTER EIGHT

BENEDICT'S pulse began to beat in his throat, and he fought vainly against that familiar rush of heat to his blood that invariably engulfed him at the sight of her. His mind blanked. He was dumb.

'Why have you come?'

It was the thread of a voice, for Theda, too, fought against the giddy pounding of her heart in his unexpected presence. She had heard the arrival as she weeded in the walled garden, but, like Taggy, she had taken it for Diggory. Only now did she recognise that there had been more than one horse. It could not have been the gig.

He did not answer. He did not even move. Only stood staring, unaware of the mix of emotions in his face: double fire in his eyes—anger and desire both; the sneer on his lips that was almost a smile; and the still-present evidence of his recent excesses—a pallid complexion and the darker skin beneath his eyes, the deeper carved lines down to his mouth.

Distress smote Theda as she took in his condition and knew herself to be the cause of it. Tears stung her eyes, and she turned as from an unbearable sight to vanish back into the garden outside.

Benedict found his tongue. '*Theda*. . . Theda, wait!'

With swift steps he crossed to the glazed door and saw her crouched before a flowerbed, apparently engrossed in the task of tugging weeds from between the flowering rose bushes.

'Confound you, can't you even face me now?' he

growled, and, walking up to her, he bent to seize her arms and drag her to her feet. 'Get up! *Look* at me!'

'Let me go!' she snapped, wrath drowning out both her guilt and the unconscious soaring of her heart at seeing him again. But she *was* looking at him, the deep grey eyes blindingly furious. 'How dare you manhandle me like this? What do you want?'

His grip on her arms did not relax. 'I came here to apologise, but if this is your attitude I'm damned if I do!'

'*My* attitude? Look to your own, you unmitigated bully! *Let me go.*'

She brought up her clenched fists to beat at him, and as he saw the dirt on them Benedict did let her go, stepping back out of the way.

'Why the devil can't you employ a gardener on such work?' he demanded irascibly.

'Because I can't afford one!' she threw at him, automatically dusting off her hands a little.

'Don't be ridiculous! I know how much my god-mother was worth. And don't tell me probate is not yet granted, for I know that too. I'm waiting for my own funds.'

'Then you should know there's not a penny in the house,' Theda retorted. 'We are living on enough credit as it is.'

'My good girl, don't you know *anything*? Ask Aycliffe for an advance.'

'I don't *need* one,' Theda returned, brushing the back of her hand at a lock of hair which was blowing across her face.

A frown came into Benedict's eyes and he reached out, his fingers closing about her wrist. Theda resisted, pulling away.

'Be *still*,' he growled. 'Show me your hands!'

Unthinkingly, Theda held the other out to him as he turned the one he had entrapped palm up. Under the brown stains could clearly be seen the white bumps of calluses.

'You confounded little fool!' Benedict uttered, somewhere between a scold and a caress. 'You've been slaving like a scullery maid.'

Theda snatched her hands away. 'What is it to you?'

His eyes blazed. 'Do you think I've lost a fortune only to see it salted away in the same nip-cheese fashion as before? For God's sake, *live* a little, woman! Haven't you had enough of drudgery?'

A gleam of humour irresistibly lit Theda's eyes. 'Am I to spend it for *your* pleasure or my own?'

'*Both*,' he said instantly, and suddenly his voice was urgent. His fingers again grasped her shoulders, pulling her closer. 'Theda, don't you see? *This* is what Aunt Lavvy intended! You *know* she meant us to marry. This is her way of bringing it about.'

Theda's lip trembled and her eyes darkened, while the amusement drained out of her face. 'Let me go, if you please, Benedict. What you suggest is—is quite impossible.'

His eyes burned into hers. 'Don't say that, Theda! We must *make* it possible. It's the only way.'

'I *cannot*,' she uttered in a stifled voice, trying to pull away.

Benedict imprisoned her closer, oblivious to her grubby hands caught against the pristine whiteness of his neckcloth. His voice was hoarse.

'I didn't mean the things I said that day, my lovely witch. I *want* you.'

His lips pressed against her hair, ran across the brow, all damp as it was with perspiration. Theda felt the warm ache inside her, and resisted the more.

'*No*. Pray, pray, let me *go*.'

His breath was warm on her cheek, closing in. She turned her face away, desperate to avoid his kiss. His voice came huskily in her ear.

'Theda, don't deny me!'

'I *must*,' she cried, and wrenched herself out of his hold, stepping back and holding one hand up in a pleading gesture. 'No, don't *touch* me, Benedict! You may *have* the house. You may have the *money*. I don't *want* them. But we must find another way. I *cannot* marry you!'

His lips formed the 'why?' but he did not speak. His breath ragged, his eyes near wild, he stared at her, and it came to him then that he wanted it *all*: the house, the money, and Theda, too. Nothing less would satisfy him!

About to speak, he paused as a distant squealing came to his ears. Theda heard it, too.

'What in the devil's name is that?' he demanded, following her as she crossed quickly to the gate and moved out into the grounds.

The squealing became slightly louder, and clearer— the yowls of an animal in pain. They glanced at each other, and the same recognition struck them both.

'*Hector*.'

Then Benedict was running, with Theda in hot pursuit, around the corner of the house towards Switham Thicket. Panting, Theda groped her way through the thick undergrowth, her direction signalled by Benedict crashing through ahead of her, and the howls of the dog growing ever louder.

She heard Benedict swearing and knew he had located the animal. Hurrying, she came upon him kneeling by Hector, whose howls had reduced at sight of rescue to pathetic whimpers.

'What is it?' she gasped out. 'What has happened to him?'

'Can't you see?' snapped Benedict angrily. 'I hope to heaven this leg is not broken!'

He moved behind the dog as he spoke, and Theda could see that Hector had caught a front foot in a trap.

'Oh, dear Lord!' she exclaimed, dropping to her knees.

Benedict was casting about. 'I need a stout stick. Hold him!'

He found a thick piece of deadwood, and broke off the twigs. This he inserted under the spring and put his own booted foot on the trap.

'Keep him still!' he commanded, heaving at the lever.

'Hush, Hector! Hush, now,' Theda crooned, grasping the animal tightly to her, and avoiding the sight of his trapped foot.

Hector squealed as the trap lifted a fraction, but Theda quickly drew the foot out and the trap sprung back with a clang. Gritting her teeth, she tried to examine the hurt, but Benedict was before her, throwing away the stick and gently taking the dog's paw in his hands.

'Is it broken, do you think?' Theda asked fearfully, still clasping Hector's shivering body to her.

'No, but badly cut. Fortunately it was only meant for rabbits.' Suddenly he turned a face of fury on Theda. 'What the devil possessed you to set traps here, when you knew the dog was roaming?'

'*I* set traps?' she repeated, stung. 'I did no such thing!'

'Well, someone must have.'

'Oh, use your wits, Benedict! It is poachers, of course. We shall have to inform the Alderleys' gamekeeper.'

'Never mind that!' he said impatiently. 'Let me take Hector. That wound must be dressed.'

Picking up the dog, he carried him, still whimpering, to the house, while Theda ran ahead to find basilicum powder and linen for a bandage. In a very short time, the two of them, together with Mrs Diggory, were fussing about the dog in the library, with bowls of warm water, blankets, an old sheet torn in strips, and even some milk laced with laudanum unearthed from the late Lady Merchiston's store of medicines in the attics.

It was early evening by the time the house settled down again, and Theda and Benedict, exhausted, found themselves alone together, one in each leather chair either side of Hector, asleep on a blanket before the fire that Adam Diggory, back from Mountsorrel, had lit in the grate in spite of the warmth of the day. Either one or the other had remained with Hector throughout the afternoon, taking turns, at Mrs Diggory's insistence, in going to the breakfast parlour to eat.

Theda had washed the dirt off her hands, but she was still attired in the old cotton gown, now stained with blood as well as dirt. She sat, leaning her cheek on her hand, gazing down at the dog, her flaming hair falling untidily down her back, and over her shoulders, and glistening in the light from the candelabrum on the mantel and the glow of the fire.

Benedict, quite as dishevelled as she, if not as dirty, sat and watched her. His heart contracted and the thought struck him that this domestic scene encompassed all he could ever want of life.

She seemed to feel his scrutiny, for she looked up, smiling involuntarily. Their eyes met and held. Time seemed to lie in suspension. When they began to speak, so softly, it was as if their mouths uttered words that did not match their thoughts.

'So much work! Why, Theda?'

'I am used to work.'

He smiled. 'The ghost passes through, cleansing the place of shadows.'

'Soon there will be nowhere to hide...and she'll have to move on again.'

'*No*,' he protested, and his voice sharpened. 'Why won't you marry me, Theda? *Tell* me.'

At once she broke the contact, looking away and rising. The intimacy was gone. A sense of loss invaded Benedict's breast, and he rose as well, taking a step towards her.

'You owe me that much!' he insisted, vehement now. '*Why*?'

'Because of what I am!' she burst out, facing him squarely. 'Let that be your answer, and ask me no more.'

'It isn't good enough!' he told her, his ire rising.

'Pray, hush! You will wake the dog,' Theda chided in a low tone, moving away to the other side of the room by the desk where they had ministered to Hector's hurt. On it lay the remnants of bandages, the scissors and a tin of basilicum powder, lit by another candelabrum.

Benedict followed her, lowering his voice, however. 'You cannot fob me off so. I *will* learn your confounded secret.'

'By what right do you demand it of me?' Theda said, turning on him. 'You are very free with your plans and schemes for *my* future. I will not be coerced! You and Lady Lavinia, you are two of a kind. If *she* thought by this means she might bend me to her will, she was as mistaken as you are now. As for you, Benedict, neither your cajolery nor your hectoring will work with me. I know that you want me, and I know why you would marry me. But I don't choose to sell myself, do you see?'

'I thought *I* was the one up for sale,' sneered Benedict. 'This is as much foisted on to me as on to you.'

'Then there is no need to pursue it! Rose suggested a deed of gift, and that will suffice.'

'A deed of gift? So that you may vanish away and hide yourself from me? Never!' He took her by the shoulders and shook her. 'Do you hear me, Theda? You are mine and I will never let you go!'

Her hand came up to strike him, but he was quicker, seizing her wrist. 'No, you don't, termagant!' He turned her about and held her imprisoned against him, the better to control her, and the better to feel her body against his own. He buried his face in the untidy tresses coursing about her twisting neck.

'Release me at once!' she panted, struggling madly.

'*Never*,' he repeated huskily. 'By God, you kept all your fires so well hidden, didn't you, witch? That passion that you know you share with me, and that fiery temper to match your glorious hair! God, how you *inflame* me!'

Theda groped about the surface of the desk as she felt his lips burning into her neck, sending the betraying heat flittering through her.

'If my hair is responsible, then I shall be rid of it!' she cried, and swung aloft the scissors which her fingers had found.

'The devil you will!' he snarled, and seized the scissors from her. 'You will never cut it, not while I'm alive!'

'Then it will *fade*,' she told him in triumph. 'So Lady

Lavinia told me, and so I have seen. Give it up, Benedict! You cannot keep it thus forever.'

'Then, confound you, I'll cut it myself,' he threatened, raising the open scissors before her face, and seizing a handful of hair in his fingers, 'and *keep* it so.'

Theda froze in his grasp. 'No, *don't*. Benedict, I beg of you, *no*.'

He pressed her head back so that it rested on his shoulder. His voice gentled her, caressing. 'Still, my fearful ghost, be still! I won't hurt you.'

'Then let me go,' she begged.

'Presently.' His lips were in her neck and she shivered involuntarily at their touch, her eyes still on the scissors in his hand. 'Theda, why are we fighting? Where's the purpose in it?'

She almost cried out as his mouth traced a path of fervid heat across her cheek. She felt his fingers in her hair and his arm tight about her, and her bones turned to liquid. Then his mouth was on hers and she groaned, turning unconsciously into him a little.

'Look at me!' he whispered as his lips left hers.

Her eyes opened and she saw that he had tugged a long strand of hair free and was playing it between his fingers. Was that all she was to him—a head of sensuous hair?

'I'll have this, Theda,' he said huskily. 'Mark me well, for I'll have you and your crowning glory, and the house, and the money, if I die in the attempt!'

A sense of hurt and outrage welled up inside her. Pain gnawed at her. What was she, that he could lay claim to her like this? Had she become part of his vaunted inheritance, too?

Benedict saw the change in her face and a frown came into his eyes. 'What is it?'

Her fingers seized the scissors from his slackened

grasp, and she snipped at the strand of hair he held. He was so surprised that he let her go, as if she had cut herself free of him.

'Take it, then!' she almost spat at him. 'If that is what you want of me, take it. You may have the rest that you covet as soon as I am able to make it over to you.'

She threw the scissors down on the table, glaring at him. His eyes narrowed, and he curled the hair about his finger.

'I'll take it,' he said curtly. 'On account. Keep the confounded house. And the money. Until you're willing to give yourself with them, I don't want any part of either!'

'Why should you dare to try and strike such a bargain?' she demanded frustratedly.

'Why should you dare to refuse me without giving me a reason?' he countered.

She caught the echo of pain in his voice. But her own was too strong to be set aside. 'I'm not to be a pawn in your game, Benedict!'

'Then be queen to my king!'

'I cannot, I cannot, I *cannot*!' she almost screamed.

'Then you can burn in hell for all I care!' he burst out, and, turning on his heel, he marched to the door and flung it open.

For a moment Theda stood where he had left her, hardly aware that he had gone. Dear Lord, he did want her! Would he really give everything up? She did not believe it, but all the same she ran to the door. He was already halfway down the hall.

'Benedict!' she called out after him, her voice rampant with the passion she could no longer control. 'Where are you going?'

'To the devil!' he yelled back, without turning round. Next moment he was gone.

Mr Beckenham, partaking of his friend Woolacombe's hospitality in that gentleman's absence in Brighton, sat over his dinner fighting the urge to go back to Theda and press his suit once more. Why the devil was she so stubborn? What was there in her murky past to raise this barrier between them?

The memory of their first meeting haunted him. They had slipped, right then, all unknowing, into an unconventional intimacy that had led them, he was convinced, to this present pass. In ordinary circumstances, persons of their order would never be permitted sufficient licence to be alone together, and so enkindle the fire that sparked between them. Had she been of any other class, he would long ago have stormed her defences and conquered.

He frowned over the glass of brandy in his hand—his fifth or sixth? He had half emptied Woolacombe's decanter, and yet his head was scarcely touched. *Was* it because of her quality? He had not thought himself so chivalrous. The *devil* it was! He slammed the glass to the table. *She* was responsible.

She knew, for she had told him so that first night, that her situation, alone, unchaperoned, *unprotected*—and that was the worst of it!—laid her open to advances. No doubt she'd had ample proof of it. The thought made his jaw tighten and his hands curl and harden into fists that might smash the unknown male faces of those who had *dared* so far! But had they, too, come up against that indefinable barrier that had stopped him?

She, contained spirit, all her fires damped, had put out to him the message that said 'stop!' And he had.

But now, with her fires so stoked that she could no longer contain them, her messages were confused. And she had him in turmoil! *Confound* her.

Snatching up his glass again, he tossed off the liquid it contained and stood up. He *would* have her. He had toyed with the idea of marriage, flirted with it only to tease her before his godmother's death. It was different now. He would have her—to *keep*—and she would put him in possession of his disappointed expectations.

The following day he drove to Mountsorrel to seek out Aycliffe.

'I had expected you before this, Mr Beckenham,' said the lawyer with a twinkle, setting a chair for his client to sit down in the drawing-room of the small house that served also for his office.

His clerks worked next door in what would have been the library, and his family used the upper floors for their own apartments. It was, he felt, one of the advantages of living and working in a small town. In London, where he had been apprenticed as a young man, the poky City offices had been suffocating.

'I was otherwise engaged,' Benedict answered shortly. Then he grinned. 'To tell you the truth, Aycliffe, I was so devilish put out that I had determined to shake the dust of this place from my heels forever!'

'That was rather the impression that I gathered, sir,' the lawyer said with a lift of one ironic eyebrow. 'What changed your mind?'

Benedict hesitated, eyeing the man. The devil! Theda would not hesitate to speak her mind. By God, she could teach him a thing or two yet! He leaned forward, resting his elbows on the table, lowering his voice confidentially.

'Aycliffe, I'm trusting you with this. I mean to marry Miss Kyte, and so gain possession of Merchiston Lodge and Aunt Lavinia's fortune.' He held up a hand as Aycliffe pursed his lips. 'Pray don't look austerely upon me. If you knew the full sum of the doings before she died, you would see that this is the result my god-mother intended.'

'Is it the result *Miss Kyte* intends, sir?' asked the lawyer shrewdly.

'Confound your impudence!' Benedict hit the surface of the desk with the flat of his palm.

'I beg your pardon, Mr Beckenham, but I am, you will recall, Miss Kyte's man of business in her new capacity.'

After a moment's glaring silence, Benedict sighed, relaxing. 'You are right, of course. It is *not* Theda's intention. But you must understand that her refusal has nothing to do with her *wishes*. There is some impediment. Or at least, so she believes. And this is where I think you may be able to be of service to me.'

'Indeed?' frowned Aycliffe.

'Yes, in point of discovering information. Miss Kyte is not, you must have realised, any ordinary female. There is a mystery surrounding her background, which she will not reveal.'

'That is her prerogative, surely?' objected the lawyer.

Benedict was leaning forward again. 'Aycliffe, this is no indigent genteel girl, forced into such a life by poverty! She has been wandering from post to post for six years, having left her home in, I suspect, scandalous circumstances. Now what does that suggest to you?'

In spite of himself, the lawyer was beginning to be interested. 'There are several possibilities for such a flight. All would almost certainly involve another party.'

'Precisely—a man!' said Benedict grimly. 'Whatever

happened to part them, she considers herself so tainted that marriage is out of the question.'

Aycliffe looked appalled. 'And you would *override* that belief?'

Benedict rose from his own chair so hastily that it almost tipped over. 'Don't *dare* impugn her! Override it? Of course I shall override it! What, am I to condemn the girl for one silly mistake to a lifetime of slights and abuse? She has been punished enough, by God, by her own dread conscience! Am I to watch *another* woman sink into her grave for want of a little *compassion*?'

Suddenly, he threw a hand across his eyes for an instant, and, turning, strode to the window and stood with his back to the room, his shoulders rigid.

Mr Aycliffe watched him in silence, his own eyes full of pity. He knew the man's history, and could not but be moved by his appeal.

Benedict spoke without turning round, his voice gruff. 'You must pardon my intemperance. It is not a subject upon which I can speak with any moderation.'

'I am aware, Mr Beckenham,' said the lawyer gently.

Turning at last, Benedict smiled a little. 'Of course you are. I had forgot.' His voice hardened again. 'But don't *you* forget this: I will never tolerate one word in disparagement of Miss Kyte's honour!'

Aycliffe bowed. 'Your sentiments do you credit, sir.'

A little shamefacedly, Benedict laughed, his colour heightened. 'In fact they don't. Not towards Miss Kyte, in any event.' Something struck him all at once, and he smote his own forehead. 'What a dolt I am! *Kyte*. It must be a false name.'

'Jupiter!' ejaculated the lawyer involuntarily. He was suddenly very alert. 'Do you really think so, Mr Beckenham? That would alter things indeed!'

Benedict stared at him blankly. 'How do you mean?'

'The will, sir! If Miss Kyte—if that is not indeed her real name, then the matter is up for dispute at once.'

'You mean it may be contested successfully?' demanded Benedict, coming swiftly forward.

'I don't say that, sir, but it certainly opens up the prospects. If she is not the person she purports to be, it may be argued in law that the will is invalid. That there is no such person as Miss Theodosia Kyte, and therefore——'

'But it is not *automatically* invalidated?' interrupted Benedict anxiously. '*That* would serve Araminta, and neither myself nor Theda would benefit.'

Aycliffe frowned portentously. 'I think it would rather be a matter of *relinquishment* of the claim. Voluntarily, you understand.'

'Oh, the devil! A day or two ago I would have welcomed this,' Benedict said irritably, beginning to pace. 'Now it seems only to worsen the coil!'

'Calm yourself, sir, I beg of you,' Aycliffe said soothingly. 'This is all conjecture. Until we have facts at our fingertips, there is no use in speculating.'

'Yes, but how are we to get these facts?' demanded Benedict, turning to him. 'Not from Theda, I'll be bound!'

The lawyer pursed his lips. 'In a legal matter, sir, she will have no choice but to reveal the truth.'

'Don't you go threatening her!' warned Benedict angrily. 'You'll leave her be, man, or you'll answer to me!'

Aycliffe sighed. 'Mr Beckenham, you are really making matters very difficult.'

'Never mind! Don't trouble *her*, I tell you. Not at this present, in any event.'

'Since the matter has been raised, sir, I have no choice but to pursue it,' explained the lawyer. He held up a pacifying hand as he saw the other prepare for battle. 'Have no fear! I may be able to institute discreet enquiries. I have a previous address. I may work backwards from there.'

'And if probate is granted meanwhile?'

'I will have to halt the proceedings, I am afraid,' Aycliffe said regretfully.

'Oh, my God! And I had it in mind to ask for an advance.'

'I can still advance you funds, sir. Although your portion would also be affected, there is still a considerable sum in trust from the late Sir John Merchiston's will. How much do you require?'

Benedict settled his own needs and the lawyer gave him a draft on Lady Merchiston's bankers.

'By the way, Mr Beckenham, I have something for you,' he said when he had done, opening a drawer and locating a small visiting card. 'I had almost forgot it.'

Benedict took the card and glanced at the name. 'It is unknown to me. Who is it?'

Aycliffe coughed. 'I believe it possible he may be an agent for one of your creditors. He would not state his business, but he had come here to find you, and came to me as having been advertised as executor of Lady Merchiston's will.'

'The devil! You are probably right, Aycliffe. Perhaps you had better increase the sum you are giving me. I must go to London, for I brought very little gear with me, so I will see him then.' He studied the card. 'This address is in the City, is it not?'

'Yes, sir. Quite a respectable neighbourhood, although he did not seem like a man of business. That is why I took him for an agent. Or perhaps a clerk.'

'Well, we shall see. I'll come straight back to you when I return to find out how you have fared.'

Aycliffe frowned a little. 'It may take some time to discover anything—if I *can* discover anything, that is.'

'Well, don't dawdle on the matter, man!' said the other, tucking both card and bank draft into his pocket book. 'My whole future is at stake.'

There was an odd glint in the lawyer's eyes as they rested on Benedict. 'Naturally you will be concerned. It may be that you need not, after all, tie yourself up in matrimony.'

Benedict's head came up from his pocket book and his eyes glowered. 'That's as may be. In any event, Miss Kyte—at least Theda, for that I *know* to be her real name—is not to lose by this. You will please to see that she has enough to cover her present needs. She will tell you she has none, but pay no attention to that! She needs help in the house, for a start, and you will inform her she is *not* to be acting like a servant. And make her buy some new clothes, for heaven's sake! *My* orders. And if she is to lose the inheritance, you may set it all to my account. But don't tell her that, or she will refuse it all!'

Aycliffe smiled. 'You may rely on me, sir. It will be better, perhaps, if she does not wholly know that the will is in question.'

'No, my God, don't *dare* reveal that to her!' Benedict said, alarmed. 'She will be off at once and I shall never be able to find her!'

Before Mr Aycliffe went to see Miss Kyte to fulfil his promise to Mr Beckenham a week or two had already gone by. He was surprised that he'd had no word from that gentleman, and even more so to find that Theda had not either.

'I had expected Mr Beckenham would have been in contact with you at least, ma'am,' he said with a frown.

Theda gave him a suspicious look. 'Why should you expect that?'

Aycliffe coughed, and his glance drifted away to rest unseeingly on the shelves of books as he spoke. They were standing by the desk in the library, where Theda had been going over the household accounts when the lawyer arrived, Hector, his wound still troublesome, laying at her feet.

'Mr Beckenham was good enough to confide his intentions to me, ma'am.'

'Oh?'

Aycliffe's eyes came back to her face. 'He was most anxious for your comfort.'

'Oh?' said Theda again.

Although her tone was non-committal, and her face gave nothing away, there was a tell-tale glint in the deep grey eyes. Tread warily, the lawyer told himself. He indicated the room with a sweep of his arm.

'You have done wonders here, ma'am! I have not seen the house look so well since Sir John's time.' He glanced out of the open door to the garden. 'If you should be in need of assistance, I can recommend an excellent gardener, for instance.'

'I thank you, Mr Aycliffe, but I have no intention of wasting money which is not my own and may never be so.'

'It is surely hardly a waste to put the place in order? Whoever comes here can only be grateful to you,' argued Aycliffe.

'Indeed? Do you include Mrs Quatt in that category?' asked Theda with a humorous look.

'Mrs Quatt is not contesting the will, ma'am.'

Theda shrugged. 'Then it can only be Benedict. Well, he said he was determined to have the place.'

'Miss Kyte, there is *no* contestant just at present,' said the lawyer firmly.

'Then why is probate delayed?' demanded Theda. 'And don't tell me it is merely a legal hitch!'

'Let us say a quibble,' amended the lawyer, smiling.

'And you cannot tell me what it is?'

'Not just at present, I am afraid.'

Theda sighed and moved to the garden door, looking out in silence a moment. Hector rose from under the desk and limped after her. As he went out, drawn irresistibly by the fresh air, Theda, with a determined air, came back to the lawyer.

'Mr Aycliffe, let us suppose that all goes through safely. How much do you think I might retain, in all fairness?'

The lawyer raised his brows. 'You intend to be rid of the main part of it?'

'Of course I do. You don't imagine I would dream of keeping what does not belong to me?' She smiled a little. 'But I am neither so foolish, nor so quixotic—nor, I may add, is my mind and resolution of so high an order!—as to deprive myself entirely of the opportunity to better my own lot. The fortune is large enough to satisfy anyone, I believe. To share a little could not be other than beneficial to the recipient's soul!'

There was an answering twinkle in the lawyer's eye, but he spoke quite seriously. 'It must depend upon what you would like to do with your share.'

Theda threw up her hands in a despairing gesture. 'Oh, but a tithe of what is in my heart! But, alas, one's head must be permitted to rule, and so I will say only this: a little house where I may be safe, with an income to enable me at least to enjoy the comforts of life, if not its luxuries. Just a simple place, somewhere... somewhere *far* from here!'

The lawyer pursed his lips. 'Your needs seem to be modest, Miss Kyte.'

'Not by comparison with what I have endured up to now,' Theda said quietly. 'Do you think sufficient to derive an income of two hundred a year would meet the case?'

'Two hundred!' echoed Aycliffe, startled. 'I was going to suggest five at least.'

Theda blinked. 'Lord above, Mr Aycliffe, I am not in the market for a husband, you know! What in the world could a single female want with such a sum?'

The lawyer smiled. 'A *companion*, perhaps?'

She had to laugh. 'Not that again, pray! But certainly a servant or two.'

'Speaking of which,' put in Aycliffe quickly, recognising his cue, 'it is quite absurd in you to be refusing to employ anyone to help improve the place.' He held up a hand as Theda opened her mouth to protest. 'The household expenses may be met by funds in trust, you know, and *not* your expectations from the will.'

'Do you take me for a fool, sir?' Theda demanded, a fresh glint in her eye. 'I am perfectly aware that the only *trust* is in Mr Beckenham's name.' She raised her brows. 'Has he told you to make me hire help? Is that it?'

The lawyer hesitated. She was extremely sharp. He must prevaricate a little. 'I think perhaps Mr Beckenham is anxious to protect his own interests, rather than yours.'

'Because he means to come by this house by hook or by crook?' She sighed wearily. 'You have it wrong, but no matter. Very well, let him bear the cost of extra servants. Will that satisfy him?'

Aycliffe shook his head, and the twinkle was once

more visible in his eye. 'You must also kit yourself out more suitably, ma'am.'

'Oh, indeed? Suitably to *what*?' She threw up a hand in a gesture of exasperation. 'No, don't answer that! Yes, I shall buy clothes, for I need them. But they are to be paid for out of my eventual share. You will keep a strict accounting, if you please.'

'Certainly, ma'am,' agreed the lawyer, relieved to have accomplished his task as easily as this. But he had still a trick or two up his sleeve. 'Have the bills sent to me, and I shall settle them and deduct the monies when the time comes.'

'You are very good, Mr Aycliffe. I will wish you to draw up a deed of gift in Mr Beckenham's favour when once probate is granted, if you please.'

'We will tackle that at the appropriate time,' said Aycliffe, adroitly side-stepping this issue. 'If you should hear from Mr Beckenham in the meanwhile, perhaps you would be so kind as to inform me.'

'I will do so,' Theda said, but with a puzzled frown. 'Are you so anxious to see him?'

'Not at all. Only he said he would return forthwith and I was surprised at his continued absence.'

Theda's frown deepened. 'Do you know where he went?'

'To London. He was only going to see a man whose address I gave him—a creditor, I believe.'

'A *creditor*!' Sudden alarm gripped Theda. 'And he is not back? Oh, dear Lord! Mr Aycliffe, have you not thought that he could have been *imprisoned*?'

CHAPTER NINE

THE lawyer blenched. 'No, I had not! Do you indeed think it possible?'

'How much was the debt?' asked Theda swiftly. 'Had he funds?'

'I advanced him a goodly sum, yes. But if the debt had been greater——'

'Lord in heaven!' The grey eyes were stricken. Theda grasped the lapels of the lawyer's coat. 'Mr Aycliffe, you must go to London at once! Pray, *pray* seek him out. Go and see this man, if you will, and search the prisons! Anything, anything, but *find* him!'

'Yes, yes, Miss Kyte,' he said, infected a little by her agitation, and putting his hands over hers in a fatherly way. 'Don't disturb yourself. If there is indeed any foundation for these fears—which I do not at all suppose, for why should he not have contacted me if he was in such trouble?—I shall settle the matter at once. A debtor's prison! I cannot credit it. I had never supposed, by Jupiter, that *that* part of the will would ever come to pass!'

The damp hair lay like a dark shroud about Theda's head, flowing down behind the chair where she sat with Hector at her feet, her back to the sun, on the terrace outside the ballroom.

'Just you take the weight off your feet, Miss Theda,' Taggy had insisted. 'Rest easy, and don't *think*!'

But how could she rest easy, Theda thought in despair, beset as she was by hideous visions? Near a

490

week, and not a *word* from Aycliffe. And daily, hourly, the picture came to haunt her: Benedict, cold and lonely. Benedict, weak from hunger, his golden hair bedraggled and grimed, his fine clothes unkempt and dirty, and, in all probability, his head foggy with the fumes of cheap gin! For there would be no silver flask of brandy. Oh, no. That would have gone to pay some meagre way towards the debt. That, and his watch and chain, and the pin he wore in his cravat. There would be no succour for Benedict if—*if*! Pray God that her fancy prove untrue!—he was immured in one of those gruesome buildings where only ready money could save its unwilling patrons from abject penury.

Oh, lord! *Unendurable*. To banish the visions, Theda had thrown herself into work—work that would at least welcome Benedict home again to a house of warmth and light.

She had not abandoned her own efforts, but she had got Mrs Diggory to fetch up a couple of girls from the village. The ballroom was now immaculate, its inlaid decorative wood floor gleaming, all the facets of the chandeliers sparkling in the sun that was permitted to stream through the clear glass of the French windows. Now they were all busily employed in setting to rights the big front saloon—a difficult task, for all its furniture was large and heavy and the carpets had not seen even a brush for years and years.

Theda had been obliged to retire from the room after receiving a deluge of dust over her person when attacking the top of a wide dresser. Coughing and spluttering, she had been dragged upstairs by Agnes Diggory.

'Out of them clothes you get, Miss Theda! I knew how it would be in that room. Just you leave them wenches to do it now. I'll fetch up the bath to you straight, and have Adam bring cans of water up here.'

Bullied into bathing, Theda allowed Agnes to wash her long hair for her, and acquiesced when that redoubtable dame dragged a chair outside that she might sit and dry it in the sun.

The surface had just begun to shimmer in the light when Mrs Rosalia Alderley came out through the French windows of the ballroom and stopped, staring in thunderstruck amazement.

The dog rose, growling under his breath. Theda, her attention caught, put up a hand to shade her eyes. 'Rose? Is that you?'

'*Theda*,' gasped the visitor. 'Good God in heaven, I thought I was seeing ghosts!'

Theda almost burst into tears, as she recalled Benedict's endearing name for her that had stuck from their first meeting. She fought down the lump in her throat, and summoned a smile as Rose came quickly forward, drawing the animal's bark.

'I assure you I am not dead,' Theda said, with an assumption of humour. She laid a hand on the dog's woolly head 'Quiet, Hector!'

The dog looked at her, and back at the visitor. Then, apparently deciding that the idyll was over, he wandered away, his limp much less apparent now that his wound was healing well.

Theda glanced up at Rose. 'Forgive my not rising, but I dare not move out of this chair until this wretched hair of mine is dry.'

Rose took the hand she held out, but her eyes were on Theda's copper crown. 'Of course there is really no resemblance at all, but for the hair. I was startled for the moment all the same. Has Benedict seen this?'

Theda's smile went a little awry as the memories

pierced her. 'Why, yes. It has—*had*—a profound effect upon him.'

'I'll warrant it did!' Rose exclaimed. 'Good God, there was a time I saw him—still but a child, to be sure—playing his fingers in her hair with such warmth and love in his face, such concentrated attention, as if it so fascinated him he could not leave it alone. I have never forgot it!'

Theda was staring at her, a pulse beginning to beat in her throat. Benedict and red hair? Had not Lady Lavinia said something of this? Could it have been. . .? Was it possible that it was not, after all, some long-gone love, but. . .?

'Rose, are you telling me that *Isabel* had hair this colour? His *mother*?'

Mrs Alderley looked surprised. 'Did I not say so? Though I fancy it was not as fiery as yours. It tended more to gold than copper, but it *was* red. Sadly, the colour faded as time went on.' She stopped, frowning. 'Why do you stare at me so, Theda?'

Theda shook her head a little, sending the fire rippling down the tresses, and looked away. 'I beg your pardon. I had not realised—it did not occur to me. . .'

Her mind was all chaos. She had never thought that her hair stood for anything other than passion and desire to Benedict. And it did do so. But so also must it stand to him for warmth, for. . .*affection*.

She touched on the word with delicacy, as if she dared not think of it. A pang went through her. Then another, of a different sort. Her eyes pricked. Might it stand also for *pain*? For had he not lost that woman's love in death? Oh, Benedict! Have I hurt you, too? What had they said at the last? 'Where are you going?' she had shouted. He had answered, 'To the devil!' Now, perhaps, the devil *had* taken him—if prison was his shameful abode. And all to be set to her account, for she had driven him away!

'What is it, Theda?' Rose was asking, concerned at the other's silence, at the distress in her face. 'What have I said?'

'Nothing, nothing, upon my honour!' Theda cried, reaching out a hand to her. She must pull herself together, make an effort. Where was that hard-earned gloss of calm efficiency that she had cultivated over the years? She tried for a brighter smile. 'Rose, I am so happy to see you! How was your stay at Brighton?'

'Never mind that,' Rose began, by no means deceived. 'What has occurred to distress you? It is to do with Benedict, I'll be bound! What is amiss?'

Theda's eyes clouded. 'Don't ask me, Rose!'

'I thought he intended matrimony,' pursued her friend, unheeding. 'I had expected to find the banns posted on my return.'

'There will be no banns,' Theda said quietly.

'Why not? Forgive me, but we *are* friends, are we not?'

'Assuredly.'

'Then I will ask you again; why not, Theda?' Mrs Alderley's eyes narrowed. 'You surely cannot hope for better?'

'Better than Benedict?' uttered Theda on a sudden half-sob. '*Never.*' She covered her eyes with one hand. 'Ask me no more, Rose, I pray you!'

Rose stood looking down at her, a worried expression in her eyes. What had gone wrong? she wondered. And where *was* Benedict? For he had certainly not returned to Brighton. Not that she approved of his plans. Far from it. She liked Theda, yes, she did, but she felt Benedict could do better for himself, even if Theda could not.

An idea occurred to her. She was fully determined that the Merchiston fortune must end with Benedict—that much she owed to Isabel's memory—but at least some provision might be found for Theda. Something better than that little house of which they had once spoken. And with that hair. . .!

'Theda!' she said imperatively.

The copper head moved and Theda's hand dropped. She was in control again, Rose saw, but her eyes were still eloquent of some turmoil within her.

'I beg your pardon, Rose,' she managed, a faint smile crossing her face. 'I was miles away.'

'Never mind that! Theda, listen to me. You must cease this nonsensical life of yours, slaving away as if you were a servant! Oh, yes, Taggy told me how you have been working your fingers to the bone.'

'She exaggerates,' Theda said.

'No, she does not! Why, I can see for myself what has been done.' She reached out to grasp one of Theda's hands, touching the calluses. '*These* show who has been doing it.'

Theda snatched her hand away. 'What does it matter, to anyone but me, and——?'

'And *Benedict*,' Rose supplied. 'You need not tell me, Theda. You are doing it for him, are you not?'

'I had to do *something*. I cannot sit idle,' Theda said with spirit, evading the question.

'What is the use of doing up the house, if you are to leave yourself in the same poor condition?' demanded Rose.

Theda blinked at her. 'I don't understand you.'

'Good God, Theda! If you mean to put everything to rights between yourself and Benedict, you must make an effort on your own account. Buy some clothes! Show your beauty—for with your hair uncovered you *are* beautiful. You will never catch a husband if you persist in looking like a dowd!'

'I have no desire to catch a husband,' Theda said frostily.

'Then you are a fool! I told you I would sponsor you. There is a deal of social activity now for the hunting season. It is an excellent opportunity to introduce you.'

Theda drew back in her chair, seeming to shrink within herself. 'No! No, I cannot.'

'Nonsense, of course you can. Even if you marry Benedict, you cannot skulk in hiding at the Lodge, you know.'

'I am not going to marry Benedict.'

'Certainly you won't, if you don't smarten yourself up!' Rose said tartly. 'You have done the house for him. Think how much more appreciative he will be of your place within it when you are suitably arrayed to complement him.'

She had struck the right note. Theda had no intention of marrying Benedict, even when—if—he returned. No, not *if*, she scolded herself. He *will* return. And yes, she *would* study to please him. For she could not *bear* him to be unhappy—even if it meant that she must. . .

She pushed the thought away. That was for the future. She remembered that Aycliffe had brought up the matter of clothes, that Benedict himself had scolded her for her nip-cheese ways. Well, then, she would buy some new gowns—just one or two, perhaps—that she might, as Rose said, fit better with the work she had done on the house.

She smiled. 'Very well, Rose. You have convinced me. Where shall I go?'

Antoinette was the best of the Leicester modistes, run by a little French *émigrée* who had set up shop and named it in memory of her martyred Queen. The mantua-maker was horrified to see Miss Kyte's ridiculously outmoded attire.

'But it is *affreux*! You ask me to improve the appearance of *mademoiselle*?' she said, shuddering. 'How can I not?'

Theda was more amused than offended, and when the assistants began scurrying about the little salon on the first floor, bringing samples for her to try, she very quickly fell into a mood of unqualified enjoyment. Nothing could better have driven her fears for Benedict temporarily from her mind.

It was very strange at first to have the tight constriction of a waist a little below her bosom, and the softly flowing folds of muslin seemed extraordinarily light about her legs. She felt almost naked, as if she were parading in her chemise. She had been too long used to plain dark colours to take easily to the frivolous sprigs and pastel shades, decorated with frills and bands, and artificial flowers.

But she fell in love with a gown set low over the bosom, and unadorned, but for a ribbon or two, in a soft peach that set off her copper tresses. She was staring at herself in the mirror in the curtained dressing-room, wondering what a certain gentleman might do and say if he were to see her in it, when she became aware of hushed voices in the salon outside.

'My dear, Antoinette positively said "Kyte", I am certain of it,' one voice was saying.

'Well, if it is indeed she,' came another, harder voice, 'I can only say that Rose Alderley is most tiresome. Bad enough when she befriended Isabel Beckenham. And now this!'

Behind the curtain, Theda froze, stiffening. But the voices continued.

'For my part,' argued the first one, 'I am very glad of it. Do you not recall what Araminta Merchiston——?'

'*Quatt*, my dear Mrs Tiverton,' interpolated her companion, with a titter. 'So vulgar, but nevertheless true.'

'Quatt, then. Do you not recall, Lady Danby, that she is supposed to have said that Miss Kyte has inherited *everything*?'

'Well, but how much is everything? You would not think from the way Lavinia lived that there was anything at all!'

'But there is!' protested the one addressed as Mrs Tiverton. 'My son had it from Woolacombe—and you know how thick he is with Benedict Beckenham—that the boy had expected more than a hundred thousand.'

'In-deed?' commented Lady Danby in quite a different tone. 'And this girl has it all?'

'All, all of it! And a very unnatural mother I should think myself if I did not make a push to secure it for Gerald!'

'Quite right, my dear,' agreed the other.

As Theda stood, rigid with wrath and dismay, the woman's voice came up in volume, and she spoke with a perfectly nauseous degree of sweetness.

'My dear Rose, we have been hearing of your protégé. So delightful to have a new face in our midst! You simply must bring her to my little soirée on Wednesday evening.'

Shock thrust Theda into a panic reaction. Flinging aside the curtain, she stepped forward.

'Oh, no!' she uttered in a far from steady voice. 'I beg your pardon, but I cannot!'

The trio before her were stricken to silence. She beheld Rose in the act of taking the hand of a middle-aged battleaxe of a woman, very fashionably attired, whom she at once deduced to be the lady who had last spoken. The third, a skinny matron with popping eyes under a feathered bonnet, gaped at her.

'Dear me!' she gasped out. 'Araminta never said you were so *beautiful*!'

Then she coloured up, as Theda's grey gaze came round to her, the mix of emotions there apparent. Mrs Alderley stepped smoothly into the breach.

'Lady Danby,' she said, reaching for Theda's arm and bringing her forward to face the battleaxe, 'you will allow me to present Miss Kyte, and she will, I am sure, be delighted to accept your invitation.'

'Rose!' broke from Theda desperately, and then she bit her lip, trying for some self-command.

'Mrs Tiverton you have also not met,' Rose pursued, indicating the thin dame as if nothing at all were amiss.

'H-how do you do?' Theda murmured, unable to help admiring Rose's social address, which enabled her to gloss over the incident so easily.

'So happy!' gushed Mrs Tiverton, taking Theda's fingers in her gloved hand. 'You *will* come on Wednesday, won't you? I know my son will be enchanted. He dotes on red hair, you know.'

'Indeed?' was all Theda could find to say. She could only wonder at the woman. How disingenuous! She must *know* she had been overheard.

Mrs Alderley was delighted. This was better than she had hoped for! She must make it impossible for Theda to refuse.

'Have no fear! I shall bring her with me on Wednesday, trust me.'

'Excellent!' smiled Lady Danby.

'Rose, I must speak with you!' Theda said in a low tone.

'Presently, my love,' was the only response.

'Oh, but I must have your promise, too, Miss Kyte!'

exclaimed Mrs Tiverton. 'For you know, we are obliged
to try to amuse ourselves during the hunt.' She tittered.
'The gentlemen are so very single-minded at this season. I have a *morning* gathering for those of us who do
not care to ride. On Friday. Do say you will come. You
will bring her, Rose?'

'Assuredly,' said Mrs Alderley. 'But now Miss Kyte
must leave you, or she will have nothing to wear for
the occasion.'

So saying, she bustled Theda back behind the curtain, bidding her change quickly that they might visit a
milliner, and prudently went away to confer with
Antoinette.

Theda was left to stare again at her reflection, all her
pleasure in the delectable peach gown destroyed. For
dread—the old, quivering dread that she thought she
had long left behind her—was settling in her bosom.
She began to shiver, feeling sick to her stomach.

Seated between Gerald Tiverton and young Mr
Finchingfield, Theda parried as best she could the
barrage of effusive compliments with light banter.
Finchingfield had turned out to be Lady Danby's
nephew, which, Theda decided cynically, explained that
lady's change of face. It had proved impossible to
withstand Rose's cajolery, and, more importantly, her
questions. Confession only would have served. But
confession was too awful to contemplate, even with
Rose.

Theda no longer knew whether Benedict's possible
plight—for still no word had come from Aycliffe—or
her own present one bore down on her nerves the
most. Attired in the peach gown, she knew she looked
well, but she felt thoroughly disadvantaged by the long
years without usage of social graces. It had taken all

her courage to come here with head held high, to converse with any degree of composure with the young men who interestedly flocked about her, thanks to Araminta's loose tongue. But that courage was becoming rapidly undermined.

On the other side of the room, an ancient dame was regarding Theda with a fixed stare while she slowly plied a fan before her face. Now and then she lifted an eyeglass up and peered through it for a moment, and, evidently finding it useless at this distance, let it fall again, shaking her head in a frustrated way.

At last Theda could stand it no longer. Interrupting without ceremony Mr Finchingfield's flow of compliments, she burst out, 'Forgive me, but this is all nonsense! I wish you will tell me instead who is that lady over there.' She added, as both gentleman turned to look, 'The old one with the fan and the eyeglass.'

Mr Finchingfield, a slight young man, rather floridly dressed for the country in a laced silk coat of purple hue, searched among the guests and had no difficulty in picking out the lady. He gave a short laugh.

'That old tabby? That's poor Woolacombe's grandmother. Dreadful woman! Devilish starched up. Always comes over for the hunting—don't know why, for she can't have ridden a horse for centuries!—and leads poor Woolacombe a dog's life.'

Gerald Tiverton shuddered. 'Don't she, though! And the poor devil can't hide a thing from her. Got a nose that wouldn't disgrace a bloodhound, and a phenomenal memory.'

Theda felt suddenly sick. 'A memory for what?'

'Gossip, mostly,' said Finchingfield. 'Remembers every morsel of scandal since Queen Anne, I dare say.'

'By George, yes!' agreed Tiverton. 'Poor Woolacombe says if he's had one story thrown in his face as an example of what bad conduct may lead to, he's had fifty. There was the devil to pay over his friendship with Beckenham.'

'You mean Benedict?' Theda asked involuntarily.

Finchingfield looked round at her. 'Of course, you know him.'

Both young men then glanced at each other, clamming up in some embarrassment as they recalled that the fortune they were at this moment vying for had been lost by Benedict Beckenham, for the story of the will was naturally common knowledge among his intimates.

'Yes, I know him,' Theda said quietly, and smiled sympathetically at both of them. 'You need not look so downcast. The matter has not resulted in a bitter enmity between us, you know. We *are* still on speaking terms.'

Finchingfield laughed a trifle self-consciously. 'Yes, well, couldn't help but be sorry for the old fellow. Do you know where he's got to, by the by?'

'By George, yes!' exclaimed Tiverton again. 'Woolacombe has been expecting him this age, and not a word from the man to anyone!'

Theda kept a tight control over the lurching of her heart. She spoke as calmly as she could. 'No, I have not heard from him for a month now.'

'Odd. Wonder where the old fellow has got to. Still, he was ever devil-may-care. Comes and goes as he pleases. Fortunate dog!' laughed Tiverton.

A shadow crossed Theda's face. Finchingfield, sensing embarrassment again, turned the subject.

'Never told us why you were so interested in old Lady Usk, ma'am.'

'Lady Usk?' asked Theda puzzled.

'Woolacombe's grandmother.'

'Oh.' Theda shrugged with an assumption of ease. 'It is rather she who is interested in me, I fear.'

Both gentlemen once more glanced round to where the old lady was still staring, but now speaking to Lady Danby, whom she had detained with a hand on her arm.

'Uh-oh!' uttered Finchingfield. He looked back at Theda and exchanged a knowledgeable glance with his friend Tiverton. 'I'll lay you any money she's checking you out with my aunt.'

'By George, yes!' assented Tiverton in his usual fashion. 'There she goes to collar Mrs Alderley.' He grinned at Theda. 'Hope you ain't got any deep, dark secrets, Miss Kyte. Old dame Usk will ferret them out in a twinkling.'

Theda managed an answering smile, but her heart was thumping like a drum. In a moment the young men were proved right as Rose came over to oust them from her side.

'Theda, there is someone who wants to make your acquaintance.'

As she approached the formidable, although diminutive figure of Lady Usk, she had to fight to overcome the hollow throbbing in her chest. She was not helped by the unnerving sight of the old woman's hugely magnified eye as she held up her glass to inspect the girl coming towards her.

But then Lady Usk dropped the glass and held out a scrawny hand. 'How de do?'

Theda took the hand, dropping a curtsy. 'Lady Usk.'

'You know me?' came sharply from the old lady.

'I asked your name, ma'am,' Theda told her frankly.

The other nodded. 'You noticed me watching you, I shouldn't wonder.'

'Yes, ma'am,' Theda agreed, adding daringly, 'Why did you?'

Beside her Rose gasped, but Lady Usk said at once, 'Your hair. I've only seen that precise colour once before.'

Warily Theda eyed her. 'Indeed? I believe it is not unique, though perhaps unusual.'

The old lady nodded. 'Very much so. Most of 'em are carroty or golden. Though, to be sure, in my day we used so much powder one couldn't always tell.'

'That is true,' Rose Alderley said, putting in her mite, and immediately came under the scrutiny of Lady Usk's interested eye.

'Remember anyone who *didn't* powder, do you, Rose?'

'Oh, yes, several,' she answered, taking a chair next to Lady Usk. 'But——'

'But only one redhead,' firmly stated the old lady, her eyes going back to Theda's flaming crown, which she had dragged into a knot on top of her head and then allowed to fall behind. 'You remind me of her very much.'

Theda produced a smile. 'Well, if she indeed had similar hair, I dare say that is not surprising.'

Lady Usk was studying her face, as if she saw there more than she spoke of. 'There is something about the complexion also,' she said slowly. 'Common to you redheads, of course. So pale, almost as if one can see through your skin.'

You mean that you see through me, Theda thought. Lord help me! Does she really know *who I am*?

'It is very tiresome at times,' she said rather desperately. 'People seem often to think one is unwell. And the sun—the sun, too, can be troublesome. One feels easily. . .overheated.'

She was speaking at random, saying anything at all, only to try to distract this acute old woman from saying what was clearly in her mind.

'Overheated?' repeated Lady Usk in an interested voice. 'Yes, I see. Rather like seizure, I should imagine. Faintness and palpitations?'

'Some—something of the sort,' Theda said in a rather husky voice, thickened with distress.

'Oh, I know what you mean,' chimed in Rose. 'One is subject to it when increasing.'

But Lady Usk paid no heed to this interjection. Her eyes were on Theda's in a look so compelling that Theda felt as if her mind were being dragged out to be read.

'Something like, I dare say,' went on the old lady, 'that seizure that attacked poor Kirtlington at the end of last season.'

Theda's eyes widened and she seemed to sway. In a hushed voice, she faltered, 'You s-said. . .*Kirtlington*?'

Lady Usk's eyes never left hers. 'Lord Kirtlington, yes. Though, to be sure, *he* has not red hair, so he cannot plead that excuse. However, his *wife* might have done so, if——'

'*Pray*' interrupted Theda in a thread of a voice, 'you said a—a *seizure*?'

'That is correct. Dreadful thing to happen to any man! His wife had to take him home to Cheshire. They say he may not live out the summer.'

Somewhere in the background, Theda heard Rose's voice exclaiming as she remembered the sad event for herself. But through the clogging pain in her breast, she could only seen the gaze of Lady Usk—dark and knowing. It was as if Lady Lavinia herself had come back to life, and sat staring at her out of the malevolence in her soul.

The protest floated at the back of her numbed mind: how could she have the heart to deal such a blow only to satisfy her own thirst for scandal? The deliberate cruelty of it gave Theda the strength she needed.

'I am happy to have made your acquaintance, Lady Usk,' she said mechanically, and then, like an automaton, turned to her friend. 'Rose, it is extremely late, and I am not used to such hours. Pray may I take your carriage and go home? Unless you are ready yourself to go now?'

Mrs Alderley, aware that something had occurred which had escaped her, and conscious of the metallic edge to Theda's voice, and the look of...yes, triumph in Lady Usk's eyes, at once lost herself in indecision.

'Oh, I don't...well, yes, I suppose—but I did want...' She drew a breath and pulled herself together. 'Yes, we will go, Theda. Lady Usk,' she added, turning to the old lady, who had resumed fanning herself and was sitting back in her chair with a smug look on her face, 'I will certainly see you again. We *must* talk.'

How Theda kept her countenance throughout the drive home she never knew, but somehow, perhaps by dint of dwelling on the attention paid her by Finchingfield and Tiverton, she managed to divert Rose from the dangerous topic of Lady Usk's strange conduct.

Once back at the Lodge, however, all her fortitude deserted her. The Diggorys were long abed, and Hector shut up in her little room, but candles had been left for her by the front door. She lit one and carried it into the ballroom, where the silver light from a large moon cast shadows on to the wood floor.

Dropping to her knees, as if she could no longer stand on her trembling legs, and heedless of the new peach gown and the pretty fawn pelisse she had bought that covered it, Theda set down her candle on the floor with quivering fingers, and covered her face with her hands.

Lord in heaven, was there no end to the burdens she must bear? It needed only this! Now must the dagger she had long carried in her heart twist in an agonising dance. Dear lord, how was she to *endure* it?

Tears flowed down her cheeks, trickling through her fingers. She tried hard to hold them back, swallowing on her aching throat.

To her came, unbidden, a desperate longing. *If only Benedict were here.* But that was madness! She must not think of Benedict. For here, thrust on her out of the darkness of her past, lay the reason she could never be his. Now how much stronger had become that barrier!

She sighed deeply. If there was any justice, it was *she* who should die. Not he! Not *he*. Dear lord, *no*. No, no, *no*!

Uncontrollable sobs broke from her and echoed on the night.

CHAPTER TEN

VISCOUNT DACRE stood by the open window of an opulent upstairs saloon, gazing out upon the vast estates he had inherited. Visible through the trees was another, smaller building. Without turning round, he pointed, addressing the man behind him. 'Is that the Dower House?'

The agent stepped forward. 'No, my lord. That is one of Lord Kirtlington's houses.'

The Viscount turned his head, a frown adding to the already sombre expression of his features. 'I have heard the name in some connection, I think.'

An explosive snort came at him from the centre of the room behind him. 'Don't ye remember the name of your own neighbours, boy?'

Lord Dacre cast his great-uncle a glance of acute dislike. 'No, sir, I do not. It is more than I bargain for to recall the names of my own. . .family.' He brought out the word with distaste, as if it soiled his lips.

'Just as I foretold!' grunted the crusty old gentleman.

He was a spare, grizzled man, who limped with the gout that made him ill-tempered, so unlike the dandi-fied figure of Lord Dacre's vague memory that he felt wholly disorientated in his presence. Not that this entire experience had not thrown him completely out of his stride! It was near twenty years since he had been here, and he had never, to his knowledge, so much as set eyes on any member of the surviving household.

'If I said to Robert once, I said to him fifty times,'

his great-uncle was grumbling. '"Keep the boy under your eye", I told him. Would he listen? No, he would not. Now see what has come of it!'

'Mr Robert could scarcely have anticipated *this* contingency, sir,' ventured his lordship's agent.

'Ha! D'ye imagine any of us anticipated it?'

Lord Dacre's eyes narrowed. 'Rid yourself of the notion, sir,' he said on a menacing note, 'that it is any more acceptable to me than it is to you!'

His uncle snorted again. 'Gammon! Because you haven't chosen to show yourself, don't think we haven't heard of you. You may cut a fine figure——' with an approving glance cast up and down his great-nephew's fashionably tight-fitting blue coat over buckskins and top-boots '—but an expensive young profligate is what you are, Dacre, and if this inheritance don't come as a windfall you may call me a dunderhead!'

A sudden grin lightened the Viscount's features. 'I should not dare, sir!'

'Humph!' grunted the old man, but a reluctant twinkle entered his eye. 'Ye've inherited something of my poor brother's humour, in any event.'

'Have I? I remember very little of my grandfather, sir.'

'Small wonder! If he'd been alive when Robert kicked up all that riot and rumpus, there'd have been a different story, I can tell you.' The old man shook his head. 'He was the only one who ever had any influence with Robert. It's to be hoped you've not come by your father's headstrong ways, boy.'

'You will be the best judge of that, sir. I hardly knew my father.' With that curt dismissal of the subject, Lord Dacre turned his back on his uncle.

But the word was not to be so lightly dismissed from his mind. *Father.* Unconsciously his hand reached for the pocket of the greatcoat he was not wearing, where he kept his silver flask. As well, perhaps. One did not take to the brandy at ten o'clock in the morning! Even if oblivion was the only way one could wipe that dread word from one's mind.

Almost harshly, he addressed his agent. 'Before we go into the matter of how much of a "windfall" all this may be, Bewdsley, where *is* the Dower House?'

Both the other men frowned, seemingly unable to understand his interest in a relatively unimportant subject. Dacre smiled rather cynically.

'Come, come, Bewdsley. Did you not tell me that all the surviving females of the family have fled there, to take refuge from my vengeance?'

A crack of laughter left the old man's lips. 'Pack of ninnies! Nothing of the sort, however. Your stepmother resides there.'

'My *stepmother*!' echoed the Viscount, and set his teeth.

'Aye, and your half-brothers and sister. Your cousins, too,' added his great-uncle, apparently unaware of his dangerous mood. 'Went off there on your aunt's death. I mean your uncle's wife, young Dacre's mother, you know.'

'It is a *little* complex, my lord,' interposed Bewdsley apologetically, seeing the frown in his new master's eyes.

But Lord Dacre was not thinking of the odd circumstance that had resulted in his stepping into his cousin's shoes. For his predecessor had been a minor, the only surviving child of the eldest of three brothers. The estate had been held in trust by the second brother. But both he and the young lord had been carried off by smallpox, leaving this estranged son of the deceased youngest brother to inherit.

All this had been carefully explained to him by
Bewdsley, who had been sent to find him. Although it
had come as a shock, for he had never made it his
business to enquire into the ramifications of his family,
he had found a morbid humour in the situation. The
gods were at their tricks again! But to hear now that
That Woman was living in the Dower House, the very
woman on whose account his mother had been incarcerated there, filled him with such distress that he could
barely find the strength to be civil.

Vividly could he still recall his nurses preventing him
from going to her there, and he knew he had stood at
a window just like this, gazing with longing through the
trees to the building where his mother was imprisoned.

But this was all in the past! There was a future now,
brighter than he had ever hoped for. He must learn to
forget. To give himself a moment to recover control, he
looked again out of the window and spoke at random.

'You were going to tell me something of Kirtlington,
were you not?'

The agent took the question to himself. 'Was I? Oh,
only that his estate marches with yours, my lord. You
have met him, I dare say?'

Dacre shook his head, his mind still on his mother.
'I've seen him, or heard of him.'

'Heard of his brush with death, I dare say,' interpolated his great-uncle. 'Not that I paid much mind to it
myself. Too many damned funerals of our own!'

'Dead, is he?' asked his lordship absently.

'No, my lord,' Bewdsley told him. 'He suffered a
stroke, but I believe he is said to be recovering.'

The Viscount nodded, although he had scarcely
heard what was said, registering it somewhere at the
back of his mind. He was more in command of his
emotions now, and he turned back into the room.

'Well, Bewdsley, since I appear to be saddled with this place, perhaps it is time you told me precisely what I am worth?'

'Difficult to say *precisely*,' said the agent carefully.

'Don't be a nodcock, Bewdsley!' snapped the old man. 'Give him a round tale and a round figure at the end.'

The agent coughed. 'Your lordship will be pleased to hear that the estates have been well cared for.'

'Aye, my brother saw to that.'

'Exactly so, sir. And his sons, too.'

'Bewdsley,' Dacre said gently, 'I am not a fool. I can see the land is in good heart, and I remember enough to know the extent of the estates. All I want is a yearly figure.'

Mr Bewdsley looked him straight in the eye. 'About eighty thousand, my lord. Excluding the investments, of course.'

'Eighty thousand a *year*?' asked the Viscount faintly.

'Perhaps a little more,' said the agent hopefully, and then his eyes popped open as Lord Dacre began to laugh.

For a moment the two gentlemen stared at him in perplexity, as he shook his head, bubbling over at some private joke, until he caught the puzzlement on both faces.

'Forgive me!' he said, his eyes still alight. 'But if you only knew—it's hell's own jest!'

'*Jest*,' echoed his uncle, affronted.

'On me, sir, on me,' said his nephew soothingly. Dear God! He had been moving heaven and earth to gain what was now little more than a pittance, in the light of what he had unexpectedly inherited. Like a thunderbolt it had come, just when he looked like losing it all. His brows snapped together. *All*?

'Hell's own jest,' he repeated aloud. 'And with a vengeance, too. Hell and the devil! Now I shall have no hold over her at all. How the devil am I to. . .?' He stopped, becoming aware of the glare from his uncle and the frank astonishment from his agent. 'I beg your pardon. I was thinking aloud.'

'Who in the name of God is *she*?' demanded the old man, shooting him a suspicious look from under frowning brows. 'You're "Dacre" now, boy. You've a duty to your name.'

The Viscount's face changed, in another of his startling alterations of mood. 'Indeed? And I must take care not to sully it, is that it? As my father did mine!'

'Now, Dacre——'

'Have no fear, sir! I have lived all my life in the shadow of scandal. I know the cost.' Then he turned to the agent. 'Speaking of cost, Bewdsley, can I afford to buy a hunting-box? There is a place I have an eye to—in Leicestershire.'

Friday came, in spite of all Theda's wishes that it might not, and, with it, a resurgence of her fears. What should she do? No word had come from Rose, and surely she would have cancelled their arrangements at the least hint of scandal? Had that dreadful Lady Usk thought better of it, or was she out to torture her victim, playing a waiting game?

If so, she was succeeding admirably, Theda thought. What little peace there had been was quite cut up. She had not even the comfort of Hector's presence, for her nervousness upset him and he had taken to roaming again, now that his leg was healed. But the dog was the least of her worries. If she was not thinking about Benedict, and seeing the most dreadful visions, interspersed with the haunting—and piercingly sweet—

memories, she was assailed by the picture which tore at her heart, of that loved face, laid in a coffin, devoid of life. It would have been better to have remained in total ignorance than to know, yet *not* know, and have no means of finding out.

With all that, must she also attend this gathering, where she might find herself exposed to public ridicule, to painful humiliation, by the dread words of that *evil* old woman? Lord in heaven, but it was too much to ask!

Nevertheless, some spark of remaining pride had driven her to array herself in a sprig muslin gown she had bought with the peach, topped by a pretty chip-straw bonnet that at least provided a little place to hide her face under its poking brim.

She heard the jangling of the bell, and hurried from the little chamber. Rose! What should she say? Should she confess all and refuse to attend at Mrs Tiverton's morning do? She heard Adam's heavy tread moving down the hall, and slowed a little, her heart shrinking within her. Next instant, the front door opened, and as she began to descend the stairs a most unwelcome voice smote her ears.

'Where is she? Where is that thieving, sneaking hag who thought to oust me from my rightful inheritance?' demanded the strident tones of Mrs Araminta Quatt.

Pushing past old Diggory, she swept into the hall, cast one angry glance around, and found Theda on the stairs. Her mouth opened, and stayed so, as her pale eyes widened under the close bonnet she wore.

Theda, stock-still on the stairs, her heart sinking, saw the discontented features pinch and harden into a mask of sheer fury.

'So!' hissed Araminta, finding her tongue. 'I catch you in the act, do I?'

'I have not the remotest idea what you mean,' Theda said coldly, all her old resentment flaring up at the woman's tone.

'Oh, have you not?' snapped the other, coming hastily forward to confront her as Theda came down the rest of the stairs. 'Have you not, Miss Thieving Kyte? And I suppose you have not chosen to *flaunt* yourself as an heiress in society. I suppose you have not squandered money which is not your own on gowns like that you have on!' Closer she came, almost spitting into Theda's face. 'And you have not removed your cap, I suppose, and displayed your *whorish* tresses that the men might be dazzled!'

Theda stepped smartly back, away from her, distress catching at the breath in her throat.

'*What* did you call me?' she managed faintly.

'I called you what you are!' Araminta almost screamed. 'Just like that *other* bitch, with her oh, so *glorious* hair that my father doted on—to *my* disadvantage! That scheming, cheating harlot, whose son you have consorted with like a cheap jade. Stealing affection, just as *she* did, as well as this house, and the money that could *never* be yours! Thief! Whore! I shall shout it to the world, if I have to!'

'You are insane!' Theda uttered fearfully, backing away towards the library, aware vaguely of the bell again jangling and of Adam shuffling reluctantly off to answer it. 'You don't know what you are saying! What do you want from me?'

'I want my dues, Madam Adventuress, that's what I want!' stated Mrs Quatt angrily. She moved forward, driving Theda before her into the library itself. 'And I'll get them! Aycliffe may not be there, but I got it from his clerks. Probate is delayed, is it not? And do you know why? Because he has set his clerks on to find you out, Miss Theodosia Kyte! Or is it some *other* name?'

Theda paled. 'He. . .*what*?'

'Oh, yes, Madam Thief! *That* is why probate is delayed. No doubt Benedict means to contest the will. But he won't succeed, because I shall contest it. And I have by far the better claim. So how do you like that, you scheming wretch?'

'I don't imagine she likes it at all,' said Mr Aycliffe's level voice from the library doorway.

Araminta swung round on him, and Theda looked past her, distress and reproach in her face as she met the lawyer's eyes.

'How do you do, Miss Kyte?' he said in matter of fact tones. Then he bowed to the other lady. 'Mrs Quatt. Do I understand that you wish to take legal action in the matter of the will?'

'What are you doing *here*?' Araminta demanded suspiciously, ignoring his question.

His brows rose. 'I have business with Miss Kyte.'

'Pah! She is as much Miss "Kyte" as I am, the wretch!'

'You know that for a fact, do you, ma'am?'

'Of course I don't, but——'

'Then I suggest that you keep your tongue, unless you wish to render yourself liable to an action for slander.'

Araminta gasped, her cheeks flying two spots of colour. 'How dare you address me in such terms?'

Mr Aycliffe bowed. 'As your legal adviser, Mrs Quatt, I conceived it to be my duty to warn you of the possible consequences of your words.'

'Pah! Don't come that nonsense over me, Aycliffe! You are on *her* side, I suppose?'

'I endeavour to serve all parties to the best of my

ability,' the lawyer said repressively. 'It is not in my brief to take sides.'

'Legal jargon!' scoffed Araminta. 'Well, if you don't favour her, I dare say you would do more by Benedict than by me.' She smiled maliciously. 'That is, if he is ever to come out of *prison*. Oh, yes, I have that tale also. You went to find him—didn't you?—for his creditors have caught up with him at last. How well my mother knew him!'

'Mr Beckenham,' stated Aycliffe in a level tone 'is *not* in prison.'

There was an intake of breath from Theda, and the lawyer glanced round at her, but it passed by Araminta.

'Pah! Much I care! Let him be in or out of prison, he will get *nothing* of mine. I am used to being ignored and slighted, but mark this well! If there is any attempt to bypass me in *this* matter, you shall all know of it!'

With which she stalked past him and into the hall without so much as a backward glance at Theda, standing by the desk, a look of new hope in her eyes. All Araminta's spite, her flooding jealousy, paled into insignificance beside this momentous news.

'Miss Kyte——' began the lawyer.

'She may not care,' Theda interrupted, coming forward eagerly, 'but I do, Mr Aycliffe.' She gave him an almost pleading look. 'He *is* safe? You were not lying?'

'Certainly not.'

'Thank the lord! Oh, you do not *know* how great a relief that is!' Her body seemed to droop all at once. 'But it seems it will avail him little. Why, oh, why did you set such enquiries in train? Could you not just have asked me?'

'To tell you the truth, ma'am,' Aycliffe said, with a wry twist of the lips, 'I would have done so. Mr

Beckenham, however, would not have me disturb you on the matter.'

Theda's stomach seemed abruptly to fall. 'He *knew*?' Suspicion kindled in her breast. 'Mr Aycliffe, was it Mr Beckenham's idea that you should delve into my history?'

The lawyer grimaced. 'I should rather say it was something he inadvertently let fall that led me to believe there might be a legal case to answer.'

'*What* did he let fall?'

Aycliffe cleared his throat. 'Mr Beckenham merely wished, if he could, to find and remove that impediment which he believes to stand in the way of a—er—union between you.'

'I see,' Theda said quietly, biting her lip. She had been foolish, had she not? She had allowed her own feelings to cloud her judgement. Ever since she had learned from Rose of his mother's red hair, she had fondly permitted her idle daydream, her secret wishes, to grow and flower as if indeed they existed.

But Benedict cared only for Merchiston Lodge and the money. In his frustration and anger, he had told her that she must give herself as well before he would take them. Yet he had since seen Aycliffe and told him of his unaltered intention to come into possession of them by wedding her. Why else should he be seeking to eliminate her past to his own advantage? Her heart twisted.

'Poor fool!' she said aloud. 'You have dug your own grave!'

'I beg your pardon?' the lawyer said blankly.

Theda shook her head. 'I was thinking aloud. It is scarcely in Mr Beckenham's interests to invalidate the will, I believe.'

'Assuredly not. He will lose everything.'

'Oh, lord in heaven! Then Araminta was right! For you are obliged to pursue your enquiries, are you not?'

'Unfortunately, yes.'

'Unfortunately?'

'Why, I believe so, ma'am,' said Aycliffe, smiling a little. 'I may have told Mrs Quatt that my position demands that I remain impartial, but one cannot entirely prevent oneself from having human feelings and preferences!'

'Very true.' Theda sighed. 'And so it is over. I am not concerned for myself. But what will poor Benedict do?'

'Your pardon, ma'am,' said the lawyer, 'but you speak as if the battle were won! So far my enquiries have drawn a blank, your tracks are so well covered. But you suggested I might have asked you outright for your—er—credentials. Do your words now mean what I think they mean?'

Distress was back in her face and her eyes widened. 'Pray, Mr Aycliffe, don't ask me!'

'I'm afraid I must,' he said, but with sympathy in his voice. 'Are you, or are you not, Miss Theodosia Kyte?'

Theda hesitated. Dear lord, what could she say? Suddenly here it was again! Had Lady Usk not been sufficient? But that was malicious. This—this was different. A legal necessity. If she did not speak the truth now, she was guilty of perjury. If she did, she was putting the knife in Benedict's back.

From the hall came a welcome interruption. Mrs Alderley's voice. 'Theda! Where are you? We shall be late!'

'Rose!' Theda uttered quickly. All of a sudden, the morning gathering at Mrs Tiverton's had lost a little of its terror, for just at this instant it seemed less threatening than Mr Aycliffe's serious face, demanding of her this fatal choice.

'Ma'am,' he said, 'I must insist——'

'Pray, sir!' Theda interrupted, throwing out a hand. Necessity forced an urgent solution—*perhaps* a solution. 'Draw up the necessary papers. I shall relinquish my claim. Will that serve?'

Contrary to the impression given by Mrs Tiverton, there were in fact several gentlemen present at her morning gathering. Although there was no hope that her own son and his intimates would forgo their day's sport, there were those less inclined for the hunt than they had been in their younger days. Their small number, however, made them more noticeable.

Theda was therefore acutely conscious of one gentleman, rather stout and red of face. *Was* it he? He must be past thirty now, but she would never have believed he could have grown to make such a gross figure of a man. He looked to be peevish, the corners of his full mouth turned down, and an irritable look in his face each time he answered some remark addressed to him by the woman at his side. She was some years his junior, not pretty, but personable enough, with brown hair, neatly dressed and a good figure.

A sharp pain twisted in Theda's guts. Had she *gold*, poor woman, so to entrap for herself that monstrous lump of selfishness? Had she thought herself fortunate to capture a thing of beauty? For if it was indeed *he*, he had been beautiful—full of lip and sensuous of eye, and reed-slim he was, six years ago. Could a man change so much?

She tried to picture Benedict thus, but the image would not form. Benedict was near thirty, and yet his face and form had withstood the ravages of time and circumstance. Perhaps because Benedict was at heart honest and true, whereas *this* man...

'My dear Miss Kyte,' said Lady Danby's voice, interrupting her reverie, 'I am certainly going to take you to task for leaving my party so early. Finchingfield was devastated.'

'I am sorry to hear it,' said Theda, dragging her attention back and focusing it on the lady.

'He has taken a marked fancy to you, my dear,' pursued the other.

'Indeed?' The cynical glint appeared in Theda's eye. He has taken a marked fancy to my expectations, she might have said. 'I dare say he will get over it.'

Lady Danby frowned. 'Don't say you prefer Gerald Tiverton!'

The glint was angry now. 'My dear ma'am, I assure you I don't look for matrimony. As for my preferences, I believe they are my own concern.'

She then rose from her seat and bowed, leaving Finchingfield's fond aunt seething. Behind her back she heard a mutter. 'Such impertinence!' But the boot, Theda thought, was on the other leg. Why had she come? She could curse Aycliffe and Rose both! Between them she had made a decision based only on panic and no common sense. Now, to confound her, there was *that man* — if she truly had recognised him in the wreck she had seen.

Passing with a smile and a bow through the predominantly female guests, she made her way through an open doorway to take refuge on the terrace outside, in spite of the slight September chill in the air.

She wished very much that Lady Lavinia had not practised this jest upon her. By now she would have been safely hidden in some dull merchant's house, forgotten by all the world — and Benedict himself. For had he not already forgotten her? If not, where *was* he? Oh, but she should have known. Men, especially handsome men, were not to be trusted!

The reminder, so sharp and painful, in the sudden appearance of that man now threw her into aching grief. Enough! She had borne enough. Better perhaps that Benedict should not return—though God send nothing had happened to him, for she could bear anything but that!—for that his lost inheritance, through her fault, must prevent his *ever* regarding her with anything but hatred. The sight of his face alone must be a reproach to her already tormented conscience. As if she were not sufficiently torn inside already by the dread news thrown at her by old Lady Usk. News that had left her prey to ancient longings added to the guilt, and a nagging anxiety that could not be relieved.

As she paced, unaware of the picture she presented of extreme agitation, she looked only at the ground, and so did not know that she was observed. She might think her identity concealed with her tell-tale tresses under the poke of the new chipstraw bonnet, but by a window overlooking the terrace a gentleman stared in horrified disbelief, his once sensuous eyes almost popping from his head.

A voice spoke at his elbow. 'D'ye not know Miss Kyte, Caswell?'

Warren Caswell turned sharply to find old Lady Usk's eyes staring up at him from her diminutive height.

'Who?' he demanded brusquely.

'Miss Kyte,' repeated the old lady, raising her eyeglass and staring through it at his face.

The man's florid complexion deepened. 'Never met her,' he said hastily. 'Don't know the name.'

'I dare say you don't,' agreed Lady Usk with a knowing smile. 'But do you know *her*?' One small finger pointed through the glass. 'Like a cat on hot bricks, ain't she?'

Caswell shuffled in obvious embarrassment. 'Never seen her before,' he muttered.

The eyeglass came up again. 'Haven't you? Pity she's covered up that copper head. You might recognise her then.'

At this there was no mistaking the alarm that leapt into his eyes. In a strangled voice, he echoed, 'Copper?'

'*Bright* copper. Most unusual.' The old lady's smile was mischievous. 'Would you care for an introduction?'

'No, no. . . I mean, my wife—must find her—,' stammered her unfortunate victim. 'Not too well lately.'

'I'm sorry to hear you say so,' said Lady Usk sympathetically. 'Let us hope there won't be anything untoward to *worsen* her condition.'

Warren Caswell paled a little now, his eyes quite frantic. Muttering something incoherent, he moved away. Lady Usk watched him wend a hasty path towards his wife and turned back to the window to find that Miss Kyte was standing stock-still on the terrace, staring in at her.

Theda was shaking, a river of ice at her back. She had been mad to come! Dear lord, one word from that dreadful old woman, and she was undone. There could be no doubt now. It *was* Warren Caswell. He had been standing large as life beside Lady Usk, and it was plain that he knew her identity. Not that she need fear him. She was sure he was no more anxious for the tale to break than she. Particularly if, as she suspected, that poor woman was his unfortunate wife. But Lady Usk had no such reticence. She was gone from the window now. Where to? Had she gone to spread the word?

Well, Theda was not going to wait to find out. Let society say what it would. She was not going to stay to hear it!

Already making her way around the house, she came to the front and asked a footman to carry a message to Rose Alderley. Then she sat on the parapet atop the wide stairway and waited.

'What in the world is the matter?' Rose demanded, running out to her in bewilderment a few moments later.

'Rose, I have to go home,' Theda said urgently, jumping up from her perch. 'Pray lend me your carriage.'

'Good God, are you ill? As if I have not had enough to worry me with all this talk of Benedict!'

'What talk?' Theda asked in quick alarm, at once diverted from her own concerns.

'Why, they say he has been thrown into prison for debt!'

'Araminta!' Theda said instantly. 'Don't fear, Rose, wherever he may be, he is *not* in prison. That much Aycliffe knew.'

'So that is why he came to the Lodge!' Rose was eyeing her frowningly. 'And why you are looking as blue as megrim.'

Theda glanced away. 'That—and other things.' She looked back. 'Rose, I *cannot* stay here, in company. I cannot explain it to you now, but I *must* go.'

Rose's frown deepened. 'Does this have anything to do with that scandalmongering Lady Usk?'

'Everything, I am afraid,' Theda said with a pathetic attempt at a smile. 'Let me go, Rose! I will not blame you if you refuse to recognise me, but *let me go*.'

Mrs Alderley was not proof against the desperation of her tone. She ordered her carriage, but assured

Theda that she would never desert her. 'Good God, if I weathered poor Isabel's friendship, I am sure I may weather yours!'

But no sooner had Theda left in her carriage than she immediately sought out Lady Usk.

'Ah, Rose!' said that bright-eyed old lady, on catching sight of her. 'Just the girl I want to see!'

'And I want to see you, Lady Usk!' said Rose pointedly.

The other's delicate brows rose. 'You do, do you? Good. Let us remove to somewhere more private.'

'Willingly,' Rose agreed, and led the way to a small antechamber that led off the main saloon.

It was deserted, and the two ladies settled together on the small sofa.

'Now, ma'am, what is it all about?' demanded Rose without preamble.

Lady Usk's eyes were eager. 'Well, my dear, it is an old tale now. You know Warren Caswell, do you not?'

'Of course I do. He is here with his wife this morning. But what has he to do with it?'

'Everything!' announced the old lady gleefully. 'There was a rare scandal a few years ago, though to be sure it was hushed up very swiftly—but *some* of us heard of it, naturally.'

'Naturally,' echoed Rose drily. 'Do go on!'

Lady Usk lowered her voice. 'Yes, a rare scandal! And Caswell was at the bottom of it...'

Theda's hands rubbed furiously at one of the posts of the bed in the second of the chambers she had tackled in the last unnumbered days. For she had no longer any mental account of time. She rubbed as if she would erase the images that flitted through her mind as she worked, like an unconnected pageant—the images, and the thoughts that crowded her mind around them.

Aycliffe's face, kind but serious, demanding of her the condemnation she *could* not give. What, was she to strike from Benedict all his hopes at one blow? She did not know if her efforts would save for him at least something from the wreck, poor Benedict.

Benedict. The smiling, classic features, topped by the golden hair. Oh, but he was so handsome! Yet, handsome? No, no. Not to be trusted. For had not *Caswell* been beautiful—his full, sensuous lips, whispering honeyed words. Love and romance to gull the wench at seventeen. For what? For her flaming tresses—burning like Isabel's on her son's sweet lips as he drew them through his fingers, drowned in them. . .

No. *No.* She shook her head, resting it against the wood, as her hands stilled. That was Benedict, not Caswell. Benedict, who wanted her for her hair. The *scissors.* She had snipped, and he had taken a lock. 'On account,' he said. But that was all there was, Benedict. *I have no more.*

A sob rose in her throat. Fool! *Fool* to weep. Angrily, she thrust herself away from the bedpost and her hands began again their energetic dance on the brightening wood. Would she could rub out Warren Caswell's loathed features! Curse him! Furiously she rubbed, unknowing that she passed and repassed over the same bright spot, while the images came and went, flitting through.

Araminta. Thin, pinched features, triumphant eyes. Words that flayed and scorched coming from her lips. For had she not earned such curses? Whore and thief, was it? A shiver ran through Theda's body—the frame that was near a shadow of itself, just as it had been that long-gone day in March. *Whore?* If not in body, then in mind. No, Theda, you are mad to talk so! Mad? True, she was not Warren's courtesan, but what of Benedict?

Benedict... Benedict...would he snarl and curse at her now, as once he had? Blenching, she closed her eyes, her fingers grasping the post. Was she not a thief? Lord help her, this was not the result Lady Lavinia had intended!

Lady Lavinia... The picture in her mind changed, and the glaring, venomous eyes looked out of the wasted features...to be succeeded at once by the smug face of another old woman. Lady Usk! With her barbed speeches and her veiled remarks. And her victim had run away, and thus *given* herself away.

The now familiar palpitating flutter in her heart made itself felt and the blood drummed unpleasantly in her head so that she feared she might lose her senses. Her eyes closed tight shut, and her forehead came to rest on the hands that gripped the bedpost.

There it was again! The threat of exposure hanging over her, so close that she had dwelled since—since when?—as if she inhabited a thick cloud of suffocating fog. How long had it *been*? Had anyone called? Had anyone written? Was Rose still her friend? Did they know now...everyone here...about her...where Benedict was...and that other, Kirtlington, was he...?

But that was a question she could not think about. That was a picture she *must* not see. Who had come here? She did not know. She had told Taggy—she *thought* she had—that she could see no one, speak to no one.

She had worked...yes, yes, she was working *now*. Her eyes opened and she made an effort to resume her futile polishing. If only she could remember... If only she could *cease* to remember. Lord in heaven, what *memories*!

Like a drowning woman clinging to a frail piece of wreckage, she hung for dear life on to the bedpost while the images cluttered her mind: Benedict smiling; Caswell shocked; a loved face dying; the wasted face of Lady Lavinia dead, eyes open; Araminta's bitter, hating mouth; Rose's pleading smile for Benedict.

Benedict. What have I done to you? *What have I done*?

Her heart felt as if it must burst. Her head was on fire, as if the copper flames outside were licking within. But she clung on to the post, her body sinking to the floor, oblivious to the groans that issued from her own throat, and the words that formed on her lips.

'The witch is *burning*, Benedict. Witch. . .ghost. . .oh, that she were a ghost indeed!'

With that came blessed oblivion.

CHAPTER ELEVEN

THEDA came to herself to find that she lay in a large four-poster bed, with the curtains drawn back, and the weak autumn sun coming in at the windows. She could feel a coolness on her brow, and would have reached up her fingers to find out what was there, but that she was possessed by a lassitude that prevented her moving at all.

'Ah, that's better!' said Agnes Diggory's voice. 'Quite a turn you give us all, Miss Theda!'

Theda's eyes focused on the face hovering above her, and she tried to speak. But the face shook from side to side.

'Don't try to talk, miss! Dr Spilsby said as how you're to rest, and rest you will. Knocked yourself up proper, you have. All that fretting and fuming, working yourself to flinders! You lie still now, for I'm to fetch you up some broth.'

'Thank you,' Theda said faintly. 'I'm n-not very hungry.'

'Never mind not being hungry,' Taggy said firmly. 'You'll eat it!'

However, when the housekeeper brought the thin soup, Theda found she was hungrier than she had supposed. She was too weak to feed herself, and Agnes had to spoon the broth into her mouth.

'How long have I been like this?' she asked in one interval.

'Too long!' snapped Taggy. Then, as Theda's eyes

clouded, she relented. 'You've only been abed these two days.'

'Two days!' echoed Theda in shocked tones. 'But I was cleaning the bedchamber. . .the post. . . I was polishing the bedpost.'

'That's where I found you,' confirmed the housekeeper, presenting another spoonful to Theda's mouth. 'And a rare taking I was in, I can tell you! I sent Adam for Dr Spilsby straight, while the maids and I put you to bed in here. Been overworking, that's what. There's to be no more of it, Dr Spilsby says.'

Theda half smiled. 'It's not just the work, Taggy.'

'I know that, Miss Theda. I'm not daft. But there ain't nothing for you to worrit your head over, do you hear me? You can't do nothing about any of it, in any event, so what's the use of banging your head on a brick wall? That's what I say. You rest easy, and get back your strength.'

Fortunately, probably due to the doctor's potions, Theda found the kaleidoscope of worrying visions had ceased to run in her brain. It was easy to sink into a sort of limbo, where nothing seemed any longer to be as important as it had been. She took little account of time, and was hardly even aware that she had been placed in Lady Merchiston's old bedchamber. She ate as directed by Taggy, and made no fuss when that dame looked after her much as she had herself done for her deceased employer—nursing her and acting as lady's maid, and combing out her troublesome copper hair, until Theda felt strong enough to perform this office for herself.

She was sitting up in bed, some few days later, tugging a recalcitrant comb through her long tresses, when a commotion from downstairs made her pause, her fingers still.

Hector, who came and went at will through her open chamber door, was in turn barking and yelping, and she could make out Mrs Diggory's voice.

'Very poorly she's been, sir, and she's still abed.'

'But what is amiss with her?' demanded a familiar male voice.

Benedict! A rush of warmth swept through Theda's body.

'Exhaustion and worry, that's all!' stated Agnes in a belligerent tone.

'*All*? Hell and the devil!'

Without thought, Theda threw off the covers and swung her feet to the floor. Through the sudden fierce pulsing of her blood, she could hear Taggy describing how she had found her mistress clinging to a bedpost in one of the spare chambers. Theda hardly took in the words. None of the thoughts that had so oppressed her came into her mind. His very presence banished them, and she responded to it with all the fire in her heart.

Her limbs were unsteady as she padded on bare feet, staggering a little, towards the door, oblivious to the fact that she was dressed only in a thin nightgown, that her half-combed hair flared untidily about her shoulders.

'Go up, Taggy!' she heard Benedict's urgent voice. 'Go up and see if she will receive me!'

Receive him? Dear lord, when she had so longed for him!

She heard Agnes begin to protest as she came through the doorway, and called out, 'Benedict!'

Sudden silence struck the voices downstairs and, as Theda reached the railings and leaned over them, she saw his handsome features turned up to stare at her from the bottom of the stairs.

'*Benedict*!' she cried, and did not know that she stretched out her arms to him.

'Theda!' he uttered throatily.

Next moment, he was racing up the stairs two at a time, and Theda was stumbling along the gallery to meet him, clinging to the railing for support.

But a few instants later, she needed no other support than the strong arms that seized her and gathered her to a broad chest, the lips in her hair uttering the words that sent the blood rushing through her veins.

'Oh, my witch! Dear ghost! I've missed you like the devil!'

'And I you,' she managed to say through the tears of relief that choked her. 'Oh, Benedict, are you *real*? Is it indeed you? Lord help me, I love you so very much!'

His hold about her tightened so suddenly that she winced and cried out. But the arms did not slacken, for his lips found hers and silenced the protest in a kiss so hard that she sagged, half fainting in his embrace.

In a moment he let her go, but only so that he might lift her bodily from the ground. With a sob, Theda flung her arms about his neck and buried her face in his shoulder. Benedict carried her through the bed-chamber door, and, with one booted foot, kicked it to behind him.

Downstairs Mrs Diggory, holding fast to the pro-testing Hector's collar, smiled to herself with grim satisfaction, and went off to the kitchen.

Benedict laid his burden gently on the bed, and sat down himself on the edge of it. Theda's hands groped towards him, grasping at his greatcoat.

'Don't leave me!' she begged hoarsely.

His fingers closed reasssuringly over hers. 'No fear of that!' He drew one hand to his lips and kissed it, but his fingers left her other hand to trace the wet that trickled over the blue smudges under her eyes.

'Don't weep, dear ghost! What the devil have you been doing to yourself? You're skin and bone again!'

Tremulously, Theda smiled. 'It is a long story. But you, Benedict! Where have you been? All this time and no word to anyone. Do you know that you are thought to have been imprisoned for debt?'

He grinned. 'No, am I indeed? In obedience to Aunt Lavvy's will, no doubt!'

'Of course,' Theda agreed, laughing a little. But her eyes clouded almost at once and she sat up, urgently grasping his coat again with her free hand. 'Benedict the *will*. All is lost! I have ruined everything, and Aycliffe says there is little hope of your succeeding in a contest with Araminta.'

Benedict did not appear to be unduly concerned. His eyes roved her features, as if he was recalling every item of the lines and planes that made up her face.

'You are more beautiful than I remember,' he murmured, his eyes alight, 'in spite of reducing yourself to a scarecrow.' Then he frowned, as if her words had only just reached him. 'The will? Oh, I care nothing for the will. Why should I?'

'Care nothing?' repeated Theda in a bewildered tone. 'But what will you do? Aycliffe and I are trying for a way to have the will stand. You *must* support us. You cannot allow Araminta to make away with all your inheritance, Benedict. I won't let you!'

Benedict grinned at her. 'My ghost, Araminta does not want the only part of this inheritance in which I have an interest.'

'Have you run mad?' Theda demanded, gazing at him blankly. 'If she has her way, she will have the house and *all* the money.'

'But she will not have *you*,' he said in a gutteral tone, and, seizing hold of her, he dragged her against him. His eyes searched hers with fierce intensity, and his lips hovered over her own. Huskily, he murmured, 'Did you mean it, Theda, when you spoke those tender words outside this room? Was it the truth?'

The grey of her eyes deepened, and she moved a little to touch his lips with her own. They felt hot and dry and her veins tingled to his fever.

'Well?' he demanded, his hold tightening. 'Answer me!'

'You see only one flame,' she said softly, smiling. 'There is another, deep in my heart. . . It burns for you.'

'Oh, *Theda*!' he uttered on a sigh, and his lips claimed hers.

At once, heat engulfed them both. Theda felt the flame lick at her loins, and the lassitude that had so possessed her was gone. Urgent now, she pressed again the strong body, thrilling to the arms that held her clamped there.

Then, abruptly, she was released, falling back against her pillows with a gasp. Her eyes flew open to see Benedict flinging off his greatcoat and throwing it aside. His coat and waistcoat swiftly followed it and his fingers ripped away the neckcloth about his throat, heedless of the ruin they effected. His shirt hung open as he sat again, and Theda's eyes were riveted to the long column of his neck, the golden glow of his chest below it.

His own eyes gazed down at her, watching the tip of her tongue pass unconsciously over her parted lips. Her gaze came up and met his.

'*Benedict*,' she whispered, in sudden realisation of his intention, her tone half fearful, half alive with longing.

He did not move, but his hand sought hers and he brought the soft fingers to his lips, mouthing them gently, one by one, turning her palm up to press a kiss inside it, passing his tongue lightly over the pink tips, so passive in his grasp.

Theda gasped as the little touches of his mouth sent flickers of heat rippling through her body. All the time, his eyes held hers, watching how his ministrations excited her. At length his other hand stole forward to play with the copper tresses that fell about the pillows. His fingers drew strands across her bosom, lightly caressing the small breasts beneath.

Theda squirmed at the feather touch, and closed her eyes. In seconds, his breath was warm on her cheek, and her eyes flew open as she felt him chest to chest above her.

'Theda,' he murmured caressingly, 'I *want* you. Will you come to me?'

She hesitated, her parted lips trembling, her eyes locked with his, their grey deepening. 'I have n-nothing else to give you, Benedict,' she faltered.

'Do you think I care for that?' he said, a smile in his eyes.

'Do you not?'

His hand brushed down the length of her body so that she shivered, then came up to cup her breast beneath the thin cotton of her nightgown. As he squeezed gently, and felt her tremble beneath him, his lips mouthed a kiss on hers, briefly, and came away.

'Will you have me, my witch?' he persisted.

She ached to say yes, but all her instincts rebelled. Why was he doing this? If he meant to take her, why did he not do so? He knew—he *knew*—that she was at his mercy, that she would not, *could* not, resist.

'Do you need my permission?' she countered.

'I have always said you must be willing,' he responded, and the smile did not leave his eyes. '*Are* you?'

Again, his fingers teased her, running a path of torturing heat about her thigh, and up over the jutting bone of her hip, close—far too close!—to that part of her where the aching need had its centre. His hand moved, and she hissed in a breath.

'Yes,' she uttered involuntarily. 'Lord in heaven, *yes*!'

His weight left her. 'That's all I wanted to know.'

Theda stared at him as he rose from the bed, reaching towards his discarded neckcloth. Her loins seemed to tear in protest, and she groaned aloud. Benedict turned his head and saw the naked want in her eyes. Fire consumed him.

'Hell and damnation!' he swore. 'Theda, you *witch*!'

Then he was beside her, laying his length, his arms seizing her to him, and his lips, no longer teasing or gentle, dragging at hers. Theda responded instantly, herself aflame, her own arms gripping his chest, her hands running up and down his strong back, as if she must feel all of him at once.

Benedict's hands tore at her nightgown, and his fingers found her flesh. He let out a groan, and his mouth and tongue pressed more deeply into hers as his hands began to roam her bare skin, which burned, tormented, at his touch.

Unknowing what she did, Theda tugged at his shirt, her own lips fighting to take possession of his mouth. Then her fingers found his bare flesh and a streak of intense heat shot through her. As of instinct, their mouths came apart, only to hiss out their passion.

'God, *Theda*!' he uttered hoarsely, burning his face

in the copper tresses that echoed the flaming fire in his loins. '*Burning*. . . I'm burning in you. . .witch. . .*witch*.'

'I'm—yours!' she managed on a gasp. 'I love you, Benedict, I *love* you. Take me now!'

He cried out then, in some species of unutterable agony, and she felt him move to cover her, while his hands signalled his purpose to her eager limbs.

She was aware of a blinding flash of pain as he mastered her, and groaned weakly. But his lips were at her mouth, murmuring tenderness.

'My ghost. . .my witch. . .my lovely one.'

The pain receded in the warmth of his caresses, and then he began to move and she found herself given over wholly to sensation. Every motion sent her senses reeling, deeper and deeper into the furnace they had entered together, until at last, as she soared to a height of such intensity of feeling that she thought she must burst, something exploded in her brain, and she was awash with the dizzying sensation of all-consuming love.

She knew, in that instant, that she belonged to Benedict, to this conqueror of her mind, her heart and her flesh. She was his, irrevocably.

She came to awareness to find Benedict's body heavy on hers, to hear his rasping breath harsh in her ears, and to feel his ragged heartbeat pounding against her own.

They stayed thus a few, pulsing moments. Then Benedict raised his head from where it rested in the wild disorder of her flaming hair, and his gaze met the misty love in the deep grey of her eyes.

To her intense disappointment, he groaned as one in pain, and dragged himself off her. He swung himself to sit on the edge of the bed, and dropped his head in his hands.

Theda sat up, shocked and mystified, and put a hand to his shoulder. 'Benedict, what ails you?'

'The devil take you!' he uttered in distressed tones. 'I never meant to do this to you.' He turned a ravaged countenance upon her. 'Theda, I swear to you, I never meant to take you! Not now. Not *yet*.'

She was hurt and it showed in her eyes. 'You said you wanted me.'

He reached towards her briefly and cradled her face. 'Don't *look* like that, my pale ghost! Of course I wanted you. But I meant only to gain your consent—if I could. Only you looked at me so, and then. . .' His fingers left her cheek and he clenched his hand, pulling away. '*Confound* you!'

His eyes raked her still half-naked limbs and fell on the sheet beneath her. What he saw there made him groan again. He dragged at the covers and threw them over her.

'Conceal yourself, for God's sake, lest I am tempted again!'

Theda huddled against the bedhead, drawing the covers up and over her breasts, as she watched him tidy his clothes and wrap the wrecked neckcloth carelessly about his throat. As he dragged on his coat, she spoke, tentative, out of the misery that consumed her.

'Benedict, you *had* my consent. . . I *was* willing.'

He turned on her. 'Not for *this*. I did not mean your consent to this. I meant for you to marry me!'

Her face dropped. 'I *cannot*. You *know* I cannot.'

Benedict seized her by the shoulders in an ungentle grip. 'I know that you say you cannot. But I know also now that you *love* me. Deny it, if you dare!'

'I don't deny it,' Theda said desperately. 'I *do* love you. I loved you *long* ago. But it alters nothing.'

He shook her. 'Don't *say* that! Especially *now*. Dear

God, as if I needed this complication! I *knew* how it would be. You will think I want to marry you only for what I have done, and you will refuse me on that score.'

'Benedict, *listen* to me!' Theda said, distress turning to anger. 'I have *tried* to tell you in the past—at least to make you *see*—I am not fit for marriage, don't you understand?'

His hands left her shoulders. 'I understand only that you have a deal of false pride. Oh, I am not a fool! I know there is something in your past of which you will not speak. I can guess its import, I dare say. But you——' his fingers reached across to take her face between his hands, and there was deep compassion in his gaze '——you, dear ghost, don't understand. Do you think I would stand aside and let you suffer, as my mother did? Do you think I could *bear* to let you sink into ignominious disgrace?'

Theda's eyes filled. 'Benedict, Benedict, don't! I could better bear disgrace in solitude, don't you see?'

'Yes, the coward's way!' he exclaimed angrily, releasing her. 'I thought you had more courage.'

'Dear lord, but we are poles apart!' Theda said in frustration. 'What is there courageous in dragging my name through the mire? And now you would have me add yours? I think you are mad!'

Benedict beat his fist on the bed and glared at her. 'I *am* mad. Mad for *you*, the more fool I! *I can't live without you*, don't you understand?'

'But you need not!' Theda exclaimed, seizing his hands. 'Benedict, you *have* me. I am *yours*. Let me be your ghost in truth. When you want me, come to me. I shall go—oh, I don't know, anywhere you wish. Only——'

'Yes, to some out-of-the-way place to hide yourself!'

he interrupted, grasping her fingers frenziedly. His eyes were aflame. 'Once before you *dared* to think I would so use you. Theda, Theda, I never meant to take you, but at least I took you in *love*. I will not violate the sanctity of that union! You *must* marry me, whatever it costs.'

'And bring you to ruin also?' she cried despairingly. 'Is that how I am to express my love? Enough that I would be publicly disgraced. Believe me, I *know*—I have reason to know now, for while you were gone I've tried it and am waiting even now for the blow to fall!— that there is *no* future for me in the world I left behind so long ago.'

'You are being foolish beyond permission!' he declared angrily, his hands dragging her to him so that his feverish glare burned into her eyes. 'What *is* this history of yours that you think it irrecoverable? Who *are* you, Theda?'

'I am your *mistress*, Benedict!' she threw at him. 'That is all I am fit for, and you have taken up that option. It is that or nothing.'

Benedict almost threw her from him, and leapt off the bed. 'Then it is nothing! For I will have you to wife, or not at all.' His eyes blazed at her. 'Are you going to tell me your story, or do I demand it of the world at large! For I *will*, if I have to—and marry you in the teeth of them all. Now *tell me*!'

'Oh, go to the devil, as you said you would!' Theda snapped. 'Or go and drag the whole affair out of that dreadful Lady Usk.'

'Woolacombe's grandmother!' uttered Benedict, his brows snapping together. 'By God, if that evil old woman has *dared* to bandy your name——!'

'She will not be the only one,' Theda told him furiously.

Unheeding, he picked up his greatcoat and strode towards the door. With his fingers on the handle, he turned his head. 'I'm not finished with you yet, Theda, so don't think it. I'll be back for you, and you had better be ready to face a pastor!'

'*Never*,' Theda yelled after him, as he slammed out of the room. Then she flung herself down into her pillows and gave way to tears of frustration and rage.

It was not many minutes before Theda's lamentations were interrupted by the eruption into her bedchamber of Hector, barking and whining, closely followed by Agnes Diggory.

'Oh, be quiet, do, you stupid dog!' scolded the housekeeper, slapping the animal smartly on his nose so that he leapt back down off the bed on to which he had just jumped.

'I'm that sorry, Miss Theda. I tried to stop him, but it were Mr Benedict coming down through the kitchens in such a bang and shouting for his groom that started it.'

Theda was too occupied in trying to compose herself and wiping her wet cheeks to notice the oddity of there being a groom in Benedict's train. But she had not spoken before Taggy took in her condition.

'Why, Miss Theda, whatever is the matter?' She set her arms akimbo, and her face flushed up. 'If it's Mr Benedict as has upset you, mum——'

'No, Taggy, it's nothing,' Theda said huskily, drawing the back of her hand across her cheeks. 'At least, it is something, of course, but——'

'And I thought all would be well, if only I was to leave you both to yourselves!' uttered Taggy crossly. 'When I see Mr Benedict——'

'Don't, Taggy,' Theda begged, stretching out a hand to her. 'It is as much my fault as his.'

Mrs Diggory shook her head as she took the hand and held it tightly. 'Six of one and half a dozen of t'other. Been that way all along with you two, ain't it, Miss Theda?'

Theda sniffed and smiled a little. 'I suppose it can't get any worse.'

'But it can, Miss Theda,' contradicted Taggy worriedly, squeezing her hand. 'That's what I come to tell you. That there traitor, Mrs Elswick, had to pick this of all days to come and visit. She's downstairs now, looking ever so knowing, just as you'd expect.'

'Oh, no,' Theda sighed. 'Do you think she guessed?'

'Well, it wouldn't be right to deceive you, Miss Theda,' Taggy said flatly, 'and she saw Mr Benedict come through, of course, and guessed where he'd come from. Sure as check, she'll tell Miss Ara he was here, and in your chamber.'

'And Araminta will tell the world!' Theda cried despairingly. 'Lord help me! Can I not take one step without falling on my face?'

'Now don't fret, Miss Theda,' Mrs Diggory began.

'There is no use in fretting,' Theda said wearily. 'What does it matter, after all? Already the world may know my story. Anyone who has heard it will declare that this is but of a piece with all the rest!'

There was a silence, while Hector, climbing back on the bed, nuzzled at her free hand. She stroked him absently, and Mrs Diggory got up in a determined way.

'I'd best straighten you out, Miss Theda. Only look at your hair! And the bed looks like a troop of soldiers has been over it.'

Realising what she had said, she flushed bright scarlet.

But Theda let out a gurgle of laughter. 'Not quite as bad as that, Taggy!'

Mrs Diggory took refuge in scolding the dog and dragging him off the bed. Then she suddenly slapped at her apron pocket.

'If all that pother has not made me forget! One of the lads come over from Switham House while Mr Benedict was here. He left this.' She brought out a sealed billet.

'From Rose?' Theda asked, taking it and breaking the seal.

'She come over while you were ill, Miss Theda,' said Taggy, with an apologetic look. 'I wouldn't let her trouble you, especially as I could tell she'd no *good* news.'

'No, indeed,' Theda agreed, running her eyes down the sheet of paper. 'For she knows it all. Lord, she had it from Lady Usk! But why so urgent!'

Next instant, she uttered a shriek that made the housekeeper jump.

'Whatever is the matter, Miss Theda?'

'Dear lord in heaven!' A pair of deeply troubled eyes were turned on Mrs Diggory. 'Why didn't he tell me?'

'Who, miss?'

'Benedict. . . He has become. . .have you ever heard of Lord Dacre, Taggy?'

'Dacre? Ain't that Miss Isabel's family? Or rather, Mr Benedict's uncle?'

'Not *Mr* Benedict, Taggy. He has himself become. . . Lord Dacre.'

'Mercy me!' uttered Mrs Diggory, sitting down plump on the bed, her eyes almost popping from her head.

'He has estates in. . . Cheshire,' went on Theda, talking almost to herself. '*Dacre*. And still he wants to marry me—but he does not know, he *can't* know. . .

Oh, dear lord, Rose will tell him! She says here that of course there can now be no question of marriage, and she is right.'

She bit her lip, crumpling the note in her hand, and into her eyes came a look so desolate that Taggy's heart contracted. In a hushed tone, she spoke.

'What is it, Miss Theda? What does it mean?'

The deep grey eyes turned to her, and a tear traced a lonely path down her pearly cheek. 'It means. . .that I shall have to go away.'

'Nothing could exceed my delight, Benedict!' uttered Mrs Alderley, beaming. 'If your poor mother had ever dreamed of this!'

'She would not have exhibited such joy as you are doing,' said the new Lord Dacre drily. 'I imagine she is turning in her grave!'

'Oh, nonsense! You know nothing of women if that is what you believe, my dear. Such a sweet revenge!'

She looked across to where the lawyer stood, quietly detached by one of the windows of her large saloon, gazing out on to the extensive gardens.

'Surely you, Aycliffe, with your wide experience must agree with me?' she appealed to him.

The lawyer turned, smiling. 'I think there is more honour among your sex, ma'am, than you give your-selves credit for.'

Benedict glanced at him. 'Is that a hint to me, man? If you think I will respect her honour to the point of releasing her, you much mistake the matter!'

'I made no such suggestion, my lord,' protested Aycliffe. 'Believe me, I have the lady's best interests very much at heart.'

'If they march with my interests, that is all to the good. If not——'

'What in the world are you two talking of?' interrupted Rose, whose perplexed gaze had been going from one to the other.

'We are talking of Theda,' Benedict said at once. 'And that is what we came for, in fact.'

'Theda? But why have you come to me? I have not seen her for days.'

'I know that,' snapped his lordship. 'She's been lying there in a state of collapse, and not a soul has been next or nigh her!'

Mrs Alderley stiffened. 'If that is a reproach to me, you are wide of the mark, Benedict. Taggy turned me away! As she has done everyone else who tried to visit.'

'Sensible woman, Taggy,' commented Benedict, with a lightning change of face. 'But never mind that. Tell me, Rose, what is all this about Lady Usk? Does she know something of Theda's history?'

'Everything!' Rose said comprehensively.

'She told you?'

'I asked her. When there was Theda behaving like a cat on a hot bakestone, what would you have had me do?'

'Well, go on! Tell us what she said.'

Rose blinked. 'Why should I? What has it to do with you?'

Benedict's eye kindled. 'You don't think, as her future husband, that the matter concerns me?'

'Husband!' gasped Mrs Alderley. 'Benedict, have you taken leave of your senses? You have no need to marry her *now*. As Lord Dacre, you certainly *cannot* do so.'

'I shall be the judge of that,' said Lord Dacre icily. 'And I don't need you against me as well as Theda herself, I thank you, Rose.'

'If Theda will not marry you, then she shows a deal more sense than you!' Rose told him roundly. 'Good God, have you *no* sense of what is fitting?' She stopped, arrested by the expression in his face. Uncertainly, she added, 'Don't look at me like that, Benedict. Anyone would suppose you meant to murder me!'

'I will, if you continue in that vein,' he promised savagely. 'What is "*fitting*"? Confound it, who am I to hold up my nose in such a fashion? The son of a woman disgraced by the scandal of divorce, brought back to respectability only by some freak of fate. To hell with what is fitting! Now do you tell me the story you had from Lady Usk, or do I go to the old witch myself?'

Rose eyed him a moment. Then she looked across at the silent lawyer. 'What is your role in this, Aycliffe?'

'His interest is in the matter of Aunt Lavinia's will, of course,' Benedict told her, answering for him.

'Not entirely,' the lawyer said. 'Officially, I must learn Miss Kyte's true identity. I am preparing papers for the relinquishment of the claim, but once she signs them she will be literally on the streets and penniless. Unofficially, therefore, I am anxious to assist her—and Lord Dacre, I may add—to come out of this coil in the best possible way.'

Mrs Alderley sighed. 'Well, I had hoped that she might still be received. I cannot tell whether or not Lady Usk has spoken out, but I suspect not. I cannot think that Taggy would have been obliged to turn away her admirers otherwise.'

'Admirers?' Benedict's steely gaze was upon her, a most ugly light in his eye. '*What* admirers?'

'Why, Taggy told me she had been obliged to deny entrance both to Tiverton and to Finchingfield.'

'Tiverton and Finchingfield!' echoed Benedict furiously. 'Hell and the devil, I'll cut both their livers out! Calling themselves my friends, too!'

'Benedict, mind your tongue!' Rose snapped, adding crossly, 'In any event, how are they to know you have an interest there yourself?'

'They'll know soon enough,' Benedict said grimly, making no apology for his lapse. 'There is no time to lose, Rose. It only needs for Araminta to get hold of the latest development, and the fat will be in the fire.'

Mrs Alderley gazed at him, appalled. 'The latest development? You mean you have...?' Understanding flooded her face, mingling with dismay and disapproval. 'Really, Benedict, how *could* you?'

He grinned suddenly, unholy amusement in his eyes. 'How could I not?' he countered. 'I am bewitched, and wholly under her spell!'

'Good God, you will have to marry her now!'

'Well, thank heaven you finally agree with me!' was all his comment.

Aycliffe bit back a laugh. 'Come, ma'am. There is no arguing this matter with Lord Dacre, as I have already discovered. Will you not enlighten us as to what you have learned?'

Outnumbered and outgunned, Rose capitulated. The story she had to tell came as no surprise to either gentleman, but Benedict no sooner heard the introduction of the name of Kirtlington than he smote his forehead.

'Dear *God*, of course! Come, Aycliffe, we must be off to Cheshire at once.'

'Cheshire!' exclaimed Rose, moving to intercept him as he turned for the door. 'But surely you would do better to confront Theda with this and demand the truth from her?'

'Don't be ridiculous, Rose! Don't you know Theda

better than that? No, no, believe me, the less she knows of my activities, the better. The only way to handle my witch is to present her with a *fait accompli*. I only pray heaven she may not take it into her head to run away while I am out of reach!'

'Oh, dear, Miss Theda, I wish you will think better of it!' Taggy said tearfully, as she nevertheless assisted to fold the clothes that had been washed and pressed, ready to pack. Hector, disturbed by the preparations, ran to and fro, whining now and then.

Theda shook her head in a determined way. 'No. Mr Aycliffe will be back today or tomorrow, so his clerks told me. If it had not been for the circumstance of his being away, I should not be here now.'

'And what am I supposed to tell Mr Benedict when he arrives to find you gone?' demanded Taggy crossly, tucking a nightgown into the battered portmanteau.

'You will have no need to tell him anything. I shall leave a letter.'

'Dear knows why he has not been back here these few days!' muttered the housekeeper fretfully.

'He has other calls on his time now, you know,' Theda said lightly, to conceal the ache in her heart, for in spite of her intention his absence could not but be painful. 'I dare say he has had to return to his estates.'

'Estates, indeed! And him with nothing to his name if it weren't for my late mistress!'

'Now, Taggy, you know well it is because of her that he had nothing. For my part, I am very happy for his good fortune.'

Taggy sniffed. 'All very well if he was inclined to share it, naming no names.'

Theda had to smile. 'Will nothing convince you that it is I and not he who is trying to escape?'

The housekeeper snorted. 'He had ought to have been here, that's all. Certain sure *he'd* have stopped you from going, even if I can't.'

A shrieking call from below interrupted them. 'Taggy! *Tag-gy!* Where are you?'

The dog immediately began to bark, and made off out of the room. Mrs Diggory froze with her hands in the portmanteau, her eyes fearful.

'It's Miss Ara! Oh, lordy, lordy, she must have heard from that wretched Mrs Elswick! I could strangle that woman, so I could!'

Theda had gone paler than usual, and she grasped at the bedpost for support. 'I had hoped to be gone so that I would not be obliged to face her.'

'Stay here!' ordered Taggy. 'I'll tell her you're out.'

She began to march towards the door, but Theda ran after her and grasped her arm. 'No! Allow me some little spark of pride, Taggy. After all, my reputation is in all likelihood blasted in any event. What more have I to fear? If I am already doomed, what have I to lose?' With an air of determination, she straightened her shoulders and put up her chin. 'I have borne enough. I will *not* cower away for fear of Araminta Quatt!'

'Bravo, Miss Theda!' applauded the housekeeper. 'Time and past someone told her what's what!'

The call came again, angry now. 'Tag-gy! Come here at once!' Then was added, 'Adam, get this dratted animal away from me!'

Gathering her dignity together, Theda turned and walked slowly out of the bedchamber. She was dressed in one of her old dark, low-waisted gowns for warmth, for she had purchased no winter clothing among the new, but her glorious hair was uncovered and half falling about her shoulders from a careless knot on top of her head. But she bore herself like a queen as she slowly descended the stairs, and knew that Araminta, staring up from below, was disconcerted by the picture she made. She saw old Diggory shuffling off to the back regions, the protesting Hector in tow.

'You want something, Mrs Quatt?' she enquired politely.

'Pah!' burst from Araminta as she found her tongue. 'Flaunting yourself again, like the low creature you are, I see! Just like Isabel Beckenham, even as that *disgusting* hair marks you. Two of a kind, you and she together. How apt for Benedict's pleasure!'

Theda flinched inside, but nothing showed in her face bar the contempt she felt for this woman. 'What is it you want?'

Araminta's smug, thin smile creased her mouth. 'I'm here to give you notice to leave. The place will be mine before long, and I want you *out.*'

'Indeed? Have you then made a successful contest of the will? I had not heard of it?'

'No, I have not. But I don't need to, Madam Harlot!'

Theda's lips whitened, but she gave no other sign of the distress this label caused her. 'You are very free with your assumptions, and your—*names*, Mrs Quatt. Pray can you substantiate any of this?'

'Don't come your highty-tighty airs and graces over me, you common baggage, you!' snapped the other woman venomously, coming close and poking her pinched features almost into Theda's face. 'Very well for Benedict to hold his head up high—though *that's* a farce, if ever I heard of one! Viscount Dacre? Pah! Viscount Muckraker, if you like— but *you*? The world knows what you are, and so does he. Taken his pleasure and gone off, has he? Well, it's all I'd expect.' She laughed jeeringly.

'Have you finished?' Theda asked quietly.

'By no means! Finished? I've not started. *He* don't want the place any more, nor the money neither, I'll be bound. So it's all *mine*, understand? I'm here to take it, and I want you out. *Now*.'

Theda stood her ground, aware of Taggy hovering on the stairs behind her, the listening ears of the maids above, and Adam Diggory's unseen shadow at the back of the hall. For she knew he had put Hector into the kitchen but remained himself. Her heart was hammering and she felt sick, but she drew a steadying breath and began to speak, as if addressing an importunate stranger, her voice icily calm, and frightening in its intensity.

'You are tardy, madam. We here have known of Lord Dacre's inheritance these three days. However, it is not for me or you to presume upon the gentleman's intentions. Therefore, until Mr Aycliffe informs me that the will has been overturned, I shall remain here. You, Mrs Quatt——' flinging out a pointing finger and thrusting it into Araminta's chest '—*you* will leave this house, not I. *At once*!'

The woman was so surprised that she fell back a step. Theda, her voice low to steady it, began to move forward, poking at Mrs Quatt as she was driven, just as she had driven Theda on a previous occasion, backwards, step by step, towards the front door.

'Ever since I entered Merchiston Lodge, Araminta, you have snarled and screeched, and torn your claws like the cat you are. Well, the worm has turned, madam! What I am, what I may be, is none of your concern. But whatever I am, you, madam, are *not* going to browbeat me, or insult me by one—word—more.' The finger jabbed for emphasis.

By now Araminta was backed up against the door, stricken to silence, and Theda came close, her deep grey eyes burning with fury in the flaming setting of her hair. Like an avenging witch, she stood over the pinched, sallow face, in which fright had at last replaced venom in the pale eyes.

'Now *go*, and leave me in peace!'

Seizing Araminta's arm, Theda dragged her away from the door. Flinging it wide, she made to thrust the other woman from the house, only to be brought up short by the sight of two gentlemen standing at the other end of the long covered porch. One was the Reverend Saul Quatt. The other was Mr Warren Caswell.

CHAPTER TWELVE

Too angry to take in the significance of the second visitor, Theda pushed Araminta through the door and addressed the vicar, who was staring open-mouthed.

'In a very good hour, sir! Take your wife, if you please, and remove her from my sight.'

'Saul!' cried out the lady in a quavering voice. 'She raised a hand to me, Saul! *Do* something.'

But Mr Quatt only grasped her arm, uttering in an urgent undervoice, 'I *told* you not to come, Araminta. You *must* wait for the law. Another time perhaps you will listen to me when I warn you of the dangerous ground you are treading.'

'But it is my *right*. This is *my* house.'

'As to that,' answered her spouse, pushing her inexorably towards the waiting gig, 'there may be another way to go to work. Now come home, do!'

Araminta paused with her foot on the step. 'What do you mean, Saul?'

'I will explain it to you presently,' said the Reverend gentleman, with a harassed glance over his shoulder to where Theda stood glaring at her second visitor. '*Get in*!'

'Don't speak to me in that tone!' protested his wife, but nevertheless responding to the pressure of his hand in her back.

Saul Quatt snapped suddenly. 'Araminta, sit *down* and be *quiet*!' he shouted.

Mouth agape, she watched him take his seat beside her and gather up the reins. Then, as the gig began to move, she started to scold. Theda could hear them arguing even as the horse trotted off down the drive. But she had no leisure to enjoy the spectacle of Mrs Quatt's sudden drop from favour. Victorious from her own encounter with the woman, she confronted Mr Caswell with belligerence.

'What do you want?'

'I—er—I had to see you, Theodosia!' he said a little diffidently, but without preamble, his voice low. 'We must talk.'

All at once Theda became fully alive to the implications of this visit. Was there to be no end? No peace? She sagged wearily. 'Oh, lord above! You had better come in.'

Turning, she led the way to the library and preceded the visitor into the room. Then she closed the door behind them both, and moved to confront him where he had gone to stand by the desk, clearly nervous.

'It has been a long time, Warren,' she said evenly.

He was silent for a moment, looking her over, his eyes clearly appreciative. 'You have changed very little,' he ventured.

Theda did not smile. 'I would I could say the same of you.'

Caswell glanced briefly down at his own person and gave a self-conscious laugh. 'Yes, I—I have altered, I suppose. Marriage, I dare say.'

Wincing inwardly, Theda asked, 'Have you children?'

'Two.' He glanced away, across the shelves of books, as if he found it hard to meet her gaze. 'It is for them—for their sake, really, that I am here.'

Theda stiffened. 'Pray do not attempt to move me to pity by a tale of innocence and woe, Warren. You will find I am hardened against all that.'

His eyes, in their now puffy setting, came back to her, and there was a trace at last of the old look that had warmed her all those years ago.

'I can't believe that,' he said, with a pathetic twist of the lips. 'You were ever tender-hearted.'

'Unlike you!' Theda threw at him before she could stop herself, as an echo of the pain he had inflicted rose again inside her.

'Don't Theodosia! I *had* to do. . .what I did. I had no choice.'

'Why?' she demanded, suddenly angry. 'Had you debts, is that it? My fortune was denied you at the last, and *that* was the spur. Was it not, Warren?'

His coarsened features reddened. 'I had need of money, it is true. But I *cared* for you, Theodosia. Can you doubt it?'

Theda fell back against the desk, a disbelieving laugh on her lips. 'Can I doubt it? Are you out of your senses? You professed to love me, oh, yes.' Her voice shook. 'With what passionate words did you not wrench my young heart from its bosom? And when my father refused consent, what then? Oh, he knew you better than I, for all my rebellious ravings! I've had time enough to learn that.'

'That will do!' cried Caswell, his anger now matching hers. 'I did not come here to rake up old scores.'

'Did you expect to find me quiescent, then?' Theda raged. The fires of her fury against him, long buried, had risen up, and were not to be contained. 'And what old "scores" have you? Was it I who persuaded you to fly from your home? Was it I who, finding your purse empty, ran from you?'

'You are beside yourself!' he uttered, stepping involuntarily backwards.

'Have I not reason?' she demanded, as the years

seemed to roll away, and she felt again the anguish his desertion had inflicted. 'You *left* me, Warren. You took my youth, my innocence—everything I had!—and then you flung me aside when you knew I could give you nothing. . .and you left *me* nothing!'

'I—I did not mean it so,' he faltered.

'You did not mean it? Is that all you can *say*?' she flared, coming at him with her hand rising to strike.

'No, Theodosia, no!' he uttered, cowering before her vengeance. 'Pray don't! Pray, pray, be calm!'

'*Calm*!' she almost screamed, ready to smash a blow into his once comely face.

She saw the terror there, and was arrested. This bloated, coarse-featured wreck was not the man she once had thought she loved. What had he to do with the woman she now was? And she *had* chosen her own destiny. Her hand came down and the fire died out of her eyes. She saw the relief that crept into his face, and a deep sigh escaped her.

'All these years,' she said in a tired voice, looking him up and down. 'All I ever cared for, all I ever hated you for, Warren, was the *lie*.'

'It was no. . .lie,' he uttered. 'I cared for you.'

'Don't compound it!' she flashed. 'And that isn't the lie I meant.'

'I tell you it was no lie,' he said in a desperate tone. 'I know it was wrong to—to leave you. But I had no choice. If you will have it, yes, there were debts that did not permit of my marrying a penniless girl. But I thought—I hoped—you would go back.'

Theda stared at him. He did not take her meaning. She was surprised to find that she felt only contempt. The anger seemed to have drained away.

'Did you? Then you were wrong.'

For the first time, she thought that her life—

wretched as it was—had been preferable to marriage with this man. She did not want to look at him, and crossed to stand before the mantel over the fireplace, gazing down into the empty grate.

'What did you come for, Warren?'

He cleared his throat. 'To—er—to make reparation. I thought—I wondered—if perhaps you might be in need of. . .' He paused, as she turned again, her expression so forbidding that he scarcely knew how to continue.

'Go on,' she said evenly.

'I have a sum of money put by, which I can give you,' he said quickly.

'Unbeknownst to your wife, no doubt,' remarked Theda. 'And in return? I presume there is a condition attached.'

Again, he cleared his throat, and his unquiet gaze moved away from her. 'I thought you might care to go abroad. Not France, of course, for we are at war there. But Holland, perhaps. Or Italy?'

Theda fought for control. 'I wonder you have not already arranged a packet for me! So I am to be bought off—like a common harpy!'

'No, no,' he began in protest.

'Don't waste your breath! Lord above, I thought I had endured the worst of insults already this day! How—*dare*—you?'

'Wait, Theodosia!' he begged anxiously. 'I meant no insult. I—I was fearful for my wife, my family. After all, you *had* shown yourself in public. And Lady Usk— God knows *when* the blow might fall!'

'Then doubtless it has not yet fallen. But did it not occur to you,' Theda said, her breast heaving with the passion she was only just holding in check, 'that I have lately *not* been seen? *Who* do you think is to be the most hurt by such a scandal? *Myself*, Warren. Not you. And you dare to come here and try to make reparation—*reparation*, you call it!—for ruining my life?'

'That will do!' he ejaculated, suddenly losing patience. 'You were willing enough at the time. And, if rumour is to be believed, you have readily found consolation elsewhere!'

Theda paled, her eyes dilating. Her voice was a croak. 'What? *What* did you say?'

'You may cease this pretence of virtue,' he said in a testy voice. 'I know what you are!'

The thought flitted through her mind that Araminta had already done her worst. If the world did not know her history, which was by no means certain, they at least knew of her liaison with Benedict. Dear lord, she *would* have to go abroad! But not at this man's expense. She would die first!

'Whatever I am,' she said, in a voice of dangerous quiet, 'it is what you made me, Warren Caswell. Long before. . .anyone else. . .came on the scene. May you take that knowledge to your grave!'

'I have a right to protect my wife and family,' he said in a blustering way.

'What do you imagine I will do—go and tell your wife my story?' Theda gave a bitter laugh. 'Perhaps I should. Why shouldn't she know what manner of man she married?'

'You *dare*!' roared Caswell, and, starting forward, he seized her shoulder and cried out, '*Bitch*!' as in his turn he raised a hand as if to strike at her.

From the doorway a furious voice stopped him in his tracks. 'Unhand my wife, villain!'

Caswell let Theda go and whirled about as Benedict strode forward into the room.

'Your *wife*!' he gasped.

'Touch her again with your filthy paws, and I'll ram my fist into your ugly face!' Benedict promised, his eyes blazing, and his clenched hands threateningly raised.

Caswell backed away, one hand held protectively before him. 'I d-didn't know you had married her, Beckenham—I mean, Dacre.'

'Well, you know now,' snapped his adversary, his tall person almost entirely concealing Theda's figure behind him where he had moved to protect her. 'And if you know what's good for you, you'll keep your mouth *shut*.'

'I'm not going to talk,' Warren said hastily, edging towards the door.

'See you don't, or it'll be the worse for you! You don't know her. You've never met her before in your life, do you understand?'

'Oh, I understand. I came here to prevent scandal, Dacre, not to start it. But you may well catch cold at it, anyway, marrying such a woman.'

Benedict took a step forward, his eyes smouldering dangerously. 'One word more—just one—and you'll face my pistol at dawn!'

Caswell blenched, and hurriedly made his exit. Benedict watched him go and then turned to find Theda leaning back against the mantel, white to the lips, one hand at her bosom. He took a hasty pace towards her, and she flung out a hand.

'No, wait! Don't come near me!'

'Not come near you?' he echoed incredulously, making to move. 'Don't be stupid!'

'I beg you!' she said desperately.

He relaxed back, his voice dropping to a tender note. 'What is it, my dearest ghost?'

Theda passed a tongue over her dry lips. Her voice

shook pitiably, but she forced herself to speak. 'Now you know...you *must* know, or you would not have spoken to him so, the reason I am *not* your wife...and can never be so, Benedict.'

To her astonishment, he smiled. Not the smile of practised charm, but one of real warmth and tenderness. 'Yes, Lady Theodosia Kirtlington, I know all about it.'

Theda gasped. 'Then you *do* know—at least who I am. But you can only have heard—who told you? Was it Rose?'

'Yes she did, but only under duress,' he answered gently.

'Then, Benedict, you have heard only the *scandalous* tale. The rumour from the lips of Lady Usk. You cannot know the truth.'

'Oh, yes, I do,' he said grimly. '*All* the truth.'

Theda's eyes were dark with distress. 'But you cannot. Only Caswell and I know the full sum of it.'

Benedict's gaze was steady. 'And one other.'

She was too overset to guess what he meant. She watched him walk to the door and open it.

'Come in, sir,' he said to someone outside.

A gentleman stepped slowly through the doorway and stood stock-still, staring at her, a not over-fashionable but well-dressed personage in late middle age, with greying hair cut short in the prevailing mode. He was of medium height, with a spare frame, a little unsteady on his feet, perhaps, and with the sallow complexion of recent illness on features that bore a striking resemblance to the girl before him.

Theda's knees almost buckled under her, and she grasped the mantel for support. Faintly, she uttered, '*Papa*?'

The Earl of Kirtlington found his tongue. 'Lord in heaven, but you are the *image* of your mother!'

Theda put trembling fingers to her lips and then stretched them out unconsciously. 'I th-thought—they said you were *dead*!'

'Almost,' he said smiling. 'But I thank God that He spared me for this!'

Next instant, he had crossed the distance between them, and enfolded his daughter in his arms. Theda raised a tear-streaked face to gaze up into the older one above her with loving eyes.

'Oh, Papa! How can you bear even to *speak* to me?'

The Earl's own eyes were moist, but he dug a hand into the pocket of his frock-coat and brought out a handkerchief. As if she were a little girl, he wiped her cheeks, and his voice was not quite steady.

'My darling, *foolish* child! Don't you think I've longed to speak to you, to hear your voice? You thought me dead these few weeks... How much more heavy has been *my* burden, and your poor mother's, do you suppose, not knowing—all these years, Theda!—whether you be alive or dead?'

Her tears overflowed again. 'I am sorry... I am *so* sorry,' she whispered.

Lord Kirtlington's hand caressed the bright copper head, gentling it against his shoulder. 'Don't, my sweet! It is myself and your mama who have cause for repentance. Well do I know that we drove you into flight. I knew your ways, that streak of obstinacy that would make you always run counter, even as an infant. We went the wrong way to work with you, and were amply punished for our mistake.'

'Papa, *Papa*!' Theda cried out, raising her face once again. 'Pray don't speak so... You will break my *heart*.'

Her father pressed a kiss to her forehead, and smiled,

releasing her at last. 'Hearts are not so easily broken. And——' with a grateful glance at Benedict, who was standing by, mute, moved as he had not expected to be by this reunion he had brought about '—thanks to this intelligent and resourceful young man, it is over now.'

Theda could not forbear a smile as she turned her head to look at Benedict. 'Resourceful, yes,' she agreed.

Benedict's eyes narrowed, but his lips twitched. 'Careful, Theda!'

She laughed. 'I shall desist, since I am again in your debt.' Her eyes came back to her father's face and she drew a breath. 'And you are truly recovered? I can't describe to you the agony of being told—and then having no means by which to find out. . . Well, no more of that! How is Mama?' Her eyes clouded. 'Do you think she will ever forgive me?'

'She did so long ago. Indeed, she was hot with me for my part in the business, and rang a fine peal over my head!'

Theda smiled. 'Poor Mama! I know what it is to be cursed with that temper.'

'You redheads!' sighed Lord Kirtlington, shaking his head, and caressing her cheek with a gentle finger. 'But she is, thank God, in high bloom, and yearning for a sight of you. She did not even *try* to prevent my journey, although she has been a perfect tyrant these many weeks, making me keep my bed! She bade me tell you that she loves you very dearly, and has never ceased to miss you.'

'Oh, dear lord!' Theda murmured, her eyes misting over. 'That is a worse reproach to me than any that she ever uttered.' She bit her lip. 'You were right, both of you, on all counts, Papa. Caswell was unworthy, just as you said, and untrue, as dear Mama would have it. And I was too stubborn to see it.'

'You were only a child, my dear,' sighed the Earl. 'You could not be expected to foresee how he would turn out.'

'Did you see him? Outside just now, I mean?' Theda asked. 'He is perfectly gross!'

Kirtlington laughed. 'I have been aware of it for some little while. You forget. We move in the same circles. Not,' he added, his voice hardening, 'that I should dream of addressing the young scoundrel! The last time I did so was when he reappeared in town, *without* you.'

'*What*?' ejaculated Benedict. 'Do you say he dared to show his face after what he did?'

'As bold as brass!' the Earl confirmed, his eye kindling. 'Having contracted, if you please, an engagement to the woman who is now his wife.'

'Devil take him! I wish I *had* landed him a facer!'

'Did you then accost him, Papa?' Theda asked, intervening swiftly.

'Certainly I did. He informed me that you had run away. I was furious that he should leave you destitute upon the world. Though I am forced to admit that his searches, like mine, would probably have been futile.'

'You searched for me?' Theda said wonderingly.

'High and low. For months. I advertised. God knows what I did not do! Except call in the Bow Street Runners, although your mama would even have had me do that, she was so distraught.' He reached out to take one of her hands and hold it between both his own. 'My child, why did you not come back to your home?'

For the first time in their interview, a trace of her old defiance came back. '*I could* not. You see, Papa, I

did not run away. After you found us, and Warren told
you we were already—he had already. . .' Her voice
died. She drew a breath and began again. '*Then*, when
you disinherited me on the spot—oh, I don't blame you
for that, don't think it!—when you said we might reap
the just rewards of our flight and marry as paupers, he
. . .he left me flat.'

'Scoundrel!' burst from Lord Kirtlington.

Behind him, Benedict's breath hissed, bringing
Theda's head round to see his face a mask of livid fury.
She put out a hand to him at once.

'*No*, Benedict! It is too late now for revenge. Pray
leave it! For *my* sake.'

He strode forward to grasp the hand she held out to
him. It clutched his tightly, and he drew it to his lips.

'Let him not cross my path, that's all!' he said curtly.
Then he looked at the Earl. 'I understand her, sir, if
you do not. She would not return to you because you
believed her to be a fallen woman, and nothing she
could say would convince you otherwise.' He kept her
fingers closely imprisoned, but he did not look at her.
'I tell you now, sir, that the villain *lied*.'

'Benedict!' Theda gasped, shocked.

Lord Kirtlington eyed his prospective son-in-law with
interest. 'Did he so?'

'He did so, sir,' Benedict said staunchly. 'You have
my word on it. If it had not been so, if I had found
that——' grinding his teeth with menace '—well, suffice
it that he may yet live his natural life out!'

'I understand you, I believe,' said the Earl, an unmistakable twinkle in his eye. 'I have to thank you, Dacre,
for your honesty in all this matter.' He looked at
Theda. 'He has told me all your story, or as much as
he knows. He even brought a lawyer to support him.

In fact, he had no need of anything more than a lock of hair he showed me.'

At that, Theda's eyes came round to Benedict's and he grinned, his expression rueful. 'The one you gave me on account, remember?'

'I remember,' she said, flashing him a look that spoke volumes.

The two gentlemen exchanged glances. But it was the Earl who said gently, 'Theda, my child. Don't let that fiery temper of yours betray you now!'

She bit her lip, but the words escaped her anyhow. 'I take it you have between you concerted your schemes for my future?'

'Well, Dacre came to find me for the purpose of asking my permission to address you,' said Kirtlington.

'*And* to find out if you *were* his daughter,' Benedict put in quickly.

'Trying to force my hand!' Theda said crossly, dragging her fingers from his grasp.

'On the contrary,' came a new voice from the doorway, and Mr Aycliffe walked into the room. He bowed. 'Forgive me, Lady Theodosia, but I could not help but overhear something of what has transpired in this room.'

'Lord!' she exclaimed. 'You, too? Is this a conspiracy?'

Her father intervened once more. 'You may rest easy, Theda. I myself will see Lady Usk. I know her all too well. When she hears what I have to say to her, there will be no question of her opening her lips on this subject. Once you are wed, and known once more as my daughter, the rest will soon be forgotten.'

'Papa, this is all very well, but——'

'Lady Theodosia,' interrupted Aycliffe, 'I think you should know that his lordship—Lord Dacre, I mean—

went to find your father not only to discover your identity for the purpose of saving your reputation, if he could. It was also because he knew that you were to become again destitute.'

'The will!' Theda said at once, utterly ignoring his words. 'Have you the papers I must sign? I have been waiting only for that so that I might go.'

'I knew it!' Benedict snapped. 'You are going nowhere, my good girl!'

As Theda turned on him, Aycliffe hastily intervened. 'Your pardon, my lord. Lady Theodosia, you mistake. Mr Beckenham—I mean, Lord Dacre—wanted you to have the security of your home so that you might have a *choice* about your future.'

'I thank you, Mr Aycliffe,' Theda said drily, 'but I know him a little better than that!'

'So I should hope!' came instantly from Benedict, as he grasped her hands again. His eyes on hers, he spoke over his shoulder. 'I think, sir, that it would be better if you—and Aycliffe also—would be so good as to leave us to settle matters to our mutual satisfaction.'

'Mutual!' echoed Theda crossly, not even noticing as her father and the lawyer left them together and closed the library door. 'How *could* you tell my father—say *that*?'

Benedict dropped her hands, but seized her bodily, snatching her to him, and holding her trapped so that she could not move.

'I said it because it was true. You are mine—and *only* mine. I knew it at once when we lost ourselves in our *mutual* passion. And if I had needed proof, it was there to be seen after. Do you think I will *ever* let you go, now that I've claimed you?'

Her heart was rioting madly, and her limbs were going weak, but a gleam entered her eye.

'You might let me go just a little. . . I know you call me a ghost, but flesh and blood must breathe!'

Laughing, he loosened his hold enough so that she could pull her arms free. Then he dragged her close again and bent his head to kiss her. Theda's arms crept up about his neck, and her lips met his.

When they came apart, she said wonderingly. 'It is all still there. You have only to *touch* me.'

He smiled. 'Did you imagine one drink would slake so raging a thirst? It will take a lifetime!' He let her go, but retained hold of her fingers as his face became serious. 'Theda, there is no other future for us, you must see that. Aside from the rest, after what I have said to Caswell—that you *are* my wife—we should make it good. Especially as your reputation is blasted already in the village. And *that* is to my account.'

'Don't, Benedict! I am ready to face all that. I told you so,' Theda said, a trifle tremulous again. 'I would do anything I could for you, save——'

'Save that which I *want* from you,' he finished. 'And you would have run from me to escape it, confound you!'

Tears sparkled on her lashes. 'I was almost packed.'

'You would not have got far!' he said grimly. 'I would have come after you, and unlike your father I'd have *found* you, had I to go to the ends of the earth!'

'You want me that much?' Theda whispered.

'I *love* you that much!' he corrected.

There was wonder and doubt in her eyes. 'You love *me*? Not. . .not my hair? Oh, Benedict, I have learned from Rose about your mother, and I see that my hair is the key, but——'

'*No*,' he burst out. 'No, Theda! The flame was there between us *before*. When I saw your hair——' touching it lovingly, fingering the fiery strands '—it was perhaps the trigger that sprang the flame. But when I was at Dacre, in spite of all the painful memories—Theda, it was *your* face that haunted me, not my mother's! I knew then that I *loved* you, more than anything in the world, more than life itself!'

Theda bit her lip, her heart turning to liquid in her bosom. She touched her fingers to his lips.

'I would like to die now,' she said shakily, 'that this moment might last forever.'

'Fool!' he uttered lovingly, kissing the fingers and taking them again within his own. 'We *have* forever.' Then he dropped her hand, and swept her back into his arms, nestling his face in the glowing tresses about her head. 'Oh, my ghost! My beloved, beautiful witch, *will* you marry me? Not to save your reputation, nor to satisfy society or your father, or even me—but only because you love me and I you?' He drew back his head so that he might look into her eyes, misty with unshed tears. 'Theda, will you?'

Her lips trembled on a smile. 'And my father called *me* obstinate!'

Benedict shook her. 'Will—you—*yield*?'

'I thought I had,' she uttered on a shaky laugh. 'Well, Lady Lavinia told me to make something of you. I suppose I had better try!'

'*Witch*!' he told her, his eyes alight.

Then his lips found hers again and it was some time before either said anything at all.

'Where shall we go?' Theda asked him at length. 'To Cheshire? You guessed as soon as you heard the name of Kirtlington, I dare say?'

Benedict nodded. 'Immediately, though I took little notice of it when I was in Cheshire, I admit. All I could think about while I was taking up that extraordinary inheritance was you.' He was playing with her hair again, curling strands about his finger. 'I realised then, you see, that, of all my ambitions, *you* were the one I could never *bear* to lose! I had to rack my brains for ways to force you to wed me. When I learned your probable identity, and knew I had Kirtlington for my neighbour——'

'Yes, I know the rest, you scheming wretch!' she said, mock-stern. 'But shall we live there?' Her eyes clouded. 'The pity of it is that Araminta will get the Lodge after all. And I expended so much energy making it beautiful for you!'

He cupped her face, his eyes tender. 'For me?'

'Of course. I never had any intention of remaining here, though I have grown to love it.' She sighed. 'I wish it were not to be lost to you.'

Benedict grinned. 'You shall have it for a bride gift.'

'Are you serious?'

'Dearest ghost, did you imagine I would let it go to that hag of a cousin of mine? All I have ever known of love has been here in this house. My mother, Sir John—and now *you*. How could I give it up, even for the splendid trappings that have fallen to my lot? You see, since I was last here, Aycliffe's clerks have been in negotiation with Quatt.'

'You mean to purchase it? But Araminta will never allow him to sell it.'

'She will have no choice,' Benedict said austerely. 'You forget that, as her husband, it is he and not she who will take possession of the money.'

'Ah, I thought there was some cogent incentive for you to seek out my father!' interposed Theda with a twinkle. 'You think he will reinstate my lost inheritance, I dare say?'

Benedict grinned. 'I was ever a gambler, remember?' He kissed her again as she gurgled. 'But in all seriousness, we understand from the clerks that Quatt is dissatisfied with his reception here—as well he might be!—and has the intention of taking up a post as archdeacon somewhere in Worcestershire, where he was living before. I gather that since he is to become a man of substance the world has become his oyster.'

'You mean that Araminta will no longer be living here?' cried Theda joyfully. 'What a merciful release! And we shall have this house! Oh, Benedict!'

His lips brushed hers. 'I don't know why you should be surprised. This is all your spells, you witch! You have been casting them from that very first night when the gods sent you to haunt me!'

Theda laughed. 'Perhaps it is Lady Lavinia pulling strings.'

'In hell? You are jesting!'

'For shame, Benedict! I, for one, shall certainly pray for Saul Quatt!'

Benedict came away and grasped her hand, pulling her towards the door. 'Speaking of Quatt, I must tell Aycliffe to go and fetch him at once.'

'Here? For what purpose?' demanded Theda, amazed.

He grinned, turning at the door to seize her once more in his arms. 'A sufficient one. And while the messenger is on his errand, you may array yourself suitably. Did you buy something new, as I instructed?'

'Yes, but under protest,' Theda said, a fleeting vision of herself in the peach gown passing through her mind, together with a swift question as to how Benedict would think she looked in it. 'But what for! Why must I change my dress? Why is Quatt to come here?'

'Why else but to marry us, my lovely one? I have a special licence in my pocket, you see.'

'Have you, indeed?' Theda said politely, the gleam

back in her eye. 'You had no doubt of carrying the day, I collect?'

'None at all,' he said, laughing. 'I had—and *have*—every intention of sharing a bed tonight. . .and every night from here on.' He kissed her again, adding softly, 'A *marriage* bed, my lady, with my beloved wife.'

MILLS & BOON®

*M*akes
any time
special

Enjoy a romantic novel from
Mills & Boon®

Presents...™ *Enchanted*™ TEMPTATION.

Historical Romance™ ∿MEDICAL
ROMANCE.